'Smart and funny'

*The Keeper of Lost Things*

'Guaranteed to melt the hardest of hearts

*Red*

'A joy from start to finish: quirky, real and moving, with unforgettable characters you'll root for from the very beginning'

Katy Regan, author of
*Little Big Love*

'Finished *Maggsie McNaughton's Second Chance* and I feel bereft. A wonderful, uplifting read'

Jenny Quintana, author of
*The Missing Girl*

Also by Frances Maynard

## THE SEVEN IMPERFECT RULES
## OF ELVIRA CARR

# Maggsie McNaughton's Second Chance

*Maggsie McNaughton's Second Chance* is, appropriately enough, Frances Maynard's second novel. Her first, *The Seven Imperfect Rules of Elvira Carr*, was runner-up in the Good Housekeeping 2014 First Novel Award and the 2018 McKitterick Prize, and shortlisted for both the 2016 Mslexia First Novel Competition and the Lucy Cavendish Prize. She teaches English, part-time, to adults with learning difficulties, including Dyslexia, and is married with one grown-up daughter.
She lives in Dorset.

Frances Maynard

# Maggsie McNaughton's Second Chance

PICADOR

First published 2019 by Mantle

This paperback edition first published 2020 by Picador
an imprint of Pan Macmillan
The Smithson, 6 Briset Street, London EC1M 5NR
Associated companies throughout the world
www.panmacmillan.com

ISBN 978-1-5290-1415-0

1 3 5 7 9 8 6 4 2

A CIP catalogue record for this book is available from the British Library.

Typeset in Stempel Garamond LT Std by Palimpsest Book Production Limited,
Falkirk, Stirlingshire
Printed and bound by CPI Group (UK) Ltd, Croydon, CRO 4YY

Visit **www.panmacmillan.com** to read more about all our books
and to buy them. You will also find features, author interviews and
news of any author events, and you can sign up for e-newsletters
so that you're always first to hear about our new releases.

In memory of David J. Westhead 1946–2016.
Artist, teacher, friend.

# 1

My name is Marguerite. Marguerite McNaughton. It's a poncy name, too fancy. My brother's called Timothy and my older sister's Petronella. That's because Dad's name was Peter and Mum was all gooey-eyed over him then. Plus she's got these posh airs and graces. Nothing behind them, that's the trouble.

There's nothing posh about me, you can trust me on that one. Or fancy. Marguerite means something to do with flowers and flowers aren't the first thing you think of when you see me. Not with my denim jacket and studded trainers. They're kids' ones, boys' – from Mothercare – and second-hand, but there's no way you'd know that.

Fancy names are the devil to spell. Trust Mum not to think about that. I can't actually write Marguerite. Can't always even *say* it right. Which doesn't create a good impression. People either think you're lying, or you're thick. Them in charge aren't allowed to call you thick nowadays, are they? It's *learning difficulties. Dyslexia.*

OK, *dyslexic* is better than thick. Still a label stuck on your forehead that says you'll never be up to much, though. As for spelling it . . . it's about as much use to me as a rubber bottle opener. Poxy word for anybody struggling with reading and writing, if you ask me.

So what I call myself is Maggsie M. That's what I put on forms. If the pen-pusher that's asking for it looks disapproving, I just give them a go-fry-yourself stare. I don't say I can't read because then their eyebrows go up and there's a pause. Take my word for it. They don't say anything, but they always give you that look.

The Job Centre wanted me to come right out and say I was dyslexic in job interviews. But even if I could say the ruddy word, you're having a laugh, aren't you, if you think I'm going to. Not something you boast about, is it? Admit to any kind of weakness and you're done for, in my experience.

You're probably good at all that Job Centre stuff, forms and that – wouldn't be reading a book otherwise, would you? Bet you're not as good as me at looking out for yourself, though. That's something I *am* OK with. Well, more than OK. Had to be with my background. Nobody else likely to do it for me, is there?

Shouting down pillocks that make remarks about my size is the sort of thing I mean. '*Poison dwarf*' I've had to put a stop to more than once.

I call it being firm but other people say different. I had to do an anger management course, last stretch, and the one before. They learnt us to breathe out slower and not to use actual violence. I've pretty much got it sorted now. Got both the anger management certificates in my holdall.

That's the way things were. But just when I was getting on with it, same as always, something unexpected turned up.

An opportunity, they said. A door opening.

Didn't expect it to be an actual door, or to be plunged head first into an emergency situation, but there you go.

*

Rattling, a *ding*, a voice droning, *doors opening*. The lift doors slammed back. I smelt scorching and barbecues. Breathed in so sharp my Nicorette chewing gum slid down my throat. Curled up tight on the metal floor, not moving, was a man in blue overalls. He looked young. His eyes were shut and he was holding a screwdriver. For a second I thought it was someone homeless kipping, but who in their right mind would choose a lift to sleep in? Security would turf you out before you'd even unrolled your sleeping bag.

A slot machine I'd seen in Skeggy – Skegness – flashed through my mind. A little doll's-house room behind glass. Red curtains and a tiny man, reading. I'd put my coin in, nose pressed up close. Darkness. Then a spotlight. And there was the little man slumped over his desk, his hair wild and a dagger in his back. Gave me the creeps even though he was only about six inches tall. Yeah, he was small, but I am small. It doesn't mean you can't have a presence. Keep people on their toes.

I couldn't see blood on this lad, and his hair was short, but he looked just as dead. And he was real!

My thumb jabbed at the lift button. The bloody doors wouldn't keep still.

I couldn't just run off and leave him. He might still be alive.

*Doors closing*. The robot voice butted in again, like a Dalek's. Made me jump, only I pretended I was just shifting my position. I glanced about. Nobody around to see me anyway – I was too ruddy early, that was why. My heart was going like the clappers. I was panicking, to be honest. Anyone would have been. I hadn't hardly slept last night. Been dreading today. Hard enough finding my way here. A lot ruddy harder finding a body and no one else around. What could I do? I was supposed to be a kitchen assistant, for God's sake, not a fireman, or a medic.

Then it struck me: say if someone thought *I* done it to him? Punched him or something. I had a record, I'd been inside. That was why I was *here*; because I'd been inside. 'A *lucky* chance,' the probation officer said. Kept on about it like I'd won something. Wasn't turning out like that, was it?

I was early because it was my first day at work. I hadn't had many of those. Even fewer second days. In fact, none. That was why I hadn't slept. Ruby, the support worker from the housing place, had come in not long after six. She'd knocked first and brought me a cup of tea. Soon as she'd gone, I pulled the covers back over. Only she came in again. All bright and breezy she was. Rosy cheeks because she'd cycled in. What time had *she* got up?

She'd hustled me out the house before seven. Big beaming smile, thumbs-up sign, the sort of person who makes you feel your legs don't hardly touch the ground.

She'd gone through the route to Scandinavian Solutions, where I was supposed to be starting work, on Google Maps. On the Friday, that was. Practically soon as I walked through the door. She printed out the way from the tube station. Inked it in red. Didn't leave nothing to chance. I did, but then I wasn't any good at long-term thinking, people said. That was why I'd been inside.

Scan-din-av-i-an Sol-u-tions. I'd looked at the road names and the tube station names on Ruby's map. The shapes of them. Counted the number of stops between where I was living and this posh part of London. It was all writ out *and* the address of the supported house because there'd be bound to be a form.

*Alright?* Ruby kept asking, red pen hovering. She said *alright?* but then she'd start on something else, before I'd even opened my mouth. If she'd given me the chance I'd have said, no, I ruddy ain't. How's someone like me going to manage all that? I've just come out of prison. Never been to London before. Never worked somewhere posh. Never even worked in a kitchen. Never hardly worked.

On my way out the door Ruby said not to frown. 'Smiling makes people look approachable, Maggsie. Alright?' Yeah, but say you don't want them to approach you? I wasn't a friendly person. And not much point anyway, seeing as they were going to kick me out after two minutes.

It was alright for Ruby to smile. She had a posh voice and a fresh complexion and tiny white teeth and nothing to hide. *She* smiled all the time. My teeth weren't white. They *were* tiny but that was because there was a couple of chips off the bottom front ones. I spoke out the side of my mouth because of it.

When I won the lottery I was going to get them fixed. When I *did* the lottery. Never been outside long enough to do it regular. *Living a disorganized life*, people in charge called it.

I was crushed up against a metal pole on the tube. Couldn't see a thing with all them bodies stood above me. Couldn't see out the window. Nothing *to* see, I know, seeing as we were underground. I was used to being shut up, inside, but not like that. A joke expecting me to cope with it all.

I heard my stop and pushed my way out. Elbowed a

briefcase out the way. I'd have to go through it all again, going back tonight. Blow that for a game of soldiers. I'd stick it for one day. Just to show willing. That's if they didn't show *me* the door first. Then that would be it. I'd find my way back to the supported house for my holdall and hitch back up north. If I could ever find my way out of London. Not that Dougie, Mum's horrible boyfriend, would let her take me in. Not without me working.

I came up the tube steps with a crowd of people behind, pushing. Made me feel small. Made me feel I could be stepped on. Stepped over. Actually, I'd felt small ever since I'd been in London. Only three days but it felt longer. I am small but I don't make an issue of it. Don't let no one else make an issue of it, neither. I keep my chin up and stride out. Mind you, they all walk like that in London. That must be why they're all thin.

My heart was going. I clapped my hand over it to slow it down. My zip-up purse with embroidery on it, fifty pence from Oxfam, was inside my bra. It was my red satin bra, my best, except the lace was unravelling from one of the straps. The purse had all my money in it. Forty-one pounds. No way was I leaving that in a supported house with girls I hardly knew around.

I spotted the name of the road where I was supposed to be working. Fernette Street, number forty-one. Ruby had underlined it in red. I knew 'street' because of the two 'e's together. And Fernette had more 'e's, three of them, and a great big 'F'.

It didn't seem real, to be honest. None of it. Me, in London, trotting off to a job. I did the special calming breathing they'd learnt us in anger management, but it made me double up coughing. I needed a fag. Best find Scan-din-av-i-an Sol-u-tions first, though. Get it over with. I chewed the Nicorette gum but it only took the edge off.

I looked around. Distracting yourself was another tip they'd learnt us in anger management – it was supposed to make your heart slow down. Useful, knowing how to distract yourself. Might work for you and all. Everyone's got something they don't want to think about.

It was a big wide road, not like the streets I was used to. Great tall houses each side, white, with no flaky bits of paint peeling off. Didn't look like somewhere someone like me was supposed to be. People in smart coats. High heels tapping. Shiny hair, like they'd just come out the hairdressers. Even the men.

On the other side was a man sitting on the pavement. That was more the sort of thing I was used to. He had a cardboard notice made out of a Kellogg's Cornflakes packet. I recognized the red chicken. I could make out the word UNWANTED on his sign because I'd seen it in the food bank, above a basket of battered-looking packets.

I was unwanted, same as him. This *lucky* chance, I was getting was just them in charge box-ticking. *Pressure* more like, teetering on a tightrope. Toppling off straight away, probably. Showing myself up while I done it. Tonight I'd be back the same as he was.

I breathed out slow like they tell you to. Must be nearly there, surely? Right at the end of the street was a big modern building. Forty-one in huge metal numbers and two great big snakey 'S's, for Scandinavian Solutions, above the door. Nothing but windows as far as you looked up. (I spend a lot of my life looking up. Puts you at a disadvantage.)

My heart was jumping about. I nearly got tangled up in the revolving door. The only one I'd seen before was in a big hotel the Job Centre had sent me to. This one would be handy for spitting me out too, later on.

The entrance had shiny floors and a big mirror right up to the ceiling. What was the point of that? Only a spider could look at itself up there. Not the sort of place a spider would fancy anyway – too clean and empty. I caught a glimpse of myself, my head and shoulders. A wisp of black hair was already escaping from my ponytail. My shoulders were hunched. I pulled them back. Breathed out.

I really, really wanted a fag. You may not have noticed but smokers get pushed into scruffy places. Next to dustbins, out the back, in car parks. Anywhere cold where there's nowhere to sit down. I already knew the kitchen was in the basement, because Ruby had said. There was no P car park sign, so most likely smokers were shunted up to the top here. I shot a glance at the reception desk. The receptionist, all swept-up blonde hair and dark eyebrows, was smiling into her phone. Ignoring me. People did. It was one of the things that made me angry. Not angry – *firm.*

I stuck my chin up again and made for the lift. I could see the word LIFT lit up in yellow beyond RECEPTION. I knew both those words. Knew *Reception* had a funny ending, the same as station. One of those endings that set out to trip up people like me.

I pressed the button.

Strange how your life can change in an instant, like that. Because of somebody you don't even know. Someone said, later on, the lad had been a *catalyst,* which means what I just said, only squeezed up into one word. And nothing to do with cats, which is a pity because I like cats.

# 2

So there I was with a body on the floor and the lift doors opening and closing soon as I took my thumb off the button. Panicking. On my own. I mean, come on, even I knew that wasn't normal for a first day.

'Help!' I shouted. My voice bounced off the marble walls. The stuck-up receptionist must still have been on her phone. I couldn't see her desk from the lift. 'Emergency!' I tried, but it didn't sound right.

Just my luck to be landed with this. Him. Him just lying there, his face all white and doughy-looking. That awful smell. I struggled with working, for God's sake, let alone ruddy emergencies. My heart hadn't had a second off since I'd woken up this morning. I couldn't think, hardly. I darted a glance over my shoulder. Still ruddy nobody.

To the other side was an open cupboard. I spotted a broom, a wooden one, and some torn-up cardboard. The sort of thing you kept your eyes open for when you were sleeping rough. Insulated you against the cold. *Insulate!* That's what wires had to be: all wrapped up in plastic in case they killed you. He might have been electrocuted! I'd done a course inside – Health and Safety in the Workplace. (Practical, see, no writing.) Never thought I'd use it. Never thought I'd be *in* a ruddy workplace.

I threw some cardboard down each side of him. Grabbed the broom. *Good girl, Maggsie*, I told myself, for remembering metal things, what was it, *conducted*, electricity. You got to give yourself credit, because no one else is likely to.

Soon as I stopped leaning on the button, the lift doors started opening and shutting again, like they had a mind of their own. I dodged in. Gave the lad a shove with the broom. He didn't move. Electricity might be leaking out all over the place. Any minute it could stop my heart stone dead.

He was big and heavy, really heavy, and, like I said, I am small (*Scrawny*, Dad used to say, but what did he know?) I wasn't that into fitness neither. If I was I'd have taken the stairs and someone else would have found the poor sod. But then, if I wanted to be healthy I wouldn't be looking for a smoking area, would I? I'd have given up the fags.

I had another go. Ran at him with the broom. Used every ounce of strength. Shouted as I did it, '*Get off!*' – something I was used to shouting. This time he rolled over, right onto his back. There was a tangle of wires where he'd been lying. And a Tupperware box with sandwiches inside, two white-bread triangles, and a KitKat. His mum had probably made him those this morning. I swallowed. He only looked about eighteen. Soft chubby cheeks. Something written on his jacket. Something with the word LIFT on it. That burnt smell again. And one trouser leg melted. He still wasn't moving.

The doors opened and I shouted again. I mean, I'm used to people ignoring me, but this was beyond a joke. The lad could be dying. Be just my luck to get landed with a dead body.

I ran back to the entrance. Screamed. 'Turn the bloody lift off! Phone an ambulance!' You had to do that first, I remembered. Even if the person was dead. The stuck-up slag's eyebrows vanished into her hair-do. She pressed buttons on her phone. Rushed over, high heels clicking, then shrank back at the lad all white and stretched out and not moving. Clapped her hands to her face. Long silver fingernails. Still managed to ask me who I was, though.

My name came out strangled but what do you expect in an emergency? I knelt on the cardboard. Got close to the lad now he wasn't touching any wires. He looked peaceful in spite of all the electric that had gone through him. His hair wasn't standing on end or anything. I braced myself and lifted his hand. Warm. Huge. Mine wouldn't stretch around it. His nails were cut straight across. I felt his wrist for a pulse. I'd done that once before, way back. It wasn't the sort of thing I thought I'd be doing again, especially in a *work* situation.

Was there a bit of a flutter? I wasn't a doctor. I was the complete opposite of anything like that. I told him the ambulance was coming. Kept hold of his hand, seeing as there was no one else to do it.

# 3

You might be wondering how someone like me got the chance to work in a posh place in London and find a body soon as they walked through the door. Obviously they didn't *choose* me. It was a charity scheme, one where they give ex-cons a leg-up in the world.

Once you'd served half your sentence there was a chat about getting a job outside. And somewhere to live. A joke, seeing as most of us wouldn't get work. Not *legal* work. And a lot of us wouldn't get housing, neither. But this time the probation officer, inside, had heard of an *opportunity*.

She took off her glasses, frumpy metal frames they had, too severe. She was getting on a bit, had grey hair, cut like a man's. Said they'd noticed *an improvement in my behaviour* this stretch. Buffed up her glasses on the sleeve of her shirt. Asked me why that was.

I shrugged. I wasn't big on thinking. 'Done a bit more reading this stretch. Maybe that.' *More.* I'd never done *any* reading before. But, this time, Enid, from the cell down the corridor, had shown me the basics.

That got her going. She blinked, all excited. But my reading was only bits and pieces from Enid's *Woman's World* magazines, not proper books or nothing.

She picked up a bit of paper. My CV. The IT tutor

had done it for me on the computer. After I'd nearly broke the mouse. I wasn't good with computers and I had dyslexia. It hardly filled a page, seeing as I'd never had a proper job, or proper schooling.

She tapped her finger on the courses I'd done: Anger Management, Food Hygiene and the Health and Safety in the Workplace one. Yeah, they'd make up for me not being able to read properly and not having any work experience, I don't think.

She put down her pen. Scandinavian company, she said, smiling, like that was something special. London, she said. Supported housing, she said.

My stomach lurched. London was a big city. I knew that. Knew it was a long way from here. I knew Scandinavian was some kind of foreign. I wasn't thick, in spite of what people said.

I'd never stuck at a job before. Hadn't been able to read that hotel's cleaning schedule when the Job Centre sent me there as a chambermaid, and I'd got sacked from a cake factory for throwing a Swiss roll at a fat bloke who'd laughed at my size. *My* size. Plus, I ask you, how can a Swiss roll be dangerous?

I'd done other things to get by: shoplifted, climbed through windows too small for anybody else, looked after empty flats and people's dogs when their owners were called away sudden.

I'd shared a flat for months with a pit-bull and a Staffie. They were supposed to wear spiked collars when I took them out, because their owner wanted them to look hard. Soon as we were back indoors though, they'd be on the sofa with me, slobbering for crisps.

I'd bought a blue scarf, spotted, at a charity shop, and cut it in half for them to wear as bandanas. When they were off duty. The charity shop was Cats Protection but I didn't think the dogs would mind. The Staffie, Mikey, always wagged his tail when he saw a cat staring down at him from a wall.

The probation officer was still smiling. Tiring having someone grin at you all the time. Specially when it was misguided. I tried telling her this *opportunity* wasn't going to happen. People have these ideas and schemes about helping the poor and underprivileged. And making sure they're, we're, grateful. But even if this one ever did get off the ground, it wasn't going to work. A different city, yeah, a different set-up, but still the same old me. But there was no stopping her. In the end I just let her get on with it. I chewed my nails, pushed down the cuticles, while she went on about this Scandinavian company designing furniture and ceramics, whatever they were, so it wasn't a complete waste of my time.

They discharge you early in prison. I was on the seven o'clock coach to London, seven *a.m.*, with a group of old biddies and a few student-looking blokes with rucksacks, sitting at the back. Noisy. Full of themselves. I gave them a *get stuffed* stare. First men, apart from screws, I'd seen in a year. Hadn't missed much.

I sat by a window. You're high up on a coach. I don't often get to look down on people. Hardly anybody about that time in the morning, though. Cold enough for Eskimos. I was wearing my denim jacket, plus a scarf and two jumpers, and I was still cold. January, see. The time of year when people go on about fresh starts even more.

Soon as we left the town I got that unsettled feeling

you get leaving prison. It was worse this time because of Enid. Her being good to me. Lord knows why.

She'd given me a hug before I left, her saggy bosom squashing my ribs, and this week's *Woman's World* that she hadn't even started yet. I'd promised her I'd practise my reading. Do a bit every day. I looked out of the window, blinking. Then I got some Nicorette chewing gum out of my holdall because you weren't allowed to smoke on a coach. I looked out of the window for the rest of the journey. Thought what a long way it was going to be, hitching back.

Vic-tor-ia, I read on the sign. I dragged out my holdall from under the seat. I was the last one off and I only got off at all because I was dying for a wee and a fag. I mean, what the hell was I, Maggsie ruddy M, doing in a great big place like London? Poxy probation officers and their big ideas. Sending people like me off on wild-goose chases. A sodding waste of time.

Outside, crowds of people were barging in different directions. Crowds and traffic are the hardest things to get used to again after you've been banged up. Someone tripped over me. I'm not that small! I scowled, but I didn't say anything, not even under my breath, because this was London and I was on my own.

I had the bus number to the supported housing place written down. Only I couldn't find the right bus stop. No rhyme nor reason in the numbering. Beyond the forest of signs I saw one I could read: tesco express. I read it straight off, just like that. Good old Enid. She'd had the patience of a saint, teaching me. I felt inside my holdall to check her *Woman's World* was still there.

I thought about going into Tesco's. I had my discharge

grant in my purse. I only thought about it for a minute and then I took a hold of myself. What helped was spotting an old biddy in a bus queue that reminded me of my nan. Same white hair – Nan swore it was ash blonde, not white – same bright pink lipstick. I showed the old biddy my bus number. She knew exactly where it went from *and* when it was due. Reckon she spent all day in bus queues.

I got out the Oyster card the probation officer had given me. A perk from Scandinavian Solutions, she said. I didn't know what you did with it. The driver snatched it out of my hand and banged it down on a little machine before I'd even spoke. Annoying he didn't seem to notice me snatching it back.

So I was on the right bus and there was a woman's voice saying the names of the stops. But London went on for miles and miles. Took me deeper and deeper into something I wouldn't be able to manage. An hour to get where I was supposed to go to and it was still London. When things went pear-shaped, which, let's face it, they would do, it was going to take for ever to find my way out.

It looked like an ordinary house from the outside. It was only a support officer coming to the door that made you realize it wasn't.

Ruby was ever so gushing, like I was a guest, rather than someone straight out of prison. One of those people who whizz about doing things. The sort of person who always has their sleeves rolled up. ADHD, I thought. Tiny (Timothy, my brother, six years younger than me) had that. But it made him do stuff he shouldn't, not be a support worker. Ruby had long curly hair which bounced about. Wore a swishy skirt and a flower-pot-coloured necklace, which made me think of Enid because she wore necklaces. Ones with plastic beads – you weren't allowed chunky jewellery in prison in case it got used as a weapon. The necklaces were supposed to draw attention *up*, away from her chest, which was massive. Ruby didn't have that problem. Didn't look no older than a teenager but maybe that was just me. I was only thirty-three but a hard life ages you.

I handed Ruby the forms that said who I was, etcetera. I'd have liked to just crawl into bed, but it was still only the afternoon. I wanted a fag and a cuppa. And, well, something else, but I was trying not to think about that. It was because of the early start and the stress and all that.

Ruby showed me the back yard where you could smoke. Said there was a cat lived out there, under the shed, but I didn't see it. Then she made me a cup of tea – not enough sugar, I take four spoons – and some toast. Sat down chatting while I chewed. Fidgeted. Jumped up soon as I'd put the cup down. Went upstairs, two at a time, in front of me.

'Blimey. How many Weetabix you had this morning?' I asked, from half a flight down.

She laughed. Said she'd had porridge, with soya milk. People thought you lived off porridge in prison, but actually, there was more cornflakes.

Ruby unlocked a door. 'This is your room, Maggsie. It's got all the basics.'

Yeah, it was basic alright. Bare, scuff marks on the walls, candlewick bedspread, threadbare patches on the carpet. But at least it was indoors and I didn't have to share it with anyone. Plus I wasn't planning on staying.

My holdall was one of those tartan ones you take

stuff to the launderette in. Didn't take me long to unpack. I folded up my T-shirts and the rest of my clothes, such as they were. Then I looked out of the window, from one of the threadbare patches. Loads of other ex-cons must have stood there, looking out at the world – well, at London.

You'd think it would look different because it was London. But it didn't, except for some tower blocks at the end of the road. Cars parked both sides, people shouting, grimy brickwork. Same as anywhere.

After I'd settled in, Ruby explained the rest of it. She'd help me with paperwork. *Monitor my progress*. Drinking or drug-taking was strictly off limits. And no going out after nine at night. Breaking the rules could mean being booted back inside. 'Alright?' she asked.

I nodded. Prison wasn't much of a threat. Home from home, more like.

Think I'd hate rules, wouldn't you? Well, I did and I didn't. Rules gave you a structure. Meant someone else was in charge and you didn't have to sort out your own life. All that stuff – bills, forms, getting things organized – was beyond me, to be honest. There was so much you had to do just to get by. It was having to start doing it all over again when you came out that made you want to go back inside.

Ruby showed me the kitchen. The other girls here marked their food with their initials. I could manage that. She gave me some cheese and biscuits to tide me over. Kept using my name like social workers did.

'I'm just out of probation, myself, Maggsie.' Training for her job, she meant, not something criminal. I'd thought she was inexperienced. I picked up on that straight away. Told you I wasn't thick.

She was more excited about my 'new start' than I was. Would have got on well with the probation officer. They could have formed a little duo, sung a song about *lucky chances*. I wasn't excited at all, seeing as it was going to go pear-shaped. It made me nervous, her keeping on about it. Made me want to get thrown out now. Save everyone the trouble on Monday. No way was I, Maggsie – *Marguerite McNaughton!* echoed from school – going to manage working for a posh design company in the centre of London.

Ruby whisked about the kitchen with a dishcloth. I put down my cream cracker and slice of cheese. The pattern on the Formica table blurred. I was homesick, if you want to know. You might think it was strange, being homesick for prison. But it was what I was used to. And I was thinking about Enid, seeing her leaning forwards, arms folded under her saggy boobs, listening to me trying to read. Remembering the way she punched the air when I cracked a new word. And all the cuppas with the girls on the wing and the chips we got on Fridays. And no decisions to make because they was made for you and no bloody forms.

Upstairs I took off my jeans and hung them in the wardrobe. I liked things neat, in spite of living in places before where I couldn't be, not always. I put on my pyjamas. Picked up Enid's *Woman's World*. Funny how a magazine can be a comfort. Never thought that would happen. I thought about writing to Enid, to let her know what I was doing. I'd never written an actual letter before, only cards. Enid would be thrilled at me writing anything. But there was no point unless I stayed, and that wasn't going to happen. I tried to get through a bit in the magazine about 'New year, new you', but I couldn't concentrate.

Plus, there were words I didn't know and I didn't have anyone to ask.

After a while I got up and pulled the blind down. Shut out the outside.

# 4

Next morning I put on the hooped earrings Nan gave me. She was supposed to have gypsy blood. First time I'd wore them in over a year and I'd forgotten the weight of them. I swung them about a bit to feel more on top of things.

Voices downstairs in the kitchen. Never a nice feeling being the new girl. I marched downstairs, pushed open the door and barged straight in because of it.

Two women, one old, one young, standing up, eating toast. The older one, Shirl – *Big* Shirl, she said – looked like she'd be the Queen Bee in here. Every place got one. She wore a frilly blouse and little pointed shoes. And make-up – powder and red lipstick. The powder showed up her wrinkles. If you read the beauty pages of *Woman's World* you'd know that. I only wore mascara and eyebrow pencil myself. And that's because I'm ginger underneath the hair dye. I'm not a beauty.

The younger one, Lucy ('*Juicy* Lucy we call her,' Big Shirl cackled), was another big girl. Baggy sweatshirt. Heavy eyelids. The sort of glasses with black frames that make people look swotty, only they didn't with her. She gave me a couple of slices of bread so I could make some toast and told me the way to the Co-op round the corner.

In prison you get what's given you. Once you come

out you've got choices again. Too many of them. I dithered for ages in the Co-op over the cans of soup. Bought tomato in the end, plus fags and basics. No point in stocking up if I wasn't staying. Threw all the stuff in my basket quick so I didn't find myself in the aisle at the end of the shop.

Ruby put scraps outside for the cat that lived under the shed. She'd already told me she was a vegetarian, so God knows what they were. She called the cat Audrey. Audrey! What kind of name was that for a cat? Ruby thought she might have been someone's pet before, way back. Someone no ruddy good then, who'd abandoned her. Or treated her bad.

Soon as I flicked on my lighter the cat dashed out and went up and over next door's wall. She was a tabby, with a white belly and paws. It was the white paws, Ruby said, that made her think of *Audrey*. Said they looked like gloves and the dark lines round the cat's eyes reminded her of Audrey Hepburn. I couldn't see it myself. Mind you, I didn't know who Audrey Hepburn was. I didn't let on, of course, but Ruby showed me a picture on her phone anyway. Film star. Dead. Looked like a deer.

Ruby said a cat charity had taken a litter of kittens off Audrey last year. They'd tried to catch her and all, to give her the snip, but she'd been too clever. Or too daft, seeing as it'd only take another Tom hanging around to put her in the family way again, even though she was just a bag of skin and bones. But that's men for you.

Ruby said Audrey was semi-feral, which meant half wild, so no use trying to make a pet of her. Blow that for a game of soldiers, I thought. I went straight down the Co-op again and bought a tin of pilchards. Tossed one to Audrey, who wolfed it down *and* came a bit closer to try and get her jaws around a second.

'Another one tonight. But you got to come out and say hello first,' I told her. She blinked at me from a safe distance away. 'Ain't much of a life living under a *shed*. Take it from one who knows.'

I put the pilchards in the fridge along with my butter. I'd bought real butter at the Co-op, although it was twice the price. Tubs of marge reminded me of being a kid. We'd lived off toast and marge because of Mum being a bad manager and Dad drinking. Bread and marge, when there wasn't any electric for the toaster.

I stayed in Sunday. Stayed near the toilet. Must be the London water. Couldn't eat much, only the tomato soup. Got through loads of fags.

Tossed and turned all through Sunday night. Why was I hanging around here when I already knew things were going to end in tears? Better to sneak off first thing in the morning. Hitch back up north, once I'd found out how to get to the motorway.

I put my jacket on over my pyjamas and went downstairs to make a brew. I didn't know what it was that made me change my mind, decide to give the job a go for a day. Get the do-gooders off my back. It might have been opening the fridge and seeing the tin of pilchards I'd bought for Audrey. Thinking of her wolfing them down. Thinking of those kittens being taken off her.

I hooked out another one now. I had to throw it through the ventilation shaft, because the kitchen door was locked overnight. I called out – 'Audrey!' – so she'd know it was from me.

*

Then it was dawn on Monday and my throat was so dry I couldn't hardly get a cup of tea down. In a couple of hours I'd be getting the tube by myself, meeting people I didn't know, posh people, having to do stuff I wouldn't know how to do.

Trouble with worrying is it doesn't prepare you for what actually happens. Stuff you've dreaded never comes up, but stuff you've never even thought of does. Because, take it from me, finding a body, soon as I got through the door on my first day, had never even crossed my mind.

# 5

Not exactly an *opportunity*, finding a young lad collapsed at your feet, is it? I tell you one thing, it didn't half put me off working. If I'd been doing one of those stress tests from anger management I'd have been off the scale.

The ambulance people stretchered him off. I was going to sneak away and all. Have another set-to with the revolving door and head back to the tube. Only my legs were shaking. I felt like a plate of melting jelly. Plus I'd been really early and now I was going to be late. Get a telling-off before I'd even started. They'd be bound not to believe what had happened. People didn't when it was me telling them.

The ambulance was out in the street for ages. I was stuck by the lift because people kept asking me questions. A posh woman wanted to know if I was OK. She had a black jacket on, fitted, and high heels. Said she was from HR. That meant Human Resources, she said, which meant staff. Blimey. Scandinavian Solutions was sounding posher and posher. A grey-haired man from Maintenance turned up to peer into the lift and ask me what had happened. Another man asked the same, a manager, he said, although he was wearing jeans and a shirt that had so many flowers on it, it might as well have been a blouse.

Then it was the police. I was used to *them* asking me questions. But not them being polite about it. Calling me Miss McNaughton instead of Maggsie.

One of the ambulance people came back. There was an awful hollow feeling in my gut. I didn't want him telling me the lad had snuffed it. Don't know why, because he was a stranger, but there you are.

He wasn't dead. In fact, he was coming to, though his left leg was badly burnt where the electric had gone through it. The ambulance man had dreadlocks, tied back. He reckoned the lad had tripped and fallen on the exposed wire. 'If it had gone anywhere near his heart, he'd have been a goner.' He said I'd done all the right things. Could even have saved his life. 'Cool head in a crisis,' he said, eyebrows raised, nodding at me.

*Saved his life. All the right things.* It was like he was talking about someone else. I hadn't done nothing. All I'd done was have a ruddy good go at what I thought was a corpse with a broom. They were all looking at me now. Smiling. Even the police. I wanted to turn round, look behind me for the person they were talking about.

The manager, the one in jeans, shook my hand. The only other bigwig who'd done that had been a prison governor. And it hadn't been to say well done, but to get me to agree to a behaviour contract. The manager smiled. 'Very lucky you were there.' Even started them off clapping. I kept my arms folded. Didn't smile. They could be having a laugh. This isn't me, you silly whatsits, I wanted to say. I got a record, I can't hardly read or write, my family don't want to know me.

My first day at work, I hadn't even *started* work, and all this was happening. Was it real? Was someone playing a practical joke? Was someone off the telly going to spring out and say I'd been taken for a mug? Made me feel dizzy.

'Go and have a sit-down, love,' the maintenance man said. His hair was thinning – well, gone at the front.

I mimed smoking – couldn't get my words out – and he showed me to the stairs. Yeah, smoking *was* right at the top of the building. I might not have had much education but I was an expert on some things.

Finally got my fag. I was nearly climbing the walls by then. I had to climb, five flights of stairs, as it was. The smoking area was a bench behind a little fence in the roof garden. A garden on a roof! They got some funny ideas in London.

I had a couple of rollies in my baccy tin already made, which was a blessing, seeing as my hands were trembling. (It was long-term thinking, actually. What they got excited about on the courses, inside.) I took a deep drag. Saw the lad's chubby face. His eyes tight shut. *Cool head in a crisis*, I heard again. I'd have written that down if I could.

Weird doing something right for once. Hard to get my brain round people being pleased with me, being treated like someone important. Being clapped! Be good to tell my sister Nella that one day. She always thought she was a cut above. I shut my eyes. Only trouble was now they'd think I was like that all the time. Talk about Imposter Syndrome. (I'd read about that in *Woman's World*. On the problem page, with Enid nodding and listening. I'd stumbled over the words; *syndrome* was a bugger with that 'y' turning up where you wouldn't expect it.)

I was still all over the place. I took a deep drag on

my rollie – it was a skinny one to make my baccy last – then I put it out and stood up. Looked over the edge of the building at London stretched out all around. Skyscrapers, all shapes and sizes, buildings, that looked like they were made of glass, shining and twinkling, dark churches with pointy roofs. It was a whole new world. It was like looking at another planet, to be honest. One where I didn't belong.

I felt shaky again going back down the stairs. Just get this one day over and done with, Maggsie. Tomorrow you can head off.

'I had given you up.' A black woman was frying eggs in a huge pan. She had bright green eyeshadow and hair braided on top of her head. Always doing each other's hair the black girls were, inside.

'There was a—' I began.

'Well, you are here now. Put on an overall.' She pointed to some kind of store cupboard in the corner. 'Wash your hands and help me with these breakfasts.' She didn't say her name and she didn't ask mine.

That kind of thing happened to me all the time. I just had to walk through a door and things unravelled. People didn't listen. Anger, no, *firmness*, began to boil. Saw myself pushing her braided head into her frying pan. I breathed out, silently counted to six. Getting worked up makes you breathe *in* too much; it's the out bit that reduces the *adren* . . . something.

I took off my denim jacket. I never felt right without it on – it put me at a disadvantage. Took an overall from a pile on a shelf. It hung off me like something draping a coat-stand. The black woman listed what I was supposed to do. Stack and unload the industrial dishwasher,

I heard. I had my arms crossed and a scowl on, only she didn't notice. Then the high-heeled woman from HR arrived and put her-in-charge – Primrose, her name was – in the picture. Rested her hand on my shoulder. Called me *a very modest young lady*. I looked at her, eyes narrowed, in case she was taking the mick. But, no, she was serious. *Modest young lady* was a first. Nella, who didn't have no time for me, would have wet herself laughing.

'I am sorry!' This Primrose put down her spatula and gave me a hug. She had a big white smile. Then she asked a big hulking guy lurking about, not saying much, foreign, I think, to make me a cup of tea. TJ, he said his name was. Too Jigantic, I thought. (It was a while before I found out it was spelt with a 'g'.) He smiled when I said four sugars, and his teeth were crooked and stained, only not as bad as mine. I didn't smile back. I didn't like big men. Dougie was big, and Dad before him. That pair would put you off for life. It was only Mum that went for great looming blokes.

Primrose had a huge backside. She swayed off to turn over a load of sausages. Then she put her hands together right there by the oven and shut her eyes: 'Dear Lord above, fill that poor injured soul with your healing light.' TJ, coming past with a trolley full of crockery, crossed himself. God botherers, the pair of them. Some of the girls inside used to do the same. Crossing themselves was supposed to show they were telling the truth. But if you need a sign to back up what you're saying, then you're probably lying.

So there I was, in a posh building, in London, being waited on – being apologized to, even. Like someone had made a mistake somewhere. I'd have given my eye teeth for Nella to see me – whatever they were. (Actually,

I wouldn't. I had enough gaps as it was. Nobody would want my eye teeth anyway.) This is what *being* Nella must feel like, I thought. People smiling at you, saying nice things, not telling you off, or laughing. Yeah, I'd always said Nella was dull and boring, but I could get quite into it, actually.

*Modest young lady*. Made me laugh, that did.

Scandinavian Solutions ('Scanda,' TJ put in, 'for shorter') staff got their meals free, so they shovelled food down all the time. Weird food. *Black* bread that looked like it had been down a coal hole, *raw* fish, brightly coloured veg that should never have been in a salad. I wasn't too keen on cooking myself. Like Mum that way. She'd never done much more than egg and chips. 'I know my limits,' she used to say. I wasn't so sure about that, looking back. She didn't with men.

The washing-up never stopped. No time to think, hardly. I spent all day scraping dirty crockery and stacking and unstacking the dishwasher. Nice how everything came out the other end, clean and dry and shiny. I got into the rhythm of it. Could do it easy.

I was exhausted by the time I got back to the house. You ever carried a stack of plates? Heavier than you'd think. I'd have arms like Popeye – like Dougie, who was a bricklayer – soon. The backs of my legs ached from standing. My hair smelt of chips from the deep-fat fryer.

I warmed up some soup and put a pilchard on a saucer. Yesterday Audrey had come a bit closer and only dodged away when I tried to stroke her head.

Ruby poked her head round the kitchen door. 'How did it go?'

'Alright,' I got out, and a thumbs-up sign. Ruby gave me one back. Both thumbs.

After I'd eaten my soup I went upstairs and crawled into bed. My eyes closed soon as my head hit the pillow.

I woke at six Tuesday morning. Strange coming to, remembering I'd saved a young lad's life the day before. Or his leg, at least. That I'd done *all the right things*. Kept going over it in my mind. And what might have happened. That awful barbecue smell and the robot voice nagging about the lift doors. I could have been electrocuted. If I hadn't managed to roll him over he could have lost his leg. Could have died if he'd fallen different.

People had been nice yesterday, but today they'd turn on me. Bound to. They'd realize what I was like. Or I'd break something, or there'd be stuff I couldn't read, or I'd lose it with someone treating me disrespectful.

Well, I still had my thumb, didn't I? Still had a gob on me. I could still do a runner, hitch back up north.

But it was OK. No worse on the tube than yesterday. In a way it was better. I was still squashed and a couple of guys in suits chatted over the top of my head, but it didn't get to me as much. Not now I was someone who'd done *all the right things*. Kept *a cool head in a crisis*. Make a good tattoo, that. I've got tattoos, everyone inside's got them, but none with writing on. *Modest young lady* on the other arm? No, maybe not. Didn't sound hard enough.

I overheard some people in the breakfast queue saying I was the person *who'd rescued that poor man in the lift*. They looked over, said it proper respectful. And I could work the dishwasher same as yesterday. Primrose *asked* me to do things. Sang churchy-sounding songs while she stirred stuff. Kept giving me little fried bits of things, crusts of pastry, a left-over sausage. *Put more flesh on your bones*, she said. I got through a lot of tit-bits. I didn't eat breakfast, but if I did I could have stopped bothering.

Make the most of it, Maggsie, I told myself, trudging up to the roof garden with my baccy tin mid-morning. Because it ain't likely to last.

TJ and I had our break at the same time. He was a smoker too so we had to share the bench. I sat right at the end. Looked at the skyscrapers. I always gave big men a wide berth. He was on his mobile, jabbering away, in Polish I think, because he was Polish, and not looking too happy at what the person back in Poland was saying.

# 6

**Woman's World, 17 January 2018**
The Joy of Flowers

There was a pile of calendars in Reception. Free ones you could just take. I picked one up. A picture of the spindly furniture or boring china Scanda made for each month. Prefer a bit of pattern myself. And padding.

I don't know why I wanted a calendar. Never had one before. I hung it from the handle of my wardrobe door. January's chair looked like a load of scaffolding. Tricky word to spell, January. And why it had to have a capital letter, I didn't know.

I ticked off all of 2018 up to today. Three days I'd done at work now. Never managed that before. Even longer since I'd, well, since I'd had a drink. Because I used to like a drink. Alcohol, I mean. Booze. You might have already guessed that. Bound to be clever, aren't you, if you can read a book?

Say if I could stick at the job? And at the not drinking. Say if I could stick at both for the whole year? Tick off *all* the days? That would be something to crow about. Something to tell Nella and Mum. If I was ever back in touch. *Modest young lady.* I'd love to get that one in.

'Don't count your chickens,' Nan used to say. Yeah. I hung the calendar back up.

\*

On Friday there was a square white envelope propped up on the dishwasher. It had my name on it.

Uh-oh. I hung up my jacket. Apart from Christmas or my birthday, envelopes were bad news. My heart thumped. Was Scanda getting rid of me? Or asking for some sort of qualification? I knew things couldn't last.

'Good morning, Maggsie.' TJ was carrying some giant tins of tomatoes in from the storeroom. He put them down and gave me a big wide smile. He was always smiling. Apart from when he was on the phone to Poland. Made him look simple, if you asked me. Plus he was always around. Took up too much space. When he had a cup of tea you could hardly see the cup for his paw around it.

Primrose pointed to the sink. She was beaming and all. Alright for them. 'Something there for you, child.'

I looked over. A huge bunch of flowers. I mean, huge – the size of a bush, practically. Orange flowers, yellow ones, purple. Like a paint-box. All done up in fancy paper and cellophane and a big pink bow. 'What do you mean, for *me*?' I frowned. Wondered, like I'd done on Monday, if it was some kind of trick.

TJ lifted a little white card Sellotaped to the paper. 'To Marguerite,' he read out. 'Is you, Maggsie?'

I nodded. Stared. Who'd send me flowers?

'Perhaps is young man in lift. To say thank you. Card may say.' TJ fetched the envelope from the dishwasher.

I folded my arms. No way was I going to try to read something with them watching. I'd just open it. The card was heavy, expensive. A picture of some cats in a circle, each holding up a little notice that said *thank you*. I could read *that*. They were looking. 'Yeah, it is from him.' I took it into the storeroom.

Three lines, big writing. I traced the words with my

finger. Took me a while to make it out. He was thanking me for saving his life. Asking me to visit him in hospital. I breathed in deep thinking about that. The rest of it was names and addresses.

I asked Primrose to read them. I didn't tell her why. I said it was because I didn't have my glasses with me. Which was true seeing as I don't wear glasses.

Primrose took the card gently like I'd gone into the cupboard because I'd been overcome with emotion. That wasn't something I went in for. It was another thing that could put you at a disadvantage.

Jack, the lad's name was. He was in Saint George's Hospital.

I ask you, how can *St* say *Saint*? A lot of words were like that. A secret code I wasn't in on.

Visiting him. My gut churned. He, *Jack*, would have bigged me up in his mind. Be expecting some willowy blonde, someone like that receptionist. Then find out I wasn't nothing special after all. I put his card back in the envelope. Plus there was having to find my way somewhere new.

I went over to the sink. They were lovely flowers. Like you saw TV stars being given when they'd won something. Nobody had ever given me flowers before. I wished I could keep them all fresh and posh-looking like they were now to show Nella one day. I had to turn away for a second, which was ridiculous. Flowers are supposed to make you happy.

Primrose squeezed my arm. I went over and switched on the dishwasher quick in case she put her hands together and brought in the *dear Lord* again. It was *me* who'd saved Jack.

\*

The flowers were heavy to carry home, well, back to the house. I had them on my lap on the tube and I could hardly see over the top. Had to go through the front door sideways.

I hadn't told anyone at the house about Jack. Hadn't had a chance. Each night I'd just warmed up my soup, fished out Audrey's pilchard and gone to bed. But now I met Ruby wheeling her bike through the hall, ready to go home. She fussed about her bike. Kept it locked up in Audrey's shed. Called it her *trusty steed*, whatever that meant.

She squealed at my flowers. Squealed more when I told her why I'd got them. Called me *a star*. (*A little star*, which took away from it a bit.)

I went to get a vase. Juicy Lucy was in the kitchen. She was always cooking. Mostly veg she'd got from the market, marked down at the end of the day. Weird veg, some of it. Things I'd never seen before. Not sure she knew what some of them were either.

'Where you get those, Maggsie?' She looked up from the chopping board. She had long hair, dark, with a blue bit at the front. When she had enough money she was going to have the whole lot done. 'Your boyfriend?'

'Not bloody likely.' There was only one vase and it was much too small so I used a plastic jug. The wrapping paper hid the measuring marks down the side. Men were a waste of space. (You may think different. If you are a man.)

Juice's mouth dropped open when I told her. Said it was like something off the telly. She'd have gone to pieces, she said. She was right: she probably would have.

I staggered to the stairs with the jug. Big Shirl came out of her room, blocking the hallway. She wasn't called

Big Shirl for nothing. She looked at the flowers, head on one side. Whistled. Didn't look the type that *could* whistle. 'A good fifty pounds those must have cost.' She jabbed me with her elbow, cackling. 'Was you worth it, Maggsie?'

I looked at her frosty. Ruby, stuffing her curly hair into a cycling helmet, filled her in. Big Shirl nodded like it was the sort of thing she heard every day. Brought in about her having a grandson around the same age as Jack. She paused like she was expecting one of us to say *you don't look old enough, Shirl,* only neither of us did. Then off she went again. All the flowers *she'd* had from *satisfied customers*, red roses every Valentine's Day from a retired judge, on and on. 'Excuse me,' I said, ever so polite, because I was still in a good mood, and heaved the flowers upstairs.

The jug only just fitted on the window sill. I pulled the blind down so the flowers wouldn't get chilled and eased some purple ones out from a tangle of leaves. There was a lovely fresh smell, like Granda's greenhouse where he'd grown his tomatoes.

I put Jack's card on the table. Smoothed out the envelope and put it away in my holdall. I stretched out on the bed – always plenty of room to stretch out when you're shorter – feet facing the window, and looked at the flowers.

I'd got a stray cat to come when I called, long as I had a pilchard with me. All week I'd managed the tube and crowds and talking to posh people. Done the right thing when I'd found Jack collapsed. Mum would never have believed I'd done a whole week working in London. 'Pull the other one, Maggs,' she'd have said, and lit another fag.

I got up and ticked Friday off on the calendar. Gave it an extra big one because it was the end of a whole week.

# 7

After tea I watched some murder thing from the olden days with Big Shirl and Juicy Lucy. They were the only two girls I'd met so far. Big Shirl's knitting needles clicked and clacked all the way through. Juicy Lucy kept asking what was happening. She said it was because she had weak eyes and the screen was too dark, but she couldn't always follow what you were saying either.

I tried some chat about Jack wanting me to visit him, and about the industrial dishwasher at work. The size of it and that. But they were glued to the screen, Juicy Lucy with a little frown on. Big Shirl got in about her grandson again. About his favourite football team. She wasn't keen on me taking the limelight.

There were two other girls on the first floor. Saturday, I met the one in the room next to mine. I'd already heard her bed creaking.

When I came out of the bathroom she was looking through my door. Nosey cow. Didn't jump back or anything, just carried on looking.

'Had your eyeful, have you?' I had to practically push past her to get into my room.

'Just seen your flowers. I wondered what the smell

was.' She had a face like a walnut, brown and shrivelled. Old – sixty, if she was a day.

'Well, now you know.' I liked my own space. And people not poking their noses in.

'Hoity-toity,' she muttered, or some such, and went back to her room sharpish. Pity it was next door.

Jack's flowers were the first thing you saw coming into my room. You could smell the perfume even in the hallway. I'd bought some Blu-Tack and stuck his card up on the wall so you could see that as well. Long as you asked first.

When his flowers were on their last legs I'd press one or two, like I'd heard you could, to keep. They'd remind me I'd done something right for once. Make it seem real.

You could be in hospital for weeks with burns, Ruby said. So I was going to visit. Well, I was working up to it. Wasn't looking forward to trying to find the hospital. Or to seeing the look on Jack's face. He'd been unconscious before. Now he'd see me in all my glory.

Ruby wrote down the name of the station nearest St George's. Printed off another Google Map. I was in her very good books because of Jack. But that's pressure, see, though you might not think it. Because then you can disappoint people.

The tube was busy although it was Sunday. I folded my arms and stared straight ahead like the rest of them. My palms were sweating. What would I say to Jack? Whatever I said was likely to come out mangled. I looked down at my old trainers. I wasn't nothing special. Anything but. Let's face it, I didn't look like the sort of person who rescued people. I brushed off my jeans. Tightened the elastic on my ponytail. Checked Nan's earrings were done up. I only wore them when I needed an extra boost. But he *wanted* to see me. It wasn't my idea. I could just scarper when his face fell.

Hard finding your way round London when your reading's not great. Puts you at a disadvantage. Makes you feel small, smaller than you actually are. But the hospital was so big, well, its chimney was, you could see it a mile off. It took longer to find the ward.

Apart from being born I'd only been inside a hospital once before. That hadn't exactly been a joyful experience. Well, it had been, for thirty-seven hours, and then it had been the complete ruddy opposite.

My trainers squeaked on the polished floor. It was the loudest noise there was. It sounded like I shouldn't be there. I felt like that in a lot of places, actually. Especially in London. The hospital TCP smell made my heart go thump, thump, thump.

A nurse pointed out a side room. Jack's bed was by the window. Buildings looming outside like there was all over London. He took up the whole length of it. He was a big lad. That's why it had been so hard rolling him off those wires. He was propped up on one elbow, playing with an Xbox. Gave me goosebumps, seeing him awake. Seeing him alive.

I marched up to the bed. Trust me, it's the best way. Otherwise, your nerve can go, dithering.

'Hiya.' My hands were in my jacket pockets, all casual. Only they were clenched. 'I'm Maggsie. From Scanda. It was me that, well, what helped you out last week.'

The same chubby cheeks and short hair, shaved

shorter at the sides. He dropped his Xbox and pulled himself up straight, wincing.

'You wanted to see me. You put it on your card,' I reminded him, seeing as he wasn't saying anything. 'Oh and thanks for the flowers, yeah. Really nice.' Probably his mum's idea, I thought.

He was sitting up now. Had on a black Darth Vader T-shirt rucked up at the side. His face was pink. 'Hi. I wasn't sure . . .'

'If it was a good idea seeing me?' I filled in for him. And now you have, you wish you hadn't, I thought.

'No! I wanted to see you. I wasn't sure if you'd come.' He stopped. His face was pinker. 'Sorry. This is weird. I didn't expect you to be so s . . .'

Scruffy, was he going to say? Stupid?

'Small,' he got out. 'I mean, they said a woman, a lady, but . . . You're really tiny. I don't know how you did it.'

I let tiny go seeing as he was in hospital and he'd said lady as well. Second time I'd been called that. He spread his hands, palms up. 'I wanted to say thank you. Like, in person. My leg's on the mend now. Could have lost it, though.'

My eyes prickled. I held the Google Map in front of my mouth so he wouldn't see my teeth. 'Nah, you're OK. I didn't have time to think, really. Made me ever so popular at work, I can tell you.' I stretched up on tiptoe. I wasn't that tiny. 'It was my first day, see. Me helping you out made a bloody good impression.'

He smiled, sank back, adjusting his leg under the covers.

And that was it really. He was a nice lad. Nice manners. I gave him an awkward sort of hug when I said goodbye. He was hard to reach, lying down.

'There's nothing to you.' He shook his head. 'Amazing you could shift me.'

'Wonder Woman, that's me. Hidden powers.'

Soon as I was out in the corridor, the TCP smell hit me again. Made my eyes sting. I had to find a toilet and splash my face with cold water. Smells are a devil for bringing things up. Things I tried to keep in a box so I didn't think about them. They hit me then like that cold water on my face.

# 8

'Out of ruddy control, you are!' Mum shouted, reaching out to grab me with the hand that didn't have a fag. She'd try and get me to stay in, half-hearted like. Dad didn't. He was always shouting at me to get out. I stood up to him, see. Someone had to. Nella was never at home and Tiny was glued to Mum.

Dad was around then. Ruling the roost from the sofa in his baggy boxers and manky Guns N' Roses T-shirt. Drinking. Poncing about with his guitar. He played in a band, and once in a blue moon they got a gig. Only in a working men's club, but enough for Dad to see himself as a rock god. I saw him more like something strutting on a dung heap. Having his neck wrung and all his Guns N' Roses feathers plucked. Roasting in hot fat with only a pile of potatoes to show off to.

That's why I went down the park. Other kids there escaping stuff at home. One of them was Al, Alex. He was a quiet type. Lovely dark eyes. Gentle. He was the complete opposite of Dad, actually.

I put loads of mascara on, chatted fit to burst, but it still took him ages to twig I fancied him. I had to catch hold of his hand – it was a chilly evening, windy, and we were running, don't know why – before he got the message. He put his arm round me then and, slowly, things moved on.

He was a soppy sort of bloke, been bullied at school. After our first snog he bought me a box of After Eights from the 99p store. The others saw it. Gave him a hard time. I had to hand them round.

A bit of the park was all rosebushes, in rows like soldiers. You could smell the roses a mile off. Old ladies, all neat white heads and pastel cardigans and clickety false teeth, sat there in the daytime. The bushes were planted in memory of their dead husbands or something.

No one there evenings, though. The old ladies were watching TV or playing bingo or knitting. Or, if they were like my nan, before she was poorly, ballroom dancing or messing about with a face pack at home.

So that's where me and Alex arranged to meet up. I arranged it really. He turned up with a bottle and a silly smile. Nearly fell over following me between the bushes. The place smelt like the Turkish Delights in the boxes of chocolates Dad brought home sometimes. When he hadn't come home the night before.

Alex took off his leather jacket – it wasn't real leather – and spread it out. Neither of us said much, in spite of the drink. In the end I thought, blow this for a game of soldiers. I sat up, pulled off my jumper and T-shirt and unzipped my jeans.

From what I could see of Alex's face he was nervous. Like I was going to bite. Very slowly, he undid his.

'Alex.' I pulled his jeans leg to hurry him up. 'You're not a bloody stripper. I ain't here to be teased.'

He fell back, giggling. Like I said, he was a limp sort of a bloke. I don't mean, well, you know . . . more that he didn't get on with things. He was worried he might hurt me, he said. Me! More like the other way round.

Anyway, we got there in the end. I don't think he'd done it before neither. He said he had, but all blokes are liars, aren't they?

Alex bent down to pick up a rose petal after. Put it in his jacket pocket. Told you he was too soft for his own good.

We didn't cuddle up, even after that, because of the others giving us grief, but Alex was always looking at me. That's why I remember his lovely dark eyes.

One evening the teasing got really bad. Alex was fed up. He'd been drinking. Had a can in his hand; said he was going to buy more booze.

He headed straight across the road. Didn't even look. There was a screech of brakes. I started running. Saw him waving at the driver with his can. I hadn't realized he was so far gone.

A car came the other way, too bloody fast. Another squeal of brakes. A horrible thud. I can still hear it when I'm feeling low.

My arms were pumping, trainers slipping on the damp grass. The others followed. 'No!' one of the girls screamed. 'This ain't happening.'

The driver had called an ambulance. Blood was coming out of Alex's mouth. To be honest, I couldn't look too close. I knew he was dead. I zipped up his jacket and kept squeezing his hand. My teeth were chattering.

One of the other lads made a move on me not long after. Called me a spitfire when I hit him. I liked the sound of that, even after spitfires turned out to be old planes, not dragons. Still given people what for, though, hadn't they?

After that, drink went to my head really quickly,

which was a good thing. Then it made me feel sick, which wasn't.

Didn't notice the first missed period. The second one I put down to not eating much. Weird the waistband of my jeans was getting tighter, though. That's when it finally clicked.

I couldn't think straight. Tried *not* to think. Only thing I did was stop drinking. Didn't want the baby not knowing where it was or what it was doing. Didn't tell anyone. Dad would have thrown me out. Mum would have made me get rid of it. No way would she want to be *Nan*. My own nan was ill. Tell a teacher? You're having a laugh, aren't you?

It was Nella who spotted it. She would. She was always a prissy little madam. Neat and tidy. All the buttons done up on her cardigans. Soon as she was thirteen she'd got herself a paper round. Bought a new school shirt with her wages and washed it herself. Bought tights, so no more sorting through our minging sock pile to find a pair that matched. Bought shampoo, with a lovely smell, that she kept hidden from Mum.

It was when I was helping her cook Sunday dinner. Roast chicken pieces – not enough money for a whole one. Mum was still in bed and Dad had just come in. Nella passed me the potato peeler and a bag of spuds. She was good at stretching out a little bit of meat. Pity she was so brisk about it. Bet she's got freezers full of chickens now, all neatly lined up in rows with a 'use by' label tied to each leg. Like the morgues you see on cop shows.

Nella's hand brushed my belly. She stopped, a bottle of corn oil in her hand. 'You're up the duff!' She slammed the bottle down. The oil made a glooping sound. My innards did the same. 'How could you be so bloody stupid? What's Justin going to say? His *mum*? They already think I'm trash.'

Justin was her boyfriend – sorry, fiancé. They'd only just got engaged. Another year and Justin would be 'a qualified electrician'. Nella, and Mum, got that in whenever they could. Justin had a car and his shirts and jumpers had sharp creases in the sleeves where his mum had ironed them. Nella wouldn't let him inside our house.

Mum came downstairs. Dressing gown, unlit fag. Nella was giving a bowlful of Yorkshire pudding batter what for.

Mum's fag fell to the floor when Nella told her. She bent to pick it up. 'If you think *I'm* going to look after it, you've got another think coming.'

She got a social worker involved. There was a mother and baby unit in the next town, other girls there in the same boat. I could carry on with my education. Yeah, right. Once I'd thought things through I'd agree *adoption was the best way forward*. Families were crying out for newborns. Give my baby away? Yeah, double right.

Mum had to pack for me. I wasn't carried off kicking and screaming, but that was only because I was so tired. All I wanted to do was sleep.

Some of the girls at the unit had already had their babies. Showed off about them. Which one had the most designer clothes and that. Gave me stick for not being able to read. So much for being *in the same boat*. The English teacher brought in a volunteer to help me. Didn't ask me if I *wanted* help. Having her there made me stick out more. She wore a long frumpy skirt and peered out from a fringe that came down to her glasses. Tutted when

I tried to read a sentence out loud. The unit was probably the only place where she got to feel superior.

That was it as far as me learning to read, of course. They couldn't make me do it.

The doctor looked at me over the top of his glasses. Called my baby my *difficulty*. The midwife asked me a list of questions and ripped the blood pressure cuff off my arm. After the first one, about smoking, I just sat there, silent, wishing I could wrap it around her throat.

And then it was the hospital. The polished floor. The TCP smell.

Alastair, I called him. Same first two letters as Alex, plus it sounded posh. Nella wrote it out for me. It had the word *stair* in it. I already knew the word because it was on signs. *Stairs* meant going up in the world.

He was small, just over five pounds, but perfect. All curled up like a little dormouse. Not much hair and the little bit he had was ginger, but you can't have everything in this life.

Hardly cried. I only put him down to change his nappy. I wasn't going to let them take him. But I was worn out, weepy, couldn't think straight, only fifteen. There were adoptive parents lined up already. I wasn't a match for Nella and Mum and all the rest of them.

I dressed him up in the yellow and white striped babygro I'd bought him and they took him off me. They had to pull him out of my arms. I wasn't going to *give* him to nobody. The last I saw of him was the back of his little head sticking out of a baby blanket, one from the unit, like they'd wrap round any baby, going out the door.

*

Back at home I didn't want to eat or watch TV. Just wanted Alastair snuggled in the crook of my arm again.

Mum and Nella were nice to me at first. They bought me a kitten. Gingernut. Like a cat would make up for not having a baby. Gingernut did worm his way in, mind. Purred on my chest. He had little ginger eyelashes like mine and Alastair's.

The two of them put towards a denim jacket. It's the one I've still got now. That was when I started dyeing my hair black. With that and the jacket, and Nan's earrings, I had a tough look going on. That was to stop people taking anything off me again.

The being nice stopped. It was *moving on. Making a fresh start*. They wanted me to go back to school. Or college. Yeah, right. That would make me feel better, when I couldn't hardly read. With people asking what I'd been doing this past year.

I had one photo of Alastair. Nella had taken it. His eyes were open and he was frowning because the light was so bright. I kept it in a box I'd got from Nan's display cabinet after she died. A little box with shells glued around the lid in a circle, and 'A Present from Margate' written in the middle. Don't laugh, but for years I thought it said 'A Present from Marguerite'. I knew *I* hadn't given it to her, but I imagined it was from some other Marguerite. Someone tall, with flashing teeth, good at cooking, a book writer.

For a while I dreamt of getting Alastair back. Then that faded. So did everything else. I just drifted, really. Drank too much. Sofa-surfed. Shoplifted. There was a hole inside me. Felt like when you lose your purse, only much, much worse.

Once things started going pear-shaped I stopped

opening the Present from Margate box. I didn't want Alastair to know what I was doing.

There were other men. They'd do anything for me, at first. But that would soon change and they'd want me to do everything for them. Got ratty, and worse, when I wouldn't. Yeah, never met a good man yet. Alex had been just a boy, really.

As things slid further downhill, I kept the whole memory of Alastair shut up in that box. He was safe there. I tried not to think about him, only sometimes things opened it up. Like when I saw a little kid with ginger hair, or someone said *my son*, or I heard the name Alastair, or there was that question: *got any kids?*

You'd be surprised how often people ask that. You might not have noticed. Medical people ask it, only they word it posher. Even people who stop you in the street to do a survey ask you. It's the next question after *married or single?*

All that went through my brain walking out of the hospital and going back on the tube. Felt like a wrung-out dishcloth by the time I got home. Took the shine off saving Jack.

I changed the water in Jack's flowers and settled the jug back on the window sill. Pictured him, pink and smiling, in his hospital bed. He must have said thank you about a dozen times.

I looked out of the window. There was a little pool of light and colour under the streetlamp. Then a bleached-out bit and then everything else was dark. I'd given Jack – or his leg, anyway – another go at life. He was keen on football, he'd said. Keen to be back playing for his works team. I'd done that for him, me, Maggsie

50

M, unlikely though it was. I pulled down the blind. I hadn't given Alastair a go at life. Someone else had. I hadn't been allowed to. I saw the back of his little head again, going out that hospital door.

I went over to the wardrobe and ticked Sunday off on the calendar. Thumbed through the other months. All those spindly Scanda chairs. Lamps like skeletons. I imagined the end of the year, Mum smiling when she'd got over the shock of me sticking at anything. Her boasting about *my youngest daughter, the one that works in London.* Saw myself crowing to Nella. Imagined flapping a *Woman's World* in the faces of all those teachers who'd written me off. *I can read this now, see, cover to cover, practically. No thanks to you.*

I imagined something else. Shut my mind to Nella bursting out laughing. Tapped the biro on my lip. Took a deep breath in. And o-u-t.

Maybe I could write to the adoption people. Ask them about Alastair. How to find him. Once he was eighteen, see, I could contact him, legally.

I dropped the biro. *He won't want to know you, Maggsie,* I heard. Not sure whose voice it was. Could have been a lot of people's.

But I'd be making things right. I could tell him how I hadn't wanted to give him up. Say sorry for not fighting to keep him. Maybe, one day, I might even meet him. See he was alright.

Yeah, he had an *adoptive* mum already, but that was different. They didn't share blood or anything. Bet *she* didn't have ginger hair. Not that that was a bonus, but knowing I did too, underneath, would be a bond, wouldn't it?

I picked up the biro. Held on to it. I could hardly

write, let alone a posh letter. God knows how much practice that would take. Three hundred and fifty more days to go. Longer than some prison stretches. But after a whole year of sticking at a job and improving my reading, I'd be as good as anyone else, wouldn't I? Maybe not my teeth, but the rest of me. I'd be a new person. I'd already done things this last week I never thought I could.

I swallowed. Could I? Never seemed possible before. But now . . .

# 9

Once I'd started thinking about Alastair again I couldn't stop. His wisps of ginger hair. The back of his little head being carried out the door. The lovely dark eyes he might have got from Alex. I'd save up, take him out somewhere posh like Pizza Hut. He'd fill in the gaps for me, since he was born, his schooling, hobbies, all that. I'd say as little as possible about my life so he wouldn't be disappointed.

I got up early and fetched down my holdall. The 'A Present from Margate' box was in there, wrapped in a baby vest. Not one of his, I didn't have anything of his. One I'd bought after. His photo was still inside – gave me goosebumps seeing it. Hadn't been easy hanging on to that box. Not in some of the places I'd been.

I was going to have to start writing letters, I thought, zipping up my jeans. Reading was bad enough, but as for writing anything down . . . I pulled on a black T-shirt, long-sleeved for winter. Turned back the sleeves a couple of inches. I'd work up to it. Start off with one to Enid.

She wouldn't mind mistakes. I'd tell her about Jack; maybe even Alastair. She'd asked me the *got any kids?* question once. 'Not so you'd notice,' I'd said, and changed the subject. But no way would I be able to put all that into words.

Audrey was waiting outside the kitchen door. Purred when she saw the pilchard coming. Didn't scarper when I scratched the top of her head. Saturday, she'd started letting me do that. She wasn't in so much of a hurry to get back under the shed neither. She sat next to it, washing her white paws that Ruby thought were like gloves. Might even be filling out a bit. Still jumped a mile in the air, mind, if anyone else got near her. On the way back home from work – don't laugh – I pictured her little furry face, her wide eyes with the black 'eyeliner', waiting for me. Well, for her pilchard.

What put a dampener on things was Primrose coming over with some stuff I was supposed to read. Health and safety, great pile of it. Small print. *Reading*. People watching while I did it. Told you that would happen. That's the sort of thing that's made me walk out before.

I could feel my face going red. It always shows because of my pale skin. Puts you at a disadvantage. I finished unloading the dishwasher. Wasn't in a hurry to make a fool of myself. I stared at the pages of writing. Yeah, I could read bits in *Woman's World*. Bits with pictures. But anything longer, whole pages, had only been with Enid helping. Sitting next to me, smiling and nodding. On my own I couldn't work out where one sentence finished and another one began. My heart would start going. Often as not I'd end up chucking it on the floor. I've already told you I got dyslexia. Doesn't mean I'm thick.

I wasn't going to tell Primrose. Not and have her look down on me. And, silly thing was, I had a Health and Safety certificate already. Never mind I'd got it in prison. I'd *used* it here, rescuing Jack!

Primrose said I still had to do it. Insurance or

something. She went back to the oven. I could see a couple of inches of bright material, orange with red and black lines, flouncing about under her overall.

Just as I was stuffing the pages in my pocket, TJ looked over. He loomed about like Dad, and Dougie after him, had. Mum was soppy with the both of them. Looked up into their eyes, snuggled into their armpits. Made me want to vomit.

'I can go over health and safety in break-time if you would like,' TJ was saying. 'When we have fags.'

I stared at him. Nearly got a crick in my neck doing it. He was too ruddy tall. And why was he always smiling? He was smiling now. Was he taking the mick? Sneering? And if he wasn't, what was in it for him? He could put any ideas of trying it on with me out of his head for starters. No thank you.

I looked at his shiny black shoes. You could tell he was foreign before he'd even opened his mouth. It was the shoes and his bristly hair, like a coconut, and the size of him. Then, when he spoke you could *really* tell.

Maybe he wanted to show off how clever *he* was. Men get a kick out of that. Well, even if he was – and I hadn't seen any sign of it so far – he was foreign. I could *speak* English loads better than him. I folded my lips tight. *When we have fags.* That wasn't right for starters. When we have *our* fags, I nearly said, only it would have encouraged him.

How did he know I struggled with reading? Because I'd said I hadn't got my glasses before? Had he read my mind? Never met a man yet who could do that.

He was still smiling. 'I read out fire precautions and sharp knives. And you explain when I make mistake with English word. Yes? Fair change is not stealing.'

'Fair *exchange* is no *robbery.*' Nan used to come out with those old sayings. I picked up the pile of plates. Once he'd given me a bit of help he'd have a hold on me. Plus he might tell other people. Broadcast I was thick. Then him asking *me* for help with English sunk in. I wanted to burst out laughing. My teachers would have done their insides a mischief hearing that.

I'd hated every second of school. Every single second. Had a gut ache every school day. Got confused from the very beginning. I could name the letters OK, but I couldn't hear the different sounds they were supposed to make. They ganged up against me. No way could I stack them together to make words.

Teachers thought I wasn't trying: *Concentrate, Marguerite!* But at home I'd spent ages staring at the words on packets and tins. Touching them, in case I could feel what they said.

One teacher, Mrs Connell, God love her – because sure as hell nobody else would – used to snatch the empty worksheets off my desk. Give me evils while she done it. Once I threw it at her first; got sent to the headmaster for that. She said I'd attacked her. Still made my gut burn, even now. Wish I *had* attacked her.

The headmaster gave me the willies, although I didn't let on. He had white hair and black eyebrows that didn't match. Glasses on top of his head. Pointed his finger at me, like he was putting on a curse. 'With that sort of behaviour I see a bleak future for you, Marguerite McNaughton. You'll never amount to anything.'

So that was it. I couldn't read. End of.

In prison, well . . . yeah, they had adult literacy classes. Went along once for something to do. But there wasn't anyone else there who couldn't read at all. I'd

56

felt like a freak. The tutor fussed around, putting coloured plastic sheets over the printed writing, plonking down wooden alphabet letters. The other girls stared. No way was I going to be seen playing with kids' toys. After that I knew there wasn't no one on this earth who could teach me to read and write.

TJ was still waiting. He handed me a stack of cups for the dishwasher. His eyes had the same expression that Lenny, Nan's poodle, used to have when I ate a bacon sarnie.

I carried on putting the cups into the racks. I was still thinking. I needed stuff read. And I didn't care what TJ thought of me. Plus, he didn't seem the type who'd make a move on you. Not with those shoes. He wore a silver ring with a dent in it; not that being married had counted for much with Dad.

I squeezed the last cup into the dishwasher. After a couple of days of using it I'd worked out a way of stacking the cups closer. Getting more in speeded things up. Scanda's staff got through shed-loads of coffee. It was because they didn't smoke much or seem to eat snacks. A lot less of both in London.

I glanced up at TJ. Big smile on his moon face. It struck me again he might be lacking in the brain department. But he could read and I couldn't, not very well. I could *speak* OK. Gobby, some people said. And he thought *I'd* be helping *him*. I pressed the button on the dishwasher. Blew out a whumph of air. 'OK, you're on.'


'Yeah, yeah.' I drummed my fingers on the bench, blowing out smoke. TJ finished the last section. Something about wiping up floor spills straight away.

He pointed to where I had to sign. *Maggsie M*, I put, like always. Looked at him to see if he was laughing at me. He was smiling but, seeing as he smiled all the time, it was difficult to say.

He put the pen back in his apron pocket. I'd never seen a man wearing an apron till I came here. They must do things different in Scandinavia. And in Poland. They definitely did in London. 'Your English ain't bad,' I told him, seeing as he'd done me a favour.

'No, no. Slang I do not get right.'

He went to English classes Tuesday evenings, he said. In Poland he'd been an agricultural scientist. 'Test soil. Help farmers.'

Blimey. He *was* all there then. 'Ain't much science in clearing tables. Ain't much *soil* in London.'

He had a big lumpy sort of face, like a potato, with little twinkly eyes that got swallowed up with the smiling. 'No, is true.' He swept his arm out at the skyscrapers around us. I ducked. One wave and he'd have me off the bench. 'Sorry!' He reached out to pat my arm. I moved away. 'But here is opportunity,' he went on, keeping his arm to himself. 'Is future.'

'Opportuni*ties*. *Are* opportunities,' I corrected, tapping the ash off my fag. It felt good correcting him. Maybe that was what teachers got off on. *Opportunity* was what the probation officer, inside, had kept on about. It meant something similar to *chance*. Only more definite.

I took a last drag and stubbed out my fag. Breathed the smoke out slow. Hugged myself against the cold. I'd found a way of not going off on one with the health and safety stuff. Alastair would have been proud of me. I looked at the new glass buildings shining in the distance. One day I'd be able to read official stuff on my own.

Enid hadn't said the word *opportunity*. Not something you'd think you'd get in prison. But that's what she'd given me getting me started on the reading. Funny how it could hurt, remembering someone doing something good for you.

# 10

Every prison's different. It's a roll of the dice who you get banged up with. When the doors slammed behind me last stretch I had no idea my life was going to change. If you'd told me I'd have learnt a bit of reading by the time I got out again I'd have said you were having a laugh. Even more if you'd said it'd be another con who'd learn me.

I'd been having a lie-down – splitting headache, cold coming on. Actually, I'd dozed off. Then *Only me, ducks.* I heaved myself up on one elbow. Enid. Chatterbox Enid. What did she want?

Enid was coming to the end of a ten-year sentence for bumping off her mum. She had done it, but it was mercy killing. Enid had looked after her for years and, when her mum couldn't get about at all, or swallow or even speak hardly, she'd asked Enid to help her out with a cushion and sleeping pills.

Enid couldn't ever find a bra that could cope with her boobs. Red marks on her shoulders. Wore cardigans, not done up, because they wouldn't stretch across and a load of necklaces and pendants. The plastic beads clicked together when she tip-tapped around the place.

She had an eager sort of expression, like she was looking for something. Always wanted to know what was going on, did Enid. And could she talk? Never stopped.

'Fancy a cuppa?' She reached out to straighten my duvet. Think it came automatic with looking after her mum.

I nodded. My throat was parched.

She came back with a strong, sweet cup of tea – four sugars, not many people remember that, or believe it – and a pile of women's magazines. *Woman's World*, she said they were.

'Thought you might fancy a read if you're not feeling well. There's a bit about Prince Harry here.' She folded back a page.

'Enid,' I slumped back on the bed. 'You know I can't read.'

'Can't read? Well, I don't suppose anyone in here's brilliant at reading. But you can read a magazine, can't you?'

I pushed it away. 'No! Can't hardly read a bloody thing.'

Enid didn't laugh. She picked up her magazine and smoothed out a crease from its pages. 'Well that's because nobody showed you how, dear. Perhaps they never had no patience at your school.' She said it very definite, like *of course* that was the reason. Like of course it wasn't because I was thick.

She turned more pages. 'Now here's an interesting bit: "What to eat for a healthy heart".'

I groaned. Peered up. 'Fish and bananas,' I said and she got excited. But that was what the pictures were about.

'Ah, but it says the same underneath.' Enid pointed to some swirls and shapes of words.

Then I guessed 'Olive Oil', because of the capital letters being big circles. Heard a chorus of teachers: *It's no good you guessing, Marguerite.*

'Nothing wrong with guessing.' Enid sat down on my bed, bouncing me up with her weight. 'When you don't know a word, just keep going until you find one you *do* know. Gives you a clue, see. Even if it's right at the end of the sentence.'

I flipped through Enid's magazine. Asked her what a couple of words were, to show willing.

'You've done ever so well, love.' Enid got up. 'Come and see me and have another go. Got to practise, else you'll forget.'

A few days later she came in when I was having a weak moment. 'Whatever's the matter, love?' As if being in prison and on my own with no future wasn't enough. She took me into her cell for a cup of tea. Fetched a *Woman's World* to cheer me up, seeing as I done so well before. Yeah, right.

Her cell was real homely. Because of all the years she'd spent inside, I suppose. It smelt of peppermints and there was a crocheted cover on the bed. Little squares, all bright colours. The other girls gave her bits of wool left over from their knitting. She crocheted while I read. Tried to read. Just as well she had something to do seeing as every bit took me ages. The hook went in, up and over. Soothing rhythm to it.

There was a collection of dolls from other countries in fancy skirts on a shelf. They stared down at me with beady little black eyes like they couldn't believe how thick I was.

The other girls in here had photos and kids' drawings

and cards on their walls. One, a right show-off, posh, had a whole wall covered with arty postcards. But Enid's were travel pictures, cut from the holiday pages of *Woman's World*. Foreign cities by moonlight, forests, mountains, castles, that sort of thing. She'd been inside so long they were going yellow.

At school my 'reading' books were nearly all pictures. I'd got teased about it. But Enid said pictures helped tell you what the writing was about. That's how I learnt about a new hair dye, one that didn't fade so quick. That was useful. And I managed to follow a recipe for scones because the pictures showed you how to make them, step by step. I was never actually going to cook any scones, but it was nice to know it was possible.

I ended up doing a bit of reading most days. Never seemed no point in trying before. Enid said she got a kick out of teaching me. God knows how she had the patience. After half an hour of concentrating I had to jump off her bed and pace about.

Sometimes letters stopped doing their own thing and clumped themselves together into words. Other days I got stuck on the simplest thing. 'I ain't never going to get it, Enid.'

'No such word as never, my girl.' Enid pushed her hair back. (It could have done with a wash, to be honest; it was always falling in her face.) 'Look at all the words you read yesterday. Couldn't have done that a few weeks back, could you?'

We moved on to the problem page. Some poor cow's hubby playing away. Read what the agony auntie said about him. Agreed, the both of us, *we'd* chop his balls off. Had a good old cackle. Interesting what you read sometimes.

One day, and it was frustrating it didn't happen every day, I read a whole sentence on my own. Without stopping. Read another, then another. I was on a roll. It was a bit from the problem page about *confidence*. There were other hard words: *positive*, *self-esteem*. (Four 'e's in that, plus a nasty little line stuck in the middle.) In the end I read the whole bit. Took me nearly an hour rather than five minutes, and Enid gave me clues, but still.

I put the *Woman's World* down and danced about. Enid punched the air, bosom bouncing. Maureen, from the cell next door, came in and asked if we were partying. Thought we'd got hold of some booze. Turned surly when we said we'd been *reading*. Stomped back to her cell.

Being able to read felt like being rescued from drowning. I knew what that was like. Gone too far in a school swimming lesson once, hadn't I, and the teacher hadn't noticed me going under. When the lifeguard fished me out I'd sat on the side, dripping, not minding the teacher shouting. Just looked at the people staring from the gallery, like I'd never seen people before.

I copied out the words *positive* and *confidence*. Long words I could read now. I'd never hardly written anything before so the letters straggled like spray-can graffiti. I tried to do them neater. There was a little word, *sit*, inside *positive*, and *con* and *den* in *confidence*. That's what I was: a con in a den.

I stuck them on my wall with blobs of toothpaste. About all it was good for with me. We weren't allowed Blu-Tack on account of it could be used to gum up the locks. I never normally had stuff to put up. Mum still sent me birthday cards and Christmas cards, but Nella had stopped bothering. One day, if I could write proper,

I'd send people cards left, right and centre. And the ones I got back I'd stick up everywhere like that posho, Louise, did with her arty postcards. There'd be whole rows of them, hanging from strings.

Think Enid was lonely, myself. She wasn't exactly street-wise. Some of the girls sniggered behind her back. No way could you see her bumping off anybody, even if it was putting her mum out of her misery.

She didn't mind talking about it. Said her mum's eyes used to follow her around the room. Pleading, like. Broke Enid's heart. She'd used a cushion her mum had embroidered to do it.

Said it was a kindness and she didn't regret it, even after years inside, because she'd loved her mum.

I looked at a picture on her wall of a desert with a string of camels. 'What you going to do when you get out, Enid? Travel?'

'Bet your bottom dollar, I am.' Her chest flopped as she sat down on the bed. 'My niece got one of they apartments in somewhere ever so foreign. Romania! By a lake. Pine forests all around. That's where I'm going. Less than eighteen months and I'll be on that plane.' She rubbed her hands together. 'You won't see me for dust.'

I didn't say anything. My release date was before Enid's. I didn't think about getting out. Out wasn't good when you didn't have plans. This was before the proba-tion officer came up with the Scanda idea. "Spect I'll get myself put back inside soon as I can.'

'Nah, reading's going to put you on the right road this time, my girl.' Enid leant towards me, her face all lit up. 'I can feel it in my water.'

*

I put down the *Woman's World* I'd bought at the Co-op. The beauty page was about making the most of your skin. *Glow* had taken me a while to work out. Think it would sound the same as *now*, wouldn't you?

That letter to Enid. I got to have a go. For her, and for Alastair.

I fetched a notepad I'd bought earlier. I knew how to spell Enid, at least. Knew it had a capital letter. Names and places had one, and beginnings of sentences. But how did you know when to start a new sentence? Why couldn't you just keep on going with the old one? I leant over the notepad, clutched the pen and made a start. I could hear myself breathing.

> *Dear Enid*
>     *I am heer in London. I am ok. There is a cat heer I am in charg off the dishwash. I save a lad in the lift. 1 day I will try and rite to somone. I hop you ok. Luv, Maggsie M.*

I crumpled up the first go. Sat back and looked at the second. I'd pressed so hard the biro had come through the other side. First letter I'd ever wrote, though. A little bit of me was on that sheet of paper now. When Enid got it she'd know what I'd been thinking. Some of it.

I crossed today off the calendar. Put down my biro, then picked it up again. Under the date I squeezed in: *rote a letter.*

# 11

I began to tick off my calendar soon as I got home from work. I got a bit obsessed by it, to tell you the truth. Looking at the ticks, counting them. In bed at night I thought about what me and Alastair would do together. I already told you about Pizza Hut.

All I had to do was keep going. Seemed pretty straightforward to me. Only, according to Ruby, I still had anger issues. I couldn't see it myself. I'd been on two separate anger management courses. Got the certificates. Knew all the tricks. Strat-e-gies, they called them, not tricks. Had the special breathing – in for four, hold for four, out for s-i-x – imprinted on my brain, practically. But them in charge had to pick on something. Otherwise it didn't look like they were doing their job.

I posted Enid's letter outside the Co-op. Heard a little soft thud as it landed inside. I'd just sent a letter. I was someone who wrote letters. Someone going places. Someone who had a goal in life. Contacting their son. Alastair.

I bought some stamps and this week's *Woman's World* and a new toothbrush, one that was supposed to work miracles, and some mouthwash. Didn't want Alastair cringing away. Plus a little tin of posh cat food for Audrey. I knew it was posh because the cat on the label had fluffy white fur and a diamond collar. And a Snickers bar for myself. It had peanuts in it and nuts were good for you. Bought a banana as well. They're more into that kind of thing in London.

Apart from me and TJ the people in the roof garden were smartly dressed. I had on my too-big overall and my jeans and trainers. I could have changed my overall for a smaller one but having it so big meant I could wrap it round me to keep out the cold, smoking. How the women who worked here ever walked in their shoes beat me. You might think I'd be one for heels, given I'm shorter, but I like the idea of a quick getaway and you can't do that in heels.

Me and TJ were about the only people who sat down to have a fag. There were a few other smokers but they stood up to do it. It was because they were posh and had jobs where they could sit down for the rest of the day.

I rolled a fag and handed it to TJ. He'd given me one of his before. I still sat at the other end of the bench. Didn't want him getting ideas. Or him knocking me to the ground when he stuck his great arm out at something. 'Read us a bit of your paper, then.' It was the *Metro* that you get free at tube stations. It was the names in the stories I struggled with.

TJ was looking at the rollie. His eyes had purple shadows underneath. He worked other places as well as Scanda. Wore himself out, more fool him. 'I *know* it's skinny. When you ain't got much, you've got to make your baccy last.'

'You use words I not understand, Maggsie. Is dialect?'

I stopped, tongue out, ready to lick my fag paper.

68

Did that mean slang? Wasn't going to let on I didn't know. Bit of a cheek him not understanding me, seeing as he mangled English soon as he opened his mouth. I nodded. Jerked my chin at the paper. 'Go on then. What's the news?'

'"Tragic Secret of High-Flying Couple".' TJ pointed to the headline. He read nice and slowly, I'll say that for him.

I peered across. *Tragic*. Now you'd think there'd be a 'j' in that, wouldn't you? I'd felt I was getting somewhere writing that letter to Enid, but then up comes a word, an everyday word, I'd never have worked out in a million years. I mean, who decided to stick a 'g' in tragic?

On my way home – well, to the house – I picked up a *Metro* myself. I'd read the article again. I'd be able to read it now, see, now I knew what it was about.

I had a couple of sandwiches in my jacket pocket. Primrose parcelled up the left-over ones at work. The weird ones nobody wanted. Dropped them off at her church, the Church of the Everlasting Light, in Peckham. She sang in the choir there. She was always singing, humming hymns and that. And she went on about her 'pastor'. I'd thought she meant spaghetti or something, but no, it was a type of vicar.

Last week she'd seen me looking at the sandwiches and offered me a couple to take home. I said I wasn't bothered, one way or the other. Didn't want to look poor. But *it is a sin to waste good food*, Primrose said, practically stuffing them into my pocket. So I let her. Saved me money and cooking so I was quids in. Don't know about 'good food', though. They weren't always sandwiches I'd have chosen myself. The bread had bits in it. Seeds. Or there'd be grated carrot where you wouldn't expect it. Once, stuck into some pongy cheese, there was actual grapes. The meat or fish ones were the best, because then Audrey could share them. I threw her little bits through the kitchen doorway. I'd got her to come right up to the door now.

Big Shirl and Juice got beady-eyed over my sandwiches because of them being free and posh. Juice said a vegetable stew – hers, she meant – had more goodness in it. Big Shirl went on about how she'd used to order in special little sandwiches and sausage rolls from Waitrose for her clients. 'Nothing but the best. And all included in the price.'

I thought she'd run a beauty salon or a posh clothes shop. 'Establishment,' she'd called it with an airy wave of her fag.

That evening, out in the yard, I found out her *establishment* was a knocking shop. An upmarket one, yeah, but still a brothel. I felt thick for not cottoning on before. Not as if I hadn't known plenty of girls inside who'd been on the game. I wasn't thick. It was a mistake anyone could have made because of the way Big Shirl looked. Wavy hair. Skirts. Pointed shoes. She had a pink cardigan on today. Pearl buttons.

Some of her clients had been solicitors, one an MP, she said, hugging herself – well, as far as she could reach. It was freezing out in the yard. She looked me up and down, telling me the details. Sizing me up. Old habits die hard. I bristled. I wouldn't be a good candidate for no knocking shop, trust me on that one. Wouldn't have no man pawing me for all the tea in China.

Funny how you can't go on first impressions. That's

not just me. That's a well-known thing. I stubbed out my fag, wondering what there was to find out about the other two girls, the foreign one – Kasia, Big Shirl said her name was – and the nosey old one next to me.

I'd looked inside her room once when she left the door open, seeing as she'd done the same. Had a good stare. I'd expected it to be messy and full of stuff – piles of old newspapers and old books and clothes like you see on TV before they bring in a decluttering expert. It wasn't messy but there were lots of ornaments and candles, like some old hippie's boudoir. The ornaments were buddhas and cats. There was a shawly thing on her bed and a cat picture stuck above it. A kitten swinging from the branch of a tree. Underneath were some torn-out pictures: cats looking smug and pleased with themselves, like the cat food adverts you saw in *Woman's World* sometimes.

I was in bed by half nine. Still got tired being on my feet all day and heaving plates about. I'd stacked them more logical in the cupboards now. In the order they got used. Breakfast bowls on the top shelf, that sort of thing. My brain worked OK doing stuff like that. Seeing the big picture. It was the little things I struggled with. Like why is it sometimes 'ie' in words, and other times 'ei'? No logic to it. Just torture. Primrose and TJ were pleased about the tidy cupboard. 'Is clever idea,' TJ said. '*A* clever idea,' I told him.

Although I was tired I couldn't drop off. The blind was moving about in the draught from the window. Yellow stripes of light from the streetlamp showed through and they moved about as well. Got on my nerves. In the end I went downstairs to make some toast.

I opened the fridge to get out my butter. Half of it was gone.

My initials were all over the packet. No way could you miss them. Someone had helped themselves. Without asking. Bet it was Big Shirl. She was just the sort of person who'd 'borrow' things. Well, two can play at that game. I bunged three slices from her loaf – it had a stick-on label with a giant 'S' on it – in the toaster. Hovis, it was, not my favourite. I slathered them all over with butter and pushed my packet right to the back of the fridge. Blowed if she was going to take any more.

I crammed the toast down before I went back upstairs. The TV was still on as I passed the lounge door. Big Shirl was probably in there, flicking through her address book, remembering all the vicars and MPs that used to eat her Waitrose sandwiches, wiping my butter from her mouth.

Being worked up don't help you get to sleep. Nor does your belly groaning.

I was pulling on my jeans when there was a rap at the door. The banging got louder. I had to hop to the door before I'd got them on properly.

Big Shirl. Looking so pissed off I wanted to close it again. But she was already in. Slammed it shut herself.

I hoisted up my jeans double quick. You don't want to be staggering about when someone's having a go.

'You pinched my bloody Hovis! Three slices you took. I counted!' Big Shirl wagged her finger in my face. I hate that. Behind the bulk of her I saw a crowd of other people: Mrs Connell from school, Dad, Dougie, a whole lot of policewomen and screws, and all of them wagging their fingers.

My heart was going. I swelled out my chest and stood feet apart, hands on hips, to give myself presence. Can't let people grind you down.

'*You* nicked half my bloody butter!' Trouble was, getting riled up made my voice go squeaky. Then people didn't take me serious. Started on about mice and that. Which got me more worked up. I lowered my chin. '*Half!*' I growled out.

Big Shirl poked her face close. She bloody hadn't. She was cutting down on her *col . . . colander*, or some such. Something butter'd got in it.

Her wrinkles looked like screwed-up paper when you'd tried to smooth it out. Like my first go at Enid's letter. I swallowed. Couldn't say I'd got it wrong, could I? Give people the upper hand and they start on the grinding. But she didn't move. Or speak. I could hear myself breathing quick and heavy.

I coughed. Then, lower, 'Next loaf I buy I'll give you your slices back.'

'Mind you bloody do.' She was still frowning. She'd drawn in her eyebrows too dark. Made her look like something out of a cartoon. They were probably bald underneath. Overplucked.

Soon as she'd gone I went over to the window. Some of Jack's flowers were still doing OK. I'd moved them into the vase from the kitchen. It had been a blow, throwing out the dead ones. I leant on the window sill. Rubbish in the gutter. An old man shuffling along. An Alsatian, with a grey muzzle, trailing behind. I shut my eyes. Not a nice feeling when someone the size of Big Shirl comes into your room and has a go. The sort of feeling that makes you want . . . well, what I've already told you, a drink. What I've told you I've put behind me. What there is no reason on this earth to go on about. *Someone* had nicked my butter, caused this kerfuffle. I did my breathing. People breathe *in* too much without letting go. You might sometimes. We all get angry; it's how you deal with it that matters.

I used to be an angry person. Had to be with my background and the places I'd spent time in. People looked up to you when you were angry. Listened. It was the only time they *did* listen. But that was before I'd done the two courses and got my certificates.

Four, four, s-i-x. I looked at the calendar, at the three weeks crossed off so far. Three weeks closer to Alastair.

After I'd sent Enid the letter, I'd written out *positive* and *confidence* on half a page torn out from my notepad. I remembered how to spell them because of the little hidden words inside. I'd stuck them on my wardrobe mirror, above the calendar. They reminded me of Enid. She'd get my letter soon. She'd be pleased with me.

I remembered a doctor's nice words to me once, said them out loud now: *keep trying and I know you'll get there.* (I haven't even told you about him yet. He was the one that helped me put things behind me. Lovely blue eyes.)

I did up the button on my jeans, wiped my face with a bit of toilet paper and went downstairs. I'd have a fag, give Audrey her pilchard – keep her special tin for a celebration, not something I was in the mood for now – and nip down the Co-op. Buy a loaf of ruddy Hovis to get Big Shirl off my back. Then I'd find out who'd pinched my butter.

I asked Juicy Lucy when I got back from the shop. She swore it wasn't her, margarine was healthier. The foreign girl, Kasia, was in the kitchen. Could have been

74

her. She was thin with dark eyes and a short skirt and too many gold chains. Brassy blonde hair that didn't match her olive skin. A read of *Woman's World*'s beauty pages would have told her that.

I'd seen her outside shooing away a great hulking bloke in a long dark coat and a woolly hat pulled down low. Tapping her watch. He hung about the entrance to the block of flats over the road. Funny the residents hadn't complained, but then this was London. Once he'd followed Kasia right up to our door and she'd shouted something and gone down the steps to give him a shove.

Now she put a funny-looking sausage in a pan to boil. *Boiling a sausage!* I kept my eye on her.

Big Shirl came in. Turned round and winked when she saw the loaf of Hovis on the worktop. Probably one of those who were OK with you, once they'd put you in your place. She took out three slices. I hoped me replacing them so quick wasn't going to go to her head. Then she asked Kasia how business was. Well, the only business Big Shirl knew about was running her brothel. So, Kasia must be on the game then. That was another thing I hadn't realized. That was another thing that might make you think I was thick. Only you'd be wrong.

Big Shirl shook her head at Kasia shrugging. Told her she'd be much better off, safer, being in an *organized set-up*. One like hers had been, you could tell she meant.

I warmed up some soup and swallowed a too-hot spoonful. Bet Kasia had taken my butter. Being on the game was breaking the rules here, but it wasn't breaking the law. Managing a brothel was, though. That was why Big Shirl had been sent down.

Juicy Lucy was sat opposite me chopping up an apple,

her eyelids drooping like sagging blinds. Didn't look safe in charge of a sharp knife. I dipped a slice of Hovis in my soup to use it up. Give me white bread any day.

Kasia slithered her sausage down onto a plate. It was still pink. A horrible link between it and what she must see a lot of in her line of work sprang to mind. Maybe that was why she'd boiled it.

She got her bread out of the fridge. Brown sour slabs, like cork tiles. Took out a jar of what looked like little cucumbers, warty things, swimming around in vinegar like diseased fish. Big Shirl told me afterwards they were called gherkins – said she'd served them with cocktails at her 'parties'. Then, blow me down if she didn't reach to the back for my packet of butter, bold as brass, and cut herself off a hefty chunk.

'Hey!' I shouted, spluttering soup. 'That's mine!'

You'd think the way Dad carried on would have turned me off getting worked up, wouldn't you? Turned me into a meek and mild sort of a person. Someone who discussed things and nodded, like Ruby. It didn't work like that. Dad, and Dougie after him, had tried to grind me down. No one was going to make me feel that way again. Powerless. That's why I always got angry – well, firm – first. The anger management tutors, therapists, whatever they called themselves, someone what tried to fix us lesser mortals, never quite got that.

'Your dad's your role model, then?' one had even asked.

I hated people trying to make me think about stuff. Like I've told you, I didn't do long-term thinking. Not forwards or backwards. Thinking spoils things in my opinion.

Another thing they'd said was, don't let your anger out. I never got that. Were you supposed to just bottle it up then? Swallow it down and pick up a piece of knitting? Yes, they said. Getting angry made the person you were angry with get angry. Lost you your job. Landed you inside. Yeah, alright for them that could just drive off, shut a door, call the police. They didn't realize that sometimes anger was all you had to defend yourself.

Kasia stared at me. Her dark eyes had eyeliner all the way round. Made them look like currants. 'Is yours? No, is woman's upstairs. Woman who not eat much.'

'No, it bloody ain't!' I jabbed the packet under her nose, what was left of it. '"MM", it says, see? Marguerite McNaughton.' For once I got my full name out perfect.

'Sounds posh when you say it like that.' Big Shirl was spreading jam on her Hovis toast. Getting it right into the corners and looking at the two of us, like she was waiting for something to kick off.

Kasia scraped the butter back into my packet. Some of it had touched her sausage.

'Too late for that!' I burst out. Her next door to me was a nosey cow. But it didn't give Kasia any right to steal her butter. She hadn't, I know, seeing as it was mine. But still.

I stared at Kasia. Someone once told me I had piercing eyes. Didn't think they'd meant it as a compliment. She was taller than me; most people were. Plus she had high heels on. She had her jar of gherkins in one hand and my butter in the other. Tottered as I snatched it back. There was a jangle of gold chains. She lost her grip on the jar – it was a big one. Smashed on the floor. Glass and warty little things everywhere; a stink of vinegar.

The others stared at the gherkins. Big Shirl shook her head. Put her jam with its great big 'S' label back in the fridge. 'Chrissie's in the office, Maggsie. She'll hear that.' Chrissie was another support worker that came in sometimes.

Kasia started to pick up the broken glass. Gave me evils while she done it. Juicy Lucy tried to rescue the gherkins. Big Shirl sighed and went to fetch the mop.

I sat back down, breathing heavy. Blowed if I was going to help. There was a red blur in front of my eyes through staring at my tomato soup. Must have been, because, since anger management, I'd kept a pretty good hold on myself. Hadn't touched Kasia, had I? Done deep breathing like they'd said. I breathed o-u-t, remembering. See?

Next minute Chrissie came in. Big-built girl. Posh voice. Single. I knew that because Big Shirl had asked her. Kasia was kneeling on the floor, surrounded by broken glass. The rest of us was dead quiet. None of us daft enough to have seen anything. But Chrissie put two and two together and made five.

# 12

**Woman's World, 7 February 2018**
Feeling Frazzled? Five Effective Ways
to Keep Your Cool

Well, that meant a sleepless night, didn't it? With my luck, just standing next to someone who'd dropped their jar of gherkins would get me kicked out. No way could I afford London rents. So lose my place here and I'd lose my job. Then where would I be? Back to square one. No chance of crowing to Nella. Or Mum. No chance of contacting Alastair one day.

Monday, after work, I got the talking-to. I put Nan's earrings on for it. Ruby's office had two swivel chairs, a desk with a load of files, probably all about us girls, and a big poster of a blonde barmaid. Old-fashioned clothes, tight-fitting, looking straight out at you with a fed-up expression. Knew how she felt. Ruby said it was a famous painting. Then her lips pressed together in the way that meant bad news was coming. I'd seen it a lot over the years.

I stared out of the window, arms folded. Here we go. The security light came on. There was Audrey walking past the shed. Much warmer inside. I still hadn't got her to come through the door. If I had to leave here she'd never manage it. I drummed my heels on the chair legs. What else can you do with your legs when they don't reach the floor? Audrey sat down to wash her face with a little white paw. Every so often she looked at the kitchen door, like she was waiting for it to open.

Ruby gave me some guff about self-control and how important it was to get on with other people, *without friction*. Yeah, but not pinching someone else's stuff is important as well. Or it ruddy should be. She'd have to report me if there were any more 'outbursts'.

My head whipped round from the window so quick my neck cricked. See, this was what happened to me. People never listened to my side of things. Ain't you got any idea what Kasia's up to when she's not stealing my butter, I wanted to say, but didn't. Snitching wasn't my thing. You don't, not once you've been inside.

I twirled one of Nan's earrings round. Stared out of the window. Saw Audrey's tail disappearing under the shed. Could think of other people I'd like to see under there and all. Ruby twitched her skirt, a long one with a fringe thing round the hem, over her knees. Big Shirl had asked her why she didn't wear short skirts, given she had the figure, and Ruby had said she *preferred an ethnic look*. That meant rusty colours and fringing and droopy skirts. And dangly earrings. 'Well, let's think how we can improve things. Alright?'

She didn't hear me mutter, 'Nah. Let's not.' Leapt in with it being bike-riding that kept *her* sane. Burnt up that *adren* . . . something. Same stuff they'd mentioned in anger management. Alright for her. She was exercise mad. She was training for a tri-ath-lon. (Try anything once, I'd thought she meant at first. Didn't know it was three horrible sports joined together. Cycling was only one of them.) I already told you how she fussed over her bike. It even had a name. Bee, short for Beyoncé. Wouldn't have a coffee out without it being chained to her table. Outside, she meant. In February. No way was *I* going to cycle in London. I'd be dead in five minutes, or anyone cutting me up would be. Ruby said *a brisk walk* would be just as good to *defuse tension*. A power-walk.

I didn't like the word *brisk*. Sounded like *risk*. *At risk*. *Power* sounded better. Useless advice, though, seeing as I'd always walked fast. Made me look like I knew what I was doing, where I was going, when I didn't always. Made me look taller. Whizzed me past people before they could have a go.

'Alright, Maggsie. Lecture over.' I nodded like I'd learnt something, when I hadn't, and I closed the door, rather than slammed it. If that wasn't self-control then I didn't know what was. That was how much I wanted to stay. Plus I'd hardly said a dicky. Not that you ever got much of a chance of that with Ruby.

I went upstairs, eyes prickling. Too many cleaning products. Juicy Lucy was always spraying bleach around.

At least I was staying, I told myself. But I *hadn't* lost it like Ruby was making out. I'd learnt a lot about keeping calm the last two stretches. All I'd done was take back what was mine.

Back in my room, I snatched up this week's *Woman's World*. Tried to focus on the cookery pages. 'Winter Warming Soups'. I knew the word *soup* alright, seeing as I had a can of it every day. Leek and ruddy potato, the recipe said. I threw the magazine down. Lay back on the bed.

I hadn't ticked the calendar yet. I'd had run-ins with two of the girls here over the weekend, plus a telling-off now from her in charge. But I was the sort of person who rescued people, wasn't I? Who held down a job.

Who kept off . . . well, what you know about now. What I don't need to discuss. OK?

Jack's face swam into my mind, all pink and healthy and grateful. Good job he hadn't seen that to-do over the butter, or Ruby telling me off. Then I saw Alastair's little baby face staring at the tiny spilt gherkins and the smashed glass. His little nose wrinkling up at the vinegary smell. Saw him turning to me and bursting out crying. Even though at one day old he couldn't have hardly focused on anything.

I wished Enid was here, doing her crocheting, looking up at her Romania pictures. She was the sort of person people told their problems to. Had that way of tilting her head like she was really thinking about what you were saying, instead of working out what *she* was going to say next, like most people. She'd have listened. Given me a little pat on the shoulder. Told me how well I was doing. *Oh, I say!* she'd have gone, seeing the *Metro* on my desk. She'd have said about Ruby the same as she had about Louise, that posh tart inside, the one with all the arty postcards: 'Who's she when she's at home with her boots off then?'

# 13

Kasia was on the other side of the road. Business must be slack if she was out and about and not entertaining clients. I sped up – *power-walked*, Ruby would have called it. Even though I'd been on my feet all day. Didn't want another run-in, did I? And there was her boyfriend, pimp, whatever, in the entrance to the block of flats, watching. Waiting. Kasia tapped her watch and frowned. He wasn't the type you'd want to meet in a dark alley. Gazed at her like a little lap-dog, though.

She came in when I was turning on my soup. Carrot and Cor-i-an-der. I'd gone up to two vegetables. It was through seeing Juicy Lucy chomp her way through loads of them. Plus London made you more adventurous, posher, without you even realizing.

Big Shirl was in the kitchen as well, unpacking a Co-op carrier bag. Her grandson, the one she went on about, lived local and helped her with her shopping. She put her fancy margarine tub that was going to give her a new lease of life, on the top shelf of the fridge. Wrote 'Shirley' on a sticky label from a roll she kept in a drawer. There were 'Shirley' and 'S' labels all over the place – on a mug, even. Like I said, she'd been here a long time. Plus she was used to being in charge.

I didn't look at Kasia. She hadn't exactly given Ruby

the whole story but I wasn't going to let her make me lose my cool. I got out a slice of my Hovis. I had the rest of the loaf to get through. Took out my butter. What was left of it. That was awkward, but blow it. I thought about taking my soup upstairs to eat. Leaving her and Big Shirl to talk business. Then Kasia reached into the fridge and handed me a packet of butter. 'I'm sorry I took. I told Ruby mistake I took.' The butter had funny writing on the label. All 'j's and 'k's. I thought it was me, reading it wrong, but, after, Big Shirl said it was because it was in a foreign language.

Kasia caught me off guard. I just nodded thanks. Then she went upstairs. Funny thing – it made me feel worse, her apologizing.

Big Shirl raised her pencilled-in eyebrows at me. 'All friends again.' People in charge, specially those that *thought* they were in charge, could come over very patronizing. She folded up her carrier bag for next time so she didn't have to pay five pence. You could see she'd run a business, even if it had been a brothel.

I had the soup with the Hovis bread and one of my sandwiches. Egg and cress, on brown bread. Bits in the bread. Told you it was the unpopular ones that got left over. Not a great dinner.

Audrey appeared soon as I went outside for a smoke. Let me stroke her while I finished my fag. Opened her mouth to miaow, only no sound came out. First time she'd done that. I went in and opened a fresh tin of pilchards. Gave her two because she rubbed against my leg while I was putting the first one down. She still hadn't had her posh little tin. I was saving it up for when I'd got her through the kitchen door.

I made a cup of tea. Might as well make one for Kasia

and all. I used my own teabag and my own milk. I got a plate for the other work sandwich, cream cheese on rye bread, which I'd fancied even less, and knocked on her door. I was putting myself at a disadvantage. 'Thanks for the butter,' I got out. There was a seed from the bread stuck in the back of my throat. Then, quicker, before I changed my mind, 'Sorry about the gherkins.' My armpits prickled. Apologizing was hard. No wonder people didn't do it much.

Kasia must have just come out the shower. She'd need plenty of those in her line of work. Her hair was wrapped in a towel. Dark roots showing at the front. She took the sandwich and the tea like they might explode in her hands. Then she gave me a grin. She had a gold tooth, near the back.

Downstairs, Audrey was still crunching her pilchards – they had little bones that were safe for cats to eat – on the step outside. I had the door half open although it was freezing. What the hell, I thought, I'll open her special tin and give her that as well. I was in a reckless mood. Be nice to see the eager look on Audrey's face and her belly blown out like a little balloon.

She went mad over the posh stuff. I sat at the kitchen table, drinking my tea and listening to her purring. It looked like the aggro had died down. And I was still here, still on the way to finding Alastair.

In a minute I'd go upstairs and tick the calendar.

# 14

'Uh?' I grunted. 'I was miles away.'

TJ looked puzzled.

I sighed. Tapped ash off my rollie. 'It means I was thinking about something else.' I had to explain the simplest things to him. Everyday expressions you'd think he'd have known already.

'Ah.' TJ took out a notebook held together with an elastic band and wrote it down. His writing was neat. Small, for such a great big lump of a man. His notebook had little foreign squares, not lines.

'You keeping notes on me?' People had done that before, the police and that. They'd only ever written bad things.

'*On* you?' He lifted off his pen. 'I learn colloquial English *through* you. *Because of* you.'

'I don't know no coll . . . English, TJ. What you said.' I didn't want him writing down actual mistakes. I was only good at *speaking* English.

'Slang, you know plenty. And I am used to write things because I am scientist.' He put his notebook away and rubbed his hands together against the cold. They were like shovels. 'When I learn English history, I write also. With date.'

I took a drag. Looked out in front of me. The

skyscrapers were brand-new. Nothing had happened in them yet. The old buildings were small and grey compared to them, but they were holding their own with their fancy windows and spiky little roofs. They must have a lot of history inside. Small things are more interesting.

TJ pointed out some of the famous buildings: the London Eye and Greenwich in the distance. Knew what they were although he was Polish. Easy for him to show off, seeing as I didn't know anything about them. He glanced at me. 'I can show London sights. If you would like.' He fidgeted his legs up and down, making the bench shake. 'Sunday is free day.'

I turned round. 'Meet up?' Was he serious?

He nodded, not looking at me. Spread his arms out at the buildings. He got his arms involved more than an English person would. There was a glint from his wedding ring. 'Shame not to see.'

I leant away, frowning. 'Got a wife at home, ain't you? Kids?'

TJ nodded. 'Yes, I have girl and boy. Teenagers.' He seemed to puff up, talking about them. Big beam all over his round face. 'They do well at school. I Skype with often.' He stopped smiling. 'And wife, yes. I still have wife.' He turned to me. 'You are not married?'

I shook my head, ponytail flicking on the collar of my giant overall. 'No bloody fear.'

He reached for his notebook, then changed his mind. Just as well. Some expressions you just couldn't explain. He smiled. 'So no children?' Like of course there wouldn't be.

I didn't answer. I was a private person although you might not think it. Wasn't going to tell TJ about Alastair.

Not when I hardly knew him. Not with him being so big and tall. And foreign. I frowned, thinking about his offer. 'I don't want no hanky-panky with no married man.' I had enough on my plate just keeping going on the straight and narrow, without some woman coming after me all the way from Poland.

This time the ruddy notebook did come out. I had to try and explain 'hanky-panky', which was awkward. Him smiling so much made it difficult to know if he was taking the mick or not.

'I will be perfect English gentleman. Wife, Sofia, will not look after that I socialize with colleague.'

'Think you might mean *care*, TJ. Your wife won't *care*.' Hardly worth him putting his notebook away. I definitely earned my side of our arrangement. We only looked at the *Metro* for a few minutes, whereas I was on the go all the time, teaching him. I tapped off some fag ash. 'I don't know. Might be busy, Sunday. I do my shopping then.' That was true except I got it done in five minutes at the Co-op. Took another drag. I'd never been a *colleague* before. Or out with a *perfect English gentleman*. Specially a Polish one. I blew out smoke. I wasn't going to let on, but it would be something to do. A lot of empty hours in the weekend, otherwise. I sighed. 'Might be able to squeeze you in, I suppose.'

I had to tell Ruby I was meeting TJ. One of the rules was you kept staff informed who you were mixing with. Didn't know how Kasia managed with that one.

Ruby was worried TJ might take me to 'unsuitable' places. Pubs and drinking dens, she meant. That was a laugh. I told her he was only interested in history and improving his English. We'd be going round old buildings.

The famous ones. And then only the outsides. Neither of us had the money to go in. And not likely TJ would lead me astray, when it was *me* what had been in prison, while all TJ had been up to, far as I knew, was doing something scientific with soil. That hair sticking up, that moon face. He looked more like a crime *victim*.

It was like Ruby was my mum. Not that Mum would have worried. She'd have been thrilled I was meeting a man. *Any* man. A *tall* man, even if he was married and it wasn't a date. Mum would have fluttered her eyelashes at TJ, like she did with every man. And I mean literally. She wore too much mascara so it was ruddy obvious. She thought a man paying you attention was a good thing. That's why she'd ended up with Dad, then Dougie. That's why she'd never minded Dad, when he'd had a few, pawing at her, his eyes bleary, long as he told her she was *a fine-looking woman*. She'd be in her dressing gown, pushing back her auburn hair. Laughing.

Mum had lovely hair. The colour was called *Tish* something. (*Titian*, I found out later. How can *Tit* say *Tish*, I ask you? It means goldy red.) Sometimes Mum wore it in a French plait. If Nella was around to do it. If Mum had a go herself her arms would get tired, plus she could never work out which bit of hair went where. 'I'm hopeless,' she'd say, giggling. Yeah, she was.

I saw men without Mum's rose-tinted spectacles, thank you very much. That's why I didn't bother with no primping or eyelash-fluttering.

On my way out to meet TJ I stopped to do up my ponytail in the hall mirror. Big Shirl poked her head round her door and asked if I wanted to borrow some make-up. When I'd told her TJ was going to show me the sights she'd had a good old cackle. She looked

89

me up and down now. Seemed disappointed I wasn't wearing a short skirt.

Short skirt? 'No way, Shirl. I don't want to look like a kid. Or the other. And I ain't got the teeth for lipstick.'

'Well, eyeliner, then. Wing it up at the corners. Them's your best feature.'

I'd always thought my eyes were a muddy grey colour but Big Shirl swore they were green. 'Thanks but no thanks, Shirl. I ain't auditioning for one of your jobs.'

Big Shirl cackled. It was that laugh that told you, yeah, she had run a brothel. 'Thank gawd, I'm done with all that. Always a nightmare getting staff, what with my girls all wanting to do different hours.'

Seeing as we're talking about mirrors and make-up, I'll give you some details of what I look like. If you're interested. You already know my teeth aren't anything to write home about, and that I'm short. Four foot eleven actually. Just *over* four foot eleven. Four foot eleven and a fag paper. Some people have said I've got issues because of it. Which is a lie. Though it is ruddy irritating, being taken for a kid. Or talked over, like right over the top of my head. Or being teased about booster cushions. Asked what the weather's like down there. Stuff like that.

Nan said the best things in life came in small packages. She was a tiny little thing herself, mind. And she might have been referring to jewellery.

I'm slim as well. Skinny, some people would say. Rude people. My spine sticks out like a row of beads. I move too quick for weight to settle.

As you know, I dye my hair black because of it being ginger underneath. *Strawberry blonde*, Mum calls it and Nan used to say *ripe corn*, but trust me, it's ginger.

Ginger hair, pasty skin, fair eyelashes, small. Only

things I *wasn't* was gay or black. Or trans. Although that was tempting sometimes. Seeing as blokes had it easier. Got bigger livers for a start. A doc, the one that was nice to me, told me that.

I've got tattoos but *everybody's* got those. Everybody *I* know. We did them to each other, inside. Needle, sterilized in a fag lighter if you was lucky, and ink from a biro, green or red if the girl doing it was artistic. I was still thinking about getting *cool head in a crisis* done one day.

TJ could take me or leave me. Actually I'd just as soon he left me. I wasn't going to doll myself up for him. Ridiculous, people treating it like a date.

# 15

I got off the tube at Waterloo. Upstairs the railway station was huge, heaving. It was Sunday; didn't people ever stop in London? People rushing in different directions, running to catch trains, shouting into mobiles. And when you glared at them they just looked straight through you. But I wasn't supposed to glare. I was supposed to *power-walk* away, Ruby said. Breathe *out*. Alastair or Jack wouldn't look up to someone who glared.

Easy to feel small when you're on your own in a great big crowded place. Not a nice feeling. Same as at the coach station when I first got to London. And when I looked out of the window too long back at the house. I stuck my hands in my pockets. I could have been back there now, reading a *Woman's World*, having a cup of tea and a fag with the girls, trying to get Audrey to come into the kitchen.

TJ said he'd meet me by the bookshop at the back of the station. I spotted him first because of him being so big and his hair sticking up. Funny, seeing him without his apron. He was wearing a donkey jacket and black trousers, not jeans.

I pulled down my denim jacket and walked over. Even though it was old, it was a good one, a designer rip-off. And my jeans were clean on this morning.

He gave me a big smile, and then, straight away, handed me a plastic bread bag. Why's he giving me sandwiches, I thought? But no, he said it was a present. Some kind of book. It was a dictionary, a school one. Big print and explained things simple, he said. He'd got it from a charity shop.

Funny giving me a present. Funny kind of present, a dictionary. He must have thought I was really thick to need something *simple*. I narrowed my eyes up at him. Nearly handed it back.

He said people in his English class had ones like it. 'They are English but have trouble spelling. Have dyslexia.' He looked at me, like I might not know the word.

I knew it alright. Hoped *he* knew it meant I wasn't thick. I stood there, holding the dictionary. It wouldn't fit into my pocket. What right did he have to give *me* a label? Come on the expert?

And it would be useless, anyway. At school, when I'd asked how you spelt a word, they'd banged a dictionary down on my desk. But if you didn't know how to spell a word in the first place, how on earth were you going to find it in a dictionary?

From TJ's expression, mind, you'd have thought he'd just handed me the Crown Jewels. 'You can look up words in *Metro* now. Help spelling. When I am not there.'

'Thanks.' I stared up at him. He was getting big ideas.

Next thing I knew he'd taken hold of my elbow. I snatched it away. 'No funny stuff.' He looked hurt. Said he was being polite. 'Pull the other one,' I said, under my breath, in case I had to explain it. Being held on to made it like he was in charge, like I was going to escape. I'd had the same on the way to the headmaster's office. And in a supermarket more than once.

We walked along the side of the river. The South Bank, TJ said. Big boats going up and down with tourists hanging over the rails and loudspeakers telling them what they was seeing. I didn't need a loudspeaker because TJ knew everything.

'Blackfriars Bridge,' he pointed out. 'New skyscrapers, the Gherkin, the Shard. One day we go up. Have cocktail. Look out over London. Twenty-five floors higher than roof garden at work.'

In your dreams, I thought, because: one, I'd stopped drinking, two, could you see me in a cocktail bar, and three, he was married.

A big reddish building came up on the right. TJ said it was an art gallery.

I followed him in to get out of the cold. I'd never been in an art gallery before. All I knew about art was Louise's wall of postcards, in prison. Inside the gallery it was nearly as crowded as Waterloo station. As usual, everyone was posh. They had guidebooks and brayed to each other, never mind if you were standing in between.

We spent half an hour just looking round the one room. The pictures weren't my cup of tea. White figures in robes. Nervy-looking women. People with no clothes on frolicking behind trees. Like the porn magazines Dad kept under his bed, only muddy colours.

TJ knew about the people that had painted the pictures. Trust him. Where they came from, who their mates were. All about their complicated love lives.

Louise had known about that stuff as well. Droned on about it, given half the chance. We were only interested in her postcards of nude men. Just Enid who'd looked at the other ones and gone *Ah look!* or *Oh, I say!*

I'd had a postcard from Enid yesterday. An arty one,

a bowl of fruit, real-looking. She'd got it from Louise, actually. One Louise had two of. *Made my day to get a letter from you*, Enid had wrote. Pity it was just a postcard.

A girl stood right in front of a painting while me and TJ were looking at it. Tossed back her hair and giggled while her friend took a photo. I told her to get out of our faces, sharpish, but TJ moved away. Looked uncomfortable. I was beginning to think he was a bit soft, the type that could get himself pushed around. The two slags scarpered. I flexed my shoulders. Result. The next painting was of a woman in a shawl, rocking a cradle. I breathed o-u-t. Didn't stay long, looking at that one.

We had a look at Shakespeare's Globe theatre after. I'd heard of *Shakespeare*. The theatre was only a copy, not the real thing. Then we crossed a footbridge with loads of little padlocks and key rings attached to the railings. TJ didn't smile when I asked what they were. His face had lit up when I'd asked him other stuff. That was why I'd kept it to a minimum. He said couples put the padlocks there to show their love couldn't be broken. Then he changed the subject to how the bridge had wobbled when it was first put up. Made me wonder what his wife was up to, all on her own back in Poland. Load of guff anyway. Plenty of girls inside who could have undone any one of those flimsy little things quicker than it took to say *I'll love you for ever, darling*.

On the other side of the river – 'Name is Thames,' TJ said. '*The* Thames,' I got in – was St Paul's Cathedral. Never mind Primrose's Church of the Everlasting Light – she'd told me it shared a building with a playgroup – this was the real deal.

Loads of steps to climb up just to get inside. Through

the door, the entrance bit was a huge high ceiling with echoes and black and white floor tiles, like in Nan's kitchen, only stretching for miles.

We had a coffee in a café round the back afterwards. TJ never went into pubs, he said. Didn't know why he'd brought that up. He didn't drink at all. Seen too many alcoholics in his own country, he said. And his own dad had died of it. Not much to say to that. I didn't tell him my dad had too. Or about my past drinking. Didn't want him asking questions. Thinking we had stuff, bad stuff, in common.

I couldn't make out half the fancy words on the menu. It put me at a disadvantage. Made me feel I shouldn't be there. Made my face burn. I looked around to see if anyone was laughing at me struggling. In the end TJ ordered me something with a fancy name, but which turned out to be just a milky coffee, the same as he'd got.

Once I'd opened all the sugar packets and finished stirring them in, I didn't know what to say. I was sitting opposite TJ and it made me nervous. Don't know why. He wasn't saying much either so I couldn't even correct his English.

He paid, which was OK seeing as I'd worked hard putting him right on his words the previous couple of hours. Our coffees cost an arm and a leg because of it being London and a tourist place. I'd have been happier with a takeaway cup. And tea, not coffee.

It was better when we lit up outside. When we weren't squashed up close together. Then it was like being on our fag break at work.

We walked back to Waterloo station. He lived *south of the river*. Lewisham. My place was north. Finsbury

Park. Big Shirl said the house was nearly in Crouch End like that was an advantage, but Finsbury Park sounded better.

TJ didn't even try to touch my elbow this time, which was a ruddy good thing.

Soon as I got upstairs I took the dictionary out of TJ's bread bag and scratched the word *School* off its cover. Didn't want the other girls seeing it and having a laugh. I put it next to the *Woman's Worlds* on my desk.

They reminded me of Enid. I'd have a go at another letter. Now, before I could weaken. She'd love to think of me seeing the London sights. Nice to have someone to tell that to. Not long till she'd be out herself.

I tried to make it better than the first one. I knew what I wanted to say, I could *say* it alright. But the words slipped away soon as my pen hit the page. Came out jumbled. And my handwriting was terrible. I was concentrating so hard on nailing down the right letters, everything else went out the window.

> *I been out and seen the sites of London I been in St Pauls I hop you allright not long to gow now I got a calendar now at the end I rite to my son I have got a son but I niver said. This is my second leter, Enid*
> *lov of*
> *Maggsie M x*

My calendar had the word *calendar* written on it, and I managed to find *sites* in TJ's dictionary so at least they were spelt right. (Like he said, it was easy to use. Words printed in blue. Nice and clear. Easier than the ones they'd thumped down on my desk at school.)

I pictured Enid reading about me writing to 'my son'. Putting things together in her mind. Her saying, *Ah, love him*. Reaching out to give me a pat.

# 16

Audrey had seen sense. Given up living under the shed. I'd moved the pilchard closer and closer to the kitchen door, and then just inside.

In the end she cottoned on it was warmer in the kitchen and we weren't going to barbecue her. She was OK as long as the door was open a fraction. The other girls grumbled about the draught, but fresh air was good for you. Plus it took away the smell of Juice's vegetables.

Trudie, the old girl next to me, was the worst. Felt the cold because she'd lived in Greece for years, apparently. Said she'd been a Mother Teresa to the stray cats over there. Thought that made her some kind of expert. Hung round the kitchen now Audrey was there. When she wasn't helping out on a mate's bric-a-brac stall down the market. That was why her room was full of junk.

She wore tie-dyed stuff. Drank her tea black. Real old hippie. When she smiled, her face was a thousand creases. Too many fags, too much sunning herself on that Greek island.

I made Audrey a bed out of a cardboard box from the Co-op. Stuck it under the radiator in the kitchen. Trudie brought down a jumper that had got scorched when she'd dropped a fag on it. Audrey's little paws went up and down on the jumper. Trudie kept on about it, when it was my pilchards that had brought Audrey inside.

Juice had told me why Trudie had done time. It was internet fraud. Stringing men along. Making out she was twenty years old and luscious.

We had a giggle over that. Juice was making some kind of sauce. She took a lot of trouble over her meals, ate all those vegetables, but then there was a lot of her to feed. Still took her a while to cotton on to things, in spite of the vegetables.

Telling me about Trudie got Juice talking about herself. There was a code inside, and in the house: you didn't ask another girl what she'd been sent down for. You didn't ask but sometimes you got told. She'd had 'issues', she said. She didn't look the type who'd go off the rails, being so big and slow, but, take a tip from me, don't go on appearances.

I put the kettle on. Juice's 'issues' turned out to be drugs. No surprise there. Nor with there being a bloke behind them. She'd worked in a post office, which was a surprise. I couldn't imagine her getting parcels off to the right places. Stolen bits of money to pay for her boyfriend's habit. Then hers. Not long before she was caught.

Off drugs completely now. Turning her life around, she said. Proving she was capable. That was why she was eating healthy.

Juice's sauce was glooping, time she'd said all that. She poured a great dollop of it over a whole half of cauliflower. It was rigid looking, like it was still on the raw side, and there was a withered leaf clinging to its knobbly stalk. I wondered, not for the first time, if she knew what she was doing. 'Fancy a bit, Maggsie?' She held out her plate. 'I've got plenty.'

'No, no, you're alright. Got my sandwiches from work. And soup. Loads.' Sat down quick before she offered again.

Ruby came in. Must have heard the kettle. She kept a carton of milk – well, soya milk – in the fridge. None of us touched it.

'Hello, sweetie.' Ruby bent down to Audrey. She got out her own teabags. Or-gan-ic, it said on the label. Kept meaning to look it up.

I'd surprised myself by actually using TJ's dictionary. Looked up at least one word I struggled with every day, no matter how long it took me to find it. Alastair would want me to keep going with my reading.

Ruby said her boyfriend, Will, had given her something for Audrey. I looked up, fishing out my teabag (Co-op Simply Value). Uh-oh, I thought. I knew he was a vegan, which was worse than a vegetarian. Didn't eat meat, not even bacon. Primrose said there were a lot of vegans at Scanda. Expect they were all over London. Will's 'something' was chickpeas rolled around in a smear of Marmite. I didn't burst out laughing, which was self-control, but I turned away to roll my eyes.

Ruby looked a bit embarrassed putting down the plastic bowl. Must have been keen on him. Audrey came running, then backed away sharpish. Looked horrified. Anybody would have. I had to give her a whole slice of roast beef from my sandwich to stop her going back under the shed.

Juice ploughed her way through her cauliflower cheese and then mooched off to watch TV with Big Shirl. Something soppy with women in long dresses. Big Shirl must have seen men at their worst and Juice had just told me about her poxy ex. They knew what men were like. So why they got a kick out of watching a bunch of them strutting round poncy great houses in long jackets and tight trousers, God only knows.

Audrey stuck up a back leg to wash her belly. Ruby sat down and asked me how things were going. Nodded like one of those toy dogs you used to see in the backs of cars. The ones with heads on springs. Mentioned TJ. 'Your friend,' she called him. We were *colleagues*, not even mates. No way was I going to get tangled up with a man. A great hulking one with a face like a potato and bristly hair. A married one.

I put the brakes on that one sharpish. 'We work on our English together.' Came out stilted rather than swotty. (Shirl would have cackled, *Well, that's* one *way of putting it.*) Ruby's mind didn't work like that. It was on posher things like *em-power-ment* and *e-quality* and *just-ice*. Words I could just about say but which I'd never be able to spell in a million years.

Seeing as Ruby was smiling, I asked her to help me get the adoption people's address. Months and months before the year was up, but I just wanted to have it ready. Ruby was into long-term thinking. Planning. She'd like me thinking ahead.

First time I'd spoken about Alastair in years. Weird hearing his name out loud. I swung my legs just saying it.

Ruby stopped smiling and put her mug on the table. She was choosing what to say. I'd seen a lot of that over the years.

'That's a big step to take, Maggsie. Are you sure you're ready? Have you thought about the other people involved?'

Audrey put her leg down and stared at Ruby.

Someone ruddy had to. It hadn't been easy telling her about Alastair. 'I *told* you. *Next year.* I ain't ready to do nothing about it *now*.' Audrey jumped out of her box, clawed the kitchen door open and vanished.

For two pins I'd have slammed out in the yard with her. You probably haven't got anger issues. But trust me, staying put is self-control. I jiggled my feet up and down and breathed out slow.

Ruby looked at me. Sighed. Said maybe it wasn't such a bad idea, seeing as it would give me time to 'consider the issues involved'. Went off to set up the computer in the office.

I clenched my hands. More or less what I'd said, only put into social-worker speak.

I printed out some pages from the website Ruby'd found. Took them upstairs. There were a lot of long words: 'Intermediary Agency', 'Registrar General', that kind of thing. Took me ages to look them up. Seemed I'd have to send in my details first. Then the adoption agency would check their records. I'd have to meet someone to discuss stuff. Prove I was who I said I was. Application forms and that as well. Quite a palaver to it.

You might think I should leave well alone. But all I wanted to do was see Alastair was OK. He might be wondering about *me*, see. Might want to find out who he was. You do when you're eighteen. Blood and that. Genes. Not things his *adoptive mum* could give him.

On the other hand he might be the sort of lad who wouldn't ever want to meet someone like me. But not after I'd done a year of living respectable, though, surely? After a year I'd be like anyone else.

I put the printouts in my holdall. Picked up this

week's *Woman's World* and turned to the problem page.

Problems! Half of them didn't know they were born. The agony aunt took half a page to answer their poncy little troubles when she could have done it in one sentence. Two or three words, even: *Ditch him!* Or *Don't believe him*.

Useful to copy out as practice, though. It took a long time. I had to keep looking back at the magazine. Bits of words vanished on their way from my brain to the paper. Other bits turned themselves around.

It didn't look too bad, written out in my notebook. But when I wrote to Alastair, wrote my own letter, it wouldn't be anything like a problem page one. It would be the complete opposite. It would be one of the agony auntie's favourite words: positive. Full of the joys of spring.

# 17

I was on my way home from the Co-op Sunday. Looking at the till receipt. I could read it easy, seeing as it was all about the stuff I'd just bought. Surprising how much information there is on a till receipt. You might only have ever checked the figures. Three soups, four tins of pilchards, milk, a new eyebrow pencil. A lighter brown one that *Woman's World* said was good. Ginger eyebrows don't have much definition. And it's too easy to overdo it with a dark one. Just look at Big Shirl.

Plus I'd bought a mug with a picture of the film star Audrey on it. I'd recognized her because of her eyes looking like my Audrey's. She had a cigarette holder in her hand. I took to her, knowing she was a smoker. That's why I'd splashed out £4.99.

The streets were empty and I was still looking at the till receipt. I wasn't concentrating on what was going on around me. That's what a quiet Sunday afternoon can do to you if you're not careful.

Nearly jumped out of my skin turning into our road. Kasia's pimp, boyfriend, whatever he was, stepped out sudden from the doorway of the block of flats opposite our house. Stood right in front of me. Taller than ever. No one else around although this was London. I rolled my shoulders. Stared up at him with a scowl on. No circumstances on this earth when it's a good idea to look vulnerable. He came right up close. Spoke through his teeth, all 's's, like a snake: 'You shout at Kasia. Smash her gherkins.' His breath stank of garlic. He was foreign like TJ, but not his manners.

My heart was going. That was nature taking over. It didn't mean I was scared. Didn't the stupid pillock know Kasia and I had sorted things out? Only yesterday she'd admired Nan's earrings. She'd got some similar. I breathed in deep. Pushed past him. Then I turned. Hissed, I mean actually hissed, like he'd done: 'Sssssss.' I said some bad words as well but you may not want to hear them. There was a special word for what he was, someone who lived off someone else. *Para* . . . something.

My chest was really banging now. I got back to the house double quick. Some people might have called it running. Ruddy great knob, throwing his weight around. Dad and Dougie were the same. No bloody big low-life was going to drag me back down. Say if Alastair, or Jack, had seen us together? I went up the steps two at a time. A bit of a stretch for my legs. Was that poxy sod going to have a go at me every time I walked down the ruddy street? I wasn't having that.

I had a fag and an extra-strong cup of tea. Used my new mug. Nice to drink out of something classy. But my chest was still tight and there was a pounding in my head. I unpacked my shopping. Labelled the tins of soup with my initials. Wrote 'Audrey' on her tins of pilchards. I was glad, now, she had that classy name. Ruby had written it out for me. It was OK to ask how you spelt a name. It was only when you asked how to write words like *because* or *there*, people looked at you funny.

I put the tins away in the cupboard. I had the bottom shelf. It wasn't because I was short, it was because Big Shirl had trouble bending. I could still smell that skanky sod's garlicky breath. Do you know what? If I wasn't careful I was going to let him ruin my Sunday. So I went up and had a shower. Let the water pour over me.

I came back down in my pyjamas. They were fleecy ones. Little hearts all over. They'd been Mum's, but she'd grown out of them. She preferred nighties anyway. Black, loads of lace. You know the type.

Kasia was in the kitchen. Had a saucepan of stew going. 'Hi.' I put the kettle on. Fluffed out my hair to dry it. Deep breath in and out. You just got to go for things in this life. Hanging about only prolongs the agony. So I told her about her rat-arse of a pimp making a scene. My heart was going in case she kicked off. Bound to be me who'd get reported, lose my place here. Her stew smelt of aniseed. Granda had had a jar of aniseed balls on the lounge mantelpiece. Nan had kept moving it back to the kitchen because it wasn't an ornament.

Kasia's narrow eyes got narrower. 'I *told* him you OK.' She slammed the lid down on her saucepan. Said something fierce in her language. Said, 'stupid', 'lazy', 'never found no customers' in English.

She reached for her phone. Her jeans were so tight she struggled to get it out of her pocket. 'He no good. I tell him. I tell him *now*!' Torrent of foreign abuse on the phone. I had to stir the stew for her. She threw her phone down on the table. 'Is finished.'

I kept my mouth shut. Blimey, don't get on the wrong side of Kasia. Just as well I'd given her that sandwich after the gherkins kerfuffle.

'I am tired of this work.' Kasia tossed some rice into

another saucepan. 'Is dirty. I want one man only. One man to look after me. Rich man.' She leant against the cooker. Heaved out a sigh. Turned one of her gold chains round and round.

'Yeah, one's plenty.' I got out a mug for her and used my Audrey one again. No need for my initials on it. Made us a cup of tea. Good luck with finding a man to look after you, I thought.

I ticked off my calendar. Swooshed the pen up with a flourish. I'd helped give an arsehole his comeuppance. Without using violence. Sorted things out with Kasia without losing my cool. Or her losing hers. I was really settling down.

# 18

Audrey was getting bolder. I swear she could tell the time, or else she knew my footsteps, because she'd be out the front, waiting when I came home from work. And she'd found her voice now. Miaowed her head off at any opportunity. Making up for lost time.

'You're supposed to be a stray, remember.' I opened a new tin. 'Supposed to be frightened of people.' She went in and out my ankles, like she was trying to trip me up. Get her jaws round the pilchard quicker.

She'd started following me upstairs. I could hear her coming. There was a stair that creaked and she'd filled out so much she set it off. It took her a few days to come right up to the top, mind. She'd kept looking behind her, all paranoid, running back down. Then she'd peep into my room, long as the door was wide open. Another week and she was marching in like she owned the place. Then she was on my bed. White paws going in and out, claws getting caught in the candlewick bedcover. Audrey was one of the things I'd done right. Jack was the other thing.

Once Audrey started to come upstairs, blow me down if Trudie didn't start leaving her door open. Displaying all her old junk: incense burners, a sparkly vase in the shape of a cat, a statue with loads of arms.

*

Audrey getting tamer meant a trip to the vet's to have done what the cat charity hadn't managed. I winced at her having her insides tied up, or taken away, or whatever they did, but Ruby wouldn't listen. Audrey was going between the pair of us in the kitchen, purring, her tail with its pale tip stuck up. She usually understood what I said to her, but not now.

All it took to get her into a cat basket was a pilchard at the other end. I felt bad about it, but Ruby was quite brisk.

Ruby's boyfriend had lent her his tiny car. The seat belt wouldn't do up round the basket so we had to put it on the back seat, loose. I hadn't thought about him having a car. I'd thought a vegan would just have a bike. There was yowling when we got going. Audrey's eyes like torch beams through the little window in the basket.

Ruby drove slowly. Cars I'd been in before had been speeding. Speeding *away*. There was always traffic and hooting in London. I couldn't drive, but if I did I'd be breathing four, four, s-i-x, all the time. And if anyone hooted at *me*, they'd regret it . . .

Funny, because in the end I lost it anyway. In spite of not being able to drive.

A cyclist, in skin-tight black clothes, like he was going swimming, flashed in front of us. Ruby had to brake sudden. The driver behind, in one of those poxy Land Rover-type cars that are all for show and no ruddy good in London, came too close. Not concentrating. Only went into the back of us, didn't he? There was a horrible grating sound and a yowl as Audrey's basket crashed to the floor.

Didn't have no time to breathe, let alone breathe slowly.

Anger burns you up inside. You get hotter and hotter. Your heart races. You're powerful. Wonder Woman.

I was out of the car. Marching up to the one behind. Instinct, see. I was defending my cat.

The car had tinted windows and music blaring. How could you see? And how the piddling poxy hell could you concentrate with a racket like that going on?

The driver jumped out before I could get to his door. Eyebrows all drooping and sorrowful. Phone in his hand and his arms in the air like I'd said *Stick 'em up!*

Easy to punch him because of that. I landed him a good one in his big soft belly. Easy for me to reach that, being short.

'That's for my cat!' I stomped back to the car.

Audrey was miaowing – at least she still could miaow. I spoke to her soothing. Put her basket back on the seat and dusted off my hands. Rubbed the knuckles where I'd punched him. Wonder Woman. The Mighty Atom. That'll learn him, I was going to say to Ruby. Till I saw she had her head in her hands.

'Don't ever do that again.' It came out muffled.

'He went into us! Knocked Audrey down.' I leant back, crossed my arms. There was a tiny sinking feeling in my stomach area. But I had to show him, didn't I? That's what do-gooders never understand.

'It was an accident. Bad driving. You're not the police, Maggsie. Far from it.' Ruby got out of the car.

I wasn't keen on the police. That weary look they usually put on when they saw me. I shifted in my seat. My stomach was working its way down lower.

Ruby was talking to the loser behind. He didn't say much, because of being winded. She got back in. Said she'd had to calm him down to stop him phoning the police. The only thing holding him back was the thought of his mates taking the mick at him getting beaten up by a woman so tiny she was practically a dwarf. Ruby didn't say that last word. 'Dw . . .' she began. But I knew what he'd said. He was just the type. Didn't make me warm to him. Bet it wasn't the thought of his mates. Losers like him didn't have no mates. Bet it was because of Ruby being young and having a fresh complexion and talking to him sympathetic.

Ruby started the car. She didn't look at me. 'He could have hit you back, Maggsie. A little thing like you wouldn't have stood a chance.'

'Size ain't everything. I'm light on my feet. He'd have to land one first.'

'If he'd called the police you'd have been back inside before your feet could touch the ground.'

That had happened to me once, actually. Two policemen, one each side, my legs kicking the air.

'It came over me sudden,' I muttered.

Ruby sighed. '*I'm* angry. Will might lose his no-claims bonus. He didn't want me to borrow his car in the first place.'

'Couldn't I have even shouted?' I asked.

'No.' Ruby shook her head, earrings flying like one of them fairground rides where the chairs swing out. 'Things escalate.'

My stomach was down at my ankles now. My Wonder Woman headband had slipped off. I thought of the gherkin episode. Saw the broken glass on the floor, smelt the vinegar. Saw Jack, with Alastair in his arms. Them shaking their heads – even though Alastair was only thirty-five hours old and couldn't hardly move, only wave his little arms and squirm a bit.

I stared out of the car window. Hard when you knew the other person was in the right and you had to sit strapped up in their boyfriend's car, a vegan, listening to it all.

We had a clear stretch of road. I checked on Audrey in the back. She was crouched low, eyes big and dark. My heart speeded up again at what she'd gone through. And she hadn't even got to the vet's yet.

Soon as I turned round Ruby was on my case again. 'Maggsie, we've spoken before about managing your anger.'

'Yeah, but . . . couldn't have power-walked in a car, could I?'

She sighed again. 'What about seeing anger as something separate from you, then. Something you *can* control.'

Social workers' gobbledegook. She was new to the job, see, had these new ideas. London ideas. How getting angry, but seeing it as me not doing it, would work, I couldn't imagine.

I didn't tick the calendar. I kept seeing Alastair's little fist, losing its grip on my finger.

I spent all evening copying out an article from this week's *Woman's World*: 'Six Different Ways to Tie a Scarf!' One they didn't mention was how to knot it round your Staffie's neck so he didn't rip it off. Another was the best knot to use for strangling cat-abusers.

I looked up the word *knot*. I ask you, who makes up these spellings? There's probably more angry people in England than anywhere else in the world, because of the spelling. It's not just me. I concentrated on keeping my handwriting on the line and it all facing the same direction. It didn't look so bad when I'd finished. I sat back. Felt better now I'd done something to improve myself. Something positive.

I looked at the calendar again. Nine more months of not losing my temper. Well, more than that. The rest of my life. How was I going to manage that?

Ruby's airy-fairy idea came back to me. Seeing anger as something separate from myself. Like, as belonging to someone else? Who could I load it onto, then? Or what? Would an animal count? That would be separate. An animal that would be angry *for* me. I quite liked that idea. Have to be something snappy, with loads of teeth. Not a cat or anything. Too fluffy. A crocodile, maybe? A small one, obviously, that I could keep in my holdall along with my anger management certificates. (*Imagine* I kept in my holdall, I mean. I ain't bonkers.) I seen a couple of crocodiles in the aquarium at Skegness. Massive things, half underwater like floating logs. A crocodile didn't take no prisoners. Snappy, I could call him.

# 19

Things kicked off on account of Audrey, even though she was just a little innocent cat. Things that got me trying out the crocodile.

I was getting my dinner ready. Not actual cooking, but I'd moved on to those plastic tubs of soup where you could see what you were getting. Juice was in the kitchen, chopping up something with leaves.

Trudie was smearing some pink fish paste onto a slice of toast. She said it was Greek but I had my doubts. Showing off, more like. Or trying to tempt Audrey. Other things Trudie went in for was olives straight from a jar and white cheese in a plastic packet that came from sheep. Audrey was watching her with the fish paste, miaowing like I starved her. I had to get out her pilchard straight away. Then Trudie had the cheek to say I was hogging her.

'Didn't drag her over, did I? Her choice.' Who'd want to be with you, I thought but didn't say. Two or three months ago I would have. I saw Alastair smiling, a tick on the calendar.

'Only, nice for the rest of us to see more of her, you know?' Trudie's wrinkles looked even deeper under the kitchen light. She added *you know?* to the end of everything she said. No, I didn't know. Then she brought in again how she'd fed stray cats in Greece. How they'd followed her about. 'Him I was shacked up with called me the Pied Piper.'

Funny Audrey don't do it, I nearly said. Funny it wasn't *you* that spent hours out in the cold, trying to get her to show her face. Instead of saying it, I conjured up the crocodile, Snappy. Put feeling angry onto him. I saw him about the size of a Jack Russell terrier. Same sort of temperament. Jaws full of teeth. He climbed out of my hold-all and crawled down the stairs. Slithered over to Trudie. I felt a bit foolish. Sort of thing a kid might do. Then I got into it. Added details. Heard his claws clicking, saw the rows of scales on his back; his yellow eyes, like Audrey's, only evil. Saw him snapping at Trudie's jeans' hems.

I nearly turned round from the fridge to watch him. A teacher told me once I had too much imag-in-a-tion. It was when I'd come up with a lie for not doing my homework. Said I'd been to Australia for the weekend, so I hadn't had time. She'd burst out laughing. Then given me a detention.

Audrey knew she was being talked about. She whisked her tail and stalked about a bit. Looked up at everyone, miaowing. She was getting to be a bossy little madam. I cut up some chicken skin I'd brought home from work. Primrose had wrapped it up for me in grease-proof. She knew I had a cat.

Audrey rubbed against my ankles and Trudie headed upstairs. Ridiculous what she'd said about Audrey. Never saw Trudie with a tin opener, did you?

'Good job that cat ain't human.' Juicy Lucy was chopping an onion now. Her heavy eyes were watery. 'Wouldn't never stop talking.'

'Yeah! Reckon she'd be in charge.' I tipped half the

soup into a saucepan. The plastic tubs had fancy names and a lot of writing on the labels. I should have been trying to work out what it said, but sometimes all you wanted to do was eat a soup, not read about it. This one was a kind of chicken, 'Something Something Chicken'. *Frag* . . . something. I looked over at Juice's pile of veg. 'Was it your mum that learnt you how to cook?'

'Yeah.' Juicy Lucy moved on to a pile of carrots. 'She's a good cook. *Adoptive* mum, she is.'

'Oh?' I stirred the soup. The spoon handle dug into my palm. 'That feel the same as a real mum? Don't feel, like, second best?'

Juicy Lucy shook her head. 'She *is* my real mum. Fostered me from a baby. Kept me on. Made me birthday cakes and that.'

I stared into my soup, remembering a birthday cake Mum had made for Nella. She'd bought flour specially, used up our marge, breadcrumbs and all, cadged a couple of eggs off a neighbour, mixed it all up and bunged it in the oven. Flour in her hair where she'd pushed it back. She'd had to put an extra £1 in the electric first to get the oven to switch on.

The cake had smelt nice, cooking. Turned out of its tin OK, although it was flatter than the ones you got in shops. Mum didn't bother icing it. 'I know my limits.' Oh, yeah? She didn't with men. She'd cut us all a big slice. It didn't taste right. Something missing. Nella dropped hers back on the plate. 'You didn't put no sugar in, Mum.' That was Mum all over. Her giggling about it after.

Little flecks of green swirled around my soup. Didn't know what they were except they weren't chicken. 'Ever thought about tracing her? Your birth mum?'

I could see Juice's lips moving, thinking. She chopped a stalk of celery. I never knew a girl what ate so many vegetables. Didn't make her look healthy, in my opinion, or slim. Last week I'd bought a loose carrot from the Co-op for eleven pence. I'd chopped it up and added it to my Scotch broth. The carrot bits were still hard, though, and one got stuck in a back tooth. Gave me gip. You can't tell me toothache's healthy.

Juice was always wanting to cook me something, only I knew what it would involve. Hours chewing. Probably hours of wind after. She looked up to me. Listened, like what I said was important. Asked me things like I'd know the answer. It was because of me rescuing Jack, and because she'd seen me using a dictionary. TJ said looking things up didn't mean you were thick. It meant the opposite. He could be right, I suppose, although he was foreign.

She finally shook her head. 'Dunno what I'd find. She had me young. Might have had a string of other kids since. Kids she *kept*. Ones that were good enough.'

I stirred the soup too quick. Some of it splashed out the saucepan. 'She might not have *wanted* to give you up.' Juice looked up. 'Just thinking about what your mum must have gone through.'

'*Birth* mum. I ain't interested. Got teased at school for being adopted.' Juice flung the celery on top of the other veg and moved on to something hard and round and orange – might have been a swede. 'She gave *me* up. And it would upset my real mum.'

I stared at Juice through the soup steam. But Juice's 'real mum' had had her all her life.

There was a skin on my soup now. I poured it out and sat down. Audrey sat by my chair. Lifted a dainty paw to wash her face. Something we had in common, being small. Not that I was dainty.

Juicy Lucy opened a tin of tomatoes and dumped it on top of the chopped veg. It turned my stomach. 'She could be a druggie, alkie, mental. Anything.'

Yeah, a druggie, like you were, I wanted to say. I dipped my sandwich in the soup. Sometimes they were a bit dry from being in the display cabinet at work. A bit of bread took its time going down. 'None of us here are whiter than white, Juice.' Stealing from a post office *was* a crime, in case she'd forgotten. I didn't say it because I liked old Juice. Liked her looking up to me. Let's face it, it was a novelty.

Another tin of tomatoes glugged out its red insides. 'But you don't want your *mum* to be like that, do you? You want to look up to your mum.'

'Yeah.' I slurped a spoonful of soup. Didn't like the taste much, in spite of its posh name, whatever it was. You might *want* to respect your mum, but you couldn't, not always.

Mum had never been much of a law-breaker. Soft-hearted in her way. But respect? What for? Her terrible taste in men, the way she'd landed us kids with them? Her flaky attitude to money and housework and cooking? Our shabby socks that was supposed to be white?

When it came down to it you just wanted a normal mum. A boring one, with no problems to take her mind off her kids. That's what Alastair would want. I couldn't tell Juice about him. Not after she'd let rip about her birth mum. She'd stop looking up to me. I dipped the last of my sandwich into what was left of the soup, but I couldn't finish it.

Audrey followed me upstairs. She sat on the window sill, both of us looking out. She wasn't brooding like I was, she was watching a pigeon strutting about on the roof opposite.

*I* hadn't wanted to give Alastair up. *I* hadn't had loads more kids.

Feeling low was a trigger for wanting a drink. I got the calendar down quick, flipped through the last three months. Ticked off today. Leant extra firm on the biro. Three more days and I'd have done a hundred.

A whole row of pigeons were on the roof now, fluffing out their feathers. Settling down for the night. Peaceful. That was because they lived in a big group, not ruddy families.

I was still off my stride next day at break. TJ and I shared the *Metro*. He had the outside bit first. I sat a bit closer now but that was only so I didn't have to keep peering over to explain things. He was reading about a Polish football player on the back page. Being slow about it. I asked him for his half, twice – he must have learnt the words off by heart, the time he was taking – but he didn't take any notice. I was breathing four, four, s-i-x, but I was still fit to burst. So I just reached over and took it off him. It was the way I'd been brought up.

TJ hung on to it, which was a mistake. The page ripped. I toppled off the bench. Someone stirring a cup of coffee at a nearby table looked over and frowned. Like I done it on purpose.

TJ was doubled over, his head practically on his knees, not in pain, bloody laughing.

I got up. 'Funny, am I? It was your effing fault!' I shouted, through swirls of red mist. I didn't say effing.

120

TJ stopped laughing. 'Sit down, Maggsie. Everyone is looking.'

He was practically telling me to calm down! I opened my mouth to give him and all the people staring what for, only he jumped up. Took hold of my shoulders and pushed me through the swing doors. I struggled, but he kept hold of me. I shut my eyes and turned my head away. A sinking in my gut. TJ wasn't supposed to be like this. I was still shouting, mind. You can shout with your eyes shut, though it might not be something you've ever tried.

'I not want you to lose *job*, Maggsie.'

Saying my name was a trigger. Snappy, I remembered, too late. Imagined him on the floor looking up at TJ. Flexing his jaws a bit half-hearted. Scuttling away.

'One day *you* good cook,' TJ winked, seeing me watching Primrose peeling some raw beetroots. Dark red stains on her pink palms. I wasn't really interested. I was pretending. I shrugged. TJ was trying to make out us arguing hadn't happened. Primrose stuck a beetroot in the food processor. I stared at it going round. Looked like roadkill.

TJ was difficult to argue with. I'd noticed it before. Just looked puzzled or hurt, didn't get angry back. Not what I was used to in a man. Dad had been the dead opposite – and Dougie. Maybe it was because he was Polish. Perhaps they were all like that over there. Al, my first boyfriend, he'd been a bit like that, come to think of it. Even worse.

That evening, I went up to my room soon as I'd had my sandwich and the rest of the soup from the day before. Wasn't going to waste it.

121

I'd made a show of myself. Shouting and that. What would Alastair have thought? Jack? And if any of those posh gits staring had complained I'd have been in trouble. Lose my job and things would go downhill fast. No way would I ever contact Alastair from prison.

Audrey was asleep. I lay on the bed next to her and stroked her little pointed ears. She started purring. They should play that at football matches to calm people down. I'd read in *Woman's World* that stroking a cat lowered your blood pressure, only I think the cat was supposed to be awake for it to work.

TJ could switch off from things. I'd seen it when he was reading the information signs on old buildings, or looking close at paintings. He got caught up in what he was doing. Shut himself off from the rest of the world. Well, from me. He'd had his nose buried in that football article. Maybe he hadn't ignored me on purpose.

I went downstairs. Fished my soup container out the kitchen bin. Rinsed the lid off and took it upstairs.

I read the writing on it this time *and* looked up all the words I didn't know. There were a lot of them. Don't laugh. How much attention *you* ever paid to a soup label? Plenty anyone could learn. It took me ages to work out the soup's name: Fragrant Thai Chicken. Well, not after ten minutes boiling, it hadn't been.

Next time I got worked up I'd start breathing o-u-t straight away. Have Snappy at my fingertips, ready to go. No. Wasn't even going to be a next time.

# 20

At fag break TJ fished something out of his apron pocket, all sheepish. 'I have something for you. Useful thing.'

Awkward seeing as I'd lost my rag with him yesterday. Felt better soon as I saw it was only an old book. Something else he'd got from a charity shop.

It was an address book, a little one. Letters of the alphabet down one side and a picture of a vase of flowers on the front. Later I saw there'd been some addresses already written in that TJ had stuck paper over.

He handed it over, smiling. 'Is personal spelling dictionary for you.' His plain potato face was pink and I swear the bristles on his head were standing up.

I wasn't good at looking pleased when I wasn't. Yeah, I was improving my English, but it was supposed to be me teaching TJ. *I* was the one that was English.

'If it's another dictionary, why ain't it got no words in it, TJ?'

'No words *yet*.' His skin nearly split smiling. 'Sandra in my class. She has one. She write tricky words in. And when she want to use word again, there is it!'

'There it *is*.' I shoved it in my pocket. 'Helpful of Sandra. Know much about me, does she?'

'No, no. I copy *idea* of Sandra. I sit next to her. Big

fat lady.' He spread his arms. 'Not leave much room at table.'

I paused, got the address book back out and handed it to him. His face fell. 'Write *your* name in it then, your *whole* name: Tad . . . what is it?'

Tadeusz Jancowitz, he wrote, under T. No one could spell that, could they? Even if they didn't have dyslexia. No wonder people called him TJ.

At home I copied some words into the address book, the *personal spelling dictionary*, under the right letters. Words I'd use again, tricky ones like *because, friend, necessary*.

TJ's face lit up when I told him I was using it. He had the sort of face that showed what he was feeling. Not a good thing, if you asked me. People could take advantage.

We'd had a couple more Sunday outings together seeing as I didn't have anything better to do. Not to places like Madame Tussauds, which is where I'd have liked to have gone. Museums and that, and parks. The outside of buildings with history.

Neither of us had much money. Reckon his wife in Poland kept all his. Bet it was her that made him have his hair so short. Bet she'd shaved it off. With a blunt razor. A rusty one. And told him it looked fantastic. Bet she'd bought his awful clumpy shoes.

TJ had said before about getting a boat along the Thames to Greenwich. It was near Lewisham where he lived. But nicer, he said, more history.

I reminded him about it now. Fixed it up for next week to show willing.


We met outside the bookshop at Waterloo again. TJ had gelled his hair up. What there was of it. Made him look like a hedgehog. When I saw him, I had to clamp my mouth shut to stop myself laughing. Pretend I was interested in a book in the window, which, trust me, wasn't likely.

We got the boat from the London Eye. I didn't let on I'd never been on a boat before. The floor moved under my feet when I stepped onto it. Felt like I'd had a couple of drinks, though I definitely hadn't. A nice feeling.

TJ pointed out the sights. Threw his arm out at the Tower of London. It used to be a prison, a cruel one, where they tortured people. Cut their heads off, like TJ's arms was likely to do to me. I hadn't told him I'd been in prison and I wasn't going to. Not something you boasted about. You might think having a colourful past is interesting because you haven't had one, but trust me, it's not. It's boring, actually. TJ didn't seem to know that Scanda gave ex-cons a fresh start in life. He wasn't the nosey type, anyway. Some people asked too many questions.

We passed Canary Wharf with all the bankers counting their millions. Weird getting up so close to the shiny skyscrapers. Squashed between them there'd be an old church, or a little thin house with tiny windows. Sometimes a statue just loomed up out of nowhere. There was history and today all jumbled up together, but it still looked OK.

The boat got up speed. Hard to keep your balance with the wind and the waves. I had to do up my ponytail again because of the wind whipping it about. TJ put his hand on my back to keep me steady. I let him, just as long as he didn't get any ideas.

Inside, there was a bar and proper comfy seats and

toilets. I didn't look at the bar. The other passengers were like the people on the tube: posh. TJ said Greenwich was an expensive part of London. All of London was posh and expensive, if you asked me.

Arriving in Greenwich was like going abroad. Well, what I thought it would be like. A two-hundred-years-old country. A huge old ship, that you could look round if you paid, was stuck in the middle of the road. Old-fashioned shops and buildings and cobbles all about. TJ took my elbow and guided me to some big white houses, palaces, whatever. He knew one that was free to look around. I only let him because I didn't know the way.

The building had a painted ceiling. Crowds of chubby people in fancy wigs floating around on clouds. Got a crick in the neck looking up at them. TJ knew who'd done the painting. Even knew who the people were. Pointed to a fat bloke with hair like a pop star from the olden days. Some British king or other, though he'd come from Germany.

I tapped his arm. It felt hard and muscly through his donkey jacket. 'You put me to shame, TJ, you do.'

'You are ashamed of me?' He looked down, his fore-head creased. Another thing about TJ was he took life too serious. In spite of the smiling. Wore his brain out, thinking.

'Nah!' I prodded his arm again. If you were talking about actual shame it would be the other way round.

I had to explain *put me to shame*. Not easy explaining things you said every day without thinking. TJ was lucky he had me teaching him.

We wandered around. It was getting warmer. I was thirsty and my feet ached. TJ whipped a bottle of water out of his pocket. He was good at long-term thinking. Then he said he was going to treat me to something nice.

He headed off down a side street, too narrow for him to hold my elbow. It looked straight out of one of them classic serials the BBC did on Sundays. The ones Big Shirl and Juice went misty-eyed over.

*Something nice.* Bound to be some kind of book. Or maybe a special Polish food. Not a sausage, though. Please. We joined the end of a queue. TJ wouldn't tell me what we were queuing for. Put his finger to his lips, smiling. 'Wait few minutes.' He had a childish streak sometimes.

I stuck my hands in my jacket pockets. The good thing about denim was you could wear it summer or winter. People came in behind us so we had to shuffle up close. 'What does your wife think about you spending money on me, then?' I asked him, just to pass the time waiting. I was trying to speak more proper. I could have said *your missus*, but I didn't. I didn't want TJ picking up mistakes.

'Mm?' he turned to me, his smile vanishing. 'Oh. I tell wife . . .'

'What's her name, again?' I knew her name but I didn't want to give him an advantage. Or her, come to that.

'Sofia.'

'Sofia.' I nodded. Sofa. I saw a big woman, stuffed into clothes loads of sizes too small. 'What you tell her then, Sofia?'

'I tell her you are my English teacher.' TJ moved forward in the queue. 'I learn formal English from text-book, from my class. I learn how people speak from you.'

I raised my eyebrows. 'So, these trips out, they're English lessons, are they?'

TJ nodded. 'I learn much from you, Maggsie. I write down words you have said.'

Sounded like a cop taking a statement. I tried to move away, get a bit more space, only we were too squashed together. I turned back to ask another question: 'Your wife work, does she?'

'Part-time, yes. In bank. She not like to say to friends I clear tables over here.' He stared straight ahead. He was tall enough to look over the queue. 'Sofia very independent woman. She have routine. When I go home Christmas, Easter, I disturb routine.'

My eyebrows went up. Where was all this coming from? TJ had never said much about his home life before. I remembered his Polish phone calls when he'd stopped smiling. Saw a sneer on his wife, old Sofa's, fat face. We moved forwards a bit. '*You're* not working part-time, TJ. You work every blood . . . blimmin' hour God sends.' As well as his Scanda job, he did two evenings a week at a college, washing out test tubes. Plus he helped a Polish mate out in his shop on a Saturday, *and* worked in another Polish mate's restaurant, Saturday nights.

TJ nodded, not smiling. 'I make most of opportunities. Is not much work in Poland.'

'What does she look like? Sofia, your wife,' I asked. It was just to make conversation. It wasn't that I was interested or anything.

'Blonde hair. Tall. Big. Twice size of you. Big since working in bank.'

'Bigg*er*,' I corrected. 'much bigger.'

We were inside the shop now. I'd forgotten we were queuing for something. A group of girls in front got served, then TJ and me were at the counter. It was glass with metal containers. Different colours inside. Cold steam coming up. Ice cream – ice cream*s*. Never seen so many flavours. I'd only had vanilla or chocolate before, Mr Whippy. His treat, TJ said. Two scoops. I asked for chocolate and coffee because I couldn't read the fancy writing on the labels. TJ had pink grapefruit and *piss* . . . something green.

We sat on a bench in Greenwich Park and ate them. Never tasted anything so good. Even TJ's weird flavours and colours were nice. I stretched my legs out in the sunshine and shut my eyes.

'You are happy, Maggsie?' TJ asked. Full of the joys of spring, he was again now. Soon as he'd stopped talking about his wife.

'Yeah, I s'pose.' Never a good idea to commit yourself. I wondered if I should tell him about Alastair. My year plan. Maybe counting chickens, though. I'd lost it – well, got too firm – only last week. No, I *had* lost it. Another step out of line and my life here would go back to being what I'd thought it was on that first day: a fairy tale. I'd be back where I started. Doing something I shouldn't just to get sent back to prison. All hope of contacting Alastair gone up in smoke.

TJ dozed off. No wonder he was tired with all his jobs. Bet his wife, old Sofa, wasn't wearing herself out like he was. Sitting on your backside in a bank for a few hours a day wasn't exactly slave labour. I imagined rolls of flesh like pink sausage-meat poking out over the top of her skirt. Imagined Snappy's jaws closing on one. TJ had said they ate a lot of sausage in Poland. I let him have ten minutes then I tapped his hand to wake him.

After a fag – well, a rollie, but still a fag, which *I*

gave *him* – we walked up a steep hill. Got out of breath. But from the top you could see the whole of London. You could see more of it than you could from the roof garden at Scanda.

TJ said people used to look at stars from up here because it was so high. They'd worked out the different times it would be around the world from here too. Alastair would want me to know stuff so I didn't mind TJ telling me things, only not all the time.

We walked a bit further. Saw a herd of deer, and squirrels and birds, and kids, posh ones, feeding them. I bought us a cup of tea from a café. The girl behind the till was eating a baguette out of a paper bag, holding it like she was hiding a bottle. I was just about to say something because she didn't give me any change from my fiver. Then I read 'TEA' on the price list, £2.50, and nearly fainted. It did come in a big cardboard cup, though, and it took a long time to drink.

# 21

Things were going OK. Too peaceful, maybe. What did Nan used to say? Plans is what God spoils when he hears you making them. Something like that.

It was like being under a nice hot shower, posh soap and all that, and then someone turning on the cold.

That someone was Louise.

It was only Enid that had sent me letters before, personal ones I mean. Then I got two more in one week. One good, one bad. The good letter was from Jack. Six lines. He was back at work. After the summer he'd be playing football again. And all thanks to me, he said. His letter was easier to read than his card had been all those months ago. *Keep in touch*, he said, at the end. Gave his address. I might. Might send him a Christmas card, written out all neat, end of this year.

The second letter, the bad one, was waiting for me at home. I knew it wasn't from Enid. Enid had round blue biro writing. This one was in black with loops and slopes.

I went upstairs to open it. Turned to the signature. *Best wishes from* . . . ? Couldn't make out the name. A real scrawl. A big *L*, then *o-u-i-s-e*. Louse? Oh, Louise. *Louise*. I sat down on the bed. Why was *she* writing?

Louise had been banged up the same time as me. Airs

and graces, and no mates, far as I could recall. I reckon she only stuck all her arty postcards up because she didn't have any proper cards or photos to show off. Neither did I, mind. Enid used to chat to her, but Enid talked to everyone.

Louise had been sent down for smuggling drugs. Travelling. In South America, I think it was. On her 'gap year', like poshos call it. She'd hooked up with a boyfriend and he'd got her passing off cocaine in bars done up as chocolate. She'd got caught with loads of them in her rucksack. Got twelve years for it. A ruddy long gap year. Her family disowned her but came round a bit after she ditched the boyfriend.

The reason Louise knew about pictures was because she got a degree or something in Art History while she was inside. A twelve-year stretch gives you plenty of time to faff around.

She'd had a job in the prison library. Thought it put her a rung above us lesser mortals. Said she was going to get a job in an art gallery when she got out. How was that going to work, I'd thought, with your record? Yawned to show I wasn't impressed. That was why I was surprised she was writing to me now.

I turned back to the first page. *Hiya Maggsie*, she wrote, like we were best mates. I didn't even like the girl. Apart from her droning on, I'd never liked the way she looked at me too long, like she was weighing me up. The way she turned away with a little smile, like I wasn't up to scratch. Just reading something she'd wrote set my teeth on edge.

I worked through her letter, saying the words out loud, going ahead when I got stuck, like Enid had said. A choked-up feeling rose in my chest. Louise's writing was big, easy enough to read. It was what she said that was difficult.

Enid was ill. A lump in her breast. (Must have been a big one, I thought, for Enid to find anything in her massive boobs.) Louise's writing got a bit blurry then, but it seemed Enid's whole boob had needed taking away.

I'd written to Enid, week before last, my third letter. Told her I'd got 'the cat here' to sleep on my bed. Didn't have the spelling of Audrey to hand, and I couldn't be bothered to go down and copy it off the pilchard tin.

Enid hadn't replied. I hadn't heard from her for a few weeks, come to think of it. So this was why.

The good thing about a letter was that you could read it again. Not Louise's, Enid's. I got her last one out of my holdall:

> *It gave me a real lift to get your letter, dear. Said you'd do well this time, didn't I? I felt it in my water when you stuck to your reading.*
>
> *Wear undies and tights under your jeans when you go out with that Polish fellow. Men are all the same whatever country they come from.*

I could see her nodding. Putting her hand to her cheek. Hear the click of her plastic beads. She was wrong about TJ, though. He'd only ever gone for my elbow.

> *I been doing my crocheting and I've got my holiday in Romania to look forward to when I get out beginning of October. It's that what keeps me going. And knowing you're doing so well.*
>
> *Write again, dear, and tell me how you're getting on. Seen the Queen yet?*
>
> *Love from your old friend Enid*

I looked at the date. More than a month ago. Had she known about the lump then? Not wanted to worry me? I folded her letter up and put it back in the envelope. Thought about her writing it, leaning over the paper, boobs resting on her knees.

Like I said before, there's no justice in this world. Enid hadn't had long to go. Another few weeks and she'd have been out of prison and off to that pine forest in *Roman . . . Romania.* My eyes stung, thinking about it.

Louise said the hospital had been going to order an extra-large fake boob for Enid to put in her bra, after, but Enid had said no, she'd always wanted to get rid of them. Gave her backache something chronic. So they'd taken them both off.

I winced and felt my own chest, even though all I'd got was two fried eggs, no matter how much I ponced them up with the lacy bras I'd bought from Enid's catalogue. You could choose from loads of pictures and you didn't have to pay straight away.

Enid, flat-chested. I couldn't imagine it. Louise said she'd been in hospital two weeks recovering, which she'd *th . . . thor . . .* something enjoyed. I swallowed. That was good then. Good old Enid.

I added a bit to the letter I'd started a couple of weeks back: *Sorry u r ill Enid get well sooNe. No mor back ake.* Sometimes I put capital letters in the middle of words, without realizing. That's the sort of thing that makes people think you're thick. I made the 'N' smaller. What I really wanted to say was: *Don't die, Enid. You can't die.*

I posted the letter in the box outside the Co-op. It was all I could do. When you were finishing off a prison sentence, which I was, only I forgot it sometimes, you weren't allowed to travel.

I thought about Louise's letter. She'd said Enid had told her I was 'working in Central London'. Like I was a managing director or something, not a ruddy kitchen assistant. Louise would be out herself next week. Her family had a flat in London. Perhaps we could meet up for a coffee? That best mate thing again. I didn't know about that. Like I said, I never liked the girl. I didn't reply. But then, in spite of London being the biggest city in Britain – eight million people living here, TJ said – I bumped into her.

# 22

It was half four, when I was coming out of work. She was walking towards me. Did a poncy sort of jump when our eyes met. Squealed.

'Oh my goodness. I don't believe it!' Same posh voice.

(It was only a lot later I thought, hang on . . . I *don't* believe it.)

'Maggsie, *is* it you?' She gave me a fancy kiss on both cheeks, like people do in London. Stood back and looked me up and down, cheeky cow. Seeing her was worse than reading her letter.

I had black trousers on, not jeans, and I'd stopped wearing my ponytail scraped up so high. It had always given me a headache anyway. There'd been a page in *Woman's World*: 'Seven Styles for Mid-length Hair'. Wearing it lower toned down Nan's earrings when I wore them. Bless her, they were on the flashy side. Mostly I stuck to my silver studs.

And I'd been using tinted moisturizer. The beauty page said it gave your skin a *subt* . . . something glow. Kept meaning to ask Ruby or TJ what it was. Alastair would want me to look smart, wouldn't he? Any son would. Primping a bit didn't mean I wasn't still as tough as old boots underneath, though, because I was.

Louise was still looking at me that few seconds too

long like she used to, inside. Like *she* was in charge. She'd changed more than I had. Well, appearance-wise she had. Put on weight since I'd last seen her – which was in prison, in spite of her airs and graces. Had her hair highlighted all different shades of blonde, and cut in fancy layers. Chin-length so didn't do nothing for her round face. She had a suede jacket on and a white shirt and a heavy gold pendant, like she was a mayor or something. And she was clutching one of those posh dangly carrier bags with a designer name on it.

'Fancy a coffee, Maggsie?' she said, all matey. 'On me.'

I hesitated. I didn't like her. All we had in common was we'd been inside. The coffee would be half foam and leave a moustache. But she might have news about Enid.

That is an important lesson in life: always go with your gut instinct. Because I should have just said thanks, but no thanks, I was putting my old life behind me. That would have put her in her place. But I didn't. I did find out something about Enid – well, she *told* me something. But it was something that led to all sorts of trouble.

Louise's loud voice didn't stand out so much in the café because they were all braying. The whole chat was about her. I didn't want to hear what *she* was doing. It was only Enid I was interested in. I went through all my anger management strategies listening. And that was before other stuff kicked off.

'Busy, busy, busy. Family stuff, you know? Pa's organized a family trip for later this year. Just before Christmas. Diving. The whole lot of us in one of those floating hotel boats. Luxury or what? It'll be a hoot. A real celebration. Give us a chance to get to know each other again.' She laughed. Only it wasn't funny, seeing as it was her being in jail that had kept them apart.

'Your family OK with you now, then?' I spooned up foam from my poncy coffee. You could get a cup of tea here but it came in a glass mug with a teabag dangling on a string. You had to fish it out and then find somewhere to put it. Blow that for a game of soldiers.

'Oh yes. They say I add colour. Even though I've always been the *black* sheep!' Louise's was the sort of laugh that makes you want to stick your fingers in your ears. Or down your throat . . . 'All the rest of them are medics or accountants. Very dull.' There was a pause.

I added five teaspoons of *brown* sugar (they didn't have white) to the coffee. Too bitter, otherwise.

'Of course, my family have gone up in the world now, you know.' Half the café must have heard that. 'Yah, Pa inherited when I was . . .' she dropped her voice for the first time, 'well, you know. *Away.*'

Yeah. And *prison* was definitely going down in the world.

She went on about the house, 'stately home' she called it, her dad had got off *his* dad. Down south somewhere. Somewhere there was more sheep than people. This house was so old it was in guidebooks. So posh someone slept there to guard it when they were away. They opened it up three days a week in the summer. *To the riff-raff*, she said, laughing. To *people*, she meant. 'And, of course, it makes a wonderful backdrop for Pa's art collection. All that dark wood sets the paintings off beautifully.'

Of course it does. I thought of Nan's display cabinet, in the lounge, the fish and seaweed patterned wallpaper behind it. Meant for a bathroom, really. Her A Present

138

from Margate box that I had in my holdall back at the house. The photo.

Louise was a daddy's girl. She'd gone on about him, inside. What car he drove, what paintings he liked. All the stuff he knew. Like an overgrown kid. Enid reckoned all Louise's studying and art malarkey was just to impress him. Make him forget she was a jailbird. Enid. It was *her* I wanted to talk about. Not sit through Louise's boasting.

She picked up her cup. 'Yes, my family won't know what's hit them, now I'm back in circulation! I've never been conventional.' She stopped laughing. 'Whereas you, you've gone the other way, haven't you? You look . . . different.' She made it sound like a bad thing. 'Still skinny, but you've lost your swagger.' A too-long look over her coffee cup.

What did she mean, swagger? Stuck-up bitch. 'I am working now,' I said frostily. 'I've been working at Scanda Solutions for more than six months.' I got a kick out of telling people that, even Louise, who had a stately home to fall back on.

She arched her eyebrows like she was amazed. I noticed some straggly hairs that needed plucking. 'Well done, you! Cutting edge in modern furniture design, aren't they? Pa's invested in a couple of their chairs.'

I nodded like I knew what she was talking about. Scanda's spiky black furniture wasn't my cup of tea. Cheap-looking, if you asked me. Basic. Mind you, you'd think they'd added another nought on the end of everything by mistake.

Louise was still on about Scanda. 'Pa says they're great ambassadors for Denmark. In fact' – she put down her cup – 'they've got quite a collection of modern Danish art, haven't they?'

Had they? First I'd heard of it. I shrugged. 'Where are their paintings then?'

'Well, in their boardroom, I expect.'

Oh. Yeah. Right up there. Come to think of it I had seen some splodges of colour through the glass of the boardroom door. I passed it on the way to the roof garden. TJ would know, seeing as he worked up there sometimes. He'd know the names of the artists better than what Louise would.

Once she'd started it was difficult to get Louise off the subject of art. She was like TJ that way. They'd have things in common. No, I tapped the little spoon on my saucer. No, they wouldn't. I let the spoon drop.

'Heard how Enid's doing?' I got in at last.

'Well,' Louise flicked her hair off her face, but it settled back in exactly the same place. Swear I could hear the clunk. 'She came back after the mastectomy. She's waiting for radiotherapy now.'

I winced. Enid liked it in hospital, I reminded myself. Nice change from prison.

'If that doesn't work then there's chemo.' Louise sounded like she was reading out a menu. 'But, after all that, well . . .' She shrugged her shoulders.

My armpits prickled. If it was anyone in *her* family Louise wouldn't be so casual. There was a heaviness in my chest. All those travel pictures in Enid's cell. Romania that was keeping her going.

When I looked up, Louise was asking more questions about Scanda. Seemed ever so interested in what it was like and what I did there. Still looked at me like she couldn't believe *I* was working there, mind. Caught her staring at my teeth more than once. Swear I saw her lip curl. Like I said, I'd never warmed to her.

She asked for my mobile number in case she got more news of Enid. Gave me hers. Not that I'd ever text her.

The only person I texted was TJ. He didn't mind my garbled messages. His weren't right neither because of being Polish.

Then, outside, blow me down if Louise didn't suggest us meeting up again. For dinner. *For old times' sake*. God knows why. 'It's been *fascinating*, Maggsie.' Waved goodbye like she was the Queen.

No, it hadn't.

# 23

I was sitting at my desk, reading a story in *Woman's World*. A made-up one. Two and a half pages long. Struggling over the names of the people in it, to be honest. Thinking of Enid, leaning forward, arms folded under her boobs that weren't there any more, smiling at me having a go at something so long. That set me off on a downer. I wanted to rip the whole ruddy thing in half. Smash something, Have a drink. Scream at the poxy stinking unfairness of it all.

Trudie poking her head round the door didn't make me feel any better. She took it being open as an invitation. It was – for Audrey. And if Audrey was on my bed it meant she was asleep. Cats needed their rest. Peace and quiet. They didn't want visitors.

I'd bought her a little beanbag bed with a fleecy pattern of mice and fish bones. Put it at the bottom of my bed, next to the wall. Audrey kneaded the furry cover, purring, eyes half closed. In a sort of trance. Preferred it to Trudie's jumper. She was on it now.

'What do you want?' I asked Trudie, narkily, because she wasn't Enid. 'Never heard of knocking?' I wasn't keen on her seeing me reading a woman's magazine with a school dictionary alongside either. My heart was going thump, thump, thump. I didn't raise my voice because I didn't want to wake Audrey.

Get out the crocodile, I thought. I sent him crawling across the carpet on his stumpy legs. Imagined him chasing Trudie out the door. She did give a little jump, like he was real. But it was because she'd spotted Audrey all curled up, one paw over her eye. Probably trying to blot out Trudie's leathery face.

'I had one just like her in Greece.' Trudie went right over to my bed. She had a tie-dyed top on. Lime green. Reliving her youth. 'Used to put sunscreen on her ears. They can get burnt. The tips, you know?'

Pity *you* didn't use some, I wanted to say. Snappy headed for her ankle.

Trudie stepped away from the bed, I'll give Snappy that. 'We don't never hardly see her downstairs, Maggsie. Cos of you enticing her up here.'

'She *follows* me upstairs. Can't help it if she prefers my company.'

'Don't own her, though, do you?' Trudie said. Muttered something I won't repeat on her way out the door.

I slammed the dictionary shut. Gave up on the story. Trudie had rubbed me up the wrong way. Couldn't concentrate anyway. Hard not being able to do something for someone who's been good to you, like Enid had.

Then, just to cheer me up, things kicked off at work. I told you that would happen sooner or later.

It was the following Thursday, half oneish. TJ was poncing about in the boardroom upstairs, waiting on the bigwigs at one of Scanda's posh dinners. He had a black bow tie on and a white shirt. Made a change from his apron. He'd

143

looked up the Danish paintings Louise had gone on about. Hadn't known they were valuable before. First time I'd been able to tell him anything about art. First time I'd been able to tell him *anything*, apart from slang.

I had to fill in for TJ downstairs. I wasn't cut out to be a waitress, out there in the canteen, on show. It was quite like a prison one, actually – no carpet, cutlery banging – but the people eating were all smartly dressed, with teeth they didn't have to cover up. None of them was wearing an overall.

I took some mushroom omelettes out to a couple of grumpy gits. One had black-framed glasses and a cardigan, which was something you saw a lot of in London, and the other one was in a suit. Reckon they'd been left out of the special boardroom dinner. I already had a down on them because, earlier, old Cardigan had snapped his fingers at me to clear their table. I did it with Snappy by the side of me, his tail lashing and both our eyes narrowed into slits, though Cardigan didn't notice.

Neither of them looked up when I put down their dinners. Didn't say thank you, even with me stood there, waiting. Just carried on chatting. It was like I wasn't there. Like I didn't matter. Because I'm small, small*er*, I haven't got much physical presence. Taking up less space makes people think I'm less important. Throw in being poor, ginger and dyslexic, and people pretended they didn't even *see* me.

Not easy to remember anger management strategies when that happens. The red mist came over. I power-walked back to the kitchen, my thumbs white on the rim of the tray.

I did try. Slammed myself into the storeroom. Stayed there for a minute, breathing o-u-t. Relaxed my shoulders.

Back in the kitchen Primrose was tetchy because TJ wasn't there to help out. Wiping sweat from her forehead with her overall sleeve. I had a good view of her giant backside lifting a casserole dish out the oven. One of her Ghanaian specials – something red and spicy with peanuts in it. By the time she'd dished out portions for me to take out, my heart had slowed down. I was cooler than Primrose. Pretty much had anger management sorted.

I served the meals OK, cleared some dirty crockery. The two ignorant pillocks had their heads together, laughing. Didn't like not knowing what they were laughing at. Then, blow me down if old Cardigan didn't snap his fingers at me again. I turned my back. Who did he think he was, treating me like the dirt on his shoe?

Snappy was scrabbling about under my overall, eager to get out, his claws tearing at the material. He was small and dangerous. You can be both. Easily.

I did know it was only me that could see Snappy. I did know using him as an anger management strategy was weird. But don't knock anything that helps you keep a hold of yourself.

'Miss!' old Suit called out. Pointed to their dirty plates, like I was slacking. I gave him a death stare. So did Snappy.

I sent him slithering through the tables, his scales rippling, his claws clicking on the laminate floor. He sat next to Cardigan, his teeth showing in an evil little smile.

I marched after him. Snatched up their plates. Made so much noise they stopped whispering. If you don't show people you're tough they'll take you for a ride. But Cardigan ordered more coffees. They were supposed to fetch them themselves from the machine. No please, no smile, no looking at me, even. No treating me like I was a human being.

I brought them out through the swing doors like a cowboy in a saloon. Guns blazing. Snappy darting ahead. The more worked up I was the more vivid I could see his open jaws and pointed teeth. I slammed the cups down with a bang that toppled them in their saucers. Half splashed into old Suit's lap. Scalding hot. He leapt up, swearing and mopping himself. Ran off to the gents.

I went back to the kitchen. Couldn't stop a little smile coming. Stacked the dishwasher, got the backlog cleared, floated on air. Wiped down every surface in the kitchen. Put the clean dishes away. Did it all smooth and efficient and careful. Did it all like a human being.

When Primrose shouted a lasagne needed taking out, and a jacket potato, I came back down to earth with a bang. Where was TJ? Them upstairs must have finished their dinners by now, surely?

I dragged my feet going through the swing doors. Those poxy twats had gone. Their coffees were on the table, left there, not touched. My stomach turned over. But at least I'd made them think twice about being disrespectful in the future, I kept telling myself. And I hadn't hit them. Hadn't even shouted.

Should have remembered I never got away with nothing in this life. Never have, never will.

TJ came back down all fired up about the boardroom paintings. Undid his bow tie. Clattered out into the canteen with his trolley. Primrose sat down for five minutes. I did some tidying in the storeroom. Forgot about the two men, except for a bit of burning in my stomach. Then, mid-afternoon, I got a message: I was wanted up at HR.

TJ and Primrose looked at me. *What have you done now, Maggsie?* I heard, without them even saying anything.

It was times like those I wished I was taller. I stuck out my chest, such as it was. Took my baccy tin and walked up to the fifth floor. I'd never got the lift, not since that first day. More burning in my belly remembering Jack lying there unconscious, and me on my own. My feet were heavy. I knew what was coming. Each step I climbed was taking me further away from Alastair.

I passed the empty boardroom. Past the sploshy paintings Louise, and now TJ, had gone on about. That brought back Enid, her being ill. I went out into the roof garden and smoked a rollie. The skyscrapers leant towards me like they had me cornered.

Knocking on HR's door was like I was back in the headmaster's office. Worse, because now I had stuff to lose.

I waited for the tube, arms folded tight, only having to keep blinking took away the effect. The doors closed behind me. I'd never felt trapped on the tube before, for all it was underground. *Doors closing.* Jack again. Months and months ago now. My eyes watered. I felt in my jacket pocket for a tissue. No sandwich there. Hadn't had a chance to take one. Hadn't even been allowed back in the kitchen. Some HR trainee, all glossy hair and lipstick, had gone downstairs to fetch my jacket.

The HR woman, her that had asked if I was alright on my first day, said there'd been a complaint. I'd been *surly*. I'd *deliberately scalded* a senior manager. Ruined his suit. 'No excuse,' she'd said, when I said they'd been rude. People like her always say putting up with rudeness is *part of the job*. That us lesser mortals should *learn to*

147

*live with it*. Them in charge wear smart clothes, though, and have a posh way of talking. Nobody's likely to be rude to them.

People got me wrong, thought I was worse than what I was. The HR woman hadn't listened to me. People didn't. I've told you that before but I don't expect you believed me. People didn't do that either.

Snappy was staring up at the HR woman with his toothy smile, but he lost heart when she handed me a form. Seemed to fade into the carpet. I'd need the form for my *next employment*. Yeah, right.

The revolving door in the front spat me out onto the street. I walked to the tube just like it was a normal day, except I was an hour early, and it was my last one.

My stomach griped all the way home. Home. Supported housing wasn't my *home*. It was one step up from a bail hostel. Not an address you could give anyone. Jack or Alastair. Even TJ. Not that it mattered now. No chance of me giving anyone any kind of address now.

I headed up the hill. Didn't have any money with me – never carried any with me if I could help it, only a pound coin for emergencies. I kept it in the little embroidered purse with the zip. That was so I couldn't buy a drink.

OK, OK. You already know about that. Yeah, I used to have a problem with drink. Lots of people do. No need to go on about it. I wouldn't sneer if I were you. For all you know, one of your friends, someone from your family might have a bottle stashed under their bed now.

I really, really wanted a drink. Quickest painkiller I knew. Might as well give in to it. No point in ticking off the calendar any more. No point in anything.

I went up to my room. Looked out of the window. Audrey was outside, on the front step, where it caught the sun, chasing a bit of Twix wrapper. If cats weren't two a penny people would pay good money to see them playing about. In zoos and that. She didn't look up. More interested in the Twix wrapper than in me.

I fetched a tenner from my holdall and went downstairs. Ignored Big Shirl's *Ain't you supposed to be at work?* and headed for the Co-op.

# 24

I bought a four-pack of Stella and headed for the little park next to the kiddies' playground in the next road. It was where the winos went.

The cans sloshed and gurgled in the carrier bag. Ages since I'd heard that sound. My belly, liver, whatever, did the same. If my brain could have gurgled it would have. A whole crowd of people flashed through it, looking disappointed. Enid, with her chest stitched up; that blue-eyed doctor who'd been nice to me. Jack and TJ. Alastair, screaming his head off in a hospital cot.

But what was the point of not drinking now? I'd already lost everything.

The lager was melted sunshine going down my throat. I drained half a can in one gulp. It set me off coughing. Forgotten how strong it was. Slowed down a bit with the other half. Felt my veins singing and a sort of shrinking under my rib-cage. Probably my liver. So much for it being enlarged, like that doc had said.

No one around, only a mum pushing a little boy with ginger hair on a swing. I felt a pang, seeing him, because of Alastair. I opened a second can, then a third. Couldn't finish the fourth.

Well and truly out of it now. Inside a warm and fuzzy cocoon. Except I needed a wee. I staggered to my feet.

The ground rose up to meet me. I had to hang on to the bench to stop myself falling. I stumbled behind a bush, giggling. After, I couldn't get my knickers up, not without toppling over. Lay there like an upturned wood-louse.

Getting up was like being on a roundabout. I tried to stand still. But it wasn't any good. I threw it all up. All three and a half cans of it *and* the remains of the jacket potato I'd had for lunch, before all that to-do. You could still see the sweetcorn kernels.

So there I was. I told you at the start I couldn't do it. Knew I didn't have it in me to stay on the straight and narrow.

I'd always liked a drink. Right from that first drop of cherry brandy in a tiny glass that Nan let us have Sunday afternoons and Christmas. That warm feeling going down. The way it made you forget things. The way you could just give yourself up to it. The way it filled up your time.

Your best friend and your worst enemy.

Before, I'd serve half my sentence and get let out. Then came the hard bit: finding somewhere to live. Never mind finding a job.

I'd kipped at Nan's sometimes, until she died. She didn't like me drinking. Sat up nights until I came home. Plus she kept on at me to come ballroom dancing with her. Can you see me, denim jacket and jeans, trainers, sailing round a dance floor? Some leathery pensioner mate of Nan's, with a bristly moustache, doing his back in, twirling me round?

I sofa-surfed until all my mates seemed to have kids

and settle down. Then I kipped in a mate's old Honda, one where you could let the seats down. Quite comfy for someone my size. Hectic, though, with all the street noise going on. And cold.

Even colder in a multi-storey car park. Concrete chills your bones no matter how much cardboard you put down. And they're lonely places, nights, especially when some tosser thinks you might like a bit of company. You have to sleep right under the CCTV camera. One eye open because you don't know what people could do to you. Well, you do know, that's the trouble.

A couple of weeks doing that and anyone would be begging to go back inside.

So then it's nicking something. Making sure you get caught. Head-shakes from the judge and the screws. The whole thing starting up again.

I always meant to go straight, but it was hard. Nothing much for me at the Job Centre. Even less after a couple of prison stretches. I pretty much gave up. Everyone else had given up on me anyway.

Coming out, the stretch before last, I'd ended up in A&E. Collapsed after my first drink and some old biddy called an ambulance. Lot of fuss about nothing. If I'd been left where I was I'd have slept if off. Hospitals don't like people coming in drunk.

But it hadn't been like that. I've spoken about him before. A young doctor. Blue eyes. This was him. He didn't look no more than twenty. Good-looking, if you were into that sort of thing, which I wasn't. I'm still not. Dark hair, those eyes, white teeth. I'd thought, uh-oh, *he's* going to be up himself, but I was in too much pain to get a snarky comment out. Anyway, he wasn't. He even asked about my pets. Pets! That was a first. I'm a cat person, I told him. They're independent, like me.

I heard about *his* cat. Then he pushed back a floppy lock of hair and asked – *asked*, mind, not told – me to put my top back on and sit down for *a chat*.

Of course it was about my drinking.

Doom and gloom. Enlarged liver. If I carried on I'd die. 'Far too young, with the rest of your life not lived.' He looked at me. 'Which would be very sad.'

Funny, him looking sorry about it brought a lump to *my* throat.

'What will be, will be. I might go on for ages. Prove you wrong.' I smiled, covering my teeth with my hand.

He smiled back, which was another thing people in charge didn't do. They looked tetchy, or tired, or their lips went tight. If they did smile, their eyes didn't move.

He touched my hand. 'Have another go at staying off it, Maggsie. Keep trying and you'll get there. I know you will.'

One chat with one person and I've never touched a drop since. It was because of the way he was. Nan had always said I'd get there in the end, but she was my nan.

Don't get me wrong. It wasn't easy. Once you stop drinking you remember all the things you've done you wished you hadn't. That's what makes you want a drink again. I had to cross roads when I saw pubs coming up. Stay away from the booze aisle in supermarkets. Just keep walking sometimes till the craving passed. Put my hand on my belly, where my liver was. Imagine it poking through my skin like it was trying to escape.

But I still ended up back inside. Nella didn't believe

I'd stopped drinking and neither did Mum. She said, Dougie looming behind her, I could only stay if I got a job. Well you know how likely that was. Dougie drank loads, but he had a job. Bricklayer. Could carry more bricks in his hod than anyone else, he said. Kept on about it, flexing his bicep, blown up to twice its normal size like Popeye. Each time the number of bricks got bigger. I didn't point that out. I wasn't daft – in spite of Dougie saying I was because I couldn't read.

The Job Centre said no chance with my record and *lack of literacy*. I wouldn't even get benefit unless I went to college. Well, blow that for a game of soldiers. I'd had enough humiliation at school. Wasn't going to sign up for more.

So, no choice but to steal something and get sent back down. Not booze. This time it was posh food from Marks & Spencer. Strawberries, cream cakes, a wodge of strong cheese that made my eyes water. I'd opened all the packets, eaten half the basket before security latched on.

First time I'd been arrested sober.

Inside, I still thought about drinking. The craving doesn't go away, even when you've got no access to it.

That's when Enid turned up in my cell with her *Woman's World*s. It was trying to read them that took my mind off things.

Then it was that probation officer coming up with the Scanda scheme.

Funny how one thing can lead to another in a *good* way.

Until now.

# 25

Now I'd thrown up all the lager, I was sober again. Pain was flooding back. My tissue was too wet to use. I dropped it in the bin, along with the cans. I was still a tidy person. There was half a can left, but I was too sick to drink it.

My legs were weak, walking home. Got in without anyone seeing me. Tomorrow I'd buy more booze, drink it slower. Get sent back down. It's simpler inside; no responsibilities, no stuck-up twats dissing you.

OK, it's good being able to do stuff, but once you can, pressure builds up. People expect more. I mean, once you can read a form you've got to fill it in. Before you know it, you'll be paying council tax. Worrying you've put your bin out on the right day.

No more seeing the sights in prison, of course. No Audrey, no Scanda, no Alastair, no future – but you can't have everything in this life.

I scrubbed my teeth to take away the taste of vomit. Splashed my face with cold water. Didn't look in the mirror.

All sorts of gurgles were coming from my insides. My liver whining, *told you.*

I didn't hang up my clothes. Just pulled them off and

left them on the floor. That's one example of what drink does to you.

I got into bed. Prayed for morning to come quick so I could get hammered proper. Audrey sat up in her beanbag. Started washing. One paw hovered in the air as she stared at me. If a cat could have put their paws on their hips, she would have.

There was a tap on the door.

'Maggsie?' Ruby's voice.

Someone come to have a go. Be disappointed. Just when I was stone cold sober.

I got up to let her in. She had a key anyway.

She put down two mugs of tea and switched on the light. Sat down on my bed, like we were all girls together, only she was posh and educated, with lovely teeth and a healthy look to her, and me, well . . .

'Big Shirl said you'd come home early.'

'Yeah.' I kept my eyes shut because of the light going on. Trust Big Shirl to gab.

'She was worried about you.'

Oh yeah?

'What happened, Maggsie? Tell me.' I opened my eyes, blinking. Her face had that pink glow *Woman's World* was always on about. Only Ruby's was through whizzing around on her bike, not make-up. 'Come on. You'll feel better for getting it all out.'

I couldn't feel any worse. I sat up and took the mug of tea. Sniffed. I had a bit of a cold. 'Lost my job. Had a drink.' I put the tea down because I was spilling it. Ruby went down to the office for a box of tissues and handed me a couple for my cold.

Shook her head. 'Oh, Maggsie.'

It all came out. Ruby didn't say much. Her eyebrows

went up and down. When I'd finished the tea she said I'd feel better after a shower. No, I wouldn't. I had one anyway. She'd only have kept on about it.

She brought up another cup of tea and the rest of a tub of soup, French onion, that had my initials on it. I'd been getting posher with my soup choices. Not that that counted for anything now.

I'd stopped feeling sick. In fact, I was hungry, though my insides were still giving me gip. Don't know why. My liver hadn't had to *do* anything, seeing as the booze had more or less come straight back up. I tied back my damp hair and slurped up the soup.

A bit of onion caught in my throat when Ruby said she'd phone Scanda *on my behalf*. 'I'll put your side of the story, Maggsie, but I can't promise anything.'

Yeah, they might listen to Ruby, with her advantages in life, where they hadn't with me. Stuff their job, I thought. Then: no, please, *please*, give me back my job.

Then Ruby got more official even though I was in bed and tired and worn out. Tomorrow, whatever Scanda said, me and her were going to have a proper talk. Go through how I could have *approached today differently*. Anger management stuff. Again. I buried my face in my pillow, head thumping.

I didn't get much sleep. Ruby phoning Scanda was a bit of hope creeping back. But drinking again so quickly was a lead weight pushing it down. I didn't tick off my calendar. Obviously.

I pulled on a black T-shirt, sleeveless. Heard Ruby on the stairs. My nails dug into my palms. She had a faint hint of a smile.

'Count yourself very, very lucky, Maggsie. It was

because of the lady in charge – Primrose, is it? – speaking up for you. She said how hard you worked. How efficient you were, she said. Very efficient.' Ruby's head was on one side. A dangly earring – a silver dragonfly and turquoise bead – brushed her shoulder. 'Alright? How are you feeling?'

I sat down sudden like I'd been winded. Audrey lifted her head. Gave a sleepy *prook*. My eyes were prickling. I wouldn't be leaving Audrey, or work, or anybody. I still might be able to contact Alastair one day.

Had the pep talk to get through first, though. I came back down to earth in Ruby's office. Felt like the barmaid in her poster. Fed up. Only smaller in the bust department.

She kept on about my drinking. Last chance and all that. It wouldn't happen again, I told her. Ever. I had a horrible flashback to being flat on my back, behind a bush, trying to pull my jeans up. The pool of vomit.

Then it was anger management. I *had* been trying, I told her. Been using her strategies. Been seeing my anger as something separate. Turned it into a crocodile, only I'd lost control of him and all.

Ruby's lips twitched. She settled herself behind her desk. Launched into *why* people got angry. Understanding the psychology might help, she said.

*Psychology*. Here we go, I thought. Try spelling that. Try *saying* it.

Because what was behind it all was fear, she said.

Fear!

Yes. Fear about feeling small, being laughed at. Losing status.

Well, that wasn't right. I wasn't frightened of anybody. Been standing up for myself since, well, since I *could* stand up.

All angry people felt like that, Ruby said. That was why they got one in first.

I gaped. Did they? Was I like that? I didn't like being laughed at. Had a lot of that because of my reading. Lack of. And because of my size. Lack of, again.

Anger showed the other person they'd got to me. That they'd scored a point, Ruby said. Didn't want that, did I?

No, I thought, frowning. I wanted to do the point-scoring. So I just had to take it then, did I? Let them get one over on me?

Ruby shook her head. One of the silver dragonflies got caught in her hair and she had to untangle it. Just don't *show* they'd got to me. Ask them, politely, to stop. Keep asking, if necessary. Then move on.

Some people I mixed with wouldn't know politeness if it hit them with a stick.

Then I'd have to show them. Keep my long-term goal in mind. My son would be proud of me handling difficult situations *in a dignified way*.

Yeah. That was a low blow of Ruby's, seeing as it was true. Not sure me and dignity were best pals.

Ruby got up to make a cup of tea. I needed to think about what she'd said. Not only now, taking it on board, but every time someone had a go.

I swallowed some tea. Ruby had got the four sugars right, at least.

I brushed my hair. The bristles seemed to scrape the inside of my brain. I fastened my ponytail. Avoided looking at *positive* and *confidence*, Enid's words, because I'd hardly given her a thought these last twenty-four hours. I didn't look at the calendar either. Tried to hold my hand steady enough for eyebrow pencil and mascara.

159

According to Ruby, you could *ask* someone, even someone posh, to treat you OK. Could you? For real? Funny I'd never thought of it.

I was ashamed about drinking yesterday, if you want to know. But we've all got something we're ashamed of. Even people who read books have. And getting even with that pair of poxy dickheads hadn't ruddy worked, had it? Maybe there was better ways of not getting ground down. Ruby's ways, even. I sighed. My head was still aching.

I went into the bathroom and gulped down a big glass of water. Going back somewhere I'd got into trouble wasn't going to be much fun. Wasn't something I went in for, usually. Well, ever.

But Primrose would need me. Twelve o'clock was the start of the lunchtime rush. She'd said I was a hard worker, *very efficient*, and nobody had ever said that before. If I could spell *efficient* I'd stick it up on my wall now.

# 26

I was in that kitchen at Scanda faster than the speed of light. Faster than anyone could see. I rushed over to Primrose to say thanks for speaking up for me. Then I gave TJ a little wave. Pulled on my overall and helped Primrose dish up. Loaded the dishwasher so quick you could hardly see me for crumbs and dried-on bits of 'specials'. I was very, very efficient. Best way to stop people asking questions.

TJ didn't ask any but in the roof garden he kept looking at me like I was a bomb about to go off. Every fag puff, then back down at his fag.

'TJ.' I stubbed out my rollie. Crossed my arms in a *finished* gesture. (TJ waving his about was catching.) 'I'm drawing a line under yesterday.' I drew an actual line in the air. 'OK? I *know* I shouldn't have lost it.' Lucky he didn't know about me drinking afterwards. My face burned. I shut my eyes. Imagined him and Alastair seeing me in that park, staggering about.

TJ's great long legs jiggled up and down. Made the bench shake. 'I was worried. It was like you vanish off face of world.'

'*Earth.*' Correcting him came practically automatic, I'd done so much of it. 'Off the face of the earth.'

He was still looking at me anxious. Had a lot of

creases round his eyes. His eyelashes were pale, like mine. You couldn't see what colour his hair would be, seeing as it was just bristles. Probably blond.

'I tried to text you but no reply. Call went to voice-mail. I not have your address . . .' He lit another fag. Didn't normally have two.

Just as well. I wasn't going to fall over myself giving him it, neither. Reckon he thought 'supported housing' was some sort of safe place for single working women. Some church thing, maybe. Like a nunnery. Nunnery, yeah right, with Big Shirl and Kasia living there . . . No way was I going to tell him we were all finishing off prison sentences. Don't know why. Don't know why it would matter him despising me. I licked the paper for another rollie. I'd have a second fag as well. 'I switched off my phone.' I'd never thought of TJ being worried. I tucked a loose strand of tobacco inside the paper, not looking at him. 'Anyway, it's not going to happen again. Onwards and upwards.'

He put his fag down. Got out his notebook. *Onwards and upwards*, he wrote. I lit up, frowning through the smoke. Things weren't going that way for Enid. Seeing as TJ had cared enough to worry, I told him about her having cancer. I even told him about Enid teaching me to read, though I didn't tell him we done it in her cell.

Next thing I knew, TJ was getting out his wallet. Offering to lend me the money to visit Enid. I had to stall him. 'Tell you what, Enid's big on the royals. If we went to Buckingham Palace it'd be like going there for her. I could get her a nice postcard.' First time I'd suggested an outing. Normally, TJ was the one with the ideas, seeing as he knew about history and that.

162

'Yes.' He was smiling now. His face was still creased up but in cheerier places. 'I would like.'

I lifted the calendar off the wardrobe handle. Ticked off today. Looked at the white space around yesterday. Thing is, I *did* lose it. Lose control. Very nearly lost my job. *Did* have a drink. Three and a half cans of Stella. Been well and truly out of it. But, I *had* thrown it all up. Reckon I was only in that park an hour. Not long enough for it to count, really, especially with all that anger management stuff with Ruby, after. Sitting through that must have wiped a lot clean. In my opinion. You might think different. But you'd be wrong.

Yeah. I took a pencil and slashed a tick through yesterday. Day two hundred and forty-eight of three hundred and sixty-five.

'Where are you off to this lovely sunny morning?' Ruby had just cycled in from where she lived. Made me tired looking at her sometimes. It cleared her head, she said, in spite of the traffic fumes. Getting places as fast as possible was training for her triathlon. Full of beans, you could say she was, and you'd be right because of the vegan boyfriend.

I mumbled about going to Buckingham Palace with TJ.

Ruby's eyes gleamed but she didn't say anything.

In case *you're* thinking the same as Ruby, TJ and I were just mates. Yeah, I saw him Sundays. Yeah, yeah, I can hear your brain whirring, but it wasn't like that. He *was* married. OK, old Sofa took all his wages and didn't appreciate him, but they were still married. I could see her, perched high up on a too-small stool in her

Polish bank. Welcoming customers in with a smarmy lipstick smile like a spider in a web.

I didn't trust men but TJ hadn't tried nothing on. So far. Didn't think of him in that way, to be honest. Maybe it was the apron. Or because he blushed easy. Where I came from, trust me, men didn't blush.

We went out Sundays so I could help him get his English right. And because he knew a lot of stuff about London – names of places, history, loads. Nella would be impressed the amount I knew now. Maybe, one day, Alastair would.

I'd got used to TJ taking my elbow. I'd even got used to him holding doors open for me. If Dad or Dougie had ever done it, it would have been so they could land me a slap.

I met TJ at Charing Cross. We walked through St James's Park to Buckingham Palace. Walked around the outside. Wasn't going to pay pounds and pounds to see poncy paintings and gold furniture that would collapse if you was ever allowed to sit on it. Anyway, I'd seen it already. Enid had a page cut out from *Woman's World* about the Queen's stuff stuck up on her cell wall.

TJ knew all about the Queen's dead relations and her art collection and her state ruddy rooms. He knew everything. Enid would have lapped all this up, I thought, with a pang. *Oh I say*, she'd have said, looking up at TJ, her face all eager. *Well, I never knew that, dear*. She'd have reached out and patted TJ like she did me.

I bought her a postcard, a big one. Buckingham Palace in the middle and the Royals, the most important ones, in little circles all around the outside. Nice bright colours to cheer her up.

There were crowds of gawping tourists, snapping away with cameras and mobile phones. Someone banged into me. See, that was London for you. People got too close. I whipped round. He had a big belly, shorts that needed pulling up. And the cheek to bark out something foreign. My chest started going, I was getting hotter, my mouth opened to swear. I clamped it shut. Saw Snappy racing up his shorts leg. Crushing his camera with one snap of his jaws. No. Moved on from a crocodile, hadn't I? Moved onto psy-chol-o-gy. *Why* I was angry. Well, barging into someone was treating them like they didn't matter. But I wasn't *frightened*, like Ruby had said. Only, not mattering was frightening, I supposed.

TJ hung back, frowning. He'd have just let himself be knocked over. He'd have probably said sorry as he fell. Too soft, see. Or maybe he didn't worry about not mattering. He was tall. Knew a lot of stuff. Maybe that stopped you worrying.

He said the flag on the palace roof meant the Queen was at home. I peered through the gates. 'Why don't she invite us in for a cup of tea then, seeing as we're showing an interest, admiring her house and that?' She had all that space. Even had other palaces, TJ said.

He smiled. 'You are socialist, Maggsie.' It meant I'd vote Labour in an election. I'd never voted. Too many forms, and prisoners don't get a vote anyway.

Juice was peeling the plastic film off a Co-op ready meal. Vegetable Stew with Dumplings – healthy, but not like her to just warm up something in the microwave.

She said it was just one of them days. I finished my sandwich – salmon and cucumber. Dark bread from Scandinavia that I'd got used to now. More or less. Audrey was going mad under the table, miaowing, dodging about for another scrap.

'There *ain't* no more, Aud.' I got up to wash the smell of fish off my hands. 'Want a tea, Juice?' It was seeing her ready meal, a tiny portion, not enough for Juice really, and only a little bit of carrot showing that made me offer.

'Yeah. No. Ain't got no milk.'

'Don't matter. I'll treat you.'

It was her that usually made me a cup of tea. That was to do with her looking up to me.

I got a Danish pastry out of the fridge. It was Friday's, from work, but I'd wrapped it up in two plastic bags. I cut it in half. 'Here. I'm more of a savoury person. Can't manage a whole one.'

'Thanks.' Her eyes were shiny behind her glasses.

'That was supposed to cheer you up, Juice, not set you off.'

A tear rolled down. I shifted on the chair. *Issues* were going to come up again and I hadn't even got a fag in my hand.

She sniffed. 'You got kids, Maggsie?'

Didn't see that coming. I paused. Shook my head.

'It's the sixth of September today. My kid's birthday.'

'Oh.' I didn't even know she had a kid. Never said before. Blimey. Seemed like we all had secrets here. Turned out Juice's little girl was four years old today. Been taken off her because Juice had put drugs and the boyfriend first. Left her alone nights. But, soon as Juice was caught, the boyfriend scarpered. 'That's harsh, Juice. She live with you, outside?' That was a mistake. Never ask questions. It only sets people off. Then they tell you more than you want to know. This was one of them times.

Turned out Juice's mum, her *adoptive* mum, had Juice's

166

kid, Shania. (Funny, Juice was so against her birth mum, for giving her up, but she'd done practically the same herself. Deluded about that, if you asked me.) Juice was going to live with her and do a parenting course after she'd finished here. To see if she could cope on her own.

Now Juice was off drugs, *and* the boyfriend, she was thinking straight. Could see all the bad things she'd done while she was out of it. It was the same with me and drink.

Shania called Juice *Mummy,* sent her drawings and that, but it was still Juice's mum that was bringing her up. I could see that would be hard. 'You're putting too much salt in that stew,' I said, meaning Juice's crying. But at least she *saw* her kid. Knew she was doing OK. Juice had had a chance and blown it. She was lucky. Her mum – adoptive mum – was helping her out. My mum would never have stood for that. She'd have hated anyone calling her Nan. Making her sound old. Nella had two kids now, girls, and they both called Mum *Susan.*

I hadn't told anyone here, apart from Ruby, about Alastair. Funny, me and Juice were both trying to improve ourselves for our kids. Hers was through cooking healthy. Impressing social workers with the amount of veg she got through. She read magazines about being a good parent as well, only it was upsetting reading about what she hadn't done.

At least Juice was trying. Plus it's hard not to like someone who looks up to you.

She started on her half of pastry. She could do with putting dark eyeshadow on her eyelids, play them down a bit. And a dot of light-reflecting stuff (there was a proper word, *illum . . .* something) in the inside corners to make her look more lively.

I put some clean washing away upstairs. Audrey followed me in, miaowing. She sounded husky, like she'd given herself a sore throat, talking. When I didn't stroke her straight away she stuck out a back leg and washed it like it was really urgent. Like she didn't want to look too desperate in case it gave me an advantage.

Soon as I sat down at the rickety table she was up there. Didn't get off till I'd paid her some attention. Getting to be a cocky little madam. Then she jumped onto her beanbag and tucked her paws under. Watched me go through *Woman's World* with the dictionary and a notebook, one pound forty-nine pence from the Co-op. Just sat there staring, looking stern, like she was in charge of my reading.

I got Enid's postcard out of its paper bag. Buckingham Palace wasn't in the dictionary. I put *where the Queen lives* instead. Then when I turned the postcard over it was written on the ruddy front. I couldn't truthfully say I hadn't had a drink, though it was more than a week ago now, but I said it was only the once and I'd thrown it up straight away: *I had 1 drink but then I was sik Never no mor Enid.* I said one day we'd go to Buckingham Palace together *and* have a cup of tea in one of them posh London stores. I didn't mention seeing Louise. I didn't know how to spell her name and I'd screwed up her letter.

# 27

Trudie still left her door open. So *my* cat could come in. In her dreams. She had a toy cat now at the bottom of her bed. A black one, all curled up. Made me jump, first time I saw it. Reckon it was to lure Audrey in.

Funny Trudie hadn't tried to make a pet of Audrey herself. Big Shirl said she had put scraps down a couple of times when she first came. Didn't keep it up, though. And *scraps*, not pilchards. Shirl said Trudie didn't like hanging round outside longer than it took to smoke a fag because of the cold. On account of her ruddy years in Greece. So I'd done the hard work with Audrey and Trudie was muscling in.

Twice I found Audrey's beanbag moved to the edge of my bed and no sign of Audrey. Trudie didn't even deny she'd been in my room. Looked up from tapping at her screen. Showing off she had a tablet. Showing off she was good at computer stuff. Not that good, though, seeing as they'd landed her inside. Said she'd thought Audrey might like a bit of company. Might want to sleep on *her* bed. Yeah, with that manky hippie shawl draped over it, and the creepy toy cat. And no comfy beanbag specially for cats. Yeah, right.

*

Audrey was miaowing on the landing, Saturday. I was working my way through this week's *Woman's World*, fashion tips for the smaller woman, so I didn't get up to call her in. I had my finger on a line. Then *Puss, puss, puss*, I heard. Miaowing from the other side of the wall. Audrey was in Trudie's room. I threw down the *Woman's World*. She was my cat! Then I sat back down. For one, fetching her back would stress Audrey out, for two, I was supposed to drag in poxy psychology. I folded my arms. Audrey strolling into someone else's room, an old bag's room, was like I didn't matter, I suppose. Yeah. Wished I'd never got her tame enough to do it, though you might think that was petty.

At home our cat, Gingernut, Nutty, had liked me best. Tiny never sat still because of his ADHD, and Nella was always out. As for Mum, well, Mum preferred men. So Nutty sat on my lap. Always.

I went downstairs for a fag and a brew. While I was there I opened a new tin of pilchards. Pilchards have got a very strong smell. I was just getting Audrey's dinner ready. Didn't know she'd come racing down the stairs, did I?

After she'd ate the pilchard she followed me back upstairs. Into my room, tail with its white tip stuck up. Didn't bother going back into Trudie's. Looked like she'd never even heard of Trudie. I got her back without even raising my voice. That was psychology for you, if you asked me.

A few days later I headed straight upstairs after work for a wash and a lie-down. It was only just five, too early to eat my sandwiches. Audrey followed me, licking her whiskers clean like she was chewing Nicorette gum.

The door of my room was wide open. I kept it pulled to, just enough for Audrey to come in and out. Didn't want the whole world seeing my school dictionary and *confidence* and *positive* stuck up on the wall.

Once you've been in prison, if something doesn't look right, you take your time going in. Don't know what you're going to find.

What I found was my pyjamas flung on the floor. Pink brushed cotton ones with white poodles. (Don't laugh, *I* didn't choose them, they were a Christmas present from Mum, three years ago.) I always folded them up. I wasn't a slovenly person, in spite of my background.

Audrey's beanbag was on the floor too. Upside down. I looked around. Nothing else touched. Trudie. Who else would have mucked up my bed? Always been jealous of me when it came to Audrey.

Sweat prickled in my armpits. I should be breathing *out*, power-walking, dragging Snappy out from my holdall, trying to read my own mind, but hang on a second, how would *you* feel if it was your stuff, your *home*, that had been messed with? *You'd* have been irritated. Plus I was tired after a day's work, and there was Enid, ill, at the back of my mind.

Audrey stared at her beanbag. I put it back on the bed but she stayed on the carpet. Reckon she knew there was trouble coming.

She put her ears back when I slapped Trudie's wall. Soon as I shouted she shot through the window. It was open at the bottom for fresh air. (Not that the air is fresh in London. Too many cars and too many people swallowing it up.)

Trudie shouted back. We went at it like a pair of

fishwives. Surprising the colourful language I can come up with even though I'm no good at English. I stopped, hearing myself. Alastair wouldn't want a fishwife for a mum. I sat back down. Call me stupid, but I was still so worked up I didn't even think about my room being on the first floor, and Audrey going out the window.

Trudie disturbing my stuff felt like being burgled. Been on the other side of *that* more than once. Always someone else who'd put me up to it, though. Got me to do it because I was small enough to get into places other people couldn't. Once someone had expected me to squeeze through a dog flap. Had his eye on doing over a big house with two French bulldogs and a swimming pool. A burglar was worse than a fishwife.

That had been part of the drinking to forget. A *vicious circle*, a probation officer had said. (*What's round and got teeth?* I remembered from the puzzle page in *Woman's World*. I'd had to turn the page upside down for the answer. Had to look up *vicious* before I got it. And *circle*.)

I fetched a cloth and some bleach from the bathroom. Wiped down everything that could be wiped. Tried to wipe away Trudie swearing at me. Had that feeling of being small again, like you sometimes get in London, like I'd felt a lot when I first came. I am small, as you know, like I just said, but I don't usually dwell on it.

One day I'd have my own place. Then Audrey would know exactly who she belonged to. I shook out the beanbag and straightened the bedspread. Two rooms and a bathroom. I wouldn't hardly need a kitchen. A cat flap. A little garden for Audrey with a little cat-sized shed she could watch birds from in comfort. And no poxy cat freaks with wrinkly walnut faces living next door.

I put the cleaning things back and rolled down my sleeves. Sat at my desk to do a bit of reading. Alastair would want me to finish the story I'd started in this week's *Woman's World*. He'd have forgotten about me shouting, wouldn't he?

I couldn't concentrate. Then it struck me: Audrey had made a swift exit from the *first* floor. She hadn't even looked. I ran to the window. No furry corpse on the path underneath. Big Shirl's window had an overhang at the top. Audrey must have jumped onto that and then down.

She wasn't in her box in the kitchen or on any of the chairs. Not in the TV lounge or out on the front step. My heart sank. Hadn't gone back under the shed, had she? I bent down and peered, but no.

I left a pilchard in the open kitchen doorway. After a couple of hours it hadn't been touched. I began to get really worried. Saw Audrey trapped somewhere, or run over, lying on her back, all four paws stuck up in the air.

I called her from the yard, went up and down the street. It was me that had frightened her away. My fault. (Trudie's as well, but she hadn't done so much shouting.) I spent ages calling but there was no sign. Audrey had vanished, *off face of world*, as TJ would say. Probably lost her faith in human nature. Hadn't done her any favours, taming her, softening her up, getting her indoors, had I? Now she was back where she'd started, living rough somewhere. Living feral. And that was if she'd survived.

I had a dragging feeling in my guts. Same as I'd had giving up Alastair. The sort of feeling that made you think about drinking. If I couldn't even look after a cat, what did it say about me as a parent? Didn't show I was fit to even contact Alastair, did it? He wouldn't like me making an innocent cat homeless.

The following day, coming home from work, I peered under the cars in our road. Spotted Trudie on the other side, doing the same. She's being *helpful*, I told myself, not muscling in.

The others girls went out the front to call Audrey. Big Shirl put a bit of corned beef on the front step. Got excited when it vanished. But it must have been a pigeon or a fox or a rat that ate it, because there wasn't no sign of Audrey.

When I said, Big Shirl put her hands on her hips. 'You're too precious over Audrey, Maggs. You should let this be a lesson. I mean, no one don't *own* a cat, do they?'

Juice joined in. *Juice*, that looked up to me. 'Yeah, I could hear that ding-dong with Trudie from downstairs, Maggsie. Aud's only a little cat. You frightened her.'

I glared at them both. 'Skin and bone she was before I came here. Living under a *shed*.' I didn't bring up brothels, or drugs, though, which shows you how far I'd come.

Kasia didn't say anything because she wasn't there. She was out with a client. A rich Russian one. We weren't allowed to say *client*. It was *boyfriend*. He was free with his money. Drove a BMW. A *sugar daddy* she called him, showing off a ring he'd given her. 'He not want me to see anyone else. Just him.' She wasn't that keen, though. He was fat and bald with bad breath.

Trudie stood there in the kitchen listening to Juice and Big Shirl having a go. Loving it, probably. She popped one of her olives into her mouth every few seconds. Tried to give me advice because of her 'cat expertise' in Greece. 'She won't have gone far, you know. Cats don't.'

I turned on my heel and went upstairs. I didn't slam my door. I left it slightly open for Audrey to come through.

Juice brought me up a cup of tea later on. Not enough sugar. 'You have been ever so good to Audrey, Maggsie. It was only that once.' Her glasses were like fishbowls, the lenses were so thick. Sometimes it didn't look as if there was any fish at home.

# 28

In the midst of all the worry about Audrey I got a text message from Louise. I'd hardly given her another thought since we'd had that coffee. Clenched my teeth when I saw her name. Never a good idea, not when they're like mine. We need to chat about Enid, she said. I didn't reply because what good would a chat with *her* do?

I had another night of dragging in my gut. It was because Big Shirl and Juice were right. And Ruby, when she'd said, *Angry people make other people angry.*

Trudie had messed with my stuff because I'd treated her like she was nothing. Easy to spot when someone does it to you. Harder when you're the one doing it. Audrey was the only person here – well, creature – who liked Trudie. I felt guilty about that now, as well as over Audrey. Ruddy psychology makes you feel like a little black beetle. If Audrey was ever found I'd let Trudie have her in her room sometimes, long as she kept the door open. Even let her have Audrey on her lap in the kitchen.

Next morning, early, I made Trudie a cup of black tea. She took it. Then she came out to the yard with me and called. Still in her nightdress. I think it was a nightdress but it might have been a kaftan. She called for a long time. Not just for five minutes like Big Shirl and Juice. Not that Audrey would bother coming to her.

I searched after work, and before. Kept the window in my room open. Kept leaning out, craning my neck. Audrey had been missing three days now.

The third day, Saturday, I went right round the shed, checking. I squeezed round the back of it where it was close to the wall. Scrambled up and peered in the garden next door. You couldn't call it a garden. More like a tip. Yellow plastic sofa lying on its side. A couple of rusty bikes, a heap of rubble. The weeds were the best bit. Them and a big old tree that leant over the sofa. A sort of fir tree, one of those that were still green in winter. Audrey used to bolt over there back in her shed days. No sign of her now, though.

I called anyway.

I turned to go back. So much for Trudie saying Aud wouldn't have gone far. I'd searched every blasted nearby place. I put my hands on the wall to jump down. Then I heard a noise. Stopped. A faint miaow. A scrabble of claws. It was coming from the tree! I scrambled down the other side. Picked my way over. Audrey was there! I could see her clinging to a branch halfway up. Trust her to find the only tree in our street, practically. Soon as she saw me her miaows got frantic. Her eyes were wide and black. She must have run straight up the trunk. It was smooth and the branches didn't start till higher up. No foothold – pawhold – for coming down. Miaow, miaow, Audrey kept on. Amazing I hadn't heard her from the house.

'Hold on, Aud!' I climbed back over. Ran inside.

Ruby was fastening the strap of her cycle helmet. Took one look at me and unfastened it.

She phoned the fire brigade but they said it wasn't an emergency. The RSPCA said she'd have to be up there longer before they came out. Cats often came down on their own.

Ruby took a sharp breath in. 'That's it then.' She got very busy putting on the yellow jacket she wore for cycling. 'No choice but to wait till tomorrow.' Began to push her bike through the hall. 'Audrey's a born survivor. She'll be OK for another day.'

'She could fall any minute,' I shouted. No food or drink. Nowhere she could sleep. I knew I was shouting. (Recognizing it was the first step in anger management. Good when you think of all the stress I was under.)

Ruby sighed. She'd ask Will. See if he had any ideas. But he was a vegan *and* a bird-watcher. Cats were his least favourite animal. What could he come up with?

Blow hanging about for a game of soldiers. Soon as Ruby had cycled off I fished two pilchards out of the tin and put them in a plastic bag. Stuffed it in my jacket pocket.

Over the wall again. The trunk was too smooth to get a grip anywhere. Plus I couldn't think straight because of the miaowing.

Back I went. Had a look inside the shed. Ruby kept her bike, Beyoncé, in there, locked up with two locks, front and back wheel, and the door closed, because of it being London and the bike being her most treasured possession after her boyfriend. Not there now, though, seeing as she'd gone home. Garden shears on a shelf, a pile of plastic pots. A sunlounger leaning against the side. A dented football. Hanging up, a hula hoop and some rope. Rope. A lot of rope, blue. I jerked it off its nail.

Got to the tree and threw the rope up. It looped itself over a branch on only the second go, because I was Wonder Woman. I pulled hard, leant all my weight on it. Heard creaking. I stopped for a second. But nobody else was coming to Audrey's rescue. Plus it was me who'd driven her up there in the first place. So I just went for it, in spite of the creaking.

I clutched the rope and sort of walked up hand over hand. My trainers gripped the sides of the trunk. Done that in the park more than once with one of them rope swings. That hadn't been straight up to the sky like this one, though. *Onwards and upwards* I suddenly saw, written out neat in TJ's notebook. A sharp twig caught on my jeans leg, then my skin, but I didn't notice until afterwards. Then it hurt.

I dragged myself up to the first branch. That's what I was doing in real life, you could say, dragging myself up. Some people would say it. Audrey's miaowing sounded right in my ear but I couldn't see her. 'Aud,' I hissed. 'Come and get your jaws round what I've got.'

I got out one of the pilchards, hanging on with my other hand. I didn't look down. I'd only have frightened myself. Good job I'm small, I told myself. In fact, I can only do this *because* I'm small. And tough.

I heard a scrabble of claws. Audrey slid down a few inches, her eyes wide and terrified. She got a grip on a broader branch, next one down. Splayed out her paws to keep her balance. Non-stop miaows when she smelt the pilchard.

'Come a bit closer and you can have it. Only there's a catch to it – I got to catch *you*.'

She leant down towards the pilchard. Purred. I grabbed her. Stuffed her into my denim jacket. Before she'd even realized. Lucky Audrey's small too. I did up all the buttons so she couldn't get out. Not easy with a cat wriggling and growling inside your clothes. I tucked the bottom of the jacket into my jeans. All this with one hand. 'Hold on tight. Going down.'

Shinning down the tree trunk was easier than coming up, in spite of my gashed leg and an angry cat buzzing around my chest area.

I hadn't told the other girls I was going to try and rescue Aud. But when we got back to the kitchen, rope burns on my hands, arms and legs killing me, there they were, all of them. First time I could remember us all being in the same room together. There was a cheer when they saw my jacket squirming. Nice, only it frightened Aud. Soon as I undid the buttons she jumped down and dashed under the table. Hard for a cat to work out what's good and bad shouting. Don't suppose they do psychology.

Big Shirl bustled off to her room. Came back with a first aid kit. She'd seen a few medical emergencies in her line of work. Heart attacks, mostly, when the old boys had got overexcited. (A lot of her clients had had heart trouble, she said. She'd even had a wheelchair ramp and stairlift fitted.)

Trudie poured Audrey a saucer of water. She'd done milk first but milk wasn't good for cats, in spite of them liking it. Ruby told me that. I don't think it was to do with Will wanting Aud to go vegan. I passed over the reserve pilchard and let Trudie give it to her.

Juicy Lucy made me a cup of tea. Never enough sugar in it. She didn't think it was healthy. When her back was turned I put in an extra couple of spoonfuls for shock.

Kasia said she'd make me some toast, *with lots of butter, yes?* – teasing – only it would be that dark sour bread and I couldn't stomach it. She came up with some Russian jam, though, cherry, I think it was. We all had some. It was quite good on normal white toast. (I let them use my bread, because I was on a high.)

Turned into a party. Trouble with celebrating was it made you crave a drink. I know I did, and Big Shirl said she'd love a sweet sherry. Juice really fancied a Snowball because of the cherry and the froth. Didn't get things quite right, did old Juice.

*The prodigal cat*, Trudie said when Audrey finally came out from under the table. When we all looked at her, she said she'd been brought up religious. (Hadn't kept to it, obviously.) Audrey wolfed down a second pilchard. I had to call a stop after the third one, in case her belly exploded. She wouldn't stop purring.

Like I said before, a cat can make a place a home.

We moved into the lounge so I could sit more comfy. Put my leg up. A couple of guys passed by outside. Black guys, one with a Rasta cap on. Big Shirl leant out, this was *without* a drink, and whistled, only she wasn't very good at it.

They looked up. Walked on, one saying something to the other. Then the one with the cap shouted something. Something I won't repeat here. Like I say, men are a waste of space. You'd have thought Big Shirl would have known better.

You could see the tree, the top of it, from the sofa. Amazing Aud had been on a branch for three days without falling off. Never mind it might have been me what forced her up there. Amazing I'd climbed up it. Sheer like that. Ruddy brave when you think about it.

181

I kept thinking about it. I'd saved a collapsed lad, and now a stranded cat.

I ticked off my calendar. Saw Alastair telling his mates his mum rescued cats from trees.

So yeah, whatever brave thing needed doing I was your woman. I was so full of myself I reckoned I could even face Louise again. The boasting. The braying voice. Her trying to put me in my place because I was on the up and she wasn't.

So I answered her text, What about dinner on me? with OK. Somewhere posh, she replied.

Maybe she'd have news about Enid. And a fancy meal. Someone I didn't like paying for it. Another thing I could show off to Nella about, one day. So, yeah, I'd meet Louise.

Big mistake, it turned out – but then you might have guessed that already.

# 29

There'd been a bit on the *Woman's World* beauty page, about eyes. Making the most of them. I followed the picture and drew in some feathery strokes with my eyebrow pencil. I'd always used mascara. Even when I was sleeping in a car. Nobody wants to look rubbish, do they? I had pale eyelashes. Goes with ginger hair. I'd look proper namby-pamby without mascara.

Building up from the tinted moisturizer, I bought some lip gloss – a pinky shade *Woman's World* said *suited most skin colourings*. Using it was like shampooing a skunk, mind. It wasn't my lips that needed improving, it was what was underneath.

You can look clean and tidy, you can do your make-up nice, but manky teeth are always going to let you down. Soon as you open your mouth people know you haven't had any education or advantages in life. Before you've even said anything.

TJ's teeth were nearly as bad. A couple of them gave him gip. He had a spicy, medical smell about him sometimes that came from sucking a clove.

I teased him about it. Made a *brr* sound like an electric drill. Waggled my fingers at his mouth till he put his elbow up as a shield. Reckon he was as scared as I was underneath.

No dentist was going to get near me. Not after a school one had jabbed my gums and tutted: *dreadful state*. I'd bitten his finger – at least my teeth were good enough for *that* – which had meant another trip to the headmaster's office.

A lot of tough people were afraid of dentists. Didn't mean I wasn't hard. Just meant I didn't like people messing with me. Someone poking and prodding about inside my mouth and me just lying there letting him do it. I mean, come on, who's going to put up with that?

Plus there'd be some snotty woman behind a desk. Her eyes widening when I couldn't fill in the forms. OK, I could read now, slowly. I'd finished that *Woman's World* story. I'd even sent letters. But only to Enid, who was thrilled with anything I did. No way could I fill in a form.

I met TJ at Waterloo and we walked to Trafalgar Square. There were statues all around like trees in a park. Two fountains big enough to swim in if you'd been allowed. In the middle, a man right on top of a great pillar. Never seen a bloke so high. Lions at each corner. Nelson, TJ said his name was. A famous sailor who stuck up for England in a war. A mate of mine – well, not really a mate – used to have a bull terrier called Nelson. White, with a black patch over one eye.

The square was crowded. Pushing and shoving and tourists taking selfies as per usual. Never any English people at these places but perhaps they'd seen it all before.

There were two free art galleries next to the square. My heart sank a bit but we only did the one, the one that was just pictures of people. I quite liked that one, only my brain got full after about twenty minutes.

We had tea from TJ's flask and some Polish biscuits and my cheese and tomato sandwiches, not ones from work, ones I'd made fresh. Before coming to London I'd have made cheese and pickle, or just cheese, not cheese and tomato.

It had been my birthday on the Saturday. I told TJ, didn't know why.

'Birthday?' He leant towards me. 'Then I will buy present.'

He didn't have to, I mean, I wasn't hinting or nothing. He probably wouldn't remember anyway.

It was still warm and we sat at the top of the steps and looked down at the crowds. I felt lucky – which was a first – that I lived in London. Suddenly realized I wasn't a tourist. Trafalgar Square wasn't a holiday thing for me. TJ and I could come here any Sunday. The pigeons were a nuisance with our sandwiches, though. Bobbing about like Granda did before he had his hip replaced. Right next to our feet. Audrey would have had a field day.

We strolled around. Found a Boots. Went in and had a look at their tooth stuff.

I didn't know what half of it was but TJ did. He could read the labels, even the small print chemical words. It was because of him having been an ag-ri-cul-tur-al scientist in Poland.

'Pity you're not *using* all them long words.' Chemical names didn't come up when you were clearing tables. I bent down to look at the mouthwashes. Wondered why they were all different colours.

TJ put two tubes of whitening toothpaste into his basket. There was a word in front of *whitening* I couldn't work out. '*Brilliant*,' TJ said it was. Ruby said that a lot. One for my personal spelling dictionary. One I could use with Enid. *London is brilliant*, I could say. I wrote to her every week now. Hadn't had a reply for a while. She must be getting loads of treatment, I kept telling myself.

TJ added a packet of toothpicks. It was three for two and he was going to treat me to the brilliant toothpaste. Was that it then? My present?

No. He strode off. Came back with a little bottle of perfume, all done up in cellophane. My face went hot. I nearly said, 'Wow!' only I stopped myself. 'Thanks, TJ. Thanks a lot.'

He smiled down at me. Then he changed the subject back to science. 'One day I use chemical words again, I hope.'

'Yeah?' I looked up at him.

He said when he'd got his English and Maths qual-if-i-cat-ions over here, he was going to train to be a teacher. A science one.

'Blimey!' First I'd heard of it. I didn't know no teachers. I mean, I'd been taught by them, and most of them I couldn't stand, but having one as a colleague, *friend*, well, you're having a laugh. Except TJ wouldn't be a colleague then, would he? He'd be teaching, not clearing tables. 'You won't want to know me then,' I said, joking like, pocketing the toothpaste he'd bought me. And the perfume.

'Of course I will want to know you. You are my English teacher.' He did his steering bit with my elbow. If anybody else done it, it would have annoyed me. 'And you are English friend.' Smiling made his plain face not look so plain. 'Important English friend.'

*

186

I didn't use the perfume. Didn't even unwrap it. I kept it in my underwear drawer. Didn't want Ruby getting ideas.

The toothpaste didn't make TJ's teeth no whiter, or mine, though I brushed them until my gums bled. Our teeth stood in our way, really. Be a handicap for a teacher. Wouldn't impress Alastair neither.

Then TJ came into work, all excited. 'Have good news.' Took him ages to do up his apron. 'I tell at break.'

That set Primrose off singing, *Find your good news in the Lord*. She knew loads of hymns. Wanted to set up a church out in Ghana. You could smell chocolate everywhere there, she said, because of the cocoa pods drying in the sun.

Mid-morning break TJ ran up the stairs to spit out his good news. Neither of us ever got the lift at Scanda. Hearing that robot woman's voice still gave me the willies. TJ took the stairs to give his lungs a workout. Undo the fag damage. I didn't run. TJ's *news* might be about his wife, old Sofa. Her coming over to pay a visit.

He lit my rollie. 'In Polish shop on Saturday . . .'

A new customer had come in while TJ was stacking shelves. Bought a load of Polish stuff. Only been in England two weeks. A dentist, he'd told TJ. Setting up his own practice.

I breathed out smoke, frowning. What was exciting about a dentist?

TJ waved his fag. He was still hyper. This dentist had spotted his sub-standard teeth.

I wasn't liking the sound of this. My tongue moved around my mouth, poking the gaps.

He'd offered to treat TJ for free in return for him doing some decorating in his new surgery. No pain, he told TJ.

Oh yeah, I thought, but I didn't say anything.

'So this Sunday I do painting. Then after work on Wednesday he treat me.'

'Bully for you,' I muttered.

'No, is not bully. Is nice man.'

'We won't be going out then, Sunday?' I could feel my voice rising.

'No. I am sorry.' He took my hand and pressed it between his. Another of his old-fashioned-gentleman sort of gestures. I knew that's what they were now. Knew they weren't him making a move on me.

I took my hand away. I wanted to snatch it back but I didn't. I lit another rollie. Blew the smoke upwards and relaxed my shoulders. Looked around the roof garden for things beginning with 'b'. An old *distraction strategy* from anger management. It came to mind now. *Bench, bird, bread* – there was a woman buttering a slice of toast, laughing – *butter, bastard, bugger, bloody fool*. TJ didn't notice me looking around. He was still raving on about the dentist and how lucky he was.

I missed two Sunday outings because of TJ's teeth. I mean, I didn't care or anything. I just walked down the park instead. Wrote my letter to Enid. I'd finally got a reply. She'd got my Buckingham Palace postcard. Said her scars were healing nicely. The radiotherapy was tiring but she was feeling better. Looking forward to Romania. I was so relieved I wrote her two letters in one week. Had more time for it because of being stuck in, Sunday.

I'd written so many letters now I started writing replies to the agony ones in *Woman's World*. I wasn't going to *send* them. It was just practice for Alastair. I kept them short, obviously. Sometimes I just put: *Leave him*. Once, I wrote *Your life is for liveing too*, to a woman whose husband took advantage. I knew it wasn't right. Crossed out the 'e'. *You have tryed your best*. That didn't look right neither. It was things like that that made me lose patience. But I finished it. Used a couple of words from my personal spelling dictionary. *Equal* was one, *unfair* was another. I was using my time productive, same as TJ.

The Polish dentist filled five of TJ's back teeth. *Scaled and polished* the others so, in the end, they did look whiter. Made mine look worse. The 'brilliant' toothpaste had been a waste of money. TJ's money.

He smiled even more now, because of his new improved teeth. Him and Primrose were like a toothpaste advert, the pair of them. It got on my nerves.

'I have suggestion, Maggsie,' TJ loomed above me, waiting for me to finish unloading the dishwasher. Any other man would have winked, stuck up an eyebrow: 'Know what I mean?' But TJ wasn't like that. Might have been because he didn't know the English words, or it might have been because he was Polish.

He wanted to run up the five flights of stairs again, but I wasn't having none of it. I walked up and he walked beside me.

'My dentist. Marek.' TJ sat on the bench. He took up a lot of room. He had broad shoulders and his legs stuck out a long way in front of him. He stank of peppermint. Sugar-free gum. His dentist mate had recommended it. And he'd bought some tiny little brushes to scrub in between his teeth. He was getting obsessive, to be frank. Boring. He was even trying to cut down on smoking because it was bad for your teeth. Reckon his dentist was taking him for a mug.

'I don't want to hear no more about no dentist.' I lit up. 'You free Sundays again, then, TJ, or you staying in to clean your teeth?'

'No, no. I do first. No, Maggsie, I think of you.'

I looked at him. Turned out the bit of me he was thinking about was my teeth. He'd told his new dentist mate about them.

'Yeah, thanks for that, TJ. Thanks for talking about me behind my back.' About the bit of me I was least proud of. I got up, fag and all, heart thumping. Couldn't go no further than the stairs, though, because I was still smoking. I stopped, breathed o-u-t. Why was I annoyed? My brain whirred. Talking about me without me being there was like I didn't matter.

'Maggsie, I only tell about you to Marek because you are important person.' TJ blinked. He looked worried. 'Person I care about. Person I want to help.'

I sat down again. Looked at the London Eye. It turned so slow you could hardly see it moving.

Apparently, this Marek had offered to treat me for free if I cleaned his surgery weekends.

'So you can have teeth like mine.' TJ leant close, flashing them in my face.

I stubbed out my fag. Squashed it flat on the bench arm. Told him I didn't want teeth like his. Or two jobs. Or him arranging things. I was an independent person. Could manage on my own.

Plus there was the slight problem of me being terrified. TJ seemed to have got over his nerves, so I couldn't admit to being scared.

*

Back at home, I looked in the mirror. Squeezed my eyes shut. To be honest, just the word *dentist* made my palms sweat. I saw myself, on hands and knees, cleaning his surgery. Scrubbing blood off the chair where he did his torturing.

Breathed o-u-t. Pictured myself smiling, looking people full in the face. Them taking me serious. Them not noticing, well, not straight away, I was poor and been in prison and hadn't had an education. Saw myself wearing loads of lipstick, a soft peach. Smiling *hello* at Nella. Saw her taking a step back, putting on sunglasses against the dazzling whiteness of my gnashers.

Pictured meeting Alastair. Him noticing my brilliant teeth. Thinking I was an ordinary, normal woman, not the shop-soiled version I really was.

Yeah, I was brave. Hard. Wonder Woman. But even she wouldn't have looked forward to going to a dentist.

# 30

Me and Juice and Big Shirl were in the yard smoking. A lot comes out over a fag. That's something doctors don't understand – it bonds you together. Reckon that was why I was telling them about Alastair. That, and because I'd been on a high since saving Audrey's life. And because Juice looked up to me.

I should have kept it to myself. Other people can put a dampener on things.

'You going to try and get him back?' First time I'd seen Juice's eyes wide open.

Well. 'Not exactly. He's eighteen, now. It's more, well . . .' His birthday had been back in June. I'd opened the 'A Present from Margate' box and got out his baby photo and had a little weep. And, when I'd ticked the calendar that day, I'd drawn in a little star above the date. I glanced at Juice and Big Shirl. Tapped ash off. 'I just want to tell him I hadn't wanted to give him up. And maybe see him again, one day, I suppose.' I was floundering. Nobody had ever asked about Alastair straight out before.

Juice's forehead creased. 'But what about his real mum, though?'

I stiffened.

'I mean his adoptive mum.' Juice bent down to stub

out her fag. 'Like I said about mine. She's the one that brought him up.'

'Yeah. Exactly.' I stared straight ahead. Juice giving me advice was the wrong way round. 'I didn't *want* to give him up. They had to pull him out my arms.'

'Yeah.' Juice nodded. 'I know, Maggsie – I felt the same when Shania went to live with Mum. But I know how she'd feel if *my* birth mum ever turned up. Not saying your little boy, no, your *son*, wouldn't look up to you. He'd be dead proud of you, Maggsie. You don't have to tell him you've been inside. Only better to tread careful, eh?'

Big Shirl stubbed out her fag with her little pointed toe. Did it so firm and thorough, I knew she was building up to some advice and all. No right to give it, but that wouldn't stop her. She had a grown-up daughter but they kept falling out. The daughter was in charge of a care home somewhere. Dead respectable. Too respectable to have much to do with Shirl. She was closer to Jordan, her grandson, the one she went on about.

Big Shirl had heaved herself up the stairs once to ask me if she could borrow a couple of teabags till tomorrow, till Jordan did her shopping. She'd picked up my school dictionary. Cheek. Seen how clear it was with the blue print. Said she might buy one for Jordan. I'd noticed him handing over her shopping bags. He had a pink pointy nose like one of them white rats you get as pets. Headphones trailing from his ears. Nodded at whatever you said.

'Can't get a job because he's . . . what do you call it? Dis something? Can't hardly read.'

*Dyslexic.* I couldn't say it neither. Wasn't going to let on that's what I was. Give Big Shirl an advantage.

I always spoke to Jordan after that. Helped him up the steps with the bags. Big Shirl got through a lot of food. The fridge was stuffed with it and the top shelf of the cupboard. Covered in sticky 'S' labels.

Poor lad had a habit of putting himself down. Reading was a sore point, he said. I told him straight it didn't mean he was thick. That, until someone with a bit of patience showed me, I'd been the same.

A magazine with pictures would help him. Big Shirl tapped her bottom lip, not looking at me. Didn't like to be told anything. Then she went out and bought him one about fishing. Loads of pictures. Of fish, mostly.

'Your son's mum's never going to be over the moon, is she?' Shirl put in now. Getting her own back if you asked me. 'Even if you was Mother Teresa. *Especially* if you was someone like that. Not going to want her nose put out of joint.'

'She'd worry you'd take over. Worry she wouldn't *be* his mum any more. That's what I think sometimes with Mum having Shania,' Juice nodded like she was an expert. Another one.

'Like how you felt when Trudie had Audrey in her room.' Big Shirl blew out a lazy curl of smoke. 'Just saying.'

Yeah, but . . . In any case had she forgotten I'd made up for that by rescuing Audrey? I had a habit of rescuing people, actually.

My face was hot. It was like they were ripping off my Wonder Woman headband. I caught a glimpse of Snappy's snout coming round the kitchen door. He yawned, gave a lazy lash of his tail. Stopped in the doorway like he wasn't sure I'd let him in. I'd more or less retired him to my holdall permanently. He'd got too keen on putting people to rights. Using his teeth. Seemed to get bigger each time he did it. I ground out my fag. 'Go away,' I breathed out slowly. Mentally sent him scuttling back upstairs.

Juice changed the subject to a bargain pack of root veg she'd got for a pound at Sainsbury's. We went back inside. Big Shirl stuck the kettle on. I took my mug upstairs.

Alastair's *mum* had had him to herself for eighteen years. So she'd be OK sharing him now, wouldn't she? I took a long swig of tea. Or were Big Shirl and Juice right about me muscling in? Look at the trouble that had caused with Audrey. I wouldn't want Alastair running off.

Ruby gave me permission to stay out late for my dinner with Louise. Plus advice to be on my guard with alcohol around.

I should have been on my guard. But not for booze.

I'd never been anywhere with a wine list before. Louise pushed it away. Wanted to keep a clear head. *Detoxing*, she said. A show-off word for staying off booze. And drugs, which were more her scene.

We had Diet Cokes, and grub that was even more poncy than the stuff Primrose cooked. Baked aubergine and a salad with little red things in it. I thought for a second, because nothing would surprise me in London, they were jewels, but they turned out to be *pomegranate seeds*. I wasn't none the wiser. I speared a couple. Even the fork was heavy, with a posh swirl to its handle. I wished, again, that Nella could see me.

Pride comes before a fall, Nan used to say. I *was* proud. First time ever. Never been so pleased with myself.

Reading, writing, working, staying off the drink, using psychology. Plus the Wonder Woman thing. No end to all the good stuff I was doing. I was practically respectable. Less than three months to make the year up and I'd be good enough for Alastair. Feeling smug makes you take your eye off the ball. I was worried about Enid, yeah. But not about myself. Should have been.

I didn't like Louise. All we had in common was we'd been inside and we knew Enid. So why *were* we having dinner together? Alarm bells should have rung from the start. She'd only want to mix with the likes of me for a reason – a dodgy one.

'Good to see you looking well and happy.' Louise clinked her glass against mine. 'To absent friends. To Enid.'

'Enid.' At least we'd got to her quicker this time. Her last letter had been cheerful. She'd said the nurses had been angels and nobody had treated her like a con. Didn't give me any details about her actual condition, though. My heart thumped. 'You heard how she is?'

Louise troughed up a forkful of salad, munched slowly. Told me, through a tangle of chewed-up leaves, the radiotherapy had wore Enid out without curing her. Now even chemo couldn't touch the cancer. 'It spreads, you see.' She swallowed a last bit of green, not looking too troubled.

I put down my knife and fork. I did know that. It was what Nan had died of. Enid hadn't told me about it spreading. She'd wanted to protect me. I stared at Louise. 'So, what will she do now?'

She smacked her lips together. 'Mm, *love* this salad dressing. *Really* flavoursome.' She shrugged. I stared at my knife. I could have stabbed her quite easy. 'Well, what *can* she do? There's a new breast cancer drug but

196

the NHS won't fund it. Too expensive.' She shrugged again. 'As far as I know Enid's got no funds, has she?' Shoved in another bunch of green leaves. 'Could be curtains for poor old Edith.'

The *pomegranate seeds* were shining and winking. Not wanting Enid to be disappointed was part of what was keeping me on the straight and narrow. All those years she'd done for her mum. The trip to Romania that had kept her going. She might never get there now. And here was this posh, porky cow not caring. A rush of heat swept through me.

'Why can't you fork out for them, then? You must be loaded, well, your dad must be.'

Louise shook her head. 'No, no.' A couple of leaves fell onto her plate. 'I'm afraid that's not possible. I have thought about it, of course. But Pa's got no cash. Inheriting a stately home means a lot of expense, you know.'

No, I ruddy didn't know. But what I did know was that Louise was a selfish cow. She picked up her Diet Coke, her eyes fixed on me, not blinking. Like a mad scientist studying a little white mouse. No way was I a mouse. I stared right back. She gave me one of her patronizing smiles. Changed the subject. At least I *thought* she changed the subject. She lowered the braying a bit. Took me a while to work out why.

'Last time we met, we were talking about Scanda. Their art collection. I don't know how much you know about modern art, but—'

That was her way of saying you *don't know sod all about modern art, but* I *am an expert.* Reminding me about her poxy degree in Art History. She'd only got it because she'd been inside so long.

'I been to the Tate Modern,' I interrupted. 'Twice.' Saying that was giving her a little tap to put her in her place. 'And I been to that place in Trafalgar Square with all the pictures of people.'

'Oh.' Her mouth fell open. 'The National Portrait Gallery. Have you?'

'Oh yeah,' I nodded. 'The week before last. And I know loads about Scanda's paintings now.'

TJ had told me what he'd found out about the artists. Bet he knew more now than Louise did. After, I'd gone and had another look at the paintings through the board-room door. Beat me what him and Louise got so excited about. Bright and cheerful, I give you that, and all from Denmark like Scanda, but just lines and circles and splodges. Blimey, if they were valuable, reckon they saw Scanda coming.

Except for one. A small one, out on its own on the far wall. A woman in a long dress, standing in a room, reading. It was the only proper painting there, if you want my opinion.

It was by Wilhelm Hammershøi, TJ said. He wrote the name down in my personal spelling dictionary, under 'H'. It had a funny line through the 'ø', like a skew-whiff no-entry sign.

The *Woman Reading* turned out to be Louise's favourite painting too, which spoilt it a bit. She was amazed I knew the artist's name. I remembered it because of the word *hammer* in it. Practically fell off her chair when I wrote it out on a paper serviette. Pow! Like landing a punch. Bet *she* couldn't have spelt it, not with the funny little line and everything, in spite of her degree. Funny seeing her trying to hide being surprised. She must have thought I was really thick.

'Didn't you used to have trouble with . . . with reading and writing, Maggsie?' She was still staring at me.

'Yeah. *Before*. But since Enid got me started I've been working on it. Studying.' I raised my eyebrows at Louise, in case she was thinking about laughing. Her own eyebrows were in a bit of a state – weird how she'd spent loads on her hair and clothes but let them straggle. *My* eyebrows matched each other. They were in a nice arched shape. Last week's *Woman's World* beauty page had showed you how. Ruby said reading women's magazines, and looking up the words you didn't know, *was* studying.

Good to bring up Enid again. Enid was why we were there. And nothing that was going to be of any use to her was coming out of this chat.

'Oh.' Me studying took the wind out Louise's sails. Second time I'd managed it in five minutes. Ruddy satisfying it was too. 'Marvellous,' she said, only it sounded like she meant the complete opposite. She stuffed in a hefty chunk of aubergine. Chewed for a bit. 'Of course the Hammershøi is the most valuable.'

I nodded. 'Oh, yeah. I know.' I didn't know. But it was the only one you'd actually want on your wall. 'How much is it worth then?' I cut off a small piece of aubergine. It had a slimy feel to it. I didn't say 'Yuk!' or mime vomiting, like I would have done before. That's self-control, see. That's *soff* . . . soph-ist-i-ca-tion. That's eating Primrose's weird concoctions these last ten months. That's London.

'It's worth about half a million. Pa looked it up. He's a big fan.'

'Half a million quid!' My voice came out in such a squeak I worried about the Coke glass shattering. Had to clear my throat to bring it down.

'Hammershøi's really collectable.' Louise spoke with her mouth full, in spite of being posh. 'Funny a painting's worth so much, isn't it, just sitting there in a boardroom, doing nothing?'

I nodded, thinking about what I could do with half a million quid. What *Enid* could do with it.

I looked up. My eyes met Louise's across the table.

She darted a quick look around. The restaurant was nearly empty because it was only just gone seven. I had to be back by nine. London people didn't mind waiting for their dinners. That was why they were so thin.

Louise lowered her voice. Leant in close. Her straggly eyebrows were practically touching each other. And she was definitely bigger since coming out of prison. Too much stuffing herself in posh restaurants. Dieting and a pair of tweezers wouldn't have hardly cost nothing. I didn't grasp what she was getting at, at first, because I was mentally re-shaping her eyebrows.

The way she was carrying on looked like we were planning a robbery.

Turned out we *were* planning a robbery. At least, *she* was.

# 31

The minute I cottoned on, I sat back. 'You're going to pinch that painting? For Enid?' My brain was whirring. Was Louise asking me to get her into Scanda somehow? Could I pass her off as my support worker, someone come to check up—

'No, Maggsie.' She smiled. She'd had work done on her teeth. White bits glued to the top front ones. So white they looked false. 'How could *I* do it? No, I've got a better idea.' She leant forwards, smile widening, like she was giving me something. Something nice. '*You* are.'

'Me?' I stared.

'You're in the ideal position. I mean, I'd like to do it, but I don't work there. And after all,' she fiddled with her spoon, looked up from under her eyebrows, 'it's *you* Enid's helped out, isn't it? Her teaching you to read must have changed your life.'

I was shaking my head. Stopped, because that last bit was true. But I had to put her right. 'I don't do thieving no more. I got a different sort of life now.'

Louise nodded and smiled. Patronizing cow. 'You have done amazingly well, Maggsie. With Enid getting you started.'

I closed my knife and fork together over the rest of the stuffed aubergine. No way would I steal from Scanda.

Not with them treating me decent. And I wasn't going to risk getting caught. It wouldn't have mattered back in January. It would have been an excuse to get banged up again. But I had stuff to lose now. Nine months of ticks, living normal, respectable. Nearly fit to contact Alastair. I still sat there, though. Why? Why didn't I just walk away?

I folded the paper serviette where I'd written Hammershøi, over and over until it was just a tight strip. Enid. All those months of her nodding and smiling while I mangled words. Tucking her arms under her chest, certain I'd get there in the end. Thing was, Enid had been more mumsy than my own mum. Mum was always patting her hair, looking in mirrors, sucking in her belly. Enid had been interested in *me*.

Me and TJ had gone into a little church in Greenwich a few weeks back. Greenwich was handy for TJ. He had a room in the flat above his mate's Polish restaurant in Lewisham. TJ wanted to light a candle for his daughter, Sabina. She was taking exams back in Poland.

Catholics light candles all the time, TJ said, not just at Christmas, or when the electric went off. Sabina would need all the help she could get, I thought, remembering what a torture exams had been. I'd just sat there while the other kids scribbled away. There'd been a clock ticking really loud. Just that and their pens scratching. I'd handed in an empty paper and the teacher had frowned at me over her glasses.

I had a nosey round the church while TJ was on his knees. There was a stained-glass window of Jesus's mother, wearing a blue scarf and holding baby Jesus. I knew who it was because Mum had made us go to Sunday school. I'd never seen her go near a church.

Reckon she just wanted an afternoon upstairs with Dad. Or Dougie.

Don't laugh but Jesus's mother was the spitting image of Enid. Younger, obviously, smaller chest, but, still, a dead spit. If you took off the scarf and gripped back the hair, stuck a mug of tea and a *Woman's World* in Jesus's place, it could have *been* Enid. (It wasn't wrong to think that because Enid's a good person, good as any church saint if you ask me.)

The candle on the restaurant table was making my eyes water. I saw Enid saying *you naughty girl* at me stealing something for her, but being grateful for saving her life. Like I'd done Jack's and Audrey's. Both times I'd got treated like someone special. Got that giant bunch of flowers. Got a cup of tea off Juice soon as I stepped through the door after work. (I'd finally trained her to put in the four sugars. I bought the sugar.) Reckon all that must have gone to my head. I stayed and listened because I was Wonder Woman. I folded my arms, frowned at Louise, but I didn't get up and walk away.

She was leaning too close. Going on about how only I could save Enid's life. How 'able' I was these days. How every posh company had insurance and Scanda could always go out and buy another painting. She had hold of the sleeve of my denim jacket and I didn't even snatch my arm away. That's how stupid I was. Looking back, Louise had me sussed, alright.

'Listen, Maggsie,' she whispered. 'No one will know the painting's even missing.'

I frowned. How did she figure *that* out?

She had it all off pat. Seemed to have the whole thing planned. Before she'd even discussed it with me. Before I'd even agreed to anything.

It must have sunk in I wasn't happy. 'I just wanted to sort things out quickly.' Her hand was still on my sleeve. 'For Enid's sake. There's no time to lose.'

So I carried on listening. She could get a good photocopy printed to exactly the same size as the painting. It could be rolled up, hidden in a newspaper. A big one. Like the one TJ read on Sundays now. (Yeah, like *I* would read it every week. Cover to cover. You seen the size of the print? How few pictures there are?)

The painting could be smuggled out the same way.

'It's in a frame. How the hell would I – how would *anyone*,' I corrected, 'roll *that* up?'

She laughed.

Take my word for it, people laughing at you is *always* disrespectful. Making you out as less than them. No matter how they dress it up. It's not just a joke, all mates together. And if you think it is, then that's because you haven't never been laughed at.

My hands balled into fists. I didn't think about breathing, Snappy, psychology, nothing. I pushed my chair back from the table. I was out of there.

Louise caught hold of my sleeve again. 'Sorry, sorry, sorry, Maggsie. I wasn't dissing you. You're a pretty bright spark, actually. No, sit down!' She darted a glance around, gabbled, 'They do a fabulous chocolate torte here, chocolate *tart*. With clotted cream and raspberry compote. To die for, honestly.'

I stood there for a second, giving her evils, and then I sat down. Stupid, stupid, stupid. I *should* have stormed out. I *should* have let rip. Like I told you, sometimes anger is a good thing. Sometimes being angry is the right thing to do. If people had kicked up a stink about Hitler earlier, there wouldn't have been a war. Granda always said that.

We had the tart. It was pretty good. By the size of her Louise ate a lot of that kind of thing – posh cakes, *patty* . . . something. She wiped a bit of cream from her chin. One of them. Then it was back to stealing the painting. Me stealing it. I'd have to cut it out of its frame with a Stanley knife.

I sat back. No way. I'd been done for vandalism in the past. Drink had been behind it. I wasn't going to slash a valuable painting. Specially one I liked.

Louise waved her hand about. The painting had a border so it wouldn't matter. Then I'd stick the photocopy inside the frame and roll the original up in the newspaper.

It didn't sound that bad when she said it. To be honest, I couldn't see why there *was* so much fuss about the actual painting. If a good photocopy looked exactly the same, what *was* the difference?

Still stealing, though. Breaking the law. Risking not seeing my son one day. Risking my job. If I kept on the straight and narrow, kept doing the work OK, Scanda might keep me on after I'd done the year. Give me a bit more responsibility. A bit more money. I'd get hold of the rest of my wages then too. They saved them for you. Supposed to be for a deposit on a flat, or to start a business, or to get educated. Stuff that was beyond me. But still . . .

I'd be crazy to risk all that, but there I was, being crazy. It was Enid, see, floating around the higher part of my mind. And, to be honest, I was showing off to Louise, a posh bint with education. Trying to prove I was better than her.

I thought of her cell, her university degree stuck on the wall, all her arty postcards. I heard her loud, posh voice now. She was rich, she knew stuff . . . This scheme she'd come up with wasn't a spur-of-the-moment, smash-and-grab thing. I wouldn't get caught, would I?

I saw Enid, frolicking, flat-chested, through a pine forest in Romania. Saw her gazing at the sparkling water of a lake, stroking a tame wolf, being serenaded by a gypsy violinist with a rose between his teeth. She'd had pictures like those plastered all over the walls of her cell. And her hair would be shiny, skin glowing. She'd be completely cured.

I put my palms flat on the table. 'I'll think about it. That's all I'm saying.'

'Yes, yes. Of course. Do that.' Louise nodded, ever so polite and considerate. 'You take your time. It's just that Enid's condition can't wait, remember. I'll be in touch very soon.'

It was a pity I'd given her my mobile number. I regretted it even more later.

She paid for the meal. With a gold card, I noticed. Then we were outside and it was all, *mwah*, *mwah*, that London kissing again that I always got wrong. We were ex-cons, for God's sake, not TV stars. Then Louise sailed off in a taxi and I got the tube.

I ticked off my calendar. Came practically automatic now. And I hadn't had a drink, even though I'd been in a restaurant where they were all drinking. Hadn't even been tempted. Been too flabbergasted. Could have done with one now, though.

Audrey wasn't in her beanbag. She'd be in her box in the kitchen or on the lounge sofa with Juice. Juice watched a lot of TV. Did a bit of knitting for her little girl – dolls' clothes, I think they were – only she couldn't always follow the pattern.

Enid's *positive* and *confidence* were on the wall above my bed. I'd stuck up *efficient* now as well. (Primrose had actually said *very efficient*. I'd put a *very* in front of it last week.) Jack's card and the little card from his flowers were both up there. And a text TJ had sent me once, which I'd written out: Tonight teacher ask where I learn colourful language and I say you. All that was stuff I'd achieved. Stuff I could lose.

I lay on the bed, arms folded behind my head. Couldn't settle. I paced about a bit. If I'd been allowed out late I'd have gone for a walk. Only I might have ended up in the wrong aisle of a supermarket.

There was no one I could talk to about Louise's plan. The girls here wouldn't snitch, I knew, but they didn't know Enid. They'd just think I was crazy. TJ? You're having a laugh, aren't you? He was a moral person. And a Catholic. Ruby was a moral person too. And a support worker.

What I should have done was write to Enid. Ask her the name of the drugs she needed. Ask her straight out how her treatment was going.

Bet you a pound to a penny that if I had, she'd have stopped me.

# 32

TJ went down ahead of me after morning break. I peered through the boardroom door. It was empty. Scanda didn't often have bigwig meetings. They were more of a *we're all equal here* type of place.

Funny, seeing the *Woman Reading* up there, now that Louise was planning on me pinching it. It *was* a very small painting. Easy to hide. Easy to steal. A quiet painting, dull colours. You'd hardly notice it was there. Or wasn't there. Amazing someone would pay half a million for it. The woman in the picture was really concentrating on her book. Maybe she wasn't a good reader, neither. And she had a cup of tea on the table. But her table had a cloth, and she had a long dress on, not a denim jacket. Plus she looked a calm sort of a person.

I tried the handle of the boardroom. It wasn't locked. Almost like the painting was asking to be took. Scanda weren't very wordly wise, if you asked me. All their spindly lamps and slippery sofas. I mean, thinking people would actually *like* that sort of stuff, *buy* it. A nice company, though. Nice to work for.

Louise had texted me at breakfast-time. Given me indigestion even though I didn't eat breakfast. I'd only seen her the night before for God's sake. Had I decided to: help save Enid's life? she asked. It's only you that can do it. Kisses at the end. Pass the sick bag. Stil Thinking, I texted back. No kisses.

Horrible being in two minds, not knowing what to do for the best. Easier when you've made a decision. Then you can just go for it, good or bad.

Ruby asked me to sign an appraisal form. It was about me. She read it out in the office and then I read it. It was like a school report except it was a good one. I'd have stuck the whole thing – two typed pages – up on my wall, only the girls would have given me stick. I signed Maggsie M at the bottom, like always. I twiddled the pen. I should be trying to write my full name by now. Marguerite McNaughton, in case you've forgotten. I leant over and added a tiny little 'c' after the 'M'. Maggsie Mc. It was a start.

Above Ruby's desk was the barmaid poster. It was a picture of a proper painting, she said. Another thing about London is that there are paintings everywhere. Paintings and posters. The barmaid looked straight out at you with a fed-up expression like she was trying to stay sober. Old-fashioned clothes, but tight-fitting. Low-cut. Crowds of people in the mirror behind her. Bottles and glasses on the bar, and a bowl of oranges, tangerines, whatever. First time I'd seen fruit in a pub. The barmaid had a bit of a look of Juice, come to think of it. Take off the glasses, add a few stone, and a blue streak of hair at the front, and she would have been very like her. It was a pretty good painting. And it was only a poster in a frame. A frame made a lot of difference.

*

209

I still hadn't made up my mind. It was hard to concentrate on what TJ was saying, Sunday, because of it. He wasn't too cheerful neither, which was unusual.

We walked along the South Bank. Enough sunshine to have the sleeves of my jacket rolled up. Too many people, though, like always, jostling, pushing, treading on your heels. Can't ever walk in a straight line in London. Aggravating. I had to stop myself from whipping round a couple of times. A woman in a T-shirt with flamingos on pointed at us and laughed with her fat mate. I've seen that before. People think the height difference between me and TJ is funny. They should take a look at themselves first if you ask me.

We turned onto the pedestrian bridge. It had a special name, a word like *million*. TJ looked into the distance, not at the lovers' padlocks. He wasn't smiling. Maybe old Sofa was giving him grief.

He never said much about her. Just spoke about his two kids, Sabina and Rudolf. Sabina's exams had gone OK. Expect she was clever, like her dad. Rudolf, like the reindeer. (I'd asked TJ if he had a red nose but he didn't know the song.) The reason TJ did his long hours was so they'd have an easier life than what he'd had. Sod's law, though, because it meant he didn't hardly ever see them. Only on Skype. That was hard, but not as hard as giving up your child altogether.

TJ carried on not being cheerful. He was so quiet I asked him if he was OK. Then it all came out. Could have come straight off the agony page in *Woman's World*. For a while I forgot all about Enid and the painting.

Sofa, *Sofia*, his wife, who looked down on TJ because she worked in a bank, not a kitchen, had been playing away. With a teacher from his kids' school.

Rudolf hadn't been doing his homework. Spent all his time designing clothes apparently. His chemistry teacher had wanted a word with Sofa. She'd taken a fancy to him and now things had gone long past words.

I pictured them together: I imagined him with thick glasses and wild hair. They'd spend their evenings mixing stuff up in test tubes. Stuff that exploded. I saw it blowing old Sofa up in the air. Onto her feet at last, in spite of her size. Saw her pink rolls of fat quivering with the vibrations. Saw the chemistry teacher's hair, even his eyebrows, all frizzled.

TJ was walking faster and faster, telling me this. Latest was the chemistry teacher moving in. Into TJ's house. Rudolf and Sabina were pissed off about a teacher living with them. Anyone would be. I felt for TJ, seeing his kids unhappy. I'd have felt the same if it was Alastair.

I had to run to keep up with TJ. I looked up at him, wanting him to stop. Got neck-ache doing it. Nearly took hold of his elbow only it would have been awkward, reaching. I offered to go over to Poland one day, when I'd served my full sentence I meant, to give Sofa a piece of my mind, but TJ was definite he didn't want that. He was seeing some Polish lawyer about getting a divorce.

That made him slow down a bit. Him and old Sofa had been childhood sweethearts. I stopped listening so close. Drifted back to the problem of Enid and the painting. Been together more than twenty years. Pass the sick bucket. He was better off without her, I said. Bound to have grown apart, weren't they, seeing as he'd been in England the last five years? There'd been a problem page letter about something similar. Who'd want to be married to a big fat woman who never got off her backside, anyway? Who looked down on him.

Who didn't appreciate how hard he worked. Or how patient he was. Or how good he was at protecting you in crowds and traffic. Another thing I didn't say was that there were plenty more fish in the sea.

'Is end to old life,' TJ said, still glum, slouching. I made him stop so we could have a proper look over the Thames. All that water stretching ahead. All those new buildings going up. Great tall things, funny shapes, windows catching the light. They made me feel small but in a good way. Like all my worries – taking the painting, if Alastair would be OK with me – were small as well. Like, not important.

TJ must have felt the same, even though he was over six foot, because he cheered up a bit. Stood up straighter and took my elbow in the crowds.

We caught a number 59 bus to King's Cross from Waterloo. TJ's suggestion. He was interested in trains, don't ask me why, and, apparently, that was a good place to see them. Waterloo was swarming with them, but he'd seen those already. With old Sofa giving him gip, I hadn't got the heart to say no.

TJ pointed out sights like the British Museum from the bus. He was like one of them tourist guides. My own private one.

We sat on a stone bench in a big square at King's Cross. TJ got a flask of tea out his rucksack and a packet of Polish biscuits. He'd remembered to pack us a snack in spite of Sofa giving him the runaround. We sat by a sort of square concrete pond and drank his tea. Had a fag, after. Looked at the kids splashing about. Last chance they'd get, probably, before winter. TJ talked about his kids, when they were small. How he missed them snuggling up, now they were older. How he hadn't

212

been able to give them stuff, like laptops, until he came over here.

I ground out my fag. Imagined it was Sofa's throat. Why had TJ had to do that, do four jobs? Why hadn't *she* coughed up for stuff, seeing as she was working? I didn't say any of that, just listened to him going on about his kids. Then I thought, if TJ hadn't come over here, I'd never have met him.

It was a relief when we got into King's Cross station and he started talking about trains. 'Is one of most famous stations in world. Home of Harry Potter.'

Well, obviously I hadn't read any of the books, but I'd seen a couple of the films on TV Christmas-times.

There was a crowd waiting to go on a tour at Platform 9 ¾. Hordes of kids but adults as well. Didn't they know it was made up? TJ couldn't afford the tour. He mooched around for a bit. Not much for me to see, not without paying. Even a wee cost thirty pence. When I got back from the ladies he was looking at the proper trains. Didn't have a ticket so he couldn't get beyond the barrier. He chatted to a guard. Nodded, smiled. Probably discussing engine sizes, speeds and that. I peered over a barrier in case I was missing something. I wasn't. It was just the front of the ruddy trains. And they were covered in dead squashed flies. I mean, is that interesting? I folded my arms and looked around. At people and what they was wearing and that, not at the trains.

Then we were off to another train station. Practically next door, but still. Saint Pancras. I'd never heard of it. Sounded like something Dad had had once, *pancr* . . . something.

It was a nice building, I'll grant you that, like a brick palace. Wasted on trains. There was loads of them inside, waiting for TJ to come over and get excited about. They all looked the same to me, but each one was supposed to be slightly different. I'm talking different-sized wheels type of thing, nothing exciting. I was losing the will to live. Not allowed to have a fag of course, like everywhere in London.

TJ wanted to get a look at the Eurostar train, which went under the sea to France. I thought he was having me on, but it turned out to be true. He showed me the poster. It went at over a hundred and fifty miles an hour. But I mean, it was just a train at the end of the day, wasn't it, even if it did go under the sea.

I sat down, stuck out my aching feet. They didn't go far – another advantage, see, of being short. I wasn't a *tripping hazard*, like Primrose nagged about in the kitchen. Only it turned out I was.

Lots of posh people about. Going on their holidays. They had poncy suitcases on wheels, some of them bigger than the toffs wheeling them about. There was probably more in one of them great big suitcases than I owned in the whole world.

A woman had the cheek to wheel one right over my feet. Too busy talking to a dumpy mate with a smaller suitcase to know what she was doing. Making swooping movements with her free hand, wristful of gold bangles kicking up a stink.

My breath came quicker. Who did she think she was, treating me like I wasn't there? My toe throbbed. I got up. Heard 'friends' from my past life shout, *Go on, Maggsie, do her!* I had to grip the cold metal of the bench to stop myself racing after her.

A crying baby in a pushchair came past. Red screwed-up face. The dad wheeling it was on his phone.

Only me taking any notice. That was how I felt. Ignored. Not worth nothing. That's why I was angry.

I power-walked after the woman. She was still chatting. Her suitcase swerved about, doing its own thing. Out of the corner of my eye I saw TJ coming, a takeaway cup in each hand. He looked nervous, which was annoying. I walked faster, in spite of my sore toe.

I tapped the woman's shoulder. She was wearing a leopard-skin jacket. I could tell it wasn't real fur, although she looked just the type to wear a dead cat slung over her shoulders.

A couple of blokes in football shirts darted glances. A woman in a beige mac stopped to have a good stare. At school, kids had formed a circle around me when I was scrapping with someone.

'Excuse me.' I pointed to her suitcase. (Don't think I'd ever said *excuse me* before without it being sarcastic.) My palms were sweating. I felt like I was taking an exam. 'You just wheeled that over my foot.' What I wanted to add was *without bloody looking*. I stopped, though, breathed o-u-t. 'Please be more careful with your suitcase in future.' It was the complete opposite of what I'd normally have said. Felt like marbles in my mouth.

She looked at me. Jabbered to her friend in a foreign language, her bracelets sliding and rattling like handcuffs. OK, she might not have understood what I'd said but I'd still said it. I turned round, chin high, and went off down the platform. Pity Ruby wasn't there to see me using all that psychology.

TJ was sitting on a bench with the tea. 'Everything is alright?' His eyes were creased and worried. 'Who was that?'

'She ran over my feet with her case.' TJ bit his lip.

215

That was also aggravating. Like he was expecting an explosion. I bent down and rubbed my toe. Another breath o-u-t. 'But' – I straightened up – 'I sorted it out. There wasn't no shouting.'

I stared after the leopard-skin woman and her mate. Would have been nice to get a *Sorry!* out of her. There was still a pounding in my head. Snappy was squirming inside the top pocket of my jacket. He crawled out. I gave him a little stroke like I would Audrey. Saw his eyes close and him roll over to have his pale belly tickled. The leopard-skin woman and her suitcase were a couple of specks weaving about in the distance. Snappy was down my jeans leg and slithering after them, only a tiny thing now. A little lizard about the size of one of Kasia's gherkins. I imagined him on the end of an extension lead, like you see dogs with in parks, so he didn't get out of control. Then I lost sight of him altogether.

I turned back to TJ. Finally got my tea off him.

Nice and sweet. He'd put four sugars in. 'You did good thing, Maggsie,' he said. Better than the breathing out, the crocodile, the psychology, the *asking* not demanding, was a bit of praise. That could stop you losing it before you'd even started.

I had a little daydream about TJ smuggling me away on holiday, somewhere hot, in a suitcase the size of the leopard-skin woman's. Free travel because I'd be in the suitcase. Bound to be illegal, though, so TJ would never do it.

The bus back to Waterloo was quiet, nearly empty. TJ started talking about the future. It came out of the blue. About my future, rather than his. Because of me being on a temporary contract.

216

'If no job at Scanda after year is up you can work for friend in café.'

'Hang on. *Your* friend, you mean?' TJ often left out important words. Small, but important, ones.

'Yes, *my* friend. Polish friend. Pavel is name.' TJ's legs stuck out into the gangway. 'I work Saturday nights there.'

'I can't cook, TJ.'

'Pavel does cooking. He need washer-up. Have machine, like Scanda, but smaller. Maybe you chop vegetable too.'

I hadn't thought beyond the year. Only about Alastair. The Pizza Hut thing. What he'd look like. Been too busy concentrating on getting through it without slipping up. Scanda might keep me on. Primrose said I was the best one they'd ever had on the dishwasher. It was why she'd called me *very efficient*. That and because I'd re-organized the crockery cupboards.

I'd have to find somewhere else to live, though. I'd already told TJ the 'hostel' was only a temporary place. Once I'd served my sentence I could live where I liked. Yeah right.

There wasn't much room on the seat. TJ had his arm along the back of it. It reached the window. The light caught a few pale bristles on his chin that he'd missed, shaving. 'That's all very well, TJ, but where am I going to live? You know what London rents are like.'

TJ had another idea. He was quite different now from earlier. 'Flat above restaurant has three bedrooms. One for storage.' I suddenly cottoned on this was his flat he was talking about. 'If Pavel not mind, I put boxes and crates in garage. I fix up hooks for clothes. We would be *flat mates*, Maggsie, I think. Is right word? Is not disrespectful?'

I shook my head. 'Thanks, TJ.' I turned to look out

of the window. That was a turn-up for the books. Ruby's face flashed into my mind, winking. I could feel myself blushing. Ridiculous.

Later, I got another text from Louise. It was only me that could save Enid's life. On and on. Well, that bigs you up and it wears you down. Louise was clever, see, where I wasn't. I learnt that the hard way.

Six days I spent, humming and hawing. Then I'd had enough. I gave in, just like that. Gave in because of Enid and because I was Wonder Woman. Not losing it with the leopard-skin woman had been another star on my headband.

OK, I texted.

# 33

**_Woman's World,_ 24 October 2018**
What Would You Do for a Friend? A Reader's Story

No time to think about things anyway because, blow
me down, there was Louise waiting for me after work
the day after. My heart sank when I saw that helmet of
streaked blonde hair.

'Hello, sweetie! Mwah.' Suffocating smell of perfume
and suede. Rich bint's smell. She pushed a rolled-up
newspaper into my hand. Made sure I had tight hold of
it because of the photocopy inside. 'Sunday's _Observer._
It's got that article you were after. Remember?' She
looked into my eyes, overdoing the smiling like she was
on stage or something. 'You can hang on to it. Text me
when you've got things together and we'll meet up.'

No need to give me a meaningful nod, but she did
anyway. And then she was off with a little wave and a
too-white smile.

Looking back, I must have had tunnel vision. All I saw
was Enid groaning in pain on a hospital trolley, clutching
a postcard of a pine forest in Romania. And me never
getting caught because of Louise's gigantic brain. My
Wonder Woman headband sparkling.

Yeah, I've had friends do the dirty on me before.
Stop letting me kip on their sofa unless I climbed through
windows I shouldn't. That dog flap I told you about.

I've had friends laugh at me for not being able to read stuff. Call me Midge. Sometimes add a 't' to the end. Lean over me, nudge each other at my shoes. You try getting size one adult shoes. Have a go at me because I couldn't take their poxy jokes.

In spite of Louise's money, her ruddy *stately home*, those were the sorts of things she'd do. Written all over her. Not Enid, though. She never would.

I'd thought Louise had time for Enid. Was sorry she was ill and that. You're thrown together in prison and Enid was the only one who'd shown an interest in her postcards. But no, it turned out to be all about her. Some people are like that, in spite of having advantages in life.

I should have asked questions. Humming and hawing for a week isn't long-term thinking. I was gullible. (I know what the word means now.) I should have gone with my gut instinct: Louise was a stuck-up cow. Should have remembered she'd just finished a twelve-year stretch through a plan *not* working.

Things didn't start off well. The *Observer* stuck out of my jacket pocket like a tent pole.

'Maggsie, you have bought same newspaper like me! I could have borrowed. Is last week's?' TJ reached out his hand.

'No!' I barked. His hand shot back. 'I want to keep it nice.' There was a pause. 'Sorry, TJ. Didn't mean to snap.'

I didn't often say sorry. He should count himself lucky. He did look surprised. Then he smiled. No one could call him handsome. His face was too round. And his nose had a squashy tip to it. He did have a nice smile, though, especially with his new improved teeth. And when he wasn't mooning over old Sofa. I wondered, for a second, what she'd think about a woman, me, moving into his flat.

At lunchtime I tucked the *Observer* into the waistband of my trousers. Good job my overall swamped me. Upstairs I took deep drags on my rollie and tried to concentrate on what TJ was going on about. E-cigs. Soon as he'd used up his stock of Polish cigarettes, he was going to start vaping. Better for your health, he said. Cheaper.

Seems crazy, looking back, that I was chatting about fags just before I stole something worth half a million pounds. Right under the noses of people I worked with. In broad daylight, bold as brass. My heart was going so much it was amazing I could chat about anything.

Louise said I should brazen things out. If I looked nervy people would be suspicious.

'Strut around like normal,' she said. No way did *I* strut. It was Louise, with her loud voice and designer clothes and stately home, who was the ruddy show-off.

'Time to go back.' TJ stubbed out his fag.

'Yeah. Be down in a few minutes. Got to pay a visit.' I headed for the ladies. Dead posh the toilets were at Scanda. Glass soap dispensers, scented hand cream. I loved those toilets.

Soon as TJ was out of sight, though, I turned right instead, into the boardroom. There were no dinners planned for today, else TJ would have said. No meetings neither, seeing as there was no notice on the door.

I had a Stanley knife in my overall pocket. Last night, once Juice had finished preparing her veg, I'd shut the door and practised slicing up a *Woman's World* on the chopping board in the kitchen. I'd bought two copies. The other one was to read and keep nice.

I'd had a chance to look at the photocopy up close too. Might seem weird, someone like me *appreciating art*, but I really liked the painting. The *Woman Reading* looked *small*. I felt like I knew her.

I had to be quick. I pushed the door shut but it would only take someone passing by, glancing in, to ruin everything. It was a real stretch to reach the painting. I hadn't thought about that. I didn't always think about being short. (*Petite*, Primrose said, which sounded better, but was still only a posh word for short.) *Petite Marguerite McNaughton*, I thought when she first said it. TJ said it would be better if everyone was my size. Better for the planet, he said. We wouldn't use up so much of things. Only he said it bending down.

My hands were shaking. Hard to line the Stanley knife up straight. I breathed out. Cut downwards. Felt I was slashing the woman in the picture. Dragging her out somewhere she didn't want to go to. She looked the kind who'd want to keep herself to herself.

Quick slice along the top. My heart was racing; difficult keeping the blade steady. No time to look behind me. A cut along the bottom and she was out.

It looked awful, that empty space.

I pulled out the *Observer*. Unrolled the photocopy. It *was* a good one, I'll say that for Louise – she did get that right. Rolled the poor slashed painting up in the paper. Stiffer than the photocopy had been. Fastened it with two elastic bands that the postman had dropped outside our place. Looked like a giant Swiss roll.

I whipped out a can of Spray Mount from my other

pocket. My overall had flapped round my ankles all morning with the weight of my equipment.

I'd practised with the Spray Mount and all. Stuck the bits I'd cut out from *Woman's World* on my bedroom door. Inside the door. I'd asked Ruby, first, if it would be OK. That's how law-abiding I was these days. Ironic, really.

I sprayed inside the empty frame. It made a terrible stink. That could give the game away. Another thing I hadn't thought of. Nor Louise. I speeded up. Unrolled the photocopy onto the glue, smoothing it down as I went. Otherwise you got air bubbles. One of my *Woman's World* ladies was a bit lumpy because of that. My arms were practically pulled out their sockets by now.

I stepped back to have a look. Very slightly skew-whiff, and the wall showed through a tiny bit at the top where my cutting line was jagged. But, pretty good. Shinier than the original, yeah, but then that was a bonus.

The rolled-up paper was too big to fit into my waist-band now. I just had to hold it and hope I didn't bump into anybody.

Downstairs the kitchen was empty. Two o'clock. Sometimes Primrose let me go early but I still had at least a couple more hours at work. Hours with the cut-out painting around, loose. Hidden in a newspaper, yeah, but not in my jacket pocket. Another fault in Louise's plan.

I rushed into the store cupboard. Looked around. Giant tins of tomatoes, beans, bags of sugar and flour everywhere. Couldn't think straight. Primrose or TJ could come in any moment. I scanned the shelves. On the top was stuff that was hardly used. Candlesticks, red and white Christmas china, an old food mixer and a funny-looking dish, long, with a lid. Fish-shaped. Looked about the right size. I thought about Jordan's fishing magazine, God knows why. He'd asked me what a word was last week – *tench*, I'd thought it was, not that I'd ever heard of it. I prayed I could get up to the top without the shelves crashing down. I put my foot on the lowest one. Good job, again, I was small. And wiry. And wore trainers. And I'd had practice climbing a tree only a few weeks back. Audrey had been stranded higher, which gave me a bit of confidence.

I climbed up three shelves. Awkward holding the newspaper bundle. Like a giant rollie, with the *Woman Reading* as the baccy. I had to keep putting it down to get a better grip. At the top now. I hung onto the edge of the shelf, lifted the dish lid. Pushed the painting in. The lid fell back with a clatter that nearly made me topple. I clambered down and jumped off the bottom shelf just as TJ came in to put a stockpot away.

'Hey, Maggsie. What you are doing? You are at gym?' Big smile like always. Nearly always.

'Oh. Yeah.' My face was on fire. My heart was hammering like it was going to burst out my chest. I couldn't look at TJ. 'Yeah. Ha ha. Keeping fit.'

He bent to put the stockpot on the bottom shelf. 'No more fags then. E-cigarettes for you.'

Second time he'd mentioned vaping. It was getting on my wick.

I glanced up at the top shelf. The painting was completely hidden. Would have been better for everyone if it had stayed there. (Even better if it had stayed on the wall, but that's what happens when you don't do long-term thinking.)

# 34

TJ left dead on four thirty because it was one of the nights he washed out test tubes at a college. Primrose was sorting through the sandwiches. I only took one. Not much room in my pockets with my equipment. Didn't feel like eating, anyway.

'You do not need to lose weight, Maggsie.' Primrose unfolded a shopping bag to put the rest in. 'You could do with more flesh on your bones.'

Like her, she meant. 'Yeah, yeah.' Like to see someone her size climbing trees and shelves. But she meant well. She swayed off to fetch her coat.

Soon as she'd gone, I grabbed my jacket and dashed into the store cupboard. Texted Louise. I was just supposed to say OK. Then meet her at five fifteen in the same coffee shop as before.

Climbing up the shelves was easier with two free hands. I reached into the dish and dropped the rolled-up painting on the floor.

Poor lady, all calm and quiet in her long dress. Bet she never dreamt she'd be thrown about. I gave her a little pat and tucked her under my arm. Headed out the kitchen door.

Or tried to. It was locked. I couldn't get out.

My heart hammered. Security must have done their

rounds early. Say if they'd already got as far as the board-room. My stomach dropped. They could be up there now, staring at the painting, thinking it didn't look right. My hands clenched. I was dying for a fag. *And* a drink, to be honest. I could murder those guards.

My phone beeped. That was all I needed, Louise checking up on me.

**Where are you?** she texted. It was only five fifteen for God's sake. Give me a chance. **Stuk in,** I texted back.

I felt like something in a cage. Ridiculous when you think how often I been locked up before. But I'd been prepared for it then. I banged on the door. Funny I was calling out for help from blokes who were only one step away from cops.

Darren and Mike, the security guards were called. One or other of them sat at the posh bint's desk in Reception at home-time. Said *Goodnight, Sir* to all the men, and *Goodnight, Miss* or *Goodnight, Madam* to the women. (Primrose was a *Madam* and I was a *Miss*.) I'd never chatted to them. I wouldn't trust anyone in a uniform.

Footsteps. 'I'm locked in!' I shouted. I didn't add, like I wanted to, You *locked me in, you silly great berks.*

'Hey up. On my way.' Mike's voice. The older one. Had a grey ponytail and no hair at the front – not a good look. Jangle of keys.

I was suddenly desperate for the toilet. I clenched every muscle in my body. Even squeezed my sandwich. Sardine and tomato on brown bread. Aud's favourite.

The *Observer,* with the Danish lady inside, was in my other hand. It was too big. Didn't look natural. I prayed Mike wouldn't look too close.

The door opened. Mike's forehead, there was a lot

of it, was beaded with sweat, 'Sorry, Miss. When I looked round earlier everyone had gone.'

'I was in the storeroom.' I pushed past him. Normally I'd have said *and ruddy check next time, why don't you?* but I wasn't going to hang around a second longer. 'Have to rush.' I headed for the stairs. 'Meeting someone.'

'Got to be carrying a copy of the *Observer*, have you?' He jerked his chin at the paper, at the painting. 'Blind date, is it?'

I stared at him, blood draining from my face. Felt faint, I put my hand out to the wall. He was just behind, swinging his bunch of keys. The sound brought back being inside. Like an awful warning. I dropped the sandwich. I was panicking. What if he saw a bit of painting sticking out? Why was he right on my heels? I wanted to run. That's what I normally did when a man in uniform was behind me.

I took a deep breath and let it out slow. Picked up the sandwich. My 'Ha ha' came out unnatural. 'It ain't a blind date.' I forced a smile, flashed him a quick glimpse of my teeth. 'I'm meeting a girlfriend.'

He wasn't put off, in spite of my teeth. Sleazy git. 'Oy oy! Like that, is it?' Like I was a lezzer. He wiped the back of his neck with a hanky. I was setting a fair old pace and he had a big gut.

Sod's law the longest chat I'd ever had with a security guard was when I had a half-million-pound stolen painting under my arm. I hadn't counted on him coming on to me.

'Nah. It's not like that. She's an old schoolfriend.' Yeah, right. *Boarding* school. One where you weren't never let out.

We were in Reception by then. Mike turned official. 'Have a nice evening, Miss. Sorry I locked you in.'

227

'That's OK,' I called over my shoulder. The revolving door turned round and round. 'Thanks.' I was so pleased to be getting out I gave him a little wave with the hand holding the sandwich. Lost my grip on the paper. Dropped the whole ruddy Swiss roll, didn't I?

My hands weren't big enough, that was the trouble. TJ laughed at them when I was cupping a cigarette, because they was so much smaller than his: 'You have hands of a child.'

I'd got narky when he'd first said it. Felt small, sub-standard all over again. Did he mean I was childish? No, he said, he only meant my hands looked cute. Pretty, he said.

There'd been a bit on manicures in *Woman's World*. (I worked out the word in the end, and some other tricky ones: *cut-i-cle, a-cryl-ic gel*. Buggers of words. *Acrylic* had the word *cry* in the middle, except, of course, it wasn't said like that. That would be too easy.)

I bought a packet of emery boards and a bottle of pale pink nail polish from the Co-op. Painted my nails one evening, when there wasn't anything on telly. Never done it before. Aud turned up her nose at the smell and stalked off.

TJ didn't seem to notice so I don't know why I bothered. And the polish wore off pretty quick anyway, with me at the dishwasher all day.

So my small hands lost their grip. Soon as I dropped the paper, it began to unroll. One of the elastic bands had burst off.

I was on my knees in a flash. The revolving door was circling behind me, panting at my heels. Why was it only me that had problems with automatic doors? They had it in for me, I swear. Wanted to squeeze my guts out, or suck me back inside, or spring open on a body in a lift.

I scrabbled at the newspaper pages. They were getting looser every second. Beginning to flap in the whoosh of warm air from the door.

Next minute Mike was over. 'You alright there, Miss? Got a mind of its own, your paper.'

'Ha ha.' I showed my teeth again. 'It's a bit awkward to carry.' My voice was a squeak. I rolled up the paper. Got it under control.

'Bigger than what you are, that is.' He stood over me, rocking on his heels.

I got up. My heart was thumping, telling me to run. My next 'Ha ha' came out snarlier than I'd meant it to. He didn't seem to notice. Men like him didn't. Stood there laughing at his own wit. My phone beeped.

'That'll be your mate,' he said.

Too right. I nodded. 'Cheerio,' I said. (*Cheerio?* Where did that come from? I'd never said *Cheerio* before, but I was under stress.) Tucked the paper under my arm and strolled down the street.

Soon as I got swallowed up by the crowd of people going home, I got a pace up. For once I was glad everyone walked so fast in London.

# 35

The coffee shop was packed. Louise was stood at a table by the window, peering out.

'Where have you been? I was imagining all sorts of scenarios.'

Her straggly eyebrows tangled themselves together when I told her about the security guard. Tutted like she couldn't believe how stupid I'd been.

That got on my wick for a start. I'd done well getting away from Mike. Done well getting the painting! My heart had been going like the clappers all day. I'd had to sneak about, climb shelves. The painting *was* here, thanks to me. It was me that had taken all the risks. (Course, I thought a lot more about that later.)

'Act naturally,' she hissed, without hardly opening her mouth. Her eyes flickered to the tables around us. 'Don't draw attention to yourself.'

Ruddy cheek. I wasn't exactly dancing on the table. She was the one with the loud voice. The one that took up so much space. I handed over the *Observer* Swiss roll. Slumped back in the chair at getting shot of it.

'Oh, thanks,' she brayed, putting it into her designer bag. 'Yes, I'll read that review you mentioned.'

I ask you, did I look like the type of person who read *reviews*, whatever they were, in posh papers? The type of person who *mentioned* things. *That* was drawing attention, if you asked me.

I'd had to ask Ruby what the word *observer* meant. She'd got excited I might be trying to *read* the ruddy thing. Looked disappointed when I said there weren't enough pictures.

Louise shoved her bag under the table. The poor *Woman Reading* was in the dark again. I wondered if her book was about science. A medical book, maybe. About cancer drugs, even. Fanciful, I know, and even more so as it turned out.

'I'll get these.' Louise bent to fish out her wallet. Hissed, 'We've got to make it look like we're really meeting up.' Then, too loud again, 'What would you like to drink?'

Silly question. What I would have *liked* was a can. Or four. What I asked for was a hot chocolate. Added, because it was a sort of celebration, 'A big one. With whipped cream. And a flake,' I called out as Louise started towards the counter, her frown reappearing.

I was suddenly hungry. I'd been too het up, lunchtime, to eat anything. And Louise was paying, and she said act natural, and I was naturally greedy. 'And a piece of cake. Please. Gat-oh.'

*Gateau.* There'd been a recipe for a 'Coffee Gateau' in last week's *Woman's World.* I'd had to ask Ruby how you said that and all. It's the French word for cake. (French looks even harder to spell than English, if you ask me – and that's saying something.)

Louise checked her wallet while she waited in the queue. She came back with a bad-tempered expression and a tiny little coffee, black, for herself. She had to go back, with a tray, for what I'd ordered. Gave me a lot of satisfaction, that did.

The gateau was lime and coconut. Lovely and light and moist. I forked up a load of it while Louise took a tiny sip of her coffee. Under the table the Danish lady had her cup of tea. 'How long will the you-know-what take to sell?' I asked Louise.

'Oh, well . . . these things take time.'

I stopped, fork in mid-air. 'Enid ain't got much of that, though, has she?'

'Well,' Louise coughed, her coffee going down the wrong way. 'They're keeping her stable at the moment. That' – she pointed a shiny red fingernail under the table – 'will pay for those extra drugs she needs. They'll kick-start, um, her immune system. Like, cure it, once and for all. Yes.' She put down her little cup. It was nearly empty.

I spooned up some cream from the top of my hot chocolate and rolled it around my mouth.

Louise's eyes tracked my spoon. 'How long since you heard from Enid?' she asked, swallowing.

'She's written to me a few times.'

'Recently?'

My eyes prickled. 'Not for a month or so. I don't suppose she's felt up to it.'

Louise set down her empty cup. 'You don't . . .' She shook her head. 'No.'

My spoon stopped. 'Don't what?'

'You don't write to *her*, do you? I know you said you'd been doing some reading, studying. But, a *letter* . . . well, you know.' She gave a little laugh.

Arrogant cow. Who did she think she was? Trying to put me down. I stabbed the gateau with my pastry fork (*Pastry fork! Get you,* I could hear the girls back at the house jeering). Wished the gateau was Louise's hand. 'I have written to Enid. Eleven letters, actually. I *can* write.'

'Oh.' Louise's eyebrows went up. She didn't look none too pleased, even though we'd never heard the end of her Art History degree. 'Only I remember you struggled with that sort of thing.' Another laugh. 'Took you an hour to read a single paragraph, didn't it? Goodness knows how Enid had the patience.' She tapped her coffee spoon against her empty cup. 'Doesn't mean you're not bright, of course.'

Stuck-up cow. *I* was the one working for a posh design company, even if it was in the kitchen. I was living independent, not relying on *Pa*. Fat chance I'd ever have been able to do that with my dad. *She'd* done more time than I had. *My* eyebrows were shaped and defined. *I* hadn't gone up loads of dress sizes.

I clenched the pastry fork. Had an urge to storm off. Didn't want to give her the satisfaction of knowing she'd got to me, though. Hadn't finished the cake or the hot chocolate neither. (It was a good cake but I never fancied gateaux after.) I put the fork down. Conjured up Snappy, that I'd thought I'd retired. He was clawing to get down. I imagined him snapping at Louise's suede jacket. Ripping off the embroidery.

I didn't need his help. I knew what Louise was doing. Trying to make me feel small. Well, I wasn't going to let her. *Rise above*, I told myself. Something Enid used to say, when a couple of girls, inside, had given her stick about her chest. Gone on about Page Three and that. Couldn't do that now, could they, with poor Enid flat-chested? Keep focused, Maggsie. Enid's why you're here.

I licked some strands of coconut off my fork. 'What happens now then? Do you send the money to Enid?

Shall I write and tell her it's coming?' Be nice to give her a boost. She needn't know where it had come from.

'No, no, no.' Louise shifted on her chair. They were little gold chairs. Fitted me perfectly. None of *me* overflowed the sides. 'No need. No. It won't be easy selling a stolen painting, you know.' She was back clattering with her spoon again. It got on my nerves. 'It has to be done privately, you see. Secretly. That's what takes the time.'

'You done this before?' Something I should have asked earlier. Let's face it, I should have asked loads of questions earlier. You probably would have.

'Oh, yes, yes.' The spoon fell onto the saucer. 'Pa's an antiques dealer. Art and antiques. I've . . . networked for him before. Found the right market.' She seemed in a bit of a hurry now. Turned to unhook her suede jacket from the back of the chair.

How do you *network* from prison, I wondered, but didn't ask. Should have. The only question I did come up with was feeble: 'You are going to let me know, aren't you, soon as you done it?'

'Yes, yes. I'll text you. Keep your voice down.' The zip on her jacket got stuck halfway. She struggled with it, then gave up. I hadn't quite finished my gateau – it was a huge portion – but she was already on her feet. Rude, that. Looked like she couldn't get away fast enough.

'Do it quick, though.' I pointed my pastry fork at her. 'We don't know how much time Enid got.'

Louise had to push some chairs in to squeeze by. At the door she turned round sudden to give me a wave. Like she'd suddenly remembered I was there.

Somehow I'd thought pinching the painting would be an instant cure for Enid. Like magic. Silly, I know.

Childish. People thought I was like that anyway because of my size. But everybody's childish sometimes. When you really want something.

I'd got the painting OK. If I had a bigger chest I'd be flashing my Wonder Woman top now. Enid was due out soon. Once we'd bought her the special drugs she'd be right as rain, wouldn't she? She'd be bustling up a gangway to Romania.

I could see her, a few months down the line, swimming in the crystal-clear waters of that Romanian lake, pine trees reflected in the water. Swimming on her back, nude, splashing, smiling. The two sewn-up lines on her chest, where her boobs had been, pink and healed.

I saw the photocopy, shining in the boardroom. Nobody realizing it was a copy. Ever.

Saw myself with my promotion. My pay rise. Treating TJ to Madame Tussauds. Saw myself contacting Alastair. Him not turning away or scarpering. Saw myself taking him somewhere posh to eat – blow Pizza Hut, we'd go to Pizza *Express*.

Sometimes I thought I had too much im-ag-in-a-tion (eleven poxy letters, same ending as ed-u-ca-tion) and sometimes I thought I hadn't got enough. If I'd had more I might have worked out what would happen next.

# 36

Taking the painting had gone OK. You've got to admit I'd done well. Done well for Enid. I was in-vin-ci-ble now. That had been in last week's *Woman's World*, on the fashion page. 'Feel invincible in this autumn's must-have – the military coat!' I had to look up *invincible*, obviously. Means *unable to be defeated*. Yeah, that was me. Funny, it had the name Vince in it, or nearly. Mum had had a fly-by-night boyfriend, one of the ones between Dad and Dougie, called Vince. He'd waited in the lounge once while Mum was primping upstairs. Trodden on a half-eaten tray of chips sticking out from under the sofa. Tapped the sofa arm and got something sticky on his hand. Never saw him again.

Seeing as I was on a roll I changed my hair colour. Been going off having it so dark. Wanted a more natural look.

Mind you, it would take a while to go back to ginger. Bleaching out black makes your hair like straw. But growing it out means looking like a racoon. So I'd have to buy a dark brown colour at the Co-op and do the roots with that. Move on to chestnut once most of the black had gone. The whole thing would be low-key. Tasteful. Once I'd got back to ginger I might put in a few blonde highlights round the front. Going blonde doesn't mean going soft.

You might laugh at me glamming myself up. But it's another way of making your presence felt, isn't it? A positive way.

Kasia cut three inches off the ends for me. She often had a read of my *Woman's World*s, to keep up with the hairstyles. She copied one she'd seen, did a good job, even put in a bit of shaping at the back. She used to be a hairdresser, used to have her own salon back in Russia. Only *bad men* over there kept asking her for money. In the end it wasn't worth carrying on.

We chatted while she got the sides even. She couldn't get a job as a hairdresser over here, not even just shampooing. That's when she'd started working as an escort.

All that was behind her now, though. Her no-good pimp – 'He just like money. Better off on my own' – had long gone. Moved up north after she'd got shot of him. Last she'd heard he was living in a caravan, picking cauliflowers. She said he'd leant around in doorways because he had a bad back. I pictured him now, bending over rows of cauliflowers, day after day, in the rain, his woolly hat getting soaked, bleak fields all around, his back going with the bending. Nobody hearing him hiss, what with the noise of the rain.

Kasia snipped into my fringe. There was a new ring, gold, on her right-hand ring finger. Bought by her Russian sugar daddy. She was fed up with him, though, in spite of the rings. Had to do stuff with him she was tired of doing. She was tired of men bossing her about, full stop. Anyone would be. She was going to go into cleaning instead, she said.

I looked up, at her nails, all shaped and shiny and perfect. At her rings. I couldn't see her scrubbing.

'Lady in Co-op already ask me if I do cleaning. She tell friend. One day I have own agency. I employ other girls. I tell them what to do.'

Yeah, she'd be good at that.

Amazing Ruby hadn't cottoned on to what Kasia had been up to when I first came. Inexperienced, see. Blind. Plus Kasia had whipped out a little foreign dictionary from her handbag whenever Ruby was around. Made out she was practising her English. 'I want get good job. Help people.' The only people she'd helped were men. But Ruby had took it all in.

Trudie knocked on the bathroom door. Saw the hairdressing set up and said she could hang on for five minutes. Chatted a bit from the doorway. Nodded at Kasia being tired of men.

Trudie was unusual, I said, what with her doing men over instead of the other way round. She'd fleeced them on that internet dating site. Promised fun-filled nights in return for them paying her fare from Greece to the UK. I wasn't being spiteful. I was interested. We'd bonded a bit since I'd rescued Audrey – which was ironic. Except maybe it wasn't. Maybe it was because I'd been nicer.

Why she'd done the internet stuff came out now like popping a cork. She'd always kept in touch with her sister in the UK. Emails, regular. Then the sister got poorly. When she got worse, Trudie raised the money from love-struck men to go over and see her. They were sort of giving money to charity only they didn't know it.

She liked my hair. Hers had henna on. Too orange. Nearly the same colour as her skin. She said I could borrow her tablet if I wanted, she'd show me how to use it. I said thanks and I asked her the cat's name. The one she'd had in Greece with the sunburnt ears. Linda, she said. That had been her sister's name. Fair-skinned, couldn't take the sun. This cat had taken on her spirit. It, she, Linda, used to lie in the sun, front paws stretched out, just like her sister had done by the pool. Told you Trudie was a hippie, didn't I?

TJ pretended not to recognize me with my new hair. 'We have new kitchen lady, Primrose. Classy lady.' He made me turn right round so he could see the back.

My ponytail had gone. My hair curled under. My eyebrows had an even better arch to them. I'd drawn in the shape first with biro, then plucked around it. Took me ages to scrub off the blue afterwards and Juicy Lucy had thought it was a bruise. I looked OK. Respectable. Until I opened my mouth and my teeth and the way I spoke let me down.

Primrose heaved a tray of sausages and tomatoes out of the oven. Looked over. She'd have been red in the face if she wasn't so dark. 'You look *smart*, child.' Flash of pearly whites. The bright-coloured African material that showed under her overall was robes from her own country. They just wrapped around so it didn't matter about her size. With her hair braided and her overall off, she looked really dignified. Important. Course, being big helped.

I hadn't heard from Louise yet, but no news was good news. I wrote to Enid but I didn't ask if she was starting the new treatment yet. I didn't want her to know I'd raised the money for it. Or how I'd done it.

Good for my English I was writing letters. And reading the stories in *Woman's World* made me feel I was getting somewhere. Didn't read them all in one go, obviously. Some of them were three pages long, with tricky names. Bit far-fetched, as well – too many happy endings. Audrey didn't like me rustling the pages in bed or leaning over to get the dictionary. She'd stalk off to the end of the bed and curl up in her beanbag.

I was improving myself for Alastair *and* trying to keep up with TJ. Well, not get so far behind. He'd started his harder English class. Took that great big paper out with us Sundays now. The *Observer*. Gave me a chill seeing its pages flapping. Plus, he was struggling through a proper book, hundreds of pages long, he said, and hundreds of years old. I think he said hundreds. Luckily, he kept it in his flat. The man in his book had lived in some old buildings near St Paul's so we had to go and look at them. He hadn't really lived there, though, TJ said; it was all made up.

Now I'd got the painting and Enid sorted, I'd been thinking about TJ's flat. Moving in after the New Year. Be a good place for Alastair to contact me. Maybe even visit. Mind you, TJ would have to watch those long arms and legs of his. Watch he didn't knock over my stuff and that. It would be weird seeing him in the mornings. Going out for our Sunday trips from the same place. Us studying together. Didn't know what old Sofa would think. The flat didn't sound big enough for someone her size anyway.

I'd been putting a few things in my holdall already, along with the stuff I'd been saving to show Alastair one day. The Present from Margate box. My appraisal, Jack's letter, leaflets from the places me and TJ had looked round, postcards. A bit I'd asked the vet to write down. (Ruby and me had taken Audrey there again to get her injections. I'd been on my best behaviour. Had to be else Ruby wouldn't have let me come. And Audrey needed me to talk to her soothing. I'd shut my eyes and stuck my fingers in my ears when some tosser hooted at Ruby for taking her time turning right. Had to drum my heels in the footwell. The vet said Audrey was *well cared for* and *well nourished*. Ruby had spelt *nourished* for me.)

It was November now, getting near the end of the year. I was whizzing so far onwards and upwards I even had a go at a practice letter to the adoption agency. I already had the proper spellings. Only, once I had the pen in my hand, I couldn't put what I wanted to say into words. Thinking about contacting Alastair made me nervous. I got into a tangle. Would he want to hear from me, even now I was doing so much better? I still had bad teeth and no exams or nothing, didn't I?

Was I being selfish like Big Shirl and Juice had said? Was it for my good, not his? Would I be pushing out his birth mum? I wanted to push her out, only everyone said it was wrong.

So I only got as far as *Dear Sir or Madam.* It was in my best handwriting, though. I put the beginning of the letter back in my holdall. Still a couple of months before the year was up.

# 37

It was a shock, after I'd pinched the painting, seeing the copy up there on the boardroom wall. Like I'd never stole it. Like I'd dreamt the whole thing. Showed I'd done a really, really good job. I leant so close to the glass – TJ had gone ahead – my breath steamed it up. People think *I'm* stupid, but it's the snooty types who'll pay hundreds of thousands of pounds for a painting, when a photocopy looks just as good, who're the thick ones, if you ask me.

I'd expected TJ and Primrose to look at me suspicious, but they didn't. As for the rest of them at Scanda, well, people don't take much notice of you when you work in a kitchen. Even less when you're smaller and you don't smile a lot because of your teeth. They'd forgotten about me rescuing Jack. Ten months ago now.

Mind you, I was smiling more. Quite full of myself since I'd saved Enid's life. Talked about her to TJ now I knew she wasn't going to die. *He'd* bored my ears off droning on about old Sofa.

I didn't tell him exactly how I'd met her. Didn't say the actual word *prison*. I just said it was a place where you go to make up for doing bad things. I said it quickly. TJ gave me a long look and didn't ask anything else. He had a little interested smile on, though. I told him Enid was going to beat her cancer. I could *feel it in my water*, like she would say. Didn't say why. Didn't say I'd raised the money to *get* her better. Or how, obviously. He said he'd say a prayer for her. A Catholic one. I was pleased, not because I believed in all that myself, but because he thought she was worth praying for.

I nearly told him about Alastair then. Be tempting fate, though. Only two months to go before the New Year.

I huddled into my overall. There was a bitter wind up in the roof garden. Reckon it was to try and put people off smoking. A clear day, though, and all London's new millionaires' towers were sparkling. I stubbed out my fag and had a good stretch. Enid would be on the mend soon with her new drugs. I'd worked here for ten months. I was going onwards and upwards. Nearer to my son. TJ was right, there *were* opportunities. You just had to look for them.

Trouble is, other people are out there looking for them too, aren't they? Opportunities to use people.

Juicy Lucy was in the kitchen, making soup. Swedes and parsnips, she said the veg were. They'd been going cheap down the market. I wasn't surprised. She'd boiled them up and now she was using a little stick blender to mash them to smithereens. It was small and powerful. *Very efficient*. A lot of small things are like that.

Her glasses were steamed up. There was a reek of boiled veg like a blocked drain. She didn't stop the whirring. I had to put the kettle on myself.

I took my work sandwiches out of my pocket. Smoked salmon on rye bread. Real posh, only it tasted just like kippers. Audrey must have smelt it, even from outside, because she scratched at the kitchen door to come in. Stared at me eating it, purring, shifting her weight – quite a lot more of it now – from paw to paw, miaowing every five seconds. I ended up giving her half.

Juice jumped when I nudged her with a cup of tea. Didn't even notice I'd made her one instead of the other way round.

She flung down the blender. She'd done her soup wrong. Put in too much water. Didn't taste of *nothing*, she said. Just as well, I thought – better than drains. 'Can't do anything right. Can't bloody think straight.' Burst into tears.

Audrey scarpered. Cats can't handle crying. Like men that way.

Juice felt better after a fag and the tea. We kept the soup boiling. I might only be able to cook egg and chips, but even I knew steam was water. After half an hour it was lower in the pan. Juice chucked in half a jar of Marmite so in the end it did taste of something. Didn't cheer her up, though.

Why Juice wasn't herself came out that evening, watching telly. Course there was a man behind it.

She'd had a letter from her ex. From prison. Loads of pages. Kisses all over them, and a heart with an arrow. You could see she was tempted. Turned your stomach seeing her goggling over them. None of us were swayed. 'Oldest trick in the book.' Big Shirl shook her fingers to dry her nails. Picked up the bottle of varnish and leant over her other hand, frowning. 'Don't you fall for it, my girl.'

*EastEnders* was on. I could watch it these days. Seeing them all boozing in the Queen Vic used to make me want a drink, but not so much now I got other things to think about.

Juice was still glued to her letter.

I turned round. 'Mention Shania, does he?'

Juice hunted through the pages. 'Um. No. But . . .'

Every single one of us whipped round. Said something along the lines of *he's bad news* at the same time. Like something out of a musical. Kasia said her bit in Russian. Sounded like she was spitting, which would have been about right. Even Trudie put in her fourpenny-worth.

Juice clutched her letter, eyes red behind her glasses. She stuffed it down her bra – leggings don't have pockets – and stomped upstairs. It reminded me of being a teenager again, only I'd have gone down the park, not upstairs.

A couple of days later Juice was in the kitchen beating up some eggs for an omelette. She had the makings of a salad on the side to go with it. Whipped up quite a froth. Seemed her mum – her *adoptive* mum I should say, only I didn't like the word – had put her right. Stick with the BF and she wouldn't ever get Shania back.

'I've torn up his letter,' Juice burst out. 'Every page. It's the only way, Mum said.'

She picked up the knife and started on the tomatoes and I got out of the kitchen sharpish.

Sunday, me and TJ went to the other art gallery in Trafalgar Square. Huge place with rooms opening off each other. Like a palace. Posher than the Queen's, probably. Everything so grand you couldn't hardly breathe. Pink marble pillars like the foreign sausage TJ liked, gold bits, glass ceilings, fancy squiggles everywhere. That sort of thing. And huge pictures that took up the whole wall.

245

Dark colours. Men mostly. Battle scenes with people stabbing each other and not wearing many clothes.

TJ had a list of six paintings he wanted to see. He didn't mean just *see*, he meant stand in front of each one for ages and get excited over it. You'd swear he'd had a drink, only I knew he hadn't. He didn't even know about my drinking days. Of course his special paintings weren't all in the same place, or on the same floor even, so there was a lot of traipsing up and down trying to find them. Waiting, seething, to get through the swing doors between the rooms, sorry, *galleries*. Crowds of foreign people, chattering fit to burst, swarming through first.

We tracked TJ's first painting down. The people in it were stiff and wound around in cloaks and robes, like mummies. Even I could see it was hundreds of years old. I stuck my hands in my pockets. Looked at it for well over a minute. Asked TJ outright why it mattered it was the original painting. 'You can get really good photocopies these days.' I didn't look at TJ, I looked at a woman in the painting with her hands clasped together. 'Nice bright colours, quality paper.' The photocopy had felt heavy and smooth when I'd unrolled it at home, with the door locked. 'Stick one of them in a frame and Bob's your uncle.'

'Bob . . . ?'

'Yeah. Means, there you go. Sorted.'

'Sorted . . .' TJ got out his notebook. I liked him writing down what I said now. It made me feel important. He put the notebook back in his trouser pocket. Proper trousers he had on, not jeans or trackie bottoms. Foreign-looking trousers. A bit old-fashioned, but smart.

'No, there is big difference.' Out came an arm, palm open. 'Artist paint this with own hand. So painting has part of artist inside. Like painted with artist's blood, almost.'

I looked closer. How did he make that out?

'Artist spend many, many hours getting painting right. Photocopy look good at first stare, but is empty.'

'At first *glance*.' Was the *Woman Reading* photocopy empty? It looked OK to me. I folded my arms. Felt a bit deflated.

I trudged after TJ as he hunted down his other paintings. He pointed out details in them you wouldn't notice. The little spot of white in people's eyes that made them look real. The different types of brushstrokes. Some of it, on the modern ones, was really lumpy.

Other people were listening to him, muscling in. Old biddies nodding and smiling. How did TJ know all this art stuff? How did he know about science as well? History? How did his brain have room? Why did he bother with someone like me? Someone who'd just stolen a painting like the ones he was getting excited about. I leant against the wall while he droned on. Began to feel I'd short-changed Scanda. I'd stolen something off them, I know, but it had felt more like swapping before.

When he'd finished crowing over the last one, he took my elbow, smiled down at me. 'You have been very patient, Maggsie.'

I heaved myself off the wall, sighing. Had I? That was a new one. Too busy thinking, more like. It's a good thing, though, isn't it, being patient?

It was a bit chilly sitting on the steps outside the National Gallery, even though we'd put down the *Observer* to sit on. We stared up at Nelson's back and had the flask of tea and my sandwiches and our fags. Well, my fag and TJ's e-cig. He'd been on them a few weeks now. I'd thought his vaping thing was a quarter-bottle of vodka at first. Same shape. Gave me a start. TJ breathed out more smoke than with a proper fag. All around himself like he was some sort of dragon. Steam, he said it was, not smoke. Been better off with a kettle.

We looked down at the people milling about like before. Felt small, with everything on such a massive scale, but sort of at the centre of things at the same time. Had to sit close to TJ, our jackets practically touching, to keep warm.

My eyes were still drawn to the painting, the *photocopy*, when I passed it on fag breaks, only not for the same reason. If TJ was with me I gabbled about any old thing to get us past the boardroom door quick. Luckily when he was up there working he was too busy to stare at the paintings.

Before, it had given me a lift; now seeing it made me feel a bit low. It looked second-rate, what TJ said all photocopies were. Empty. To be honest it looked like a photocopy. I'd thought shiny, bright colours was better. More cheerful. But maybe the artist, old Hammershøi, hadn't wanted flashy.

Enid, I had to keep reminding myself. The original's gone to save Enid's life. And TJ was unusual knowing so much about art. No one else would spot the difference.

# 38

**Woman's World, 5 December 2018**
New Ways with Cheese!

I still hadn't heard from Louise. I kept checking my phone. Hardly bothered normally. No text or call. Maybe she was too busy trying to sell the painting. Maybe no one would buy it. Maybe Enid was running out of options.

Hadn't heard from her either, come to that. When I let myself weaken I thought she might be wasting away in one of those special places people go to die, waiting for a wonder drug that wouldn't never come.

I was still writing to her every week. It was easier now because most of the words were ones I'd used before. Soon as my sentence was up, January, I'd go and visit Enid. Ask Ruby to help me find out which hospital she was in. I had enough put by for the fare and that. I'd do it soon as I'd sent off that letter to the adoption agency.

For a few weeks the boardroom wasn't used. Then, beginning of December, there was a posh dinner for some bigwigs. Primrose banged about the kitchen with saucepans. Big backside bumping into me. No hymn singing. I took more notice of that than about the stuff that might be going on upstairs. Sounds strange but I'd almost forgot I'd taken the painting.

No TJ to help Primrose out in the kitchen, seeing as he was upstairs. So no chance she could spare me to clear tables in the canteen. I hadn't done that since those stuck-up tossers nearly lost me my job. They got a young girl in from an agency instead. Polish, she was, like TJ. Red hair. Dyed. She was quick, I give her that, and after she said she lived with her boyfriend, I warmed to her a bit. Plus she didn't have time to get matey with anyone.

About three o'clock TJ came down, undoing his bow tie. The Polish girl went off then. They only had time to say *hello* and *goodbye*. Funny how hearing them few words, in a foreign language, could make you feel lonely.

TJ was bursting to tell us something. Don't say he's met another dentist, I thought. His arms were going. Even more dramatic than usual. I saw the two of us in his mate's flat. Squeezed together in a tiny kitchen. Only the size of a cupboard, TJ had said. That was because it had used to *be* a cupboard. Saw my Audrey mug going flying. Then I heard what he was saying: 'There has been theft! Theft from boardroom.'

I was grating a block of cheese for tomorrow's sand-wiches. Primrose froze it after. The cheese skidded on the metal teeth. I rasped my knuckles. My heart was beating so fast I felt faint. I leant against the table. *Theft* was the painting. Must be. There wasn't anything else to steal up there. The boardroom was practically empty, except for a big table and some spindly Scanda chairs.

Primrose was stood in front of the store cupboard, making notes with a pencil. She looked up. 'What is that you say, TJ? What has been stolen?'

'Painting! Valuable painting.' He looked at me. 'The one you like, Maggsie.'

My face was on fire. Showed I'd taken it. They'd know it was me.

Primrose frowned. 'How could that happen?'

I was drowning. Louise had said it would be years before anyone found out. Probably never. *There's absolutely no risk, Maggsie.* Yeah, right.

'It was cut from frame.' TJ made a slashing movement with his hand.

My head whipped up from the cheese. Wasn't like *that*, I nearly said. I was *careful*. I didn't want to hurt the lady.

Primrose tutted. 'Too many knives about these days. But why did security not see them?'

'It is inside job, director said. Is someone who works here.' TJ paused, like in *EastEnders* before the end music comes on. 'One of us.'

I swallowed. The smell of cheese was making me want to puke. How many other people working here got a record? They'd definitely know it was me.

'Police are coming. They will question everyone.' TJ was all puffed up and important with his exciting news and me and Primrose hanging on to every word. Pretty soon he was going to feel like a burst balloon. Worse. Angry. Like I'd tricked him.

'Not at lunchtime, I hope.' Primrose moved her finger along a row of jars of spices, counting. How could she be checking what she had in when I was going to be sent down for a million years? When I was never going to be able to contact Alastair? 'I do not want them under my feet.'

I didn't want them ruddy anywhere. I sucked my grazed knuckles.

'A lot of fuss for a painting.' Primrose walked over to the fridge. She walked very graceful for a bigger-built woman. Held her head up high. Funny I thought of that with all the prison stuff going through my brain. 'I do not like those splattered things. You should not steal, but . . .' She counted the eggs on the top shelf and made a note on a piece of paper.

'No, is different painting.' TJ's arms were still going. 'It is the Hammershøi, *Woman Reading*. It is worth half a million pounds. More, perhaps.'

I've stolen half a million pounds, I thought. Felt a flicker of pride. I could see, well, *imagine*, Enid, in a Romanian castle, her *own* castle, thanks to all that money. The money I'd got for her. Frisky and full of life because of a blood transfusion from a Romanian virgin. TJ had told me about Dracula.

Then I thought, *I'm going to be sent down for life.*

The painting must have been stolen a while back, TJ announced. I tried to look surprised.

'Stupid I not notice myself,' TJ banged his chest. 'But I have not been inside room for weeks.'

It was only today someone sitting opposite it had noticed something wrong. 'Danish man.' TJ nodded. 'Had seen other Hammershøi paintings before.'

Pity this Danish know-all hadn't ruddy kept it to himself. Snooty git had thought the colours were too bright. Spotted a little gap between the painting and the frame. Up close he saw it was a photocopy stuck in.

'Spray-mounted!' I burst out. I done a good job. No one else had noticed. 'Most like,' I added quickly. I was losing it.

TJ and Primrose stared at me. The cheese slipped out my hands again. 'That's what you said earlier. Spray-mounted.' I bent my head. Kept my eyes down. Normally I'd have stared back.

'Yes, you are right. Spray-mounted.' TJ paused, went on, 'This man, important client, slapped Mr Holstrom on the back. Said, was joke I think, Mr Holstrom could not afford real thing.'

Mr Holstrom was the big boss. The one that had shook my hand the first day. The one that wore jeans. The one you could be stood next to, mouthing off, and you wouldn't realize. A couple of weeks ago he'd come down to the kitchen to praise our *high standard of food and cleanliness*. My face had gone bright red. Primrose had pulled me to her, laughing. Said I should be proud not embarrassed. Only it was shame, as well as embarrassment.

Primrose shook her head. Turned back to the fridge to see what she had left in there to make soup with. How could she think about soup when my whole future was going down the pan?

Mr Holstrom called a meeting. The canteen was the only place that had room for everybody. He stood by the chilled section, next to the sandwiches. Primrose had nudged me to the front because I was smaller. Thanks, Primrose. I stuck my hands in my overall pockets. Hard to stand there in the front with your heart thumping. Like being in the headmaster's office all over again. Worse, because Mr H was a nice bloke who'd given me a chance. Worser, because it was *me* that had done it.

Mr H was disappointed a *trusted employee* had stolen from a company that *prided itself on its good treatment of staff*. A painting that was *the star* of Scanda's art collection. A well-known, *distinctive* painting that would be difficult to sell. My blood ran cold. Why hadn't Louise told me that?

He spoke without looking at us. Stared over our

heads. Said the police would be speaking to everybody, but his office door was always open.

For snitching, I thought. TJ had looked at me funny when I'd said about the spray-mounting. Hadn't guessed, had he? No, he couldn't have. But if he had, would he tell on me? Have to, because of being a Catholic? They had to confess stuff every month even if they hadn't done anything.

'Thank you, colleagues,' Mr Holstrom finished. I couldn't breathe properly till I was back through the swing doors.

At break I shot a look through the boardroom door. The far wall was empty. Frame and photocopy gone. The empty space was bare. Reminded me of a prison wall.

Where *was* the *Woman Reading*? By rights she should be off saving Enid's life. If it was hard to sell, what had Louise done with it? My belly was burning with the stress of it. What the hell was Louise doing?

# 39

I woke with a start, heart racing. Two a.m. on my phone. Something had come to me while I was asleep. TJ had said they'd sent away six months' worth of CCTV footage. A camera I'd never spotted was trained on the revolving door. So they'd find out exactly when the painting had been taken. Who'd taken it. They'd see me struggling to keep hold of it. Mike might even remember me dropping the newspaper. Might take them a couple of weeks but then . . .

Trudie was snoring next door. Got so I couldn't focus on anything else. I threw back the candlewick bedspread. Got up and looked out of the window. All there was to see was the pool of light under the street-lamp and the darkness all around. Not a soul about, even though this was London. I was dying for a fag. Took a couple of deep breaths, o-u-t, then got back into bed, shivering. I was going to get sent down. Knew it in my water.

I stared into the darkness. Felt small and on my own. I *was* small and on my own. I still hadn't heard from Enid. The dragging feeling of it already being too late for her came over me again. Might have risked everything for nothing.

I'd trusted Louise – well, not trusted, put blind faith

255

in her poshness and education. That they'd make things go right. Thought she was as fond of Enid as I was.

I'd thought ticking off the calendar regular showed I was getting better at long-term thinking. But I'd been reckless to trust Louise.

Lying bitch, saying her plan was foolproof. Soon as I'd handed over the painting she'd backtracked on when Enid would get her money. Might even have sold it, kept the money herself! Spent it on diving holidays, designer clothes. Or found out she couldn't sell it and kept it stuck up on her wall. Either way she'd used me.

The bedclothes got untucked with me thrashing about. Then I was freezing. I put the light on. Picked up this week's *Woman's World*. Ripped out an advert for reclining chairs. Tore it into shreds. Imagined it was Louise's suede jacket. I was properly worked up now.

Sod Snappy. Sod psychology.

I picked up my phone. Sod Louise telling me not to contact her for *security reasons*. She'd contact *me*, she'd said. Yeah, right. Sod my text beeping her in the middle of the night.

I worded it careful. No point in signposting myself:
They know the lady is not who she shoud be. Are you helping Enid now?

I even remembered there was a silent 'k' in front of 'no' and a silent 'w' at the end. *Shoud* didn't look right but who cares about impressing a con artist?

Nearly two hundred people worked for Scanda Solutions. A lot of people for the police to question. A waste of their ruddy time, seeing as it was me. They were in a room on the top floor. The door was closed but you could see a cop, with his hat off, sat behind a table through

256

the glass bit. Every time I walked past my innards turned to water.

Things were closing in on me.

Scanda had given me a chance and I'd blown it. People had said I'd done *all the right things*, had *a cool head*, was *amazing*, *very efficient*, and I'd proved them wrong.

No option but to do a runner. Nothing to stay for. The supported house felt like prison. Scruffy, noisy, all us girls squabbling over petty things. Them kicking up a stink when I woke them early, pacing about. At least I didn't snore. Had to keep a hold of myself so I didn't fly at them. So much for us being *a team*, like Ruby beamed about sometimes.

Audrey was about the only comfort I had left. When I patted my lap now she jumped straight up. Once, when Juice's back was turned, she'd helped herself to one of her yogurts. Hooked it out with her paw. Don't tell me cats aren't clever. Scarpering would mean leaving her behind.

TJ? Running off would save him turning against me. I saw him looking puzzled, running his big hand over his bristly hair. His smile dying.

He probably still had a thing for old Sofa anyway. He'd probably forgive her playing away. Drop his divorce thing. Go back to Poland. When he found out what I'd done he wouldn't want anything more to do with me.

He'd thought I was like he was, someone going onwards and upwards. He'd thought I was improving myself. Seizing opportunities left, right and centre.

I was. Well, I had been. Been doing it for Alastair. But what was the point now? Never going to be able to contact him now, was I? Not from prison. That was another thing to run away from. That was the worst thing.

What had been the point of all that struggling? Avoiding booze? I might as well have been out of it every ruddy day. My calendar, all those wasted ticks I'd been so pleased about? All those packed tube journeys to Scanda, the hours on my feet, the baggy overall. The hours I'd spent looking up words, writing them down. Even taming Audrey had been for nothing now I was going to abandon her. All of it a bloody waste of time.

I was on edge the whole time. Smoking like a chimney. Trying not to snap at people, or to murder anybody who knocked into me or walked too slow. Even Aud's miaowing got on my nerves. She put a lot of expression into it. Mostly it was to do with demanding a pilchard, but I could hear, *Oh no!* and *What now?* as well.

When I wasn't tetchy, I was a zombie through not sleeping. I didn't have much to say to TJ. Wasn't interested in the *Metro*. Couldn't concentrate.

Friday fag break he put down the sports pages. Breathed out his fruity-flavoured steam. Rested his e-cig on the bench-arm.

'You so quiet, Maggsie. You have problem? Family problem? Your friend Enid is bad, yes?'

'Enid is *good*,' I snapped. 'A *good* person. If you mean, is she *ill*, she's got cancer, remember.'

'Yes. It is worry for you.'

'Yeah.' I sucked in a great lungful of smoke. Breathed it out over London. Fogged over its opportunities. My only one was prison.

Booze was calling to me. An ice-cold pack of Stella would take away all my worries. I'd looked round the drinks aisle in the Co-op yesterday. I'd avoided it all

258

year, practically. Stopped thinking about it. Now I was drawn to it again. Let's face it, drink was all I had left.

The police had interviewed the managers and the arty types. They were on the first floor now. Then it was the ground floor: Reception, the furniture showroom and security.

Next floor down was the basement. My floor.

I only had a couple of days of freedom left. And not exactly freedom, seeing as I was stuck with the same old brain. It went over and over what Louise had done. Got me worked up. Told me how stupid I'd been. Bet you're thinking the same.

Saturday morning Ruby brought in the post. All smiles, rosy face, bright eyes. Just come in on her bike. She'd done a really good time, she said. Who ruddy cared?

'Don't give me no bills.' Big Shirl heaved herself up from the only kitchen chair with arms.

'There's a postcard for you, Maggsie. Pretty stamp.'

Ruby handed me a card with a picture of a lake surrounded by pine trees. I turned it over. Enid's writing. Enid's name at the bottom. I stared at it.

Enid was still alive.

*Hello dear, I'm here, in Romania.*

Enid was well. Enid was out. Enid was doing the thing she'd dreamt of doing all these years.

*I'm all clear now, ducks. No further treatment. Just a yearly check-up.*

I sat down. Enid was OK. She'd got better. She'd got

better without those special drugs you couldn't get on the NHS. The drugs I'd stolen the painting to buy.

It had all been one big con.

I'd thought Louise was taking her time, might be keeping the money for herself. Or keeping the painting. Never thought she'd use Enid's cancer to trick me.

I'd put everything on the line. For nothing. No: much, much worse than nothing. I was heading for prison. Alastair was just a pipe dream now.

Now you're definitely thinking how stupid I've been. I know you are. Why didn't she ask Ruby about breast cancer drugs, google it herself? Check the whole thing out with Enid? Why did she let herself get taken for a mug by an ex-con? Just because she got a posh voice and a stately home and a degree stuck up on the wall?

I should have. Of course I should. I do know that. Yeah, Louise had been rushing me and I was worried about Enid, but I still should have *questioned* things.

Don't say you've never got anything wrong, though, because I bet you have. Maybe stuff you don't even know about yet. Could happen to anybody. Didn't mean I was thick. Meant I was *gullible*, like I said before. I'd put *gullible* in my personal spelling dictionary. Too late now. I remembered a seagull snatching a chip off me in Skeggie. Years ago. *Easily tricked or fooled*, gullible means. Yeah, that was me. My mind flashed back to another time, another 'friend'. A night when I'd been hoisted through a skylight. And that dog flap. Yeah, I was hard as nails, gave as good as I got, but none of that protected you against being conned.

I sat there holding Enid's postcard. Felt a flash of guilt because the first thing I'd thought wasn't, *Thank God, Enid's OK*, but, *F—ing hell, that bitch has done me over!*

Ruby breezed off to the office.

'What's up with you, gel?' Big Shirl got up to rinse out her mug. The ink from her 'Shirley' label had smudged and run. 'Bad news?'

I shook my head. Couldn't get no words out.

Soon as I got to my room it hit me.

Rage.

I grabbed my phone. Texted Louise again. You c–, you conned me. Where's the f–cking painting? F–cking giv it bak or ill hunt you down till my dyeing day. I didn't use dashes. I put in the actual swear words. The phone jumped in with red lines everywhere like it was a teacher. I didn't do what it said. I threw it down on the bed.

No reply. I snatched up the phone again. Texted her four more times. Never going to reply, was she? She'd have ditched her phone soon as she got her scabby hands on the painting. She was clever. She'd planned all this.

I stomped around my room. Not much room for stomping. How did you keep going when your life was in ruins, when a poxy great lying cow has ruined it for you, tell me that?

I thought about what I could do to Louise. Tear her highlighted hair out in clumps, scratch her face to ribbons, shave off her bloody eyebrows – only that would improve her. Smash up her stately home, set fire to it. Except I didn't know where it was.

And none of it would be enough for what she done to me. My heart was jumping out my chest. Red mist all around. Snappy cowering in my holdall.

Being conned makes you angrier than anything else. Take it from me, because you might not have experienced it yourself. Yet. When you think about it, use psychology, it's treating you like you don't matter, like you're nothing.

Yeah, psychology was good up to a point. Couldn't exactly ask Louise nicely to give me back the painting, though, could I? Take the blame for me at Scanda? That's where it was limited, see.

Yeah, she'd taken me for a mug. But I was never going to be made a mug of again.

Seeing as she'd lost me everything, I didn't have nothing left to lose.

I was going to do that runner.

Head down south.

Kill her.

# 40

Monday. The police had spoken to everyone on the ground floor. Tomorrow was our turn. My life had already gone for a burton. I was going to make ruddy sure Louise's did too.

I couldn't go without telling TJ.

I wrote him a letter. Harder than the ones I'd done to Enid. Even since knowing she had cancer. I poured out my heart in the letter, much as I could with the words I knew. Couldn't concentrate on looking anything up in the dictionary. I was like a Catholic. TJ said you could do that, get stuff off your chest and the priest wasn't allowed to tell the police.

> *I been stupid and I thought I wasn't any mor. I did it of Enid It was Louse who put me up to it. I'm going after her, TJ. Dont worry. I can look after myself. I'm going to be sent to prison* [I didn't put 'back'] *TJ, so you wont ever see me again. That's a pity because you been a good frend.*

Writing doesn't half take it out of you. I felt drained after and my eyes were sore.

I sent Enid a postcard of Trafalgar Square. I'd bought

it when I'd gone to the Portrait Gallery with TJ. When my life was different.

> *I have blown it Enid. I am off. I am very glad you are OK. Fantastick you are in R.* [Romania wasn't in the dictionary and I never thought about copying it off her postcard. I just put a capital R.] *Glad you got a good life now Enid. You deserv it. Love of your frend Maggsie M xx*

I didn't bother putting the little 'c' after the 'M'. No point now.

No idea how much it would cost to send a postcard to Romania. I stuck on three second-class stamps and hoped for the best.

I took the letter into work. My last day, only no one else knew that. Last time I'd see TJ, Primrose, the roof garden, the toilets with the posh soap dispensers, the fancy sandwiches. The dishwasher that always worked so smooth. Dwelling on it wouldn't do any good. Dwelling on anything doesn't.

TJ noticed me light a second fag at break. I normally just had the one. I turned away. 'Alright, alright, you ain't my nan.'

Actually Nan had smoked like a trooper. Said it kept her slim for her ballroom dancing.

TJ thought I wasn't myself because of Enid.

'Nah,' I snapped, licking the paper to roll another fag. 'Enid's better. Out of hospital, out of prison. In Romania.' I looked down, concentrating on the rollie. I'd said 'prison'. TJ would guess that was where I'd met her. Well, who cared now? Now that was where I was going back to.

TJ didn't seem to twig about prison. 'Is good news, no?'

'Yeah. Fantastic.' I clicked my lighter, frowning.

'But . . . ?' TJ's eyebrows were raised, focused on me.

'But what?' I snapped the lid of my baccy tin shut. It was annoying TJ knew something was wrong when I hadn't even said anything. When he was foreign. And his English wasn't perfect. And he was a man. It gave him an advantage. I couldn't tell him to his face. Not have him angry, ashamed of me, with me sat there listening to it all. I should have been open about it. To a lot of people, a lot earlier. Then it would never have happened. I made a mistake, OK? No need to go on about it.

TJ looked at me funny when I said goodbye that afternoon. Shook his head. 'You talk to me tomorrow, yes? Talk more.' He undid his apron and hung it up. 'A trouble shared is a trouble split.'

I buttoned up my jacket. 'Halved.' Came out automatically, only my heart wasn't in it.

He dashed off to his English class. I propped the note on the peg where he hung his jacket. Then I got out of the building quick as I could. 'Goodnight, Miss,' said Mike at Reception, with a little salute like I was as good as anyone else.

I'd leave first thing next morning. I was desperate, yeah, but not desperate enough to go hitching in the dark.

I woke at five. Put on two pairs of jeans. Two extra T-shirts. God knows where I'd be sleeping tonight. Two pairs of socks, which made my shoes tight. Three pairs of pants in my rucksack, a small one I'd got in the pound shop. My phone. Yesterday's work sandwiches that I hadn't felt like eating. My comb and toothbrush, although

265

my teeth were a lost cause. Another one. Never had got myself in the right frame of mind to see TJ's dentist mate. Another wasted opportunity.

I left my holdall and the things stuck up on my wall. The evidence I'd been respectable. What good was it now? The only thing I took was the A Present from Margate box. Then I snatched up my make-up bag. Stopped. *You're either going to be banged up or homeless, Maggsie.* I only took my eyebrow pencil and mascara. I left TJ's bottle of perfume behind. He wouldn't want to know me and I didn't want to be reminded. I remembered Nan's earrings just in time. I'd need them. They were like Nan pushing me forward.

I had over a hundred and forty pounds saved and there was still a bit left on my Oyster card. I took a quick look round. My personal spelling dictionary was on the table. I hesitated. Picked it up.

I dithered over the Scanda calendar. Eleven months of ticks. Written proof I'd lived normal and hadn't had a drink. It was the last little bit of hope. Yeah, but what for, now? I couldn't waste time deciding so in the end I took it. I ripped Scanda's furniture pictures off first to fit it in the rucksack. I left my other stuff, my new black trousers, my school dictionary, my pile – eleven months' worth – of *Woman's World*s, behind. You got to travel light when you're running away.

I took a knife from the kitchen. A small one, but sharp, the one Juicy Lucy used for slicing veg. Tucked it into my sock.

I opened a new tin of pilchards. Audrey was in her box, all curled up. She opened one eye at the sound of the tin opener. Closed it again and curled up tighter. Out for the count. I gave her a last stroke. Her fur crackled and she put her ears back like I'd done it on purpose. Like she knew how stupid I'd been. I wanted her to wake up, have the warmth of her settled on my lap. But that would be mean, seeing as I'd have to go straight off again, seeing as I was running away. She'd have Trudie fussing over her now, I told myself. Only that made me feel worse.

I walked to the tube. I was heading for Osterley. It was south-west and near the motorway – I'd checked with a guard at the station yesterday. The south-west was where Louise lived. I'd trawl round all the posh places down there, looking for her.

Six a.m. A glitter of frost on the pavement. Glad I'd put on extra clothes. I walked to a clear bit of road. Each step was one nearer to finding Louise. And killing her.

I picked a stretch, under a streetlamp, where a driver could pull in. Stuck out my thumb and waited.

Yeah, yeah. I know what you're thinking. I did know hitching was dangerous. But it was getting light now. And I was past caring, anyway.

It was only a couple of minutes before a lorry slowed down, the driver staring. He pulled in ahead and I ran towards him.

You've probably never been in a lorry cab. People that read books aren't likely to have. But, take my word for it, they are really high up. You got to haul yourself in, especially if your legs are shorter.

'Thought you were a little kid.' The lorry driver looked in the mirror, setting off again. He was dark and sweaty-looking. Had a gut that reached the steering wheel. 'Where you going then? Early bird, aren't you?'

'South.' I put down my rucksack. 'South-west. Dorset.'

I wasn't sure if Dorset was a town or a county. I just remembered Louise saying that's where her dad's place was, *in the wilds of Dorset.*

Being in a lorry cab is like sitting on the top deck of a bus. Right at the front. You own the road, you're in charge, special. I leant back, legs dangling. At least I was doing something. Always better to be doing something. Especially if you are a practical person. Which I am. Have to be when you're dyslexic. Like at work it had been my idea to heat up the breakfast beans in the microwave. Left more room on the hob for Primrose to do the eggs and fried bread. *Eased congestion* like they were always going on about in London. I could come up with good ideas sometimes, see; ways round things. Clever ways. You might think trusting Louise showed the opposite, mind. But what would you have done? Go on. Tell me. In my situation, not yours? Yeah, exactly.

'Got friends down there, have you?' the driver asked, his eyes on the road.

Lorry drivers don't have to concentrate on driving because everything else just gets out of their way. Quite fancied driving one myself. It gives them plenty of time to talk, though. That's one of the drawbacks of hitching.

'Yeah, got a mate down there.' My lip curled on the word *mate.*

'Expecting you early, is he?'

'*She* ain't expecting me at all,' I growled, under my breath.

He only heard the *she.* Seemed to think it was a green light to get matey. Fumbled in a door compartment.

He offered me a fag from a crumpled packet. 'I'm on the e-cigs now, myself. Vaping.' He lit up and the cab filled with mint-flavoured steam. TJ's e-cigs smelt of fruit. I'd never see him again. I bit down on my lip because it didn't do to weaken.

Soon as I lit up, John – that was his name; I told him mine was Mary – started on about his ex-wife. That is another drawback of hitching. Another way you pay for it. Drivers tell you their problems. You're alone, just the two of you, see, and they're not looking at you, they're looking at the road. They don't know you and won't ever see you again. So you're their psychiatrist. But at least when they're telling you their problems, they're not asking you about yours.

John's ex-wife had kept the house and the two kids and the two dogs. He seemed more worried about the dogs than anything else, how she was turning them against him, how one had snapped at his trouser leg last time . . . The cab was warm and stuffy and John's voice went on and on. I hadn't slept properly for days and I felt my eyes closing. I must have dropped off because when I lifted my head we were pulling into a service station. It was past nine by then. Snarls of traffic.

'Wakey-wakey.' John tapped my hand. He must have only just noticed I was asleep because he didn't seem riled. He said he'd ask if any other drivers were going on to Dorset because he was headed for Portsmouth.

I had time to go to the toilet and have a drink of water. Wasn't going to waste money on overpriced tea. When I came out John had fixed me up with a young bloke that had a truck and was going to the ferry in Poole, which was in Dorset.

The new bloke looked me up and down when I came out of the toilet. Bad sign. I'm not much to look at – and not much of me to look at neither. Not that he was anything to write home about himself. Shaved head and a squashed-looking nose. Normally, I would have given him a go-boil-your-head stare, but I couldn't because he was doing me a favour.

'In you go, missus,' he opened his cab door. Practically pushed me in.

'Good luck, John,' I called out to the lorry driver because he wasn't a bad bloke, just lonely.

I wasn't so sure about this new one, Steve – 'Stevey-boy', he called himself. He texted while he was driving, laughed at the messages he got back. And when he wasn't looking at his phone he was looking at me, at my legs, my legs in their two pairs of jeans. They were so tight they felt like they were cutting off my blood supply. Like the waistband button could pop off any moment. Glad I was wearing them, though, the way Stevey-boy was leching.

He could attack me, you might be thinking. Could be a serial killer. You probably got a good life going on, which is why you'd worry about stuff like that. My future had just vanished down the plughole – though that didn't mean I wouldn't fight back with every bone in my body. Takes people, men, off their guard when a woman stands up for herself, especially one that is smaller.

# 41

The truck rattled along. Stevey-boy drove too fast. Laughed when he went over bumps and dips and I flew up in the air. Kept talking. Took his eyes off the road. Pushed his great ugly mug up close. I ain't deaf, I wanted to scream.

We passed a sign for Southampton. He asked me what I was going to *get up to* in Dorset. Would have given me a nudge only I was right up by the passenger door.

I'm going to kill someone, I nearly told him, to shut him up. Instead I came out with the 'meeting up with an old mate' story. Got the same old spiel from him too. No, *she* was a woman.

'Where she live then, your mate?' Stevey-boy leant right over. He was staring at my chest – probably trying to spot it, because what little there was of it was covered up by three T-shirts, a jumper and a jacket.

'Out in the wilds somewhere.'

'Yeah? Hippie, is she?'

'Nah. She's into . . . um . . . art.'

I shifted on the seat, trying to get comfortable. It was mostly the jeans digging in. No way was I undoing anything, though. Stevey-boy was seriously getting on my nerves. Nosey, too close, staring.

'What's her address, then? I'll put the postcode in the sat-nav and take you right there.' He gave me a wink. His broad nose got even wider when he smiled. Made me want to flatten it. Another wink. 'You scratch my back and I'll scratch yours.' I waited for a *know what I mean?* but it didn't come.

Yeah, right. I looked out of the window so he didn't see me rolling my eyes. Then I had to tell him I didn't actually know Louise's address.

He handed me his phone. 'Google your mate's name and it'll tell you. I've got an app for it.'

Mine was pay as you go. Didn't have no internet. Or no app, whatever that was. It was switched off anyway, just in case TJ texted me. He'd have got my note by now. Be in shock, probably. Wouldn't want anything more to do with me. But just a chance he might text to try to put me off hunting down Louise.

I fumbled with the phone. I wasn't good with technology. Plus I didn't know how to spell Louise's surname. Not that I'd tell Stevey-boy that. I just knew it was a long one with a poncy little line in the middle. Trust her.

'Here, you do it.' I handed it back. I said her name. Made me feel sick, saying it.

Doing seventy, no hands on the wheel, Stevey-boy tapped in her name. And there she was:

*Foxholes*

*Melbury Weston*

*Dorset*

*DT2 0LW*

I hadn't expected it to be that easy. Hadn't been sure I'd ever find her. Definitely didn't expect to be delivered to her doorstep. And you can bet your bottom dollar Louise wouldn't be expecting it either.

'See how good Stevey-boy is to you,' he winked again. 'Know what I mean?'

I had to nod, mutter, 'Yeah, thanks.' Try to smile, which isn't easy when all the time you're turning over in your mind exactly how you're going to kill someone.

The roads got more winding. I felt sick even though it had been hours since the piece of bread and butter I'd eaten on the hoof earlier. Not long till I'd be banging on the door of Louise's stately home.

I reached down to feel the knife in my sock. Hadn't used a knife on anyone before. Only the painting. Louise had tricked me. Lost me nearly a year of being good. Lost me Alastair. She'd lied about Enid, *used* Enid, even though old Enid was frolicking in Romania now, not knowing anything about it.

I worked myself up so much I couldn't hardly breathe. I'd been trying to keep a lid on things for weeks. Now I felt I could explode, boil over like one of Juice's stews when she turned it up too high. Felt I could fly out the cab, into Louise's stately bloody home's bloody window and stab her in the heart. And before I killed her I'd hold the knife to her throat and make her tell me where the painting was. Her fat chins would wobble, her hair would be all over the place. But she'd give it back.

I'm going to stop calling her Louise. Spell her name wrong on purpose, not through being dyslexic. Put the 'i' the other side of the 's' and you get lousie. Someone had spelt Louise like that on one of her certificates. It had given me and Enid a giggle. Lousie. That was her.

It was getting darker outside, which was odd seeing as it was the middle of the morning. Tree branches scraped against the cab's roof. I looked at Stevey-boy. Wasn't getting ideas, was he? Looking for somewhere quiet, out the way, to pull in so we could get to know each other better? I bent down to straighten my sock. Pulled the knife out a fraction.

But he'd stopped leering. Even put his phone down. He was swearing at the sat-nav. 'Where the fuck have you taken us, bitch?' and 'I'm going to be fucking late!' The sat-nav stayed calm, in spite of him swearing. She behaved like they tell you to in anger management. 'Turn around where possible,' she kept saying. Nice to hear her bossing Stevey-boy about.

The narrow road was like a tunnel. Trees overhanging it on both sides. No space to turn around. No time neither because Stevey boy wasn't slowing down. We shot along. Flew up a hill, the wheels banging and crashing because the road was more like a track. Stevey-boy kept on about being in trouble at the depot if he was late again.

I pushed the knife back in my sock. No time for hanky-panky then. What a pity. Not. I could just concentrate on killing Louise, *lousie*, now. (I know she should have a capital letter but she's not going to get one.)

Only it turned out there wasn't time to concentrate on ruddy anything because the next second we flew off the top of the hill into outer space and it was only something coming up the other way that brought us back down to earth.

Just before everything went black, I felt a tingle of pleasure. I'd read the road sign, even though we were going so fast. It was a red triangle with a big exclamation mark. And the words BLIND SUMMIT.

I woke up to Stevey-boy groaning and the doom-laden nee-naw of a police car. To murky light like I was underwater.

I tried to get out of my seat. Had to get out. Else I'd be caught before I even got to lousie. But I couldn't move.

I wasn't hurt. I could wiggle my toes. Move my arms. My head ached and I'd kill for a drink and a fag, but that was normal. There was a heaviness in my chest. It was because my life had gone down the plughole. No, something was pressing *on* my chest. Something soft. I struggled. Felt panicky to be honest, but I had been through a lot.

It wasn't a body. It was the airbag wedging me in my seat. The truck's bonnet was all stove in. I was trapped. A sitting duck.

Weird when a person in a uniform is nice to you. It took me back to finding Jack in the lift, all those months ago. Before this year, they'd have been dragging me off somewhere. Clutching a notebook and not ruddy listening.

I sat inside the ambulance, getting my head together. There was a gash on my leg that I hadn't even noticed. A paramedic, a no-nonsense sort, with a swinging ponytail, bandaged it up. Gave me one of those shiny blankets like what you wrap round a turkey at Christmas. I'd seen them on the ads. We'd only had a turkey once and that had been a present from Nan. Other years we'd had chicken, and not always a whole one, neither.

At A&E they shone a torch in my eyes and felt me all over. No young doc this time taking a personal interest. I got off with just a minor leg wound because of the airbag and wearing a seat belt.

Stevey-boy, *not* wearing a seat belt, had had his ribs crushed. He was going to be very, very late at the depot. The other car was a write-off, they said, but nobody hurt.

I was shook up, thanks to Stevey-boy. Tired. Thirsty. And still off my head with anger, of course. You name a bad feeling and I was feeling it. I'd have given anything for a Stella or four.

Next stop was the police station. Sitting on a swivel chair and answering questions, seeing as I was a witness to the accident.

A cop brought me an extra-large, extra-sweet mug of tea. And a sandwich from the canteen. Gave me a friendly wink. Chatted about it being his turn to pick up his daughter from school later. She'd test him on what she'd learnt in her lessons today, even though she was only six, going on sixty.

I ate the sandwich and drank the tea. Felt less shaky. The cop didn't bring up the painting. TJ must still be keeping schtum. I'd taken the knife out of my sock soon as I'd got in the ambulance and put it in the rucksack. I wasn't daft. Reckon it was the knife that had cut my leg, come to think of it.

I spun round on the chair like I had nothing to hide. Don't expect I looked like someone gearing up for murder.

The cop asked me to slow down answering his questions about Stevey-boy and his sat-nav. 'My spelling's not the greatest. The missus says I'm dyslexic.'

'You and me both, mate.' First time I'd ever called a copper 'mate'. I brushed the sandwich crumbs off the desk. Cheese and pickle. Don't think I'd had such a bog-standard sandwich since I'd been in London.

I got my personal spelling dictionary out of my rucksack to show the cop. All that had gone for a burton, but I was still a show-off. He looked at it, then at me, not taking a note for a minute. Then, when we had a break, he brought me another mug of tea and a packet of fags and a KitKat and a woman's magazine, not *Woman's World,* unfortunately. This one had TV stars looking chubby and pissed off all over the front of it. He must have nipped out specially. Gruff-like, when he handed them over. I got out a *thanks, mate*, and took a hot gulp of tea so I didn't weaken.

When he asked what I was doing down here I nearly told him. Reckon the accident had fried my brain. Made me think we really were mates. I said I'd been visiting a friend. Made out I needed to get back to London. Said I couldn't get my bearings. I knew me and Stevey-boy had been close to lousie's gaff. Gone off course since, with the hospital and that.

The cop was helpful. 'Give me a map any day, rather than a notebook,' he said. Spread a local one out on his desk.

He pointed to the nearest railway station. Dorchester. I nodded like I was going to head straight there, but out of the corner of my eye I saw the capital M and W of Melbury Weston. Where lousie's stately home was. It only looked a few miles off. I could walk it. Power-walk it. Walk over there and kill her.

# 42

A few miles is further than you think. My leg stung a bit. It was afternoon now, what with all the faffing around with forms and statements at the police station. The cop had filled them in. (Had to keep looking at a checklist at the back of his notebook.) Still only afternoon and a whole lot had happened. Getting dark, though, as it was December. I hadn't given the cop my real name and address (wasn't sure I even had an address any more). Yeah, he'd been OK but old habits die hard. Besides, TJ might have told someone what I'd done by now. Pretty soon the police might be looking for Marguerite McNaughton, known as Maggsie. It wasn't that TJ was a snitch. But he was into all that confession stuff. Plus he worried about people. Even people like me. He used to, anyway.

The road was narrow. No pavement or streetlamps. I had to keep flattening myself into the hedge as cars whizzed past. A big person would have found it more difficult. In between the noise of the cars there were creepy rustlings in the undergrowth.

I was worn out. Head still thumping from the collision. Cold, tired. Close to giving up, actually. I smoked one of the cop's fags, walking along. Dark now. Just the odd flash of headlights as a car roared by. The hedge got higher. I stubbed out my fag and stopped for a moment to breathe in the fresh air. Faint whiff of manure to it.

There was a rustle of wings, something hooting. Cows mooing from a barn. A dog barking. Then another one answering. Stuffed with animals, the countryside. I stepped over a muddy patch. And then I remembered, with an awful jolt, worse than what I'd got in the crash, something lousie had said first time we met. She'd been showing off about her family welcoming her back. Yeah, right. Boasted about a family holiday, *before the Christmas mayhem*. Diving off some tropical island. We were pre-Christmas now. Bet she wasn't even *in* her ruddy stately home! I stopped. Stamped my feet with the frustration of it. I even growled, seeing as there was no one around to hear me. That would be just my luck. Yeah, bet she was bulging out of a bikini somewhere hot. Ruddy hoped she drowned.

So what was I doing scrambling about in the wilds and the cold and the dark if she'd already gone? It was hunting down lousie that had kept me going. What the hell was I going to do now? No way was she going to get away with ruining my life!

I started walking again. All over the place in my head but still heading for Melbury ruddy Weston. Didn't know what else to do. Fewer cars now so at least I could walk in the road. Pitch black, though. I switched my phone on for the light. Three texts from TJ. Probably telling me to come back and face the music. Having a go at me for being a criminal. Lucky he'd never know I'd planned on being a murderer as well. No good reading them. I had to get even with lousie somehow. And I didn't want TJ putting me off, thank you very much. I deleted them. Really quick to save my battery.

I stumbled in the dark. An idea struck me. Lousie might have wanted the painting so she could give it to her dad. Boost his art collection. Posh up his ruddy stately home. She'd gone on about him inside. *Daddy's girl*, Enid had said. So lousie wouldn't be there, but the painting might be. In a private bit of the house, probably, seeing as it was stolen. By me. Suddenly I knew in my water – as Enid would have said – that was where it was.

So I carried on heading for her stately home. Only now it was to find the painting, not her. Getting it back would be putting things right. That was better, wasn't it? Yeah, I saw the people I looked up to nodding their heads, even baby Alastair, whose head could only wobble. Killing lousie was the sort of thing that got you locked up for years and years, anyway. Look at what had happened to poor old Enid.

I was good at rescuing things. I'd saved Jack from all that electric, rescued Audrey from starving to death up a tree. Now I was going to take a painting away from a lonely life shut up in some toffee-nosed crook's stately home. Put it back where it had come from. (From where I'd *stole* it, but I glossed over that bit.) Wonder Woman, that was me. I had a sudden vision of a grown-up Alastair, arms wide, running towards me.

No, too early yet to think about Alastair.

I walked faster now I had a plan. A respectable one. The sort of plan you read about in the *Metro*, under a headline like Plucky Maggsie Saves the Day. I swung my arms. A bit more traffic now. I had to walk close to the hedge again. Brambles seemed to have it in for my jacket. I ducked my head each time a car passed because a white face shows up in the dark and I was on my way to do a bit of trespassing. Annoying taking the painting *back*, putting something right, might be illegal.

A sign: MELBURY WESTON. I walked past a straggly row of thatched cottages. At the end was a board for Iousie's house: FOXHOLES – SIXTEENTH-CENTURY HOUSE, OPEN FRIDAYS, SATURDAYS AND SUNDAYS, CREAM TEAS, REFRESHMENTS. A smaller sign underneath: CLOSED OCTOBER TO MARCH. I read it all easy-peasy.

Then a long gravel drive. It was quieter, walking on the grass. A car park, empty. Just one car, a Land Rover, close to the house.

No lights at the front. Lousie had said 'a family retainer' lived in while they were away. Probably watching TV in some tiny back room full of spiders and cobwebs.

As I got closer the security light came on, which was handy. The house was faded red brick, windows with diamond-shaped panes of glass, ivy, the lot. Like you see on biscuit tins at Christmas.

I spotted a little window on the first floor that was half open at the top. A bathroom or toilet, then. You'd be amazed how often they're left open.

Bathrooms have drainpipes. Shinning up that would be my best way in. There was a concrete footpath underneath. My heart thumped. It might not hold my weight. Didn't fancy smashing my head open. That's when I had to give myself a talking-to. *You've done a lot of climbing recently. And years of experience before, getting into places you shouldn't. You're small, Maggsie. And this is where being small really comes into its own.*

I nodded at myself. Got both arms around the drainpipe. Shook it. Firmly attached. So I just went for it. My fingers scrabbled for a grip on the smooth metal.

All I could do was pray I didn't fall. Didn't have no time to actually pray. Even Primrose wouldn't have. I just said *God, God, God* over and over again. Can't remember if I said it out loud, or if it was in my head.

One foot each side. Hand over hand like I'd done with the rope on Audrey's tree. Ruddy tiring. I was out of breath time I got to the window. I hung on to the ledge for a minute. Not many people could do what I'd just done.

Pushed the window wider and I was in. Inside lousie's house.

Yeah, it was a bathroom. A huge old bath, deepest I'd ever seen. I could lie flat out in the bottom of it if I needed to hide. I stood behind the door now, chest heaving. Switched on my phone for the light. More texts from TJ. No time to read them. What was I doing, flashed through my brain for a second. What would I do if that old servant heard me? I listened. No TV or nothing. Nobody moving around. Got my breath under control. Then I heard a bark. Oh, no. That was all I needed. A ruddy dog poking its nose, and jaws, in.

I still had yesterday's sandwiches in my rucksack, or was it the day before's, I'd lost track of time. What with the policeman giving me grub, and that *adren . . . adrian . . .* something, firing me up, I hadn't been hungry. I took off my rucksack and got them out now. Roast beef with something hot and peppery, and a vegetarian one. I could see a bit of green poking out. They'd keep a dog at bay. All dogs were dustbins, weren't they? Not as bright as cats.

Another bark, nearer. Panting. I drew back, holding out a sandwich. A dog shambled in. A big dog as far as I could see with just my phone. A black Labrador, like toffs have. Bit stiff-legged, grey round its face. Drooping jowls. It didn't seem to see too well. Banged into the bathroom door on its way in. Smelt the sandwich, though. Four halves, I had in total. It wolfed one down in two snaps. Nothing wrong with its teeth. Snappy came to mind with the smell of vinegar that always seemed to be about him, because of the smashed gherkin jar. I'd seen him as a real person – well, reptile. Company, even, not just an anger management strategy.

I tucked the knife back in my sock and stashed my rucksack in the bath. Kept the sandwiches and my phone on me, though. Tiptoed down a corridor. The dog followed me, its nose much too close to my bum.

A big, big house. The painting could be anywhere. Anywhere not open to the public. Pity poor old lousie's pa couldn't show it off. Not without him or lousie getting caught. He must have *known* it was stolen. Must have. He was supposed to be a ruddy art expert, wasn't he? Well, here I was, stealing it back. Not to keep for myself, like that pair of selfish gits, to return it to Scanda's boardroom. Put her back with her other mates from Denmark. Looking out over the London skyline and getting on with her book.

Most likely the painting was upstairs. Most likely not even on this floor. I hunted for the stairs. Lousie had been right about one thing: it was a very old house. Creaky floors, smell of musty wood and lavender polish everywhere. No carpets, just rugs. When I put my hand out to the walls they were covered with rough, bumpy old cloths.

The dog made more noise than I did. It trailed after me, its nose still poking my backside. I stopped and gave it a little bit of sandwich, the vegetarian one, to get it off.

A slobber and a swallow, then it was off again. Further along the corridor it gave off a loud series of farts. That's the trouble with vegetarian food, well, vegetables full stop. Juice was always moaning about bloating. Will, Ruby's boyfriend, being vegan, ate nothing but. He must be ruddy explosive in bed.

Ruby. Jingle of earrings, swish of an ethnic skirt. I'd texted her earlier from the police station. Told her the truth. Well, a bit of it. Told her I'd been in an accident. I wasn't hurt but I couldn't get back tonight. That was against the rules. Let's face it, everything I was doing was against the rules. I'd thought my text was a sort of goodbye to Ruby, seeing as I'd been on my way to give lousie what for. But now . . . I stopped. The dog bumped into me and I had to give it another bit of sandwich. It snuffled around the rug for crumbs. Could I even go back to the supported house? Would I be allowed? I pushed the dog away with my knee. If I brought the painting back, would I still have my job? Nah. No chance. I'd stolen from Scanda. No way would they have me back. That was a downer after I'd been so fired up at doing the right thing.

The stairs were very steep. The dog struggled. Gave up and stood at the bottom. I could hear its tail wagging and another fart. It whined. Then barked. 'Shh!' I threw it down another piece of sandwich. Course it couldn't see it, so there was a lot of sniffing and slobbering.

I made my way along the upstairs corridor. I could see by the light of my phone that all the doors were closed. Like Russian roulette opening them. The first door was a cupboard full of bedding. Lots of white sheets, all folded up neat. Reminded me of the hotel I'd got sacked from on my first day for not being able to read the cleaning schedule.

The next door was another bathroom. An old-fashioned bath again, but a modern shower over. A modern-looking toilet. The one on the first floor had had a wooden seat and a dangling chain. I had an urge to use this one. Opening all these doors with who knows what behind them turned your insides to water.

I breathed out. Opened another door. Late-night horror films – Kasia had a weakness for them – sprang to mind. A four-poster bed like they had in the olden days. Its curtains drawn. Could be someone behind them. Could be a nest of rats. Could be a skeleton. I almost wished the dog was up here with me. Could be someone inside who'd been trapped there for hundreds of years.

# 43

*Marguerite McNaughton*, echoed from school, from Mrs Connell, my horrible teacher, *you can put that idea out of your head for a start.* Funny – it pulled me up, although I'd hated her.

I turned away from the bed. Flashed my phone round the walls. Wood panelling. Paintings. I moved close. Dogs with dead things hanging out their mouths. Bowls of ancient-looking fruit. Not half as good as the barmaid's bowl of oranges in Ruby's poster. Even though it was a photocopy. A hot wave of shame flashed through me, remembering I'd thought photocopies were as good as the real thing. No *Woman Reading* here. Perhaps lousie *had* sold it. Perhaps it had paid for her family's diving holiday. I was thinking negative like they went on about on the *Woman's World* agony page. I didn't *know* she'd sold it. Keep going, Maggs.

How many more rooms? How many people lived here usually? Who did the cleaning? I tiptoed on. Opened the next door a crack. Listened for sounds of breathing. Pointed my phone inside, covering the torch bit with my hand because it was so bright. Twin beds. A wardrobe with its doors wide open. An old-fashioned alarm clock on a bedside table. More pictures. I shone my phone in a slow circle. A couple of red-faced men in wigs. Another man in tights and a hat with a curly feather. A bad-tempered-looking woman, in black, with a black hat clamped to her head. I wanted to turn her to face the wall, only TJ said that paintings in galleries had alarms behind them that screamed if you touched them. I flashed my phone above the beds. And there she was. The *Woman Reading*. Glowing in the darkness in the light from my phone. My legs trembled.

I moved close. She looked OK. Dull colours, but deep; drew you in, like. Not shiny. Blushed again at TJ being right. Lousie's pa had stuck her in a heavy carved frame. Show-offy. Didn't suit her. I climbed onto the bed. Tweedy cover pulled up. Bet this was where he slept. Bet he lay there, looking up the woman's skirt. When he wasn't wheeling and dealing, or diving, or showing off his posh house and his art collection.

I reached out to touch the frame. I didn't want an uproar. Even though the whole house seemed to be deserted. An alarm would be linked to the police station. Probably the one I'd been in earlier. As I leant towards the painting someone shoved the back of my knees. I heard heavy breathing as they gave way.

The ruddy dog had somehow hobbled up the stairs. It sat down by the bed, whining, slobber dripping from its jowls.

I sat up. My heart was still going. Funny I wasn't angry. I was almost pleased to see the dog. It was the relief. Made me realize how much I didn't want to get caught. OK, I'd strayed off the straight and narrow, but there was still a faint chance Alastair might be at the end of it. 'They ought to retire you, mate.' I tossed the dog the third half-sandwich, the roast beef. 'You're more of a ruddy receptionist than a guard dog.' Then I stood back up and checked there were no wires behind the painting. Gently unhooked the lady. Spoke soothing and stuffed her inside my jacket like she was Audrey.

Now to get out. I pushed past the dog, still hunting crumbs on the carpet. Crept down to the first floor. Paused. Silence, only a faint whimper from the dog at the top of the stairs. I heard it retch. That would be the peppery sauce hitting the back of its throat. Best to go out the same way I'd come in, via the drainpipe. The 'old family retainer' had probably dozed off in front of the TV. Probably exhausted by all the work lousie's family made her do. Bet they kept her chained up.

I threw the last sandwich up to the dog and headed for the bathroom. Slung on my rucksack and pushed open the window, far as it would go. Climbed out onto the sill. My fingers scrabbled on the bricks. The surface took a bit of skin off.

I crouched, clung to the window frame. Couldn't see much in the dark. No spare hand for my phone. Eased my legs off. They swung free for a second, like I was a ruddy trapeze artist. Then one foot banged against the drainpipe.

I shifted my grip along. Got one arm around it. Then both. Slid down in a rush. Landed in a heap at the bottom. Took too much weight on one ankle. Nice to have my feet on the ground, though. Nice to have the painting. Rescuing it was putting things right *and* getting one over on lousie. Didn't even mind the bits of me throbbing. They were war wounds. I dusted off my hands and headed for the empty car park and the road. The *Woman Reading* banged against my chest each step I took like she wanted to get out.

Midnight now. No one around. The air was cold and

damp, fresh-smelling. You could see the stars really clear as well, because there were hardly any lights.

I remembered there'd been road signs in the village. DORCHESTER: HISTORIC COUNTY TOWN, one said. (See, eighteen months ago, inside, I wouldn't have been able to read that. I'd have been completely lost.)

The cop had told me Dorchester had a train station. I could get a train back to London. Didn't know how late they ran. Might have to hang about. If the police caught up with me I'd have some explaining to do. They'd never believe I was taking the painting *back*. I'd only missed a day at work, so far. Didn't want it to be any more. Hang on. I'd probably already lost my job even though I'd risked my life saving the painting.

*A painting you stole*, I heard someone who tried to keep me on the straight and narrow say. *How could you have been so stupid?* My sister, Nella, putting her oar in.

Another long walk. No cars, so I could walk in the road. Easier than wading through brambles and long grass. No light, though. I couldn't use my phone too much because of the battery going. I saw a couple of foxes, chasing each other. Gave me a fright hearing them crashing about. I imagined it was the old retainer coming after me, or, worse, whatever had been behind the curtains of the four-poster bed. An owl swooped over-head like a police helicopter. Made me jump, that did, but it didn't matter because there was no one around to see me do it.

Another olde-worlde village. Grey stone houses huddled together, a village pond with ducks. Heads under their wings. Curled up like Audrey. Even the pub had a thatched roof.

I was tired. Must have walked near on ten miles in all. I'd been in a crash, been in a police station, been thieving – sort of – in a stately home. Been in the country. Hadn't slept. Hadn't hardly slept for days before. Blimey, how much more can you pack in, Maggsie, I asked myself. I flicked out my hair like I'd seen lousie do, only mine was under an imaginary Wonder Woman headband.

DORCHESTER ½ MILE, a sign said. Thank God for that. Then I'd have to find the station. Avoid the police, avoid anyone asking awkward questions and avoid anyone staring at my rigid chest. Lucky I had all those T-shirts on. I'd have to get on the right train. Have to buy a ticket, now I was back on the straight and narrow. I still had most of the money I'd taken with me yesterday morning. It felt like weeks ago.

Dorchester wasn't as big as it made itself out to be. Old-fashioned place. No skyscrapers. Some of the shops looked like they'd been there hundreds of years. Bristling with museums. I peered in at one, marching past. Not free, though, not like in London.

Found a signpost on the next corner. Spotted the railway logo. Two train stations, though! Only a little place, but with ideas above its station. Hah! Funny I was cracking jokes when I was on the run. It was because I was on the run *back*. Not that the police would see the difference.

# 44

**Woman's World,** 5 December 2018
The Romance of the Train!

Dithering over the two stations pulled me up. Made me doubt myself for a minute. I had done the right thing, hadn't I, getting the painting back? *The right thing, but the wrong way*, I could hear Ruby saying. I wasn't going to stand there and listen to her.

South then. Dorchester South.

Trains to London this side. Phew, I'd been right then. Saved me a bit of walking. I was getting so tired I couldn't hardly put one foot in front of the other.

Never thought I'd be relieved to see the word *London*. That it would give me a thrill, even.

I was glad no one was around. Till I realized it was because there were no ruddy trains. The lit-up sign said the next one wasn't until 3:33. No drinks machine neither. I would have killed for a hot, sweet tea. Would have been almost better than a Stella. Nowhere to buy a ticket. There was a widdling little machine but if you think I was going to faff about pressing buttons, trying to *select* poxy *options* late at night, you're more stupid than I am. There was a windswept sort of shelter. I lay on a bench for some shut-eye. Too ruddy cold, though, plus I didn't want to be out of it when the train came. I huddled up, sitting, and dozed, my chin resting on the *Woman Reading* tucked inside my T-shirts.

I was the only one getting on the train. The guard was red-faced and chubby. Cheerful. Too cheerful. Said he'd been up since two a.m. and how it was the best time of the day. Only if you were an owl.

When he said how much a ticket to London cost, I nearly passed out. 'Child's ticket?' he'd asked first and I wished I'd nodded, instead of giving him a frosty stare. 'Peak time, see,' the guard said, when I gaped at him. How can minging three thirty a.m. be peak time? Not exactly rush hour, is it? But he meant the time we got into Waterloo. Even six thirty is rush hour in London, seeing as people go to work all hours of the day or night. So bang went half my savings. But not buying a ticket was a kind of stealing. And I'd stopped all that. Alastair wouldn't want a fare-dodger for a mum.

A jolt of electric went through me hearing *Waterloo*. Brought home I'd be facing a lot of angry people back in London.

I had a good wash in the toilet. Not much room and the hot-air dryer hardly worked. But nice to have no one queuing outside. Three of us squabbling over the upstairs bathroom back at the house sometimes. Kasia spent hours shaving her legs and God knows what else in there. I pushed away the thought that I might never use that bathroom again.

I propped the *Woman Reading* on the floor and put on fresh clothes. Best chance I'd had of taking off the extra pair of jeans. I looked like I'd been dragged through a hedge backwards. I had, more or less, but at least it had been me doing the dragging. I cleaned my teeth. Combed my hair. It didn't look too bad, considering I'd been in a crash and up and down a drainpipe. Kasia had done a good job there. My ginger roots were only just showing through. Another packet of brown dye to fork out on. I fastened the lady back into my jacket and went back to the carriage. Lay down on a row of three seats. I took my shoes off first, so I could curl up. Reckon you can only sleep proper on a train if you're small.

The train took its time. Seemed to stop at every station in Britain. When I woke up it was five fourteen on my phone. Still dark outside. I didn't know where I was. There were other people in the carriage now. I could hear papers rustling, someone chatting on their mobile.

I was stiff all over, especially my right ankle where I'd slid down the drainpipe too sudden. The top of my chest was sore from where the *Woman Reading*'s frame had rubbed. Like lousie's pa was getting his revenge. I sat up and stretched; well, as much as you could when you've got a half-million-pound painting down your jacket.

I peered around the seat. All the rest were full now. People with earphones, reading papers, frowning at laptops. They'd given me a wide berth. Maybe they'd thought I was a tramp because I was sleeping on a train. Showed how much they knew. I had a job and a home. At least, I hoped I did.

A voice came over the tannoy. The next station was Winchester. There was a map of the train route by the window. I could read it OK. That was one of the best things, maybe *the* best thing, that had ever happened to me, being able to read. Win-*chester*, I found on the route map, like Dor-*chester*.

I texted TJ. Just to let him know I was still alive. He was a worrier. And too late now for him to stop me doing *bad thing*. I said I was on the train 'with her'. Hoped he'd realize I meant the painting.

I hauled up my rucksack and headed for the toilet again. Had to wait this time. Smartly dressed people staring. I smoothed down my hair. Stared back.

Hard to keep my balance, putting on eyebrow pencil and mascara. So much for people thinking I was a tramp. 'Beggars can't be choosers,' Nan used to say when she gave us sugar sandwiches Sunday teatimes. I'd never been a beggar but I'd come close. Used to think I'd end up as one, seeing as I was too thick to do anything else. There was a thump on the door. Cheek. I gave the door-thumper, a woman in a suit jacket and too much lipstick, a frosty stare when I came out.

No more texts from TJ. He'd probably lost interest. If he'd snitched, the police might be waiting for me at Scanda. I might be walking straight into their arms. Might not even get past Reception. Might get locked up. Nah, my imagination was going into overdrive. Not enough sleep. Not as if lousie and her pa could press charges, was it? But Scanda could. I mean, I *had* stolen *Woman Reading*. Giving it back might not change that.

I went round and round like that for ages. In the end I was so tired I dozed off.

I woke up near London. Knew we were near there because of all the high-rises, lit up. Began to feel jittery.

Hordes at Waterloo. Worse than Sundays. I got through the ticket barrier without being crushed. Looked around for the tube sign.

'Maggsie!' I heard. 'I am here.'

I stopped. Looked up, heart pounding, heat rising in my face. A bearded man behind, with a briefcase, didn't stop when I did. Carried on striding. Practically pushed me into TJ's arms.

His eyes were so screwed up with smiling, you couldn't hardly see them. His fair eyelashes were damp. Always been too soft for his own good. Good job he was a law-abiding citizen. Wouldn't last five minutes banged up.

He took my hands. Pumped them up and down. That was the kind of thing that showed he was foreign. The kind of thing that made people look at him. That and his height. And his shoes.

'What you doing here, TJ? How did you know what train I'd be on?'

He shouldered my rucksack and took my elbow through the crowd. It was a relief when he took it. And not just through having nothing to carry. Amazing he wasn't angry. Amazing he was here.

'I google timetable. Work out time from Winchester.' He looked down at me, his eyes creasing into grooves, like the ones Primrose forked onto her shepherd's pies. 'We go back to Scanda together, yes?'

'Yeah.' What would Scanda do with me? I saw them all in Reception, waiting: the HR woman; Mike and Darren, the security officers; Mr H, in his jeans. None of them smiling and clapping. A police car lurking outside.

We had an hour before we needed to leave. It was still only six thirty, for Heaven's sake. Good of TJ to get up so early. Good of him to come. 'We've got time for a cuppa first, ain't we, TJ? I've been dying for one all night.'

We had one upstairs near Waterloo East where TJ got his Lewisham train from. A bit quieter up there. Nice to look at all the people dashing about and not be down there with them. TJ had brought me some fags even though he'd given up smoking. I couldn't smoke here, but I turned the packet over and over in my pocket.

Tapped my rigid chest to check the *Woman Reading* was still OK. It – she – gave off a hollow sound.

When I hadn't turned up for work yesterday, TJ had told them I was out of sorts. Which was true. He hadn't told them anything else, not about the painting or me going off to hunt someone down. He was too dizzy, he said. Dazed, I think he meant, only I was too tired to correct him. He hadn't understood all my note. And I'd spent ages over it, trying to word it right. My handwriting wasn't *that* bad. 'But I trust you to sort things out. Only I worry because you not answer texts.'

I nearly told him I was busy roaming *the wilds of Dorset*. Recovering from an accident. But, like I said, he was a worrier. He didn't have to know all the details. And, blimey, he'd trusted me to sort things out. He was the first, then.

Just as well we did have an hour. I poured everything else out. It was the lack of sleep. Plus still being in shock from the accident, plus months of reading and writing agony letters, where people poured out stuff all the time. In the end, well, before the end, TJ had to go off and buy us another cuppa, my throat got so dry talking. I told him everything. Even about prison. Even about Alastair. I wanted him to know everything. First time in my life I wanted to tell someone something I was ashamed of.

He didn't say much. Nodded. Touched my hand a couple of times. Blinked when it came to me trying to stay a year on the straight and narrow for Alastair. He'd just thought I wanted to get on in life. He sat there with his tea. Didn't walk away or nothing.

He was amazed I'd taken the *Woman Reading* without him even noticing. Amazed she'd spent nearly three hours in a big old serving dish at the top of our store cupboard. He slapped his thigh. Even more amazed I'd stolen it back. He hadn't understood my text from the train either. What was it with him? He'd thought *with her* meant I was sharing my train seat with that skanky rat-arse lousie. I'd rather wrestle a pig than go anywhere with her. Made my skin crawl the painting still linking us together. And that I was going back to a rollicking, and she was going to get off scot-free. Only her pa that was going to be pissed off with *her.*

'You climb up drainpipe?' TJ's eyes were like saucers.

'Yeah. And down.'

He shook his head. 'I would not have courage.'

I took a nice deep breath in; my chest, behind the painting, puffing up. No need to tell him my original plan had been to kill lousie. That I still had Juice's vegetable knife tucked down my sock. Next to the bandage. Nice being Wonder Woman again. Even if it was only for an hour. Weird he saw that in me even after I'd told him about prison and giving up Alastair.

He reached over and took my hand.

There was something else to tell him. 'TJ, if I lose my job at Scanda . . .'

He nodded. 'My friend Pavel give job at restaurant. I have already told hard worker.'

'Yeah. Thanks. Thing is . . .' TJ didn't know I had a problem with drink. He was dead against alcohol because of his dad. Pity it hadn't affected me the same way. 'I've got a weakness, TJ. I don't want to work with booze.'

Even that didn't put him off. 'But restaurant not have licence. *Is* no booze.' He spread out his free arm, nearly knocking over his cup.

'Yeah?' I took another swig of tea. Hours since that

cuppa in the police station. 'Don't know if I'd be up to it, though, TJ. Scanda's the first job I've had.'

'You will be fine. You hard worker. Quick.' He still had hold of my hand.

My eyes were sore and tired. Made it hard to look at him. 'I been reckless, TJ. Gullible. This year thing hasn't gone to plan. Don't even know about contacting my son now. Don't know if I'm good enough.'

TJ didn't let go of my hand. 'You have had hard life, Maggsie. But now you do well. More important is you *try* to do things. You should be proud. Your son would be proud. The year does not matter.'

I had to fumble for a tissue so my mascara didn't run before I faced them at Scanda. Like I already told you, TJ was too soft for his own good. Just as well he got someone like me to look out for him.

My old headmaster had told me I'd never amount to anything. But TJ said as long as you *tried* to do stuff, kept trying, you were OK. On your way to being something. It was like he'd undone a curse.

He looked at his watch. 'Is nearly seven thirty. We go now to Scanda? I will be with.'

'With you. I mean, with me.' My insides turned over. I stood up. 'Got to pay a visit first.'

That was thirty pence like at King's Cross. I was running through my savings. Lucky I had my Oyster card. I half expected TJ to have done a runner, after the things I'd told him, but no, there he was, outside the toilet, smiling. Waiting for an ex-con, ex-alkie, with a stolen painting down her T-shirt, and smiling.

# 45

**Woman's World, 5 December 2018**
Here's How to Move Forward!

Coming up the tube steps near Scanda I had the same nerves as on my first day. Only now it was because I had a half-million-pound painting down my top.

Say if Mr H got the police involved when he'd heard the whole story? Wanted me punished for damaging his painting, abusing his trust? Even though I was bringing it *back*. Even though I'd *rescued* it. Risked my life.

TJ kept looking down at me. I was still there. He didn't have to keep checking.

'I wish I could do for you. Stand in shoes.'

I nearly fainted with shock when the blonde receptionist gave us a friendly smile. Never seen it before. Then I saw the grin on TJ's big round face. He was always smiling. That was the trouble. I drew myself up straight – having a chest like a ramrod helped – and jabbed him with my elbow. No time for socializing.

He went with me as far as the stairs. Then I went up the five flights on my own. Walking up I thought about my first day at Scanda. Finding Jack. How he'd sort of started things off. Then it had been the calendar. Later, that reference from Primrose. Audrey. My practice letters. All that could still go for a burton.

Mr H's door was right at the end of the corridor. Weird passing the boardroom. Weirder for the *Woman*

*Reading*. I didn't look in. My heart was hammering and it wasn't because of the stairs.

I knocked on the door.

'Come.'

I marched in. I didn't want to go in. What I wanted to do was leave the painting outside his office and scarper. Only then what? That's why I marched in.

He looked up from his computer. Geeky-looking glasses on the end of his nose. A V-necked jumper. Pink. Men did wear pink in London. He smiled. Perfect teeth, of course. He smiled because he didn't know why I was there. 'Marguerite, isn't it?'

I didn't smile because of my teeth. And because I had a painting I'd stole from him down my top. I nodded. 'Maggsie.' My face was burning.

'And what can I do for you, Maggsie?'

'I've got something. Something of yours.' I tugged out the painting. The frame got caught on my bra strap and there was a bit of a tussle. My face was scarlet now. 'Here.'

'Oh my God.' He stood up. 'The Hammershøi. My *Woman Reading*. Is it the real thing?' He touched it gently. Took it over to the window. Turned it over. 'It *is* her. How did you get hold of it? Tell me, tell me. Sit down.' He gestured to a chair, a spindly black one. I sat down, carefully.

He propped the lady against his screen. Looked younger now he'd taken off his glasses.

I shifted in the uncomfortable chair. My legs were dangling six inches off the floor. 'You ain't, aren't going to like it.'

He ran his hand through his hair when I told him. It stuck up after. I had to repeat the bits he didn't believe.

I told him everything except lousie's name. You might think I should have done. Thing is, you learn, inside, never to snitch. It's just you cons against the rest of them, see? So you don't drop people in it. Even if it's all their fault and they deserve everything they get like bloody lousie. That hefty wazzock was probably still swimming off a tropical beach somewhere with all her posh family. I imagined her struggling to get underwater, because of her size. Imagined her keeping popping up like a cork. Saw her surrounded by a sea of jellyfish. Stung to death, her skin a mass of little boils.

He shut his eyes when I said why I'd wanted to help Enid out. 'What a tangle.' When he opened them again his thrilled expression had gone. He shook his head. Stood up. 'You go back to work, Maggsie. There's a lot to sort out here.' *Go back to work* was a glimmer of hope.

Primrose was short with me. Thought I'd just taken the day off yesterday and hadn't let her know. TJ was rushed off his feet. Only had time to smile and raise his eyebrows. I only had time to shrug.

Thank heavens for the dishwasher. The rhythm of it, the whoosh and rumble as it got everything clean, the unloading of all the shiny plates and glasses.

Mid-afternoon I got a call to Mr H's office.

He didn't ask me to sit down this time. It was more of a headmaster's study scenario. He'd talked things over with the police.

I shut my eyes. Clung to the back of the Scanda chair. It tipped like it might buckle.

Given the value of the painting it had taken a lot of talking, he said. He'd had to persuade them not to prosecute me. They'd 'invested time and resources' in the case. Interviewing people, I suppose he meant.

The chair legs scraped on the floor. I kept my eyes shut.

Mr H's voice got louder. He'd had to 'varnish the truth', lie, basically, tell them the painting had been 'temporarily borrowed without his knowledge'. It had all been 'a dreadful misunderstanding'.

You could say that again. Only not in the way he meant.

He paused, let out a long sigh. Sounded very tired when he said the case had been closed. I wasn't going to be charged.

My legs sagged with the chair. Puts you at a disadvantage, being grateful.

Then a *but*. There's always a *but*. He was *concerned* I'd been *taken advantage of so easily*.

Like I was weak or something! Thick!

He was worried I hadn't thought things through. *Apprehensive about my recklessness.*

I put my hands in my jacket pockets. Didn't say anything. Another first for me.

He was in two minds about keeping me on. Long, long pause.

Talk about a rollercoaster. I held on to TJ's packet of cigarettes.

Another but – I looked up – he had decided to give me another chance because I had tried to put things right.

I still had my job.

It had been much easier scrambling up and down that drainpipe. Less scary. I couldn't get out of his office quick enough. I ran down the stairs to the kitchen.

*

I'd thought I'd never see Audrey again. She was sitting on the top step, waiting for me, or for her pilchards, when I got back from work. Even though I'd been away. Ran down, gave one of the two-toned miaows that meant *hello*, front paws lifting off the ground to be stroked. In and out my legs, tail up like a question mark. Didn't hold a grudge. If Ruby didn't let me stay on here she'd feel abandoned all over again.

I had to open a new tin of pilchards, which meant someone had fed her yesterday. I was even pleased about that. That was how far I'd come.

I put the kettle on and went out for a fag. No one knew I was back yet. Then I sat down at the kitchen table with my mug of tea. Looked at it still swirling round and round after I'd stirred in the sugar. Audrey jumped onto my lap. Sniffed around in case I had something interesting in my sandwiches – I hadn't even looked to see what they were yet – and then settled herself down. Dug her claws in when I moved. I couldn't eat a thing till I knew I was staying. Knew Aud still had a lap to sit on tomorrow.

I rolled up my jeans leg to check how the gash from the accident was healing, only I couldn't bend down enough to see it without disturbing Audrey. I could feel the knife by the side of it. My other ankle was still swollen from where I'd landed slithering down the drain-pipe. I could see it, looking down. Two injuries I'd got rescuing the painting. And what had lousie got? A ruddy great holiday of a lifetime!

I'd been on high alert for days. Takes it out of you. Audrey was purring her head off. Nice, just stroking her. A tear dropped onto her fur. One of mine. Lord knows why. Ridiculous when you think how much better things had turned out, so far, than I'd thought they were going to a couple of days ago. Maybe it was delayed shock. *Marguerite McNaughton, you're getting soft*. I wiped it off. My stroking got slower, my head nodded onto my chest. Then I jerked up.

Ruby was standing by the fridge, shaking her carton of soya milk. Her necklace rattled. She wasn't happy. But support workers have had training not to shout. Got psychology oozing out of every pore. I carried on stroking Audrey. That cat therapist thing again. I *had* told Ruby I wouldn't be back last night. I reminded her about that. OK, I'd switched off my phone after, but that was to save the battery. Yes, it was against the rules, I know. Even more so having a knife in your sock. Being eager to use it.

'Where *were* you, Maggsie? What were you doing? Were you on a bender?'

No, I ruddy wasn't. 'Ain't touched a drop, I swear. I had to sort something. Something to do with work.' I didn't go into details. I hadn't committed a crime, only going into Foxholes without being invited. No charges or nothing. No point in worrying Ruby. No point in losing my place here.

I told the girls more later. I mean, I liked Ruby and she'd helped me out loads, but we weren't all girls together like she thought, not really. She'd always be the one in charge. It was only because she was new and young she hadn't realized that yet.

She had to note everything down. Her mouth went all pursed and her skirt flounced about as she filled the kettle. She hadn't said I wasn't staying, though. I gently dislodged Audrey and offered to make Ruby a cup of tea. While her back was turned I sneaked the veg knife back in the drawer. Juice must have missed it yesterday.

Upstairs I got the calendar out of my rucksack. Hung it back up on the wardrobe knob. Two days to tick off. Once I'd done that I wrote: 'Got paneting bak' under yesterday.

The *Woman Reading* was back in Scanda's boardroom, getting on with her book. She had an alarm behind her now. If she was so much as breathed on, all hell would break loose. Her border, where I'd cut it, had been repaired and she had a new frame paid for by Scanda's insurance. Only next year they'd have to pay more. A small amount of my wages was going towards it. I wasn't quite as keen on Mr H as I had been. I'd been going to buy him a bunch of flowers for keeping me on but I changed my mind.

TJ didn't tell Primrose, but she found out what I'd done. I had to tell her the full story. Well, nearly all of it. She brought me in a bookmark with something from the Bible printed on it after. And wrote down when her church services were on. Like my soul needed rescuing. When it was me that did that sort of thing.

People in the canteen and the roof garden looked at me like I was some sort of wild animal. Not at all like they had when I'd saved Jack's life. More like any minute I was going to pinch their handbags. (Even men have handbags in London. They're called 'man-bags' but otherwise they're the same.)

Doing the right thing isn't easy. Which is why a lot of people don't.

Lousie getting away with everything still ate me up.

'Do not waste energy on low-life like her,' TJ said.

*Low-life*. Low-life in spite of being posh. In spite of having a degree and a stately home.

I liked that – but it still ate me up she'd got away with it when it had all been her idea. And I'd only done it to help Enid, but lousie had just been out for herself.

Nice the girls here were so dead against her. Juice said she felt the same about her ex. Now she knew he'd used her. But her mum, *adoptive mum*, said the best revenge was a successful life. 'And I thought, yeah, she's right. Me getting worked up is just letting him carry on getting to me. I got to move on. Think about Shania. Do stuff for her.'

She'd given up the knitting. Now she was trying to sew dolls' clothes for Shania's Barbie. I'd seen her making a little mini-skirt out of a piece of ribbon and a press stud. Holding it right up close to her eyes, working out which bit of the press stud went where.

She watched kids' programmes on the telly. CBeebies. *Peppa Pig* and all that. Said it was to keep up with what Shania was into but you could see she enjoyed them. She knew all the songs. Hummed them sometimes when she was cooking.

What she said hit home. Festering over lousie using me gave her more power. She'd be thrilled if she knew she was still getting to me. Well, not any more.

A couple of weeks later Mr H came down to the kitchen. My heart turned over when I saw him. He had some news I *might be interested in*. He told me in the storeroom. I *was* interested because it was about lousie. Her getting her comeuppance.

Mr H said he thought the police might not have quite believed his story – him covering for me – the 'dreadful misunderstanding' thing. They'd put two and two together. Checked records. There was only one girl, banged up the same time as me and Enid, who'd done a degree in Art History. Funny that. They found lousie's address, just like I done. Well, like Stevey-boy had. Headed off to her stately home. Lousie and her pa denied everything. As *art historians*, they'd heard of Hammershøi, of course. Of course. But they'd never been lucky enough to have one of his paintings in their home. They'd made out they were bewildered by the whole thing.

If only she'd been in her ruddy stately home for me to use my knife on! I told you there was no justice in this world, but you might not have believed me.

'But' – Mr H held up a finger – 'the police think there could be something fishy there.'

They were going to look into exactly where all lousie's pa's art and antiques had come from. Because, once you put the lights on, apparently Foxholes was more like an Aladdin's cave.

# 46

Enid sent me another postcard from Romania. This one had her mobile number. Then she Skyped me. Ruby let me use the computer in her office.

The screen was a bit blurry and I couldn't see the top of her head. Funny seeing Enid squashed into a screen. Mind you, she was a different shape anyway, because of the surgery. Smaller all over. First time I'd seen her without a cardigan. First time I'd seen her outside prison.

'Hello, dear.' She gave me a wink and a thumbs-up. 'Look at us two, all hunky-dory. Spreading our wings.' She pointed to her chest. 'I've got two lovely neat scars there now, lovey. Don't miss my boobs at all.'

Always been very open, Enid. Even about her mum and that. The mercy killing. 'I'm not ashamed of what I did for Mum, but Julie, my niece, says I should stop going on about it now. We're not Dignitas over here, she says.'

She had two tortoiseshell combs in her hair to keep it off her face. Perhaps they all wore their hair like that in Romania. Her cheeks had some pink to them. Could have been blusher or could have been all the fresh air they got over there.

Lovely to see her, even if it wasn't in the flesh. And hear how things were going well for her over in Romania.

'I mostly got bad memories back home, Maggsie, and there's such a lot of lovely country and open spaces here after all those years inside.'

Her niece had bought five self-catering log cabins. Enid was crocheting the bedcovers. She helped with the cleaning and the bed-making on changeover days. Sometimes did stints on Reception. In her element now, with all the locals keen on practising their English.

'I'm ever so proud of you, Maggsie. How well you're getting on. Told you, didn't I? All those lovely letters you wrote. All your London news. Now, what's he like then, this bloke that's been showing you the sights? Don't let him drag you down, Maggs. Not a drinker, is he?'

The complete ruddy opposite.

Enid hadn't a clue about all the to-do with lousie and the painting. Turned out she'd never got my postcard of Trafalgar Square, in spite of the three stamps. And I hadn't written since – I couldn't put it all into words. So this was a *real* catch-up call.

'I'll be jiggered.' Enid got out a hankie. Not a tissue, a proper hankie with a big red 'E' embroidered in a corner. Perhaps her mum had done it for her years ago. 'You silly girl. Silly, silly girl.' She mopped her eyes. 'You've got a heart of gold, Maggs. Doing all that for me. All those risks you took.'

I told her about the police checking out lousie's dad's art collection down in Dorset. *Outrageous*, he'd called it, apparently.

'You wait, dear. That one will get her comeuppance. Don't waste no more time over her. Specially now you been doing so well.'

She brought her face up close to the screen, like she was sharing a secret: 'Whatever happens, get yourself some proper learning, dear. Keep going with it. I'll write. And you come on over to Romania and see me. There's a job in my niece's complex for you any time. Bring that handsome hunk you've been going on about with you!'

No one would call TJ handsome. And I'd hardly said a word about him.

Christmas. Only a week before my year of living respectable, more or less, was up. TJ had gone back to Poland for the holiday. He'd been looking forward to seeing his kids. And getting old Sofa's signature on his divorce papers.

I'd gone round all the charity shops in Finsbury Park looking for something to give him for Christmas. I'd got five history books in the end, and only one of them cost more than £2. They were for my benefit as well. Sooner or later, I'd be hearing all about the stuff inside.

TJ had bought me a pink make-up bag with a cat wearing a crown on it and my initials: MM. I'd never had anything like it before. It's not exactly *hard*. But it's classy.

Christmas is when you get in touch with people. I bought a pack of ten cards in aid of the homeless from the Co-op. Gold around the outside and Jesus, Mary and Joseph in a stable. Never needed ten before. I sent one to Jack. His address was on the letter he'd sent me back in the summer. *Hope you're back playing football*, I put inside. Checked the spellings first. I sent one to Mum saying I'd visit soon, *if I can get the time off work*. That was just a taster to rub it in with Dougie. I'd never written anything in a card to her before beyond *xxx Maggsie M*. Mum would fall into a faint when I turned up with TJ. Plus my new hair and eyebrows and that.

My sister Nella hadn't bothered sending me a card

these last few years. I'd send her one now. In fact I'd write her an actual letter. Have a go anyway. Give her a shock. Catch her up with what I'd been doing. The good bits. Being off work over Christmas, I had plenty of time to do it.

I had a look at the problem pages in *Woman's World* to see how to start it off. Not that I had *problems* any more. That's why I was writing. My letter was going to be like the problem page *answers*.

I put in some bits the agony auntie said was a good idea to repeat to yourself: *I have turned my life around. I have learnt to value my unique qualities.* (I knew they were spelt right because I copied them straight off the page.) *Life is* brilliant *for me now.* I got that off TJ's toothpaste tube. The one that hadn't worked.

I put in the words stuck up on my mirror as well. I am *positive* and *confidence*, I got in. Changed it to *confident.* Then, *efficient. Very efficient. As you can see I have been working on my reading and my writing*, I added. It took me ages to check the spelling of *writing* because I was looking under 'r'. (I ask you, what *is* the point of a silent letter? If I was in charge I'd dump the lot of them. Squash the smug little pillocks like flies. Those silent 'h's in *what, when, why*, all those stupid 'k's in *know, knife, knee*. What are they for except to trip up people like me?)

I put the Polish Corner Café's address on the right-hand side. Told Nella I had a job, at Scanda, the Danish Design company. I copied that bit off the calendar.

I only had to rewrite the letter once and that was because I'd left off the capital letter from Greenwich. I enjoyed writing it. Never thought *I'd* say that. Nice to crow to someone who'd always thought I dragged her down.

I'd learnt more than just useful words, reading all those problem pages. They'd got me thinking different. Nella was a pain, yeah, but she hadn't had it easy neither. Not when she was young, anyway. She was the oldest girl, see, so she got landed with things. It was always Nella who'd had to take over when Mum was out with a bloke or wrapped up in one at home. There'd been other men, besides Dad and Dougie. Fly-by-nights, who didn't stick around.

And when they didn't, Mum got low. Reckon that was why she let Dougie and Dad get away with murder. She'd take to her bed, and Nella would have to go to the chippy. Stretch out the little bit of cash left in Mum's purse. Take cups of tea up to her like she was an invalid. I slopped the tea in the saucer or scalded my hand, so it was mostly Nella that did it.

I thought about all that but I didn't know how to write it. At the end of the letter I said, perhaps we could meet up for a coffee in Greenwich sometime? Like I hung out there all the time. I put *love from* and *xxx* at the end because she was my sister.

# 47

I finished the calendar. A whole year of ticks. It was scruffy now with the furniture pictures at the top torn off and all the pages worn and creased. I put it away in my holdall anyway because it was still a record. A good one.

Now I'd done the year I could contact Alastair. I'd bought a new notepad from the Co-op. Had a first-class stamp stuck on an envelope ready. I'd copied out the adoption agency's address. I was all set. Only a jolt of electric seemed to go through me each time I picked up the pen. Almost as if I was nervous about it.

'Giving up your baby's for the best,' them in charge had said. Like I'd had nothing to give Alastair. Like I wasn't good enough to be his mum. A horrible feeling. One that stayed with you. One that added to the aching hole without him. 'Now you'll have a chance to make something of your life,' was another thing they'd said. Like, soon as I was shot of Alastair, I'd be buzzing off to university, or to a job on TV or something. When all I'd made of my life after was a mess.

Sometimes I thought, if I'd been able to keep him, I'd have pulled my socks up. Bettered myself. Tried to get some education. I'd have read him little books. Made him clean his teeth three times a day. Wouldn't have wanted him to have the struggles I did.

I put my pen down. There'd been some chat in the kitchen yesterday. About New Year's resolutions. 'Most things don't come out right first time,' Ruby had said. She meant giving up smoking, but you could say it about a lot of things. Everything, really. My life certainly hadn't.

My resolution, of course, was to contact Alastair. I mean, that's what this whole year had been about.

'But that's about you, isn't it?' said Big Shirl. 'What *you* want. It's Alastair this, Alastair that, Alastair wouldn't want me to . . . when you don't even know him.'

Big Shirl liked keeping people in line. It was what she'd done managing a brothel. Only that had involved whips. As for going on about Alastair – well, she never stopped talking about Jordan. How well he was doing with his fishing magazines. (My idea, in case she'd forgotten.) How he'd learnt what bait different types of fish liked. How he was actually fishing now. On and on. Ruddy boring. I saw poor little Jordan crouched over a seedy canal somewhere. Somewhere where he could get away from Big Shirl. Dangling a fishing rod and his pink nose going when he felt something on the line. 'Excuse me,' I said, putting the kettle down firmly. 'What is wrong with bettering myself for my son?'

'Good to better yourself, yeah, Maggs. Not a baby now, though, is he? He's a grown man, practically. You tracking him down sounds a bit heavy to me. Two-handkerchief sort of job. TV show.'

'It is like *he* is adult. And you are child,' put in Kasia. She was munching a slice of her dark bread. Same colour as my hair was now. Smelt like the yogurt Ruby was so keen on. She'd just come in from cleaning for the lady who worked in the Co-op. Kept looking at her nails and frowning.

314

My shoulders were hunched, heart thumping. I breathed o-u-t. They're not *deliberately* riling me, I told myself.

'Bit of a burden for him, if you ask me.' Big Shirl slathered some of her healthy spread on two slices of Hovis toast. Then spoilt it by covering it with strawberry jam. She looked up. 'Must be difficult, Maggs. Difficult decision to make. I'm not saying it isn't.'

If you ask me, Big Shirl didn't have enough to do. That was why she was always ready to sort other people out. She only had another couple of months to go here. Then she was off to a job as relief manageress of a bar in Soho. Cackled each time she said the word *relief*. Looking forward to it so long as she could sit down. Dispensing advice to lonely men over the counter. Good luck to them, I say.

Ruby stirred her organic teabag round her mug. She'd won it coming 160th in her triathlon. I'd thought she was joking, but no, she said there were over five hundred competing and it *was* an achievement. Stirred other stuff up as well as her teabag. Put her fourpenny-worth in. 'Sounds like you want him to forgive you. But you were fifteen, Maggsie. A child. You *couldn't* keep him. He's not going to blame you. He probably would be proud of what you've achieved. But that's not the point. You should be proud of yourself. How you've turned your life around.' A bit like what TJ had said. Why did everyone have to have an opinion on me? *And* ruddy give it?

'But I've done all that *for* Alastair.' She didn't get it. None of them did. It was the thought of seeing him that had kept me focused this past year!

'And that's great. But now keep going for yourself.'

315

'You saying I shouldn't never see him?'

She shook her head. 'I'm just saying don't rush things. You don't know anything about his life now. How his adoptive parents are going to feel, for a start—'

'But they've had him to theirselves all this time.'

'Exactly. It could be a minefield.'

'That's what I've always said,' put in Juice. Alright, alright.

I gave a long breath out. It was a sigh, really. Saw Snappy, upstairs in my holdall, open one eye and close it again.

Ruby got out her soya milk. It had never seen a cow. Bet she only drank it because of Will. A lot of writing on the carton. Which I didn't fancy reading. 'Why not write that letter to the adoption agency? Once you've sent in your details the rest will be up to him.'

'Then is about him, not you.' Kasia adjusted her sparkly top. She'd probably had to wear an overall earlier. And maybe even an apron over that.

'You look after number one.' Big Shirl chewed her toast.

Juice blinked at me. 'You deserve a good life, Maggsie.'

They all nodded. Even Trudie, coming in from her volunteering. Ruby had sorted that for her. Got her into a cat charity shop, selling bric-a-brac in aid of cats. Made for her. Now they'd offered her a trial in a cat adoption centre, stroking cats. Socializing them, they called it. That was going to make her think she was even more of an expert. I could see it coming. But I wouldn't be here to see it. I'd be moving into TJ's flat. Just as ruddy well.

I put some bread in the toaster. I'd only be standing there scowling at the lot of them otherwise. Took it upstairs. Ate it looking out of the window. Funny not having a calendar to tick. Usually the high spot of my day, doing that. Bit scary not having a focus. Scary not having Alastair to aim for.

Maybe they were right. Hard to admit it. Hard to do stuff just for yourself. I leant against the glass. I could just see the tree in next door's garden. The one that had been Audrey's downfall. Only it hadn't, thanks to me. It was still green. Nice to see a bit of green in London. I'd see more of it in Lewisham, with it being near Greenwich.

I wrote to Alastair – well, the adoption agency – later on that evening, when the house was quiet. It had to be perfect even though he might never see the letter.

> *I am writing to you because I want to trace my son. His name is* [. . . is or was, I wondered] *Alastair McNaughton. He was born on 22 June 2000 at Chesterbrooke Hospital, Nottingham. He is eighteen now. He was adopted. I would be grateful if you could add my details to his file.* Ruby had wrote that last bit out for me to copy.

I gave the restaurant's address. Didn't want the adoption agency to know I was in supported housing. Exactly the impression I didn't want to give. Anyway, in two weeks' time I wouldn't be.

I signed the letter with my full name: Marguerite McNaughton. First time I'd done that. Don't laugh but I showed it to Audrey. I was dead proud I'd written it straight out. She had her paws folded underneath. She looked at it, eyes half closed, gave it a sniff and then turned away like she was going to vomit. It did look a bit stark, just my name and address. Maybe I could add one sentence. Something personal. I'd ask TJ.

'Write something like what you have told me.'
'I won't be able to spell what I want to say.'
'You have go. Then we look at together.'

*I only had you for thirty-six hours and three minutes but I loved you for every second of them,* I wrote, with TJ checking the spelling. So between us we got it right.

Ruby called me into her office Saturday morning. Uh-oh. But it was to *signpost* me to *future goals,* a bit like she'd done with Trudie. (I wasn't sure if Ruby had fixed up that Soho bar job for Big Shirl. It was more the sort of thing you'd find for yourself. If you were an in-charge sort of person. With Shirl's background.)

I'd done something along the same lines myself, I supposed. Or TJ had. And I'd done something for Kasia. Unofficial, obviously. Someone in the canteen, a girl, had asked TJ to ask me where I'd got my hair cut. I'd peered at her through the swing doors. One of those big glasses, slash of red lipstick, types.

I passed on her number to Kasia. She'd been rubbing hand cream in from a tube in her bag. Perked up straight away. She went round to the Scanda girl's flat to cut her hair. Then she told *her* friend and Kasia got some regular clients. The right sort of clients.

'What about some proper classes for you now, Maggsie?' Ruby asked. 'An English qualification? Not like school these days.'

Go to college. Like TJ. He'd always said his classes were OK. Other people there with dyslexia. Chubby

Sandra with her personal spelling dictionary, I remembered.

'Possibly.' I wasn't going to commit myself. My heart had started going just at the word *English*.

'And, maybe, after that' – Ruby leant forwards. I could see the little damp curls of hair around her face, from where she'd been sweating, cycling – 'some training? You enjoy reading the beauty pages, don't you? In your women's magazines?'

'*Woman's World*.' It wasn't any old magazine. It was what Enid had taught me to read with. I was going to read it for the rest of my life. 'Yeah. So?'

'Well, is that something you've ever thought of pursuing?'

I pointed to my chest. 'Me? You having a laugh?' I wanted to look behind me, like I had that first day at Scanda when they'd clapped me. There'd be a willowy blonde with flashing teeth, towering behind me. Probably making a rude gesture. I almost turned round to tell her to piss off.

'Why not you? You've got an interest.' Ruby tilted her head, looking at me. She had beady eyes, like a bird's, that didn't miss nothing. 'You're bright, you work hard, you're willing to learn.'

I wasn't exactly an advert for beauty treatments. I reminded her about my sub-standard teeth, in case she hadn't noticed, my smoking. Plus I was an ex-con and an ex-alcoholic (if you ever could be an *ex*-alcoholic). And then there was my dyslexia.

But beauty therapist.

*This is my birth mum. She's a beauty therapist*, I heard Alastair say.

*My youngest daughter*, Mum chipped in, primping

her Titian hair. *She's a beauty therapist. Yes, up in London, you know.*

*This is my good English friend. She is beauty therapist.*
*A* beauty therapist.

*What nail varnish would* you *recommend, Maggsie?* (That was Nella.)

'I don't know about that,' I muttered. 'Anyway, I can't do exams.' I had a horrible flashback to school. Sitting there, like I'd been beamed down from another planet, with all the other kids writing as fast as they could.

Ruby said I'd get extra time because of my dyslexia. Help with reading the questions. 'You're a bright girl,' she said. 'You'll be fine.' She said I was bright *because* of my dyslexia. It had made me more intelligent because I'd had to problem-solve.

I wasn't so sure. But, *bright*. Second time she'd said it. *Intelligent*. Blimey.

'Better at keeping your cool now, too.' Ruby brushed some hair out of her eyes. A bit of wax would separate those curls nicely, I thought. There'd been a bit in *Woman's World* on curl management. 'I should think you'd need anger strategies for beauty therapy!' Her earrings swayed when she smiled. 'Lose your temper with a client and you wouldn't have any left.'

I imagined throwing melted wax at someone stretched out on a couch. Someone who'd just said, 'Hey, Shorty, you're doing that all wrong.' Swallowed. No. That was going to be tricky. But beauty therapist, I thought. A little white coat with my name on the pocket.

A beauty therapist would be like Wonder Woman. They both put things right.

# 48

**Woman's World, 9 January 2019**
A New Life in Our Dream Home!

Today's the day I move the last of my stuff to the flat above Pavel's restaurant. He's cleared out the storeroom. TJ's put in two rows of coat hooks. Hung up proper heavy curtains with stripes and flowers on. Got them from a charity shop. Found a *futon* from somewhere. (I had to look up the word. A poncy foreign word for a poncy foreign mattress.)

I went over there last weekend. Saw the yard at the back. The bins are out there and a few things growing in pots. It's where I'll have to go to smoke. Wouldn't you know it? Next to a dustbin like always.

I've hung up the new calendar Enid sent me. Cats. Loads of them. Kittens on every page: in baskets, scrabbling up trees, sleeping in slippers. *Ah, love them, the pretty dears*, I can hear her saying. I'm not going to tick off the days this year. I don't need to.

I've re-organized the bits of furniture. Good at seeing the big picture, see. Blu-Tacked Enid's postcards from Romania on the wall above a little rickety table that'll do as a desk. I wasn't copying lousie. Mine are *real* postcards. Ones that have actually been posted. With stamps. From a friend. A real friend. Enid. Lousie didn't have any of those. Never likely to either, the way she carries on.

The cops had found loads of dodgy stuff down in stately old Foxholes. Stashed on the second floor where the public weren't allowed. Paintings that had been reported missing. Some of them from years and years ago. Lousie's this-is-outrageous pa had been charged with theft and harbouring stolen goods. Lousie with being an accessory. Both of them were awaiting trial.

Even the crockery in the café where they served cream teas in the summer had been stolen from a posh hotel somewhere. Yeah, her getting me to take the *Woman Reading* had opened a whole can of worms for Lousie. Satisfying, that.

The only fly in the ointment now is leaving Audrey behind. TJ's not sure if Pavel will allow a cat. I'm going to work on him. I've moved in Aud's beanbag already. Meanwhile Audrey's fine staying here at the house, Ruby says. She's planning on making her a new bed out of a crisp box that's got a round hole in the front. Just right for a cat, she says. Don't know about *that*. Sounds cramped. And there's always the worry that Will might get Ruby to stop Aud's pilchards. Put her on tofu or some such.

TJ took me to Lewisham Library, end of last year. It's only five minutes from the flat. I'd never been to a library before. It looked a bit like a Job Centre, only stuffed with books. There were two floors of them and miles and miles of shelves. Took your breath away, looking at them. All those words.

I had to fill in a form to join, wouldn't you believe it. Anyway, I did it – TJ only helped with *ethnic origin* – and signed my name at the bottom. Marguerite McNaughton.

TJ had started on another of his big books. Four

hundred and seventy-six pages. Small print. Gave me the willies just looking at it. 'But four years ago I begin with Quick Reads. Short books.' He beckoned. Showed me a stand with paperback books. I'd never read any kind of book before. They scared the shit out of me, after school.

'Quick Reads shorter books but good stories.' Nothing wrong with being shorter. I picked one up. On the front was a picture of a dead body washed up on a beach. That'll cheer me up, I thought. Not that it would be a ruddy 'quick read' for me. Not with thousands of words inside. A hundred and thirteen pages.

We'd – well, *they'd* – read books at school. Round the class. *Walkabout*, one was called. Funny thing was, I'd *liked* the story. I'd had a week's exclusion before they got to the end but, later, I saw the film on TV. Wished I hadn't in a way because it was sad.

My hands would be slippery with sweat waiting for my turn to read. Because teachers can do things easy they forget other people can't. And that's being, what do you call it? Char-it-able. Soon as I stumbled old Mrs Connell would go, 'For goodness' sake, Marguerite! It's a simple word! A child of six could read it.' I'd sit there, face burning, words swimming and dancing all over the place. It was throwing the book at her that got me the week's exclusion.

Now I'm reading a book at home on my own. Plenty of white space on the pages, thank God. If there's no white space in a piece of writing I'm done for. Mind you, the first couple of pages took me ages. I kept losing track of what had happened. But some of the words were the same. I kept going. Never thought I'd read a book.

I went back to the library, on my own, when TJ was working. Spun the Quick Reads stand round to look at the covers. Thought which one I'd get out next. Onwards and upwards. On the way out I picked up a leaflet about evening classes. English and Maths. I needed to learn stuff properly. After lousie, no one was never going to make a fool of me again. That's another upwards thing.

It's half past eight in the morning. TJ's borrowed Pavel's car to move the last of my stuff. Not that I've got much, but I've had to buy another holdall for all my *Woman's Worlds*, my dictionary, library books, all that.

If things go OK and I don't mess up in the kitchen, Pavel will let Aud move in, surely? She's a small cat. Been used to not having much. Plenty of food scraps in a restaurant. With her name and her airs and graces she'd add a bit of class, if you ask me.

I stop myself. Don't count your chickens, Maggsie. One day at a time.

I'll have to get used to sharing with a man. TJ. A man who's stopped smoking. Who won't hardly be there because of his other jobs. A man who reads long books and big old Sunday newspapers. Seizes opportunities left, right and centre. Who's going to train to be a teacher one day. A man who needs help understanding English slang. Needs listening to, looking out for sometimes. Specially when his wife has a go at him. She'd asked him for money when he went over at Christmas. Ruddy cheek. What about the poxy chemistry teacher's wages? She'd just have to cut down a bit, wouldn't she? Eat less.

But you can't have everything in this life.

I smooth down my hair. I've grown out a couple of inches of the black now. Looking at me you'd almost think I was a brunette. I run my tongue over my teeth. TJ's made an appointment for me to meet his dentist mate. Just *meet*. I'm not going to commit myself. *You see he is nice man. Then you feel better lying in chair.* I could use some of my Scanda money, the lump sum, to pay for my treatment. Fund myself without cleaning. I'll be working in the restaurant Friday nights and Saturdays. (No way am I going to take on a third job. I'm not TJ.) I swallow. Blimey, I'm going so far on and up I'm going to end up in outer space.

I can see TJ outside now. He's wearing a hat. Why is he poncing about in one of those? It's one of those hats you see in black and white films. With a brim. It's tipped to the side. He bends down to stroke Audrey. Then he looks up and sees me at the window. Something in my belly, heart, liver, some part of my innards, anyway, turns over.

He'll carry my holdalls to the car. Hold my elbow and guide me across. Even though I'm perfectly capable of crossing a road. Eight thirty on a Sunday morning. He's driven halfway across London. Worked in the restaurant the night before.

I go downstairs, a holdall in each hand. The girls are in the kitchen. Amazing they're all up. Only Trudie dressed, but still. Quiet for them. Hugs all round. I show Trudie the row of pilchard tins I've got in for Audrey. Fifteen should see her through till I've persuaded Pavel. Aud's just come in from out the front. I scratch the top of her head and she makes her *prook* noise. I don't hang about. Don't do to weaken.

*He's a bit of alright, Maggs.*
*Be good, and if you can't be good, be careful.*
*Bye, Maggs.*

*Good luck, girl.*

This is the last time I have anything to do with supported housing, probation officers, prison. When TJ said, *You should be proud. Your son would be proud,* I'd felt all the bad stuff – thicko, and worse – floating away. Backwards and downwards. Him and Enid and Ruby, even that young doc, seeing the good bits inside me, not the rubbish, made them real.

It's like I've been through the dishwasher at work. Like I've come out the other side scrubbed clean and pure and shiny.

I close the front door behind me and walk towards the car. TJ's waiting.

# Acknowledgements

Thanks to my agent Juliet Mushens for her energy, hard work and for the incisive suggestions that transformed this book. To my editor, Sam Humphreys, for her encouragement, tact and kindness, to desk editor Natalie Young, to Amber Burlinson for her sharp-eyed copy-editing, and to all at Mantle books.

Thanks to Dave, who gave me access to his library and guidance on Hammershøi, and who suppressed his horror to discuss how you would slash a painting out of its frame.

Thanks to Tamasin Perkins for her expert legal advice – any mistakes my own.

Thanks again to Eileen, Monique and Celia for getting me started and to Jenny E for opening the door.

And thanks to Ed for his patience, support and for all the many cups of tea.

Unfortunately, the 3.33 train from Dorchester South to Waterloo is imaginary.